Journey *to* Michipicoten

Journey *to* Michipicoten

A NOVEL

Patricia Kay Lucas

FIRST PERSON PRODUCTIONS MADISON, WISCONSIN

First Person Productions, Publisher
50 S. Fair Oaks Avenue, Madison, WI 53714
Copyright ©2010 by Patricia Kay Lucas
All rights reserved.

ISBN 978-0-9844413-1-0
Library of Congress Control #2010927185

Book design, Sarah E. White
Cover photograph, Gregg Riemer
Chapter icons, Jeanne Gomoll
"The Fish and the Cormorant," in *The Complete Fables of Jean de la Fontaine*,
translated by Norman B. Spector, Northwestern University Press, 1988.
Used with permission.

Trademarked names mentioned in this book belong to the holders.

www.journeytomichi.com

Printed in the United States of America

For Gregg, life partner, best friend,
and co-voyageur on many a journey.

Author's Note

Today, Michipicoten is usually pronounced **mish**api**COTT**en. Aside from Edward and Frances Anne Hopkins, all the main characters in this book are fictitious. Readers are encouraged to read these pages outside, if possible, with fresh air on the face and the sounds of birds, water, and wind in the ear.

I am indebted to Paul Shepard for his extravagant ideas about our biological need for wilderness and to Frances Anne Hopkins for her beautiful and inspiring pictures.

I wish to thank Carolyn Gilman, Gregg Riemer, Ann Lacy, Linda Newman Woito, Rebecca Lee Williams, Lisa Hunter, David Wells, James P. Roberts, LaVon Lucas, Nancy Hoene, Marg Sumner, Joan Donovan, Jeanne Gomoll, Sarah White, and Corey Caswick for their kindness and astute suggestions. I own, free and clear, any errors or missteps that remain.

May 1, 2010

Contents

Cast of Characters ix
Prologue: The Synthesist 1
1. Welcome 6
2. The Fur Trade. 9
3. Déjà Vu 16
4. Turning Around. 24
5. Xavier Speaks. 33
6. Seventeenth Century Europe 41
7. A Young Man from Anjou. 45
8. Fort Atkinson, Wisconsin 58
9. The Three Voyageurs 70
10. Marinette, Wisconsin 82
11. The Ocean Dreams. 105
12. A Sea Journey 106
13. A Nudge from Kitchi Gami 115
14. The Nebaunaubaewuk 121
15. The Honorable Men. 122
16. Seventeenth Century Canada 125
17. Settling Accounts. 132
18. A Great Adventure 144
19. The Conspirators 161
20. Dégradé 180
21. The Northern Forest 186
22. Pukaskwa 194
23. Little Ice Age. 209
24. The Trials of Garamond 212
25. Gallantry 225
26. The Dakota Sioux 232
27. Grand Père Shows Up. 255
28. Lichen 272
29. The Prize. 278

30. Montréal 292
31. A Bird Out of Place 299
32. The Artists. 309
33. Lake Superior 314
34. A Revelation. 320
35. What I Know About Michipicoten Island 327
36. A Tweak of Fate. 332
37. Frances in Paradise 337
38. The Approach 341
39. Elusion. 350
40. Passing, Not Stopping. 355
41. Mercy. 359
42. Michipicoten Island. 367
43. The Seed Exchange. 377
44. How Matters Stand 384
45. A Drive in the Dark. 386
46. Hampstead. 390
Epilogue: Chasing Synthesis. 392

Sources for Quotations 395
Further Reading 399

Cast of Characters

The Synthesist – old man on a quest

20th Century:
> Frances Bookstaff – middle-aged woman on a quest
> Herb and Janet – her parents
> Jerry – her ex-husband
> Michael and Walt – her sons
> Christine Kinney – her cousin
> Cora and John – Christine's children
> Grandma Beth – Janet's mother, Frances's grandmother
> Pete Schiller – Herb's hunting buddy
> Irv Klein – the boyfriend
> Nicolette Poggi – grad student and lichen survey boss
> Captain Bergquist – owner of Edward Bergquist Fisheries
> Warren – Bergquist employee
> *Palmina* – Bergquist's fishing boat

19th Century:
> Frances Anne Hopkins - artist
> Edward – her husband, Hudson's Bay Company chief
> Mr. Baker – Hudson's Bay Co. clerk
> Mr. Marsh – Hudson's Bay Co. clerk
> Will Armstrong – artist and engineer at Silver Islet
> Xavier La Fourche – storyteller and steersman of the
>   Hopkins's canoe
> Denis – bowman of the Hopkins's canoe
> The White Shell – Iroquois voyageur
> Patrice – voyageur and budding artist
> Peter Bell – proprietor of Michipicoten Post
> Mrs. Eileen Bell – his wife, Frances Anne Hopkins's friend

Mrs. Marjorie Kinney – student of Frances Anne Hopkins,
    great-grandmother to 20th century Frances Bookstaff
Mrs. Turner – fellow artist of Frances Anne Hopkins
Miss Beatrice Brooks – art student
Louise – art student

17th Century:

Jean Garamond – young man on a quest
Andrée – his mother
Auguste Michon – his stepfather
Jean and Annebette – his stepbrother and stepsister
Brother Romain – his mother's brother and a Jesuit scholar
Father Marcel – Jesuit priest
Little Ugly – the Poitevin colt, a draft horse
Claude – student at the Jesuit college
Bernard Cornet – merchant in Canada
Pauline – his wife
Frances – his stepdaughter, a willful wisp of a girl
Father Hennepin – Recollet priest, author of
    Description de la Louisiane
Sainte Anne – ship to Canada, named for the patron saint of
    travelers
Master Chaviteau – captain of *Sainte Anne*
M. Dubois – Cornet's agent in Québec
Charles Laverdure – Cornet's partner in Montréal
Mathurin Cadot – Cornet's associate for the fall run
Michel Miron – Cadot's employee, Garamond's canoe
    partner
Frère Bouleau – Ottawa elder, Garamond's canoe partner
Little Owl – young Ottawa man, Garamond's adversary
Doucette – French trader
Jules Mercier – French trader at Missilimackinac

Yellow Deer – Dakota Sioux woman, Garamond's adopted
  mother
Shining Heart – Dakota elder
Mitahansi – young Dakota man, Garamond's tutor
Mamehnese – Dakota warrior
Sitka Toh – Dakota woman
Wasu – her husband
Grand Père – old French Jesuit and trader, Garamond's
  partner
Saint Pierre – French-Huron trader, Garamond's associate
Snow-in-his-Hair – Cree trader
Singing Woman – his wife
Maeengan – Ojibwa youth, Garamond's canoe partner and
  guide
Marc – Frances Cornet's friend in Montréal
Jiwatena – Huron man
Blue Wing – elderly Huron woman
Dawn – her daughter
Tiron – Dawn's new husband

Journey *to* Michipicoten

Prologue:
The Synthesist

Winter 2020

CONSIDER THE SUBTLE glamour of a journey by birch bark canoe. To cross watersheds and traverse vast tracts, to dance down rapids or float upon mirrors. To see what one has not seen, and then to see again and again what becomes indispensable—wilderness. The skin of the canoe is rough and brown and warm in the sun; the bow, arched like the neck of a swan, slips artfully along some secret way to, perhaps, the head of a portage trail, or a connecting stream barely inches deep. Or the canoe, stalwart and bold, rides the waves of a Great Lake to safety. All these waters form a network across North America, by turns watering and draining the land like the blood vessels of a body. The canoes of the old fur trade went everywhere thereon, only discouraged, but not entirely stopped, by the ramparts of the Rocky Mountains.

Myriad portage trails stitch all of this together. Some of the longest: the twelve-mile Methye Portage between the Churchill and Athabasca river systems; the nine-mile Grand Portage between Lake Superior and the Rainy Lake country. That animals first made these trails is a deep irony. The Indians, and then the explorers, priests, and voyageurs entrenched their use, and indeed, there are many portage trails that lie a foot or more below the surrounding terrain. They are still used in these modern days. That's another thing; maybe we remember the old days by remembering the canoe because, although much has passed away, it is still possible to paddle a canoe to places unfamiliar, even, perhaps, *sauvage*. Mixed up in all this is the allure of long-distance trade, wherever it has figured, which would be most of the globe; think of the Phoenicians, the Hawaiians, the Hanse. Well, let's call it glorious adventure—isn't that really it? Something the imagination grabs on to?

Before the fur trade, the Indians made canoes in as many styles as there were nations and personal preference. These of course, were northern Indians, whose homelands coincided with the range of *Betula paperifera*, the white birch. The bark of white birch is peerless for making canoes; it is flexible, strong, water-proof, rot-resistant, and easy to fix. The Europeans, and especially the Nor'Westers, developed their own variations of the native canoes peculiarly suited to the needs of the fur trade. Most famously, the *canot de maître*, the thirty-six-foot flagship, carrying four tons of cargo and paddlers from Montréal to Grand Portage or Fort William, and back. But also the *canot du nord*, perhaps twenty-five feet, still big but nimble enough to maneuver the streams and portages of the far northwest. There were intermediate types, such as the *canot bâtard*. There were express canoes, which were simply any that were lightly loaded and manned for speed. All of them gorgeous to the eye. Here are the words of one supposedly cool and calculating trader, one Malcolm McLeod, describing George Simpson's North canoe in 1828:

> The Governor's was the most beautiful thing of the kind I ever saw; beautiful in its "lines" of faultless fineness, and in its form and every feature; the bow, a magnificent curve of bark, gaudily but tastefully painted, that would have made a Roman rostrum of old hide its diminished head. The paddles painted red with vermilion, were made to match, and the whole thing in its

kind, was of faultless grace and beauty—beauty in the
sense of graceful and perfect fitness to its end.

I am stopped here for the ninth time this week. There's something
about the phrase, "graceful and perfect fitness to its end," that fills
me with longing. I wonder if this emotion is an evolutionary adapta-
tion, the restlessness of a species that is never satisfied. I am not
satisfied. Despite everything, I still wish to ride that ever-flowing
horizon and to swim the deeps of time. Ah me! It is not to be.

Until now, I've thought of myself as an encyclopedist, even though
encyclopedism is not generally an activity that leads to gainful em-
ployment, *per se*. My purpose has been simply to gather knowledge.
I have been working for days now on this entry about the North
American canoe, a subject of epic romance to be sure, but the usual
approach is not working.

I am suffering from my knowledge; it has become a mob of in-
vested and often competing interests, dangerously confined within
an overheated brain. A manifestation, perhaps, of my illness. Nothing that will kill me—please do not think this a plea for sympathy,
my dear reader. Yet, this whirl in my head has at last driven me,
blinking, into bright sunlight. I am, in fact, disoriented enough to
seek your help.

As a boy, I loved to play on beaches and stony shores, where I
seemed always to see things I could not explain. Those margins of
lapping water, long ago, before the days of fear and complaint. Ever,
as a man, have I sought to understand the world around me. Years
and years have I done so, and let the sand flow down the throat of
the hourglass. Is it too late to change my tactics?

The canoe has led me astray, you see, into a series of exotic landscapes. I find myself wondering how people evolve with landscape,
and so make peace with it. And whether this tie of evolved peace is
carried around inside us no matter where we go, but is stirred by our
return to an ancestral home. And conversely, are we more vulnerable in landscapes where our ancestors never were? (And is there yet
time for me to find *my* place?)

Specifically, I am intrigued by the convergence of these elements:

- the sense of place felt in a sacred landscape,
- the evolutionary ties between people and place,
- ancient myth and legend,
- history, as far as we know, and
- synthesis in modern events and people.

I can sense but not explicate parallels between the past and present, myth and legend. Parallels and links that defy common sense, much less description. I long for a time/place in which all of the above tie themselves together into one coherent and functional realization, but encyclopedism is not the means, I am ready to admit, to achieve this. I need a new trick if I'm going to aspire to *synthesis*. I need, even at my age, to become somewhat lighter on my feet. I need to learn how to dance.

What would you think if I brought everything into juxtaposition? An experimental juxtaposition of all the elements bearing on, for example, the relationship between human beings and wilderness? History, art, economics, science, religion. Not only essay, but music, prose-poem, fiction, doggerel, even—dare I say—World Wide Webbery? What would come of such a concoction? In this fractured world of intractable problems, would it not be worthwhile to try for even the faintest illumination of one question?

I am too old for this. But there's no turning back.

It shall be necessary to recruit assistance, and so, being a bookish sort, my first inclination is to recruit a bookful of characters to portray an adequate range of humanity. I promise to maintain tranquility in the midst of this crew, the better to nurture a sensibility conducive to dancing, to weaving. But key to the whole endeavor shall be you, a gentle reader, I hope, but not a passive one.

No, I am not naive, and yes, it pains me that this mad project is bound to stray into imperfect terrain. So be it. My plans are laid, and there is nothing left to do but to put aside pride and bad habits. I bid goodbye to the encyclopedist. I am out; I am in the sun, humbly seeking partners for the dance. And so, with apologies to all poets and gods of poets, I give you:

No specialists, we—
H. sapiens free,
Compelled to seam
This synthesist's dream

1.

Welcome

July 1, 1992

MY NEW HOUSE is filled with the art of Frances Anne Hopkins. I have made the rooms, halls, and all the odd corners glow with her favorite colors: russet, distant blue, deep gold, and green. In the kitchen, a voyageur camp wakes to mist and dawn on a Lake Superior beach. In the living room, a *canot de maître* shoots a rapids, descending precipitously over my couch. When I open my eyes in the morning, the first thing I see is Frances Anne, her husband Edward, and eight glorious, paddle-wielding men in a canoe. They are gliding past a waterfall that spills down a wall of rock. She is holding a white water lily—her favorite flower—as one of the paddlers bends to pick another. I have maybe a dozen of these pictures in my house. Prints, of course. The originals, wrought in oil, watercolor, pencil, and ink, over a hundred years ago, are secured in museums and private collections. There are some in England and the U.S., but mostly they're in Canada—*O Canada*! She spent just twelve years there, but how she loved its rivers, its lakes, and the forests—the vast *bois fort* of the north. The wilderness: she loved it with her artist's eye and left its images to tease me.

To think that a woman of the nineteenth century, a woman of

means and style, would cast aside her comforts and all that was familiar and easy to camp for weeks at a time in the Canadian wilderness. To tramp portage trails in little black shoes and billowing, bush-snagging skirts. The white lace! She went several times, at least twice on canoe trips long enough to stamp her will and imagination forever. She went as the privileged wife of Edward Hopkins, Chief Factor of the Montreal Department of the Hudson's Bay Company. It was the twilight of the H. B. Co., back in the 1860s when Frances Anne went canoeing. The old firm had scrounged and squandered who knows how much natural wealth for centuries, but it was all coming to an end. Frances Anne painted the last days of the voyageur's world.

She was a woman and an artist, and somehow she cut her way out of Victorian England to leave us these pictures. Unbearably, there were many that were simply lost. I have fantasized about finding them, even just one, in an attic in a tenement on a dingy, ancient London street. Or a flea market in a New England town. What would I do? I'd be wracked with guilt and end up giving it to Canada. No, I'd give it to Hampstead village in London, her last refuge, where she ended her days painting through the nightmare of the Great War.

Sometimes I walk from picture to picture studying them so intently I'm surprised to see my own face in an intervening mirror—a tall woman with short straight hair, middle-aged, wide staring eyes. My hair is dark and cut pixie-style, just as it's been for twenty-five years. Can you believe that?

I am supposed to be packing for the dream trip to Pukaskwa, but I'm distracted by the spectacle of voyageurs gamely repairing the skin of their birch bark canoe in the flickering, orange light of a torch. I've been pacing from picture to picture, my little route, wasting time as usual. What am I trying to see? Clues? Just for once, I wish I could hold everything together long enough to make an informed opinion, one confident decision about the direction of my life, my own route. Surely, if I collected all the threads and spread them out on the table and closed off the drafts, surely I could make some sense of, as my Grandma would say, "this dreadful *mélange*." Because, you know, much as I love them, clues aren't enough.

Over the desk in my bedroom, there is a print of a watercolor, *Portrait of a Young Boy*. His features are delicate, sweet, but he is turning away. Frances Anne lost two of her sons, one in 1864 and one in 1869. I have two sons, healthy and grown-up now, and I am strangled at the thought of her grief. Each of her Lake Superior canoe trips followed in the wake of a death. You have to hand it to the Victorians, though; they didn't stint on what they thought would heal. A bracing holiday in the wilderness? Yes, let's try that. But how infinitely more tragic that second trip must have been, and just how good a healer is wilderness? I suppose it could either kill you or cure you, but it is likely an open-ended question if there ever was one.

In July of 1869, Edward and Frances Anne took a steamer from Lake Huron to the Company's old stronghold on Lake Superior, Fort William, near present-day Thunder Bay. From there, they rode in the canoe with the voyageurs, first along the north shore of Lake Superior, then past Sault Sainte Marie, and all the way back on the old trade routes—the rivers and lakes of the back-country—to Montreal. Just a couple months later, they left for England, for good. It was on the 1869 canoe trip that a Canadian-Ojibway *métis* of their crew told the tale of another Frances, a girl who made a similar journey in an earlier time, the last years of the seventeenth century, when the northwest wilderness was a landscape of endless possibility.

I know about this because my great-grandmother heard it from Frances Anne Hopkins herself. This story has been passed down through my female relations from Great-Grandma Marjorie to Grandma Beth, then to my mother Janet, and finally to me, Frances.

2.

The Fur Trade

Winter 2020

Gentle Reader,

IT IS A curious notion that the most valuable commodity of the North American fur trade was a product comprised of the pelt of *Castor canadensis* and the sweat and oil of human skin. A beaver's pelt is lustrous and beautiful, consisting of close, ripply wool overlain with shiny, much longer guard hairs. The Indians made garments of these pelts and wore them fur side in—how luxurious—and thus, the guard hairs fell away with use, leaving only the wool, nicely conditioned by Indian bodies, but perhaps less handsome to Indian eyes. There were no worries on that score, for glossy new pelts could always be had, blessed windfalls that accompanied animal flesh, that is, food.

It happened that the wool of *C. canadensis* was precisely what was wanted by the fair-skinned traders from the east, who had their own unfathomable notions of fashion. The wool was the best material in the world for making felt on account of its minute barbs, which, when steamed and pressed together, bound the whole into a sturdy, malleable fabric. Handsome to Euro-American eyes. So it would seem that the fur trade was a match made in heaven, though certainly not to animal eyes.

All this really began because people like to make things and travel, and to sit and talk when they get "there." People *like* to trade. And what with necessity and coercion of one form or another, it was inevitable that fair-skinned and dark-skinned traders would converge in North America. Well, necessity: the dispersal of the peoples of Europe, as inevitable as the flow of anything from high to low pressure. They came and landed north and south on the long American coast. To the south, their landing brought plantations and towns, inimical to the presence of Indians. To the north, the fur trade, or "this adventurous Traffick" in the words of one trader, brought wealth *dependent* on the presence of Indians. In pursuing this trade, the fair-skins were forced to cope with wilderness, an entity so appallingly inconvenient, profligate, disorderly—and irresistible—that they themselves were changed forever.

As were the Indians. "*Le Castor fait tout,*" they said. The worn-out pelts of beaver bought everything, anything one could desire from the realm of trade: tools, adornments, alliances, and especially weaponry with which to punish one's enemies. That last was key. All too soon it was necessary to kill too many animals for their pelts, for guns. This was not happily done, but it was done, and to no avail, for the Indians were at least temporarily conquered, not by old foes, but new. By the end of the fur trade era, the Indians were reduced to playing the roles of supplier, market, and labor for the business endeavors of the fair-skins.

They'd begun as suppliers, markets, *mentors*, and *hosts*. In the sixteenth century, first Portuguese, then Norman, Breton, and Basque fishermen found their ways to the Grand Banks fisheries off Newfoundland, and thence to the river mouths to trade with the exotic peoples gathered there. This went on for decades and likely caused the first waves of European disease epidemics among the northern Indians. The trade itself was not seriously regulated until Samuel Champlain arrived with government sanction at the dawn of the seventeenth century. This was the beginning of New France: Canada. The French called the Indians, "*les sauvages,*" meaning wild, untamed. Perhaps even free. There was a distinct sense of equal standing between the French and the Indians, though they deplored each others' morals and superstitions. They journeyed and traded and fought together for about one hundred fifty years.

To the south, first the Dutch, then the English, and then the Americans dealt rather less successfully with the Indians, and in any case, the good furs were to be found in the north. Far north on the rim of Hudson Bay, the English planted a few small, tenacious outposts, beginning in the year 1670, and there they stayed through thick and thin as "The Governor and Company of Adventurers of England trading into Hudsons Bay." As part of their charter, they were given Prince Rupert's Land, which was all the land whose rivers drained into the Bay, for their own. This most conservative of firms preferred for long years that the Indians journey to them, and never vice versa, so that the interior of Rupert's Land remained indigenous. The Cree, the Assiniboine, the Chipewyan. To the English and Americans, the Indians were "savages." Make of it what you will. Yet there were many fair-skinned men who married Indian women, both in the temporary and the permanent way, because people *will* mingle. Early on, there appeared the people of mixed blood, *les métis*, and these formed a prominent and unique block of interests in the fur trade. They were brides, clerks, interpreters, canoe-men, everything. They built their own traditions. But they battled the edifice of racism along with their full-blood relatives, and they still do.

The European luminaries of the early days included men with names like Radisson, Groseilliers, Du Lhut, Kelsey, La Vérendrye. Many of these live on as place names on maps, along with the Ottawa, Dakota, Huron, Mohawk, and all the rest of the Indian nations. The old days ended when the French succumbed to the British in 1760. Then there were new faces in Montréal, and these were Scottish. Soon the French and the Indians were working for *them*.

The H. B. Co. men called them "pedlars," derisively, for the newcomers seemed a bit low rent at first. They brought a different kind of energy to the trade, whether inspired by greed or astounding ambition or both. They went themselves to the Indians and woe be unto anyone who got in their way. By 1778, they had reached as far northwest as the Athabasca country, the *ne plus ultra* of fur-bearing terrain, sixteen hundred miles from Montréal; from there it was but a skip over the Rockies to the Pacific, and thus the whole continent was in their grasp. But that is facetious talk. There is no skipping over the Rockies or anywhere in the wilderness. In fact, they toiled, often failed, and sometimes perished in their attempts to grasp all. But the Scottish pedlars could not be stopped, and to the envious eyes of the Bay men, they did seem sometimes to skip across the country much in the way of an infection. In 1784, the independent pedlars formally congealed into the North West Company, and so, like Coke and Pepsi, the race was on between giants. All this in time of revolution, first in America, then in France.

These were the glory days of the fur trade and how we usually think of it: the fancy, thrifty gentlemen, the voyageurs singing their voyageur songs, the heroic feats of travel, and of course the annual rendezvous—Mardi Gras of the north—at the N. W. Co. depot, the Grand Portage on Lake Superior's northwest edge. Here, the winterers, all haughty with prowess, came down with their furs from the farthest backcountry. Here, the lowly summer help, the pork-and-beans boys—the voyageurs—came up in mammoth birch bark canoes with provisions from home, that is, east. They met with a flourish at Grand Portage. "Huzza!" they all cried, and exchanged their burdens, raised hell, conferred, schemed, and drank. They made love with local Ojibway girls. When the Americans made noises of sovereignty, the N. W. Co. simply moved the post forty-five miles north to undisputed British land, and built there Fort William at the mouth of the Kaministiquia River.

And what did the Indians make of all this? For one thing, they adapted to and sometimes controlled the fur business. They bought on credit, which was not as nice as family ties, but just as effective at binding the loyalties of the traders. Certain European goods proved admirably suited to Indian purposes and were taken up with enthusiasm. Others were tried and discarded. Alcohol was a problem: it opened a way to ecstasy and sometimes communion with other realms, but also sickened and killed without pity. The depletion of animals was a problem: it rocked ecosystems and drove people constantly to farther terrain. European diseases continued to wreck havoc, alas. Despite all of that, the northern Indians held their own for long years as linchpins of the trade and models for living in wilderness. They left an undying impression on every fair-skinned soul; they still do. One thinks of the Greeks and the Romans.

It was the horrendous competition between the two great Companies that finally brought things to a head. How strange; they were different but the same in the end. *Pro Pelle Cutem*, the H. B. Co. motto, meant, roughly, that they wanted the skin for the sake of the fleece—so utilitarian; it reflected their whole cautious, dogged image. Picture this: the Bay men sifting sand on their warehouse floors for every last hair. In contrast, the competition had *Fortitude in Distress*. The Nor'Westers forced the H. B. Co. to meet them in the backcountry and soon, rival posts speckled the maps. Hunters killed without mercy while anything was left and rum flooded the land. There was murder and unaccountable greed. Cheating was briefly profitable until, when things went too far, the enraged hunters turned on the traders, themselves victims of the machinations or ignorance of the agents and senior partners back east.

By 1821 the fair-skins gave in to the inevitable: coalition between the two companies. Subsumed under the name and charter of the H. B. Co., the rivals gritted their teeth and shook hands, and thus the fur trade in Canada solidified into a monolith. Ironically, the Indians were then plagued not with rum but low prices on furs. Racism built to a towering wall, one which neither love between men and women, nor old friendships could easily surmount. The fair-skins were duped into the general striving for upward mobility characteristic of the times (still), which did not admit of inter-racial parity. This little scurvy was promulgated especially vigorously by the

Company's new governor—George Simpson. This man, who began with no direct experience in the trade, became its conqueror before whom everyone, it seemed, must give way. How curious that a force of nature would have so little feeling for the real thing. He went everywhere at the most incredible pace, dispensing instructions to "destroy" the country—that is, to hunt out all the animals without regard to the future—in one place, and in another, to "nurse" the country or to leave off hunting entirely. These policies were driven by profits of course, but in the face of fluctuating political boundaries, simple expediency, and, eventually, the march of settlement—this last a foe to the fur trade. Furs needed wilderness and Indians. Farms, towns, ranches—no. Logging, mining and ditching—not at all. But the Dominion of Canada was stirring and *would* be born, so that by mid-century, the venerable Company was making its last stand against the onslaught.

It could never have lasted anyway, for if anything ever bore the stamp of temporary extravagance, it was the North American fur trade. Imagine the folly of basing anything—much less the penetration of a continent—on fashion. One wishes they could have found their northwest passage to the Orient, if only to distract from the thought of furs piled in warehouses, rotting. The vagaries of the Market; the waste of Life. But wasn't there always ruthlessness beneath the refinement of Western civilization? No different than China, Egypt, Peru, no doubt. In the mid-1800s, the British Empire, blithely oblivious and ruthlessly efficient, surveyed the globe from its heights. It was the rule of Victoria, and especially so in the sphere of outlook, mores, expectations. The world was changing swiftly and utterly, much as it had at the end of the seventeenth century or the end of the twentieth. In Victoria's time, there were massive, smoking industries and transcontinental railroads. Some people had most of the power (still), and these were delighted by toys and bedazzled by money. In America, there was Civil War.

The world of the Indians and the traders did not withstand this pressure, though circumstances varied according to latitude. In the south, with the conclusion of the war, westward expansion reached crescendo and the Indians were trapped on reservations, whether by means of false treaty or relentless persecution. To the north, somewhat the same. The buffalo plains were ploughed for grain, though robes and pemmican could still be procured there, at least for a while longer, from the *métis* at Red River, a settlement fraught with troubles, it is true. The numbers in Canada were fewer to begin with, the pressure a hair less, and the great forest, though logged and probed, remained and still stands. Yet the arc of three hundred years of trading for fur was poised, in the mid-1800s, to find its end, and dwindle thereafter to an insignificant sidelight, a small arcane thing. The Hudson's Bay Company took to land sales, then retail, then sold off its fur operations in the 1980s. And so the obscure finish of a most bittersweet intertwining of cultures.

* * *

In the summer of 1869, the last summer the Company would possess Prince Rupert's Land before the coming of Dominion, Edward and Frances Anne Hopkins waited at old Fort William for a pair of resplendent *canots de maître*. Edward had spent twenty-eight years of his life in the country, had crossed its expanse countless times, and weathered all of its trials. In the spring of that year, he had retired at last, and would leave behind him all that was bad, and take in his memory all that was good. It was fitting therefore that Edward's farewell to the North should be from a beautiful bark canoe, by the side of his wife, Frances, and in the company of fifteen voyageurs and two loyal clerks of the Hudson's Bay Company. Let us wish him safe journey! But it was not the Bay that bore his canoe that summer, but rather, Lake Superior, Kitchi Gami, that is, in the Ojibway tongue. Which is to say, *the Great Lake*.

3.

Déjà Vu

Summer 1869

OUT OF THE corner of his eye, Edward Hopkins was dismayed to observe his wife huddled on the shore like a common waif. It was an uncharacteristic pose, to be sure. Pretending not to see, he resumed his inspection of the bales and boxes heaped on the wharf. As if it were necessary. Everyone there—the laborers, clerks, sundry voyageurs—accorded him the deepest respect, but their eyes said clearly, "Sir, you're no longer in charge." How vexing. He glanced over his shoulder. Frances had straightened into her usual elegant self and now held her pencil poised delicately over a sketch pad. Thank Heaven, he thought. Perhaps she will draw a view of the river.

Graves, the bow-legged, quick-witted proprietor of Fort William, soon came down, unable to pass up a chance to gossip. For Edward, it *was* diverting to dissect the petty lunacies of the trade without feeling, for once, responsible for their resolution. Thus, he whiled away an hour or so, as the heat of the day waned and the colors deepened.

By six o'clock, Graves, in his excitement at having guests—especially the Hopkinses—went off to bother the cook, leaving Edward alone. The wharf by then was nearly deserted, the only sound, laughter from a handful of Indian wigwams at the end of the palisade. One last clerk walked away, writing diligently in his book.

Edward meandered back to Frances, who had not stirred. He could see that her hair, a dark amber gold, had been mussed by the breeze. This pleased him, though he could not say why. "My dear, Graves tells me we shall dine at eight. I hope you can carry on, though it's hours yet, I know."

She looked up at him and smiled faintly. "Of course." He noted the paper was blank.

How tiresome that she was still encased in full mourning crepe. Black upon black upon black. How he wished she would wear the lighter gown that evening, the one he'd insisted she bring, still black of course, but lighter and relieved with gray stripes. He was not sure how to broach the subject; he knew it would not do to push. "What about that pretty collar of yours, have a bit of white lace under your chin tonight? What do you say to that?"

"It would hardly be expected just yet, Edward."

"Ah." He cleared his throat. "I shall just go for a smoke, all right?"

"Yes, of course."

The pipe helped, though it was filled with cheaper tobacco now. A shame, but he might as well economize where he could, he thought, for he was retired. Retired! Retired, the little child dead, and his wife inconsolable. Edward heaved a great sigh, the kind of thing he never did unless alone. He could not deny that her sadness prolonged his own, but there was no help for any of it, was there? He was old enough to recognize his old ploy—impatience, which he used to cover sadness, remorse, even wrath, depending. He was old enough to know his own wily ways, and, he thought, To keep them hidden. He must not let out the awful *impatience*. In the still of the early evening, he could just hear the steamer far out on Thunder Bay, making for Isle Royale. He sighed again and muttered, "Damned dismal trip so far."

It had begun well enough. Agreeable, decent people, some old friends, all of them gathered for a pleasure trip on the Great Lakes. The Falls, Erie, Huron. At Collingwood they'd taken on business passengers and a band of hardy settlers returning to their homes on the upper lakes. Frances got on famously with all, as usual. But she'd quieted when they reached the Sault and had not recovered. Dutifully, they'd called on officials at Fort Brady and the Company's little post; she'd performed flawlessly, but without warmth. He supposed the sorrowful memories of the earlier trip had caught up with her, but what could he do? Hadn't she leapt at the chance for this voyage, this last adventure in the north? And here they were. At the Sault, he'd tried to interest her in the Indians fishing the rapids, surely an exotic sight and perfect for painting, but his wife was unmoved. This worried him more than anything; she had not made one sketch, much less a picture, yet, on this trip. It had always been what she *did*, and now she did *not*.

"Cheer up, Hopkins, she'll get better by and by," McCrary had said, not helpfully. Edward felt the impatience simmering. He refilled his pipe.

There had certainly been subjects enough. After the Sault, they'd advanced north into Whitefish Bay, with its treacherous wind and the dramatic view across from Gros Cap. There'd been lighthouses, as picturesque as any artist could wish. Lovely hanging waterfalls on Grand Island, and so on. Had it not been she who taught him to see these things? To truly see them? They'd had one terrible storm and after that, rain, rather dreary but not unendurable. After all, they could stop off if they wished at any of the little towns. There was much bustling on and off the steamer round Marquette and La Pointe and Superior City. But she preferred to stay on deck, or even in their berth "resting."

A movement on the shore caught Edward's attention. It was Frances; she had risen and now trekked slowly up the path toward him. The light had gone enough, he supposed, so that it was no longer practical to sketch—how convenient. He winced and thought, I must leave her be! I'll end up an ogre, thinking like this— He went to meet her and offered her his arm. "Shall we make our preparations then?" He would still try to tease her, after all.

She rewarded him with a soft chuckle. "Yes, we must. Who will be there, do you know?"

"The usual assortment." He ran through the list, so much shorter than in the old days. Hardly anyone lived at Fort William anymore, though it still served as a way mark for government officials, adventurers, tycoons. One or two of these would surely turn up at dinner. Edward pressed his wife's hand, as if to convey an apology. "You must try to summon your appetite, Frances," he said, "I believe they've killed the fatted calf."

"Oh dear." She leaned heavily on his arm, but only for a moment.

Frances wore all the black she could muster that night, for she was feeling distinctly low. A necklace of jet, her only concession to Edward's wishes. The diners, seven men, including the priest, du Ranquet, and one country wife—a full-blooded Cree, so they said— were on their best behavior. For perhaps half an hour, they kept their voices low and their remarks studied. But the wine flowed, and soon Graves was arguing with his guests, in particular, the Port Arthur man—a booster.

"The silver is just the beginning, I say!" cried the booster. "Soon we'll have a metropolis here on the north shore, and only a fool would try to stop it—"

"Ridiculous," the proprietor retorted, albeit with good humor, "Pride goeth, you know, *et cetera*."

Edward began to chafe and pull at his collar—confounded thing pinching his beard! He could not reconcile himself to the idea of a metropolis *here*. Oh, he was all for going home to London, Britain's great city of Empire, but he did not wish to see anything like that in Canada. Canada should remain as it had always been— open, empty, beautiful, a refuge for his memories. All this talk of *towns*—abominable! Rudely, but not caring, he broke in, "What of the Yukon returns?"

There was a short pause. An Indian girl, shy and very young, sidled in to clear the table. She and the Cree woman exchanged a fleeting smile.

"Ah, I didn't look up the exact figures yet, Mr. Hopkins. It wasn't half bad—"

"You have all grown quite lax." Edward pretended to be stern, but everyone was feeling far too comfortable to react. "Or is it that now you don't hide it, eh?"

"I dare say." Graves winked and called for port.

"I shall report you to the proper authorities."

"Who are they now?"

Edward gave up. "I've no idea."

"Mrs. Hopkins," ventured the senior clerk, a sun-burnt whip of a man, "Did you enjoy the falls at Grand Portage?"

"Oh yes, very much."

The Cree woman watched the English woman carefully, as if imagining how it must feel to inhabit that impenetrable black cloud of a dress.

"It was a devil of a climb," Edward put in, "and slippery, what with the mist. Had a proper nip at the top, too."

"We'll soon be in ruins like the Nor'Westers' old place down there. Come, what is your best guess, Hopkins? Shall we hang on here for very long?"

"Shouldn't wonder," he replied with a vague glance around. The lamps had burned down and a tall boy with a troubled complexion came in to trim them. They watched him solemnly. Then Graves and the Port Arthur man resumed their barely polite debate about local politics and the future of the trade. Du Ranquet nodded and murmured to himself. Edward's thoughts wandered back to the falls on the Pigeon River. How fine it had been! And she'd hardly noticed. He frowned and threw her a stealthy glance. He thought, Look at her, picking away at her food. He'd moved heaven and earth to get them to stop for the falls, and she'd hardly noticed!

On the contrary, she'd noticed everything. The wild strawberries and roses by the path. May apples and white-flowered bunchberry. The warm perfume of balsam fir. The sound of the falls, a froth over thunder; the edges like cascades of women's lace. The center cataract exploded over the top and plummeted, Edward had said, 120 feet. Below, dun-colored rapids raced down the gorge, all sheer black rock. Glossy, wet. In the gorge, there were ravens soaring and crying, and beyond, Lake Superior, so big and blue, it stretched above the trees where there should have been sky.

She saw everything. The problem was that she no longer knew how to put it on paper. Where to begin? This problem had become an absolute mystery.

She'd watched the water rush to the brink as if it could hardly wait to jump. In spite of herself, her gaze would fix on one discrete patch, a small gather of water, and follow it down. Then another patch, again and again. First, leap, then bloom. She couldn't help but wonder—what would it feel like? She'd counted three heartbeats before the water hit bottom.

She'd been stuck, in fact, on the inexplicable movement of water for several days. She was drawn to it, perplexed by it. There'd been the long, sinuous brown waves at La Pointe, rippling through reeds. And later, the waters of the lake moving east in unison, without waves. And the boy's face everywhere, confusing the issue. He was a child! Innocent and open, just as all children were, but he, so completely guileless as to frighten her sometimes. Then the fever, and so he was gone. There'd been Isle Royale's sleek silhouette and later, the cliffs, gray as iron, as they approached Thunder Bay. She could not paint any of it; she'd begun to despair.

She thought, I must just stop this.

She turned then to the sun-burnt clerk and asked in her most encouraging voice, "Mr. Shaw, what have you heard of your charming *fiancée*? We saw her in Lachine a fortnight ago. She was wearing a blue frock and said it was your favorite."

The clerk's face flamed with pleasure and everyone gave a great laugh. He said, "I'd be most grateful, Mrs. Hopkins, if you'd take a letter to her on your way down—oh blast!" He'd spilled his drink.

At that moment, there was a shout from outside the Hall. They could just make out the words, "Brigade coming!"

"At last!" Edward cried, forgetting to hide his impatience.

The diners rose, crowded out the door and down the steps of the grand-but-now-shabby Hall. They crossed the courtyard, and joined the few excitable souls left in Fort William to greet the brigade. It was not really a brigade; there were only four canoes, two for the Hopkins party and two to stay at the Fort. It was dark by then, moonless and mystical, and the only sign of the canoes was the flickering of their torches far out on the lake. Soon there were fragments of song, louder, then fainter, then louder again, as if borne by gusts of wind. But there was no wind. Frances, like everyone in the trade, knew the old French voyageur songs. This one's English approximation: "Friend, would you travel the water in all winds? The waves and the storm growl cruelly. The waves change with each day." To Frances, these melancholy words were full of an import she could not name outright. Unconsciously, she mouthed the words floating over the water, *"Ami, veux-tu voyager sur l'onde de tous les vents? Les flots et la tempête grondent cruellement. Les vagues changent tous les jours. . ."*

It was like a dream, drifting. A cannon shot cracked the dream briefly, in salute. Frances peered toward the canoes, expecting them to vanish at the boom, but they remained, coming nearer until quite suddenly the sound of paddles, dipping and stirring in water, came to the fore. Small waves like corrugations streamed toward them, limned in the torchlight. She thought, A scene such as this is full of possibility. She did not dare to think of what, but clung to the delicious sense of suspense.

The canoes appeared like phantoms, swiftly unmanned as the crew hopped overboard with a startling splash. News was exchanged; desultory orders ignored. Within an hour, the unloading was accomplished, leaving the wharf empty again. All were abed by midnight:

voyageurs in their makeshift shelters, clerks in their bunks, guests in comfortable quarters.

But in the bright and luminous morning, all suspense fled, and none who'd been lost were found. Weary *engagés* packed two very earthly canoes and prepared the gentlemen's breakfast. Frances longed to return to the dark of the night before. But that was not to be, of course. Hastily, she dressed.

"Tighter, Edward," she commanded as he wrestled with the corset. "No, tighter." For that was how she contained herself, pleasure trip or no. "Thank you, dear. I shall be out at once."

Edward looked at the heap of black on the bed. "All right," he said, and went out.

4.

Turning Around

July 1, 1992

I HAVEN'T LIVED in this house very long, but already it is more my own than any other place has been. I've only lived in three houses my whole life: my parents', my husband's, and this one. To our relatives, it's already "Chrissy and Franny's house." We tend to turn up the music here, like we did in those passionate old days, our stereo speakers turned out to the streets. Except we're so much wiser now—first there was music, then there was sex, then there were babies, *et cetera*. Oh yes, we get it now.

My first self-evident clue came in 1969, the year I got married in a brilliant white pantsuit, my pregnancy just barely showing. Long legs, so cute. I was eighteen and Jer was twenty, about to be drafted. He got out of it though, because of me—because of *us*—and his lousy lungs. Everything happened so quickly that year, events colliding into each other, each overwhelming what had just gone before. Woodstock, astronauts, morning sickness. I was dancing up 'til the eighth month, and after that, I still kept moving; I just swayed. Really, to me life seemed good. It was harder for Jerry; too many of his buddies went to war; too many didn't come back.

He could never get away from the razzing: "Pretty convenient condition, ya got there, Jer." My poor, freckle-faced husband couldn't hide that stricken look of frustration and guilt when the topic came up. He couldn't help that heat and mold left him breathless, and even though I hate his guts now, I will say the asthma was not made up. He had it, all right.

But together, we took it in stride. He started working half-time at Highsmith, a nice, clean place, and I got bigger and meaner and slower until Michael finally was born. He was seven pounds, four ounces, and it's funny, I know I'll never forget that one little statistic, no matter what else happens. Our world was the world of Michael; he was our small, squalling tyrant, but oh, when he laughed. At night, Jer and I would lie on the living room floor with Michael on a blanket between us, and we'd just watch him; we'd just eat him up with our eyes. We didn't want to do anything else.

We rented a tiny, two-bedroom ranch with a carport. Eventually, I had another baby boy—that was Walter, six pounds, eleven ounces. Jer's asthma got better over the years, and eventually he left Highsmith to teach gym at our old school—his way of dealing with old devils. Lucky him. Did I say yet that all this happened in Fort Atkinson, Wisconsin? Our home town astride the Rock River, right in the beautiful middle of America's Dairyland? Both our families lived there with us, and all our friends and relatives, and all the people we knew by sight, or at least by reputation. It was small, but I truly loved it. I still love it, but I don't live there anymore.

As a child in Fort Atkinson—we called it "Fort"—I used to love to search for the clues so skillfully set by my mother Janet, who put on the best treasure hunts on earth. When I was older, my girlfriends and I saw clues and signs and symbols in everything. It was a kind of addiction, so looking back on things now, I am dumb-founded that I missed it all with Jer. In my defense, I was pretty damned busy raising two boys, zipping around my house, keeping that firm but light grip on the reins. It's a trick to keep children alive and to cultivate their spirit, too. Maybe it's not such a trick; I could be just saying that for sympathy—my God, I am still riddled with doubt.

Because in essence, clue-hunting is nothing more than taking notice of details. I could tell you anything about my house, my boys, the intricacies of family politics, because I noticed everything that occurred in that domain. But I did not notice that Jer had become a different man until it was too late.

What kind of fool would just take it for granted he was doing his share? Of course, we both knew from the beginning that if it hadn't been for Michael, Jer and I may never have married. But so what? He arrived and we did, and for a long time, it worked. We had our little ship, we braved the seas, and my husband was right there with me. For sixteen years. So, was I a fool to believe it would go on? This is going nowhere, as usual.

The fact is, he did change, gradually, but, at least from what I hear, irreversibly. Because he taught gym, it didn't seem strange when he started subscriptions to, oh, half a dozen fitness magazines. Then he joined the health club in Madison, forty miles away, even though he had infinite access to the school gym and our basement full of fitness toys. His job was to teach kids to play softball, but after hours he really disappeared from that scene. I know he loved our boys, I can't deny that. What I want to know is, where did the cynicism come from? My freckle-faced Jerry with that darling, quizzical smile, became at some point a cynic and a deceiver, hard as his chiseled little bod.

Here are the obvious clues I missed.

- fussing with his appearance
- a bizarre concern with cleanliness
- driving all the way to the club two or three times a week
- fascination with vampy women on TV

And here are the subtle clues I missed.

- the blank looks
- unfamiliar gestures
- new jokes

- a sudden regard for respectability
- the absence of his favorite expression, "freaky," which he dropped utterly (when?)

But this tiresome list is not really the point, is it? The question remains, not how, but why did I miss all those clues? The only thing I remember is feeling, just now and then, uneasy. That's it.

In June 1985, my dad took the boys on a fishing trip to Canada. I made them take a wildflower book, but of course they were only interested in walleyes, rapids and bears. What a pang I had when they rolled away down the street! Yes, it was tough seeing my sons go off like that with Dad, but really the killer was that it used to be me who went with him. You know, I was jealous, but I kept that to myself. Then I forgot about it because, while they were gone, Jer and I had a little honeymoon. Oh yeah. He treated me like a queen and I so graciously accepted every last morsel of love. My doubts, if I ever really had them, were gone.

Things were still great when the boys came back a week later and we all crowded into the kitchen to hear about the trip. The campers radiating sun and high spirits, and even the kids smelling pretty bad. My dad leaning quietly in the doorway, looking apologetic because he knew who'd be doing the laundry.

"The flies were so bad!" Walt was shouting, "We had bloody chunks in our hair!"

"Yeah! Mom!" This from Mike. He was sixteen and had forgotten to be cool. Walt, thin as a post, was just turning twelve.

"Did you catch some walleye?" This from Jer, and so they really let loose about the fishing and campfire cooking and the eating of the giant, warrior walleyes. This was all pretty fun, but Mike, who knew how to please me, broke it off to give me the wildflower list: bluebead lily, pink lady's slipper, corydalis, bunchberry.

"Violets and marsh marigolds," he finished with a flourish, while his little brother cheered. You'd better believe I was proud of those kids.

"Geez, it was nice up there," said Dad. "The pollen was thick as yellow smoke on top of the water."

I said, "Oh Dad, I want to go camping again."

"You can come, Franny, any time."

But I had very little time to fantasize about camping because just a few days later, Jerry, my newly relished husband, got careless. It had to happen, but why did it happen in front of my boys? It was late, maybe 9:30 in the evening, and pretty hot, and I was going to pick him up at his office at school. So typical. I left early and took the boys, thinking how good it would be to stop and get ice cream, all of us, together. It's weird how I feel that I somehow messed up. So we pulled into the back lot and surprised him. He was leaning way, way into a nice new Camry, very sleek and gray, and when he backed out, the face, and in particular, the red lips of a woman I'd never seen before, followed. But you know, I think she had her seatbelt on, so she couldn't hang with him too long. She saw us first, then he did.

"Who's that?" Walt wanted to know.

By my side, I could feel Michael's embarrassment like a searing heat. I did not look at him, but said, very carefully, "Dad's still busy. I'll just pick him up later."

Then, in absolute silence—silence like a vacuum—I turned the car around and slowly drove away, as if the asphalt of the parking lot would crumble into a field of bottomless pits if I drove too fast or made any sudden moves. We went home.

So I lost Jerry to, not just one, it turned out, but countless young women of the '80s. With their big hair and sly, narrow eyes, their suits, and red lipstick. I felt like an infant, I was too ashamed to be angry, I was unsophisticated, naive, old-fashioned with that ridiculously innocent '60s look. I didn't deserve a modern man. Shit. We had several devastating scenes that occurred approximately at two-week intervals throughout the summer, and started divorce proceedings in the fall. Jerry moved out, and really, by the holidays, it was all pretty much over; it ended just as fast as it started. I shed Jerry's last name and regained my own, or rather, my dad's: Bookstaff. I was Frances Marcia Bookstaff again. It seemed very strange.

We tried to tell the boys that "sometimes grown-ups fall out of love, but you know, Walt, Michael, we'll always, always love our boys." They never bought it, and in fact, I think little Walt took a swing at his father. Mike snapped shut and wouldn't talk to either of us for a year. But through the whole wretched business, I have to say that my in-laws, Jack and Linda, really came through for the boys when I was about to lose my mind. And my dad of course, it goes without saying. He was the one who called me every day to find out what we needed: groceries, oil changes, plumbing tips, money. And my mother? Well, she'd always had her own way of looking at things, we were used to that. Turns out her hero, the painter Marc Chagall, died that same year. What the hell, she seemed to think it was some kind of sign. Just what I needed to hear about then. Anyway, I was thirty-four, a divorced mother of two, and life had changed. When Chernobyl blew up in the spring, I thought, Well, that fits.

My mother was an artist and my dad was a hunter, so you could say I'd been immunized against the plastic and fake smiles of popular culture at an early age. You have to be tolerant, though, or you'd just die, drowning in that crap. But after the divorce, my tolerance level took a dive. I couldn't watch TV anymore and even ads on the radio nauseated me. Really, nothing pleased me—every little pothole jarred my bones; sad saps like our neighbor put me in a fury. I reverted to a pre-marriage habit I'd had—walking alone in all kinds of out-of-the-way places. Places full of dust and litter, sparrows, crickets. I'd say I was taking shortcuts, but that wasn't it. I was reverting all right, picking up where I'd left off seventeen years before. I didn't realize right away that it was the girl Frances—not the artist Frances Anne Hopkins, or my own younger self—but the legendary girl from my grandmother's stories, coming out in me.

I started waitressing part-time days when the boys were at school, just to keep my head straight. This was an excellent strategy because, A.) I was good at it, B.) it brought in a little money, and C.) it kept me from thinking. If given the chance, I'd waste all my time and precious energy thinking bad thoughts and searching backward in time for all those damned clues. Yeah, that was healthy. Revenge was my favorite fantasy. I did not change my hairstyle.

In '87, Grandma Beth turned eighty and we gave her a fabulous party. All kinds of people showed up and even Jerry sent flowers. It was the first real fun I'd had, although, out of habit, I was still hiding behind snide comments and various attitudes of self-defeat. But I had noticed the terrible effect that kind of messing around had on the boys—it had really worn them down by then—and so when Grandma said to me, in the only English accent in all of Fort Atkinson, "Darling, you must cheer up and make plans," I was ready to listen.

"What are you going to do when the babies grow up?" she asked in her most silky, sympathetic voice. "It will simply not do," and she earnestly took my hands in hers, "to continue to stew."

The party was at my parents' house, so spacious compared to ours, almost decadent with its long halls and whole rooms set aside for specific purposes: the art studio, the gear room, the pantry, the added-on room for cleaning fish and butchering deer. I was wandering around, sipping punch and daydreaming, and stopped in front of the old print of *Canoes in a Fog, Lake Superior*. It had been hung in the same place for as long as I could remember, floating in its fancy gilt frame. It had belonged to my great-grandmother Marjorie. There was Frances Anne Hopkins's "FAH" signed in the corner; my mother named me Frances for that woman, I think, and not for the girl in Grandma Beth's stories. I'm pretty sure that day of the party was when I started thinking again about Frances Anne Hopkins's journeys and all those stories I'd heard when I was little.

I started working more hours. I waitressed nights at our only really nice supper club and made good money, which I socked away. I didn't know what for, yet. I had to trust Mike and Walt to stay out of trouble, which for the most part, they did, and just once in a while,

Dad checked in on them to make sure. So a new little wind started blowing.

We had a terrible drought in southern Wisconsin in '88. In '89, we watched the Berlin Wall come down. Mike moved out and got a job on Dad's crew, and Walt buckled down in school. He wanted, he said, to be an engineer, or maybe a rock star, but either way, he'd be leaving soon, too. During all this time Jer paid his alimony faithfully—how ironic—and scrupulously on time. I spent barely enough money to pay the bills and the rest of my pitiful income I saved. Finally, I had enough to set Mike up with a carpentry apprenticeship, and then Jer came through for Walt's education. Things were looking good for the boys.

And me? I took over the books at the restaurant during the day and hauled in tips at night. I went on a few ridiculous dates, and every now and then, had furtive, unsatisfactory sex with some other lost soul. When Walt and his gang moved to Madison to get ready, despite all the partying, for school, I was forty years old and my house was empty. I couldn't stand the place anymore. It had been six years since Jer and I split up and I was still mad, but that was a given, part of the scenery, so to speak. Nibbling away at my conscience was Grandma Beth's gentle, genteel prodding, "What are you going to do now, Frances, darling?" No matter how hard I worked, I couldn't get rid of my energy.

"The same as when you were a kid." This from Dad. "Geez, we couldn't get you to sit still. You never knew what was going on or even what you wanted, Franny, because you couldn't sit still for a minute."

I agreed with him; I wasn't stupid, just nervous, and I tried very, very hard to slow down enough to think. But that pace, that deliberate control eluded me, and so I floundered on. That summer, the big old Midwestern trees began to feel ponderous and overbearing. I'd always loved to watch wind stir the maples and oaks and elms, but now it only irritated me and amplified my restlessness. It got so that the sight of the whitish undersides of leaves, blown up and sideways, sent me back indoors, scowling in despair. It was nearly July when my mother came to the rescue.

She and I were studying the picture, *Canoes in a Fog*, for the umpteenth time, each of us silently appraising in our own ways, for our own reasons, and suddenly she said, "You know, Chrissy could use some help. You might like it in Marinette."

5.

Xavier Speaks

Summer 1869

THE HOPKINS PARTY was allowed a late start on that first fine morning, in deference perhaps, to the effects of the previous night's party. Mr. and Mrs. Hopkins took their places—comfortable seats arranged especially for them—in the middle of the second canoe. The sun was dazzling and so Frances unfurled her small parasol of black, lacy shade. They watched the brief tobacco ceremony and called out goodbyes to the Fort Williamites left on shore.

"*En avant!*" the steersman cried and in unison all fifteen paddles bit water. It was a relief to be underway. There was something in the crisp, steady motions of the paddlers that both soothed and sharpened the senses of their passenger observers, that is, the Hopkinses and the two Company clerks. Frances studied the casual physicality of the men in front of her, sighed inaudibly, and felt herself relax for the first time in a week. At last—she could brood in peace.

Edward, aware of her mood, did not trouble her with conversation. His head throbbed lightly; he was content to smoke and take in—perhaps for the last time—the passing scene. They advanced into the wide bay at the mouth of the Kaministiquia River and made for the cape at the tip of the great sloping mass of Paquanah, the peninsula that bore the sleeping giant. It would be a twelve-mile crossing, but Edward didn't care; he could feel in his bones that the weather would hold.

The bark canoes, emblazoned with colorful emblems, creaked and flexed agreeably to the exertions of the voyageurs. Not really voyageurs in the old way; these were Iroquois from Caughnawaga, near Montréal, for the most part, as well as several *métis* of obscure provenance. And, except for the French Canadian brothers in the lead canoe, the crew were not so well versed in the good old songs. They would give it a try now and then, but really they preferred to chat and tell stories. Some sly, off-color jokes they thought would go unnoticed, but there they erred. Frances gave no sign, of course, but she smiled inside, a little, and closed her eyes to savor the feel of floating on water. Mergansers fled before them and before long, the canoes had accelerated subtly until they were muscling their way through the water with the sort of high energy that is born of auspicious morning departures. The cape loomed ahead.

Edward was eager to see the already fabled silver island off the far side of the peninsula. A mere barren rock, just ninety feet across, it was said, the improbable site of a fantastically rich vein. Macfarlane had only found it the year before and now it was rumored to be for sale. Though surely not deserted, surely not, for when the canoes rounded the cape, the smoke of numerous campfires was instantly visible, both on the mainland and hovering over seemingly open water.

"No, there it is," Edward fumbled with the glass, steadied it and remarked with surprise, "It is barely above the waves, by God."

"Shall we pay them a visit, sir?" asked Mr. Baker, the elder clerk. They were all curious, voyageurs and *bourgeois* alike, glancing expectantly between Mr. Hopkins and the spot on the lake.

"Yes, certainly."

They recommenced paddling and soon drew up to the lee side of the island, or islet, while two surly men watched them, arms folded over their chests, glaring, trousers hitched high. A kettle slung over their fire wafted an unsavory odor toward the canoes. The fair-haired man took one step forward and said by way of greeting, "Private property."

Said Edward, "I am, you might say, a representative of an interested party. Perhaps you have heard of the Hudson's Bay Company?"

The two men sneered, but they were outnumbered by chuckling Bay men, and so the fair one made an effort to be civil. He pointed to the camp on the mainland.

"You'll find the boss over there."

"Very well, we'll just make a circuit 'round. Where is the vein?"

"Can't say."

"Ah."

In truth, there was nothing that portended a mine, only scattered piles of implements and broken rocks. The Bay canoes backed off and paddled slowly around the perimeter, lingering above a shelf of solid rock that fell away into the lake until lost in an aqua haze. The men on shore walked even with their visitors, all the way around, but their faces gave no clues.

"What say we call on 'the boss,' my dear."

Frances said nothing. She needed to stop after the long crossing, but did not wish to meet anyone. She was tired of courtesies, tired of social maneuvering. But the visit to the boss was inevitable, so she put on the guise of a Company wife and got ready. On the mainland, her worst fear was realized.

"What luck," her husband enthused, "There's Will Armstrong."

Armstrong was a modern man, one of those whose ambitions knew no bounds. An engineer and an artist of some repute, he was congenial, sharp, gifted, challenging, and unfortunately just the sort of person of whom Mrs. Hopkins was most weary. They'd met him through friends, and because Armstrong never dreamed of passing a chance to better himself, they'd ended up spending a long afternoon together, talking of trade and the nuances of angling for patronage.

Now, here he was, midway through his summer on the north shore of Superior. He was taking views of notable locations, such as the silver island, with the plan to either publish or sell them. It was not so precarious a living, for his topographical studies complemented his skill in the arts of engineering, and in fact, he was highly sought after for both. Thus he had established himself, but he, like everyone then, thought there must be something more—were not the riches of this world inexhaustible? One had only to ferret them out.

He strode now to meet the canoes, and in recognizing the Hopkinses, hurried to assist them. "Hallo, hallo! What a chance, sir!" He gave Mrs. Hopkins his arm as she was let down by two voyageurs. "We shall have a luncheon and tour the site," he said. "You must stay and look at my sketches, madam."

"How kind of you to offer."

Half a dozen men had now gathered around the visitors. The boss, stout and waist-coated, conversed self-importantly with Edward and the clerks. "We have christened it Silver Islet," the Bay men were informed. "It was just Skull Rock, before, but that's no fitting name for the richest silver vein in the world!"

Frances and Will Armstrong stood to one side, listening. She could tell he wanted to join the others, so she grasped the opportunity, and asked, "Would you be so kind as to show me where I could rest?" This was code of course, but Armstrong knew it well enough. He escorted her to a secluded place. She thanked him and said firmly, "Please don't trouble yourself; I shall rejoin my husband shortly." So he was released and she gained perhaps half an hour to herself.

Pushing through the dense balsam and spruce at woods' edge, she found herself in a cool, shady hollow where she could squat in peace. Through the screen of vegetation, she could still see the beach, very bright and cheerful with the blue lake beyond and the knot of men, a handful of canvas tents, a couple smoldering campfires. Before long, the mosquitoes discovered her, and rather than fight them, she pushed deeper into the woods to a clearing of lichen-crusted rock. She sat down on a flat, sunny spot and looked around with contentment. The clearing was ringed with wildflowers: columbine, small bluebells, buttercups, bunchberries and thimbleberries still in flower, and a riot of ferns. A single white-throated sparrow broke the silence with its wistful notes, and far off came the long complicated trill of a winter wren. She stayed thus as long as possible, until she knew Edward would be glancing around for her. Not long enough. She rose with a practiced shifting and levering, all hidden beneath the black skirts, and set off for the camp.

The luncheon was an over-civilized affair, with everyone, even the old rough cook, putting on airs. They paddled back out to the island and made a proper inspection. There was much talk, and finally, it came as no surprise when Edward decided to make camp for the evening right there with the boss and crew. Everyone was enjoying himself, so Frances was obliged to make the best of it. Still it wasn't so bad, she admitted at one point. Armstrong showed her his sketches and they were good, though she noted the human figures were not correct. As evening drew near, the clear atmosphere softened, then thickened, and then began a gentle rain as the encampment settled down for sleep.

She woke in the morning to diaphanous, white mist under a turquoise sky, and for a while she felt positively hopeful, for here was something she could paint. She went in search of her sketch pad and took a perch in her usual preferred spot, a little above and behind the camp. She began with a few light pencil strokes, hesitated and stopped to study the magnificent wall of Paquanah. At this juncture, her husband came ambling toward her with Armstrong at his side.

Edward was feeling a certain amount of self-satisfaction. He thought the trip was going better and he'd been most stimulated by the company of the silver speculators. He clapped Armstrong on the back. "Well, if I can't make a living off the beasts, I may just as well try precious metals. Perhaps we'll find some likely specimens as we go, can't ever tell."

Armstrong laughed politely, thinking, Fancy these old fur traders grubbing for ore. Still they had plenty of money to invest— He said,

"Watch out for greenstones, sir; it's said they're the best indicators."

On the beach, the canoes were being loaded with parcels. Voyageurs and clerks milled about; no one seemed hurried. Edward decided he liked these relaxed departures, so different from the usual Company routine. And, with his wife along, there was no worry of impudent voyageurs pulling down his tent around his ears, covert revenge on the pretense they needed the poles for the bottom of the canoe! His crew was leisurely enough on this morning. Edward checked his pocket watch; almost seven o'clock. He was gratified to see that his wife was drawing again at last. Excellent! he thought. Foolishly, he approached her, Armstrong in tow, and said, "You know Will, Mrs. Hopkins showed at the Royal Academy in May. What do you think of that, eh?"

"My congratulations, madam!" The engineer bowed low, unfortunately with a patronizing manner, as if she were a child who had done rather well. Frances gave them a frozen smile. She had worked for years to have a painting accepted at the Academy.

Armstrong made then a fatal error. "It is a sign of the times that the august Academy opens its doors to *paintresses*. What next?"

Edward winced. She would think *he* was trying to goad her with Armstrong's bumbling, the last thing he wished at that moment.

"Very clever, Edward." She did not even spare him a glance; she was furious. Meanwhile, Armstrong, puzzled but blithe, continued his wretched train of thought.

"I met a paintress in New York last year," he said. "Flowers, babies, that sort of thing. She was a fright, herself—"

Frances closed her sketch pad and rose to her feet.

"Well, old man," said Edward, "we'll be off. Good luck on your tour." He rose and hastened after his wife. Damn, he thought, I'm back in gaol.

The steersman of the Hopkins's canoe was a thin, raven-haired *métis* by the name of Xavier La Fourche. The "La Fourche" element was rarely remembered for he was always called "Xavier" and nothing else. "Xavier, Xavier, let's have the story of *La Maudite*." "Xavier, take us into the far channel," *et cetera*. He was an excellent steersman, a *gouvernail* of the old days, though he tended to daydream on long, sleepy crossings. He'd been watching with interest the little drama between Mr. and Mrs. Hopkins, and now, as the mist cleared before a fresh breeze and the paddlers doubled their pace, he was mulling the idea of a modest experiment. A line of black cormorants streamed overhead and disappeared in a fogbank. He wondered, Is it a sign? But his expertise did not extend that far, so he continued to hold his peace. As usual, the small cramp in his side made itself known, and he frowned, for he knew it would not ease for hours. If only he could distract himself; the experiment would be perfect for that.

Edward Hopkins remarked, then, over-loud and edged with frustration, "Fine day!"

An uncomfortable silence followed, and into this breach Xavier decided to plunge. "What about a tale to pass the time?" he suggested in his most noncommittal voice.

"Ah, Xavier the *raconteur*. Splendid! What do you have in mind?"

"I am thinking of the legend of—" he paused dramatically, gazing into the sky, "Frances and Garamond."

"What? Never heard of it"

However, appreciative murmurs rippled through the boat. The Caughnawaga Iroquois were thinking, in so many unspoken words, That's a risky one, Xavier, given the company, but you must give it your all for our sake, we who do all the work!

Mrs. Hopkins twisted around to look at the *métis*. He still regarded the sky, deftly plying his long steersman's paddle, silver ear-ring flashing.

"Which 'Frances' do you refer to, eh? Mrs. Simpson? Surely," Edward gave a strained laugh, "not my wife."

"*Non, non, Monsieur.* The Frances of the legend was a young girl, a wild young thing who journeyed here, long long ago." Xavier smiled broadly. He knew he'd taken the right tack. He shifted around in his place, unseen in the narrow stern.

"And Garamond was a young man from France, a man of gigantic character and strength, and immense kindness. There are none like him in these days, no, none at all. I must warn you, Monsieur, it is a long tale, and perhaps not a simple one."

Edward glanced at his wife. "Well?" he said. He no longer wanted to coddle her. And then she surprised him.

"Please, I would love to hear a tale." She turned to smile at Xavier.

"I would be honored, Madame."

The sun burned away the last of the mist. Frances opened her parasol, lightly touched her husband's arm, and settled down to listen.

"The people of France were very poor in those days," began the *métis*, "even as poor as some of us are now."

The Iroquois paddlers exchanged cautious looks. Edward wondered, What's he up to?

"And here on the waters of Kitchi Gami, the Ojibway, the Ottawa, the Cree, and even the Sioux paddled their canoes everywhere. They were rich in those days."

Frances, undisturbed by the implications of Xavier's words, closed her eyes and let herself be lulled by his exotic accent, a blend of French and the cool, musical cadence of the northern Indians. It was good to not think, to simply coast over the sun-shot emerald depths of the lake while listening to a story. Without opening her eyes, she knew that Edward was filling his pipe, and she felt for a moment, just a hint of her old serenity.

Xavier, said, "It is hard, so hard, for us to understand how they were in those days." He was glad no one could see him for he couldn't help smiling, which did not jibe with the story at all. But the little cramp in his side had eased a bit after all, and he knew he'd hooked his audience. "Let us start then with Jean Garamond," he said, "the young hero, trapped in his miserable hut in a land enslaved by the Sun King of France!"

6.

Seventeenth Century Europe

Winter 2020

Gentle Reader,

WHAT DOES IT mean to say that in the year 1689, Europe held some one hundred million people? In essence, it means that Europe was full. It hadn't been so since three hundred years before that, when the exuberant growth in human numbers was about to be crushed by the Black Death. Those plagues took one out of every three souls. The land had been emptied and gradually refilled, until there they were again, awaiting catastrophe, cheek by skinny jowl.

A biologist would say that the land had reached or exceeded its carrying capacity for human beings (other predators having long been eradicated). The ways and means then available to wring sustenance from land were pressed to the furthest limits. The fields of most villages abutted fields of the next. The ancient European forests had long been stripped for fuel and building cities. What was left was a landscape of tired plains, eroded uplands, pastures, and marshes eyed hungrily by peasants and engineers. Despite the best efforts to drain the marshes, build polders, or till mountains, the fact remained: land that was fertile and friendly for human habitation was used up.

By any account, seventeenth century Europe was a nasty test-tube for demographic experiment. In the usual situation, there was no leeway, no cushion, no nest egg, no nothing to fall back on when luck failed. A few good years, and then an epidemic, an early frost, a broken leg, famine, fire, or a visit from a self-appointed tax collector.

How was one to live in such a world? Why, people simply persevered. They suffered, laughed, prayed, demanded justice, and took to the highway. They—meaning the rural peasants who comprised most of the populace and produced virtually all of the food—were efficient, tough, hungry, and smart. They took such precautions as they deemed wise and spread their chances. They worked endlessly and died suddenly.

People were accustomed to living on the edge of starvation. Malnutrition was a common condition that produced both overt and subtle health problems. The stress of crop failure, illness, or accident was more than enough to loosen a peasant's hold on life. Girls' bodies, struggling to grow, did not have enough reserves to shelter new life and so menstruation was delayed into the late teens. This last was a blessing.

Sometimes, there were alternatives in the cities. Civic leaders in this period were known to maintain stores of food for the poor in times of famine. Sometimes it was enough. In the city, with luck, one could turn a trade into a business, join a guild and command respect. One could set aside a little dab of wealth. Or more likely, join the ranks of the urban underclass and die like a dog.

People everywhere waited to marry and have children until they were twenty-going-on-thirty. Children, of course, consumed scant resources, and usually only two out of three survived. Overall, the population of Europe was slowly declining, seeking more sustainable ground.

As one would expect, misery was intensified by unequal distribution of wealth and power. The peasants lost roughly half of their sustenance to taxes, tithes, and rent. Their wealth was sucked into the cities where it fueled industry, trade, art, and war. The agents of this transfer were kings and nobles, bishops, financiers, unsavory government officials. These were the classes who skimmed the cream and best half of the milk of the land of Europe. Had it not been so, the cities could have nurtured perhaps millions more happy *bourgeois*, trading and tidying. Peasants could have lived long and wanted for nothing. Yet, the land would still have been full.

Certainly one must own that there were evils—war and religious fanaticism—that waylaid anyone. No one was safe from these. Charles I, the stingy, stubborn King of England had died as easily as any pauper or secret confessor of sins.

How many died in the chaos of war? The Thirty Years War in Germany, the Bishops' Wars in Scotland, the Civil Wars in England, the Northern War, wars against Ottoman Turks. There were spurious revolts instigated by nobles; trade wars and piracy on the high seas; devastation wrought by vast, aimless armies of mercenaries; and peasant rebellions everywhere, savagely put down. There was waste beyond all reason.

With each disaster, people died or endured and prayed for heaven's justice. For in heaven they would learn who won: the Pope, Martin Luther, John Calvin? The Puritans, the Jansenists, the Levellers, the Covenanters (surely not the savages, Turks, or Quakers)? Everywhere, people wrestled for their souls with priests and elders, righteous know-it-alls, visionaries, and hacks. If they lost, they could be killed or at least punished, so practical people went their own ways in the secrecy of their hearts. Have pity for those who were co-opted, intimidated, hustled. Pity as well those who surrendered *so that* they could believe there was only one way to heaven.

Enough! It was time for the wheel to turn.

And so, by the last lean years of the seventeenth century, throughout the land of Europe one could detect a diffuse and persistent striving for order out of the chaos. Some people began to speak their minds, and surprisingly, they were not so often punished. These were usually people with leisure to burn, fortunate souls, or those in any age driven by genius. Scientists, philosophers, statesmen, playwrights. They thought: Perhaps we could dispense with inquisitions; perhaps we could make fun of our rulers; was it not possible that life could improve? *What if* the world obeyed natural laws that anyone could understand? Then there appeared a great abundance of ideas—published in pamphlets and debated both in royal societies and rowdy coffee houses. The *leitmotif* was everywhere the same: reason, order, tolerance, peace!

This first inkling of the Enlightenment was a fitful thing. It advanced and receded haphazardly, dependent on the whims of the powerful. Yet there was a growing sense of its inevitability. What was most difficult to keep down was a general self-awareness that seemed to infect everyone. The inhabitants of Europe knew very well they were hemmed in—by their past, their numbers, their rulers. Like all people they knew they were potentially brilliant. Imagine how they longed for a clean slate!

There were a very few of these restless people, who, with luck or money, escaped altogether. They made their tenuous ways to Brazil, the Carib, Virginia, Canada or elsewhere (to the woe of the inhabitants therein). And there, they found what was missing: freedom and land—rich, spacious land. The obstacles in their way were formidable, of course. But these would be dealt with somehow. The first and most essential matter was to secure passage on a ship fit for sailing the far westward reach of the sea.

7.

A Young Man from Anjou

Spring 1689

LATE IN HIS nineteenth year, Jean Garamond stood propped against a wall in the corner of his Uncle Romain's room, safely tucked in a wing of the Jesuit college in La Flèche. The stone was rough and cold, but it felt good to Garamond. He was dark-haired and, except for one lazy eye, good looking, and immensely strong for his age. Though his stance was nonchalant, he was listening intently to the conversation between his step-father Auguste Michon, his mother Andrée, and her brother, Romain, for they were deciding his future. Or so they thought.

His mother's voice was rising now, afraid that Romain would refuse the seriousness of their plight. After all, he'd found his own refuge here, long ago. Why should he risk disturbing anything, family or no?

"I tell you brother, the wolves have come! I know you know this." She forced him to hold her stare. "The King's men are pounding every door, looking for recruits, our poor boys to throw before the bayonets of some enemy, we know not who. I'll allow, our Garamond mayn't be quite ready to begin his novitiate, but could you not speak for him?" She was pleading now, her fingers squeezing the edge of her brother's desk. "He looks up to you! He adores you, Romain!"

Garamond remained still, his face showing a noncommittal earnestness, an expression he'd perfected as a way to keep his options open without offending. He didn't adore Romain, but he didn't dislike him either. He actually didn't mind the prospect of soldiering either—he pictured himself riding mounted into battle, wearing a uniform, carrying a pistol—though he knew that was a foolish dream. With some amusement, he thought of all the things that were being left unsaid in this meeting.

Uneasily, Romain glanced at his nephew, then down at his own hands folded on his lap. I've neglected my sister's son, he admitted silently, and now King Louis calls us to account. But my life's work is arduous! My duties intrude, my health fails, and he is bright but interested in girls and boats, not Latin—I did the best I could.

"If only you'd brought him here earlier, Andrée."

She shot a reproachful look at her husband.

Auguste shrugged and said, "He is good with the beasts." Though he loved his wife's son, his first concern was his other son—his *own*—who was older than Garamond, and ardently wished to marry and take over the farm. His second concern was his daughter, older yet and marriageable, but spurned by a flighty suitor. Auguste's house had simply become too crowded. Five adults on fourteen acres could only be a temporary state of affairs; it was time for Garamond to go. If the boy could find a place with the Jesuits, rather than wandering off to war or the highway, all the better. Such connections, thought Auguste, would pay off eventually.

"He is good with beasts but even better with books, eh Garamond?" Auguste waggled his finger at Garamond, pumping his brows up and down.

All this was beside the point to the young man. What *he* really wanted was to be a fisherman on the sea, which he'd heard was wide and blue and without demarcations of property, without landlords or haughty *seigneurs*. Each time he and his stepfather and brother had gone to the nearby city of Angers, Garamond would sneak down to the docks to watch the flat-bottomed boats and barges toiling upstream from the Atlantic. Sometimes they were towed by horses, sometimes sailed before a brisk wind. He studied every detail of these emissaries, ignored the jibes of their seasoned crews, and plotted his escape from the lush, ordered land of Anjou. Now it seemed this escape might take an unforeseen turn, deflected by war and his mother's power of persuasion. He held steady and waited.

Andrée leaned forward and clasped her brother's thin hand with her gnarled one. "Anything you want him to do, he will do, I promise."

Romain smiled faintly and withdrew his hand. I have no time for this boy, he decided, and said, "I will speak to Father Marcel about it. Come back in a fortnight and see he goes to Mass in the meantime."

"Shall I come next Thursday as usual?" Garamond asked.

"Yes, yes!" Auguste stood abruptly. "We need him for sowing, of course, but he may come to do chores for you, and we'll see he goes to church, depend on it! You won't be disappointed in our Garamond, Monsieur, he is a fast learner when he decides he must be."

Romain nodded once, thus ending the interview on a condescendingly tepid note.

The three peasants took their leave. As they started down the path to their farm, a light drizzle started, softening the already fuzzy outlines of a landscape tinged with green and filled with the birds of spring. Garamond stepped lively, unaccountably optimistic in the way of those lucky few blessed with utter confidence in themselves and their futures. He was, he felt, indestructible. He put an arm around his mother's waist and said, "The Jesuit brothers go everywhere —"

"Never mind that," she snapped. "God willing you'll teach right here at La Flèche with your uncle."

Auguste hid a smile and deadpanned, "Or perhaps you'll be right here, mucking the Jesuit stables." Then he laughed good-naturedly as Andrée cuffed him.

Garamond laughed too, but persisted, "To be accepted with them, you must always obey—it is part of the oath. They may order you to go anywhere, and you have to go, you know? Whether it's to save souls or muck stables, you have to go."

Andrée frowned and tightened her grip on her son's encircling arm. For a moment, no one spoke; only their breaths puffed in the cool, humid air.

"We'll see about that," she said.

Auguste changed the subject. "Well, you can't go away just yet, Garamond. I need you to take the colt to sell in the Poitou. It was bad luck we couldn't spare it last fall, and the creature ate more than its share this winter, greedy wretch; it's been a near thing this spring, bones showing on every beast. The colt has got to go," he finished, unconsciously echoing the lot of his stepson.

"Yes, *papa*. After the sowing."

Late in the afternoon, they returned to the farm with its familiar sounds of bleating sheep and lowing cattle, and smoke curling up from a roof of turf to disappear in the sky. They each noted this beauty but did not speak of it. Husband and wife headed for the cottage, while the son cut away for the barn where his brother tended the animals.

"Jean!" Garamond shouted as he ducked inside, for these stepbrothers shared the same Christian name. That was why Garamond was called by his family name; Old Garamond, they'd called him when he first arrived with his mother, long ago, on account of his wizened little face.

The step-brother, Jean Michon, was tall, plain, twenty-four years old and craving his father's farm. Jean knew as well as all of them that there was no room for his step-brother. "How did it go?" he asked, and winced. There was no question that he loved Garamond with all his heart. Yet he needed him to leave.

"So much hand-wringing and talk," Garamond answered. He moved swiftly to retrieve a ewe that was heading for the door. "We're to go back in a fortnight. You know, it wouldn't be so bad if they'd send me to Nantes, or any port, with a few sols and new clothes. I could slip away easy enough, sign on with a ship, and there I'd be sailing off to La Chine." He grinned at Jean and tossed him a sack of grain. "We're sowing tomorrow, Jeanette, huh?"

"Don't spill it, fool." Jean laughed. "Did you see Marthe on the way home? She was supposed to be in the village. I'm going to her tonight, I think."

"No, but I saw her crazy cousin."

"Phew, what a bitch."

"Where's Annebette?" Garamond asked. He referred to their recently snubbed sister.

"She's sulking, of course. Making tallow candles."

"You know, Jean, we should beat that son of a bitch for her."

"Yes, but when?"

"Next time we see him—we won't have to go out of our way."

They worked together happily, each knowing the other's rhythms and the rhythms of the animals. It turned completely dark so Jean lit a rush light, and they finished their chores in its smoky, unsteady light. Before they left, Garamond went to the colt—Little Ugly—he called it, and stroked its huge, shaggy neck.

"*Papa* says you'll be taking a trip to the marshes soon," he informed it. "Back to the land of your fathers, eh? They'll put you to work all right, digging and trenching all day. But you'll bring a better dowry for Annebette if we sell you there, no arguing." The colt stood with complete serenity; its grave, round eyes seemed still to gaze at ancient forests.

"I'll steal some oats for you on Thursday, what do you say? You'll be the strongest beast in the Poitou." He kissed the colt on its gigantic nose and went out.

The sowing that spring was a resounding success. A string of calm, mild days followed by soaking rain, then sun. The soil of Anjou was extraordinarily fertile and coddled by a most benign and temperate climate. Now, with such an auspicious beginning, what wealth might the harvest of 1689 yield? The face of every peasant glowed with hope, all the more radiant because, every soul knew deep inside that even a record harvest would never be enough.

The Michon farm was sown before most, what with its surfeit of personnel. There was plenty of time left to discipline Annebette's lover, but the atmosphere of good will pervaded the hearts of the brothers, and so they let the idea go. "He may still well be my brother-in-law," Jean reasoned. "Best to wait and see what the colt brings."

The day that Garamond was due at the college, he woke early, while the brightest stars still burned, and with only a long drink of milk to fortify him, set out for La Flèche. If he got there by dawn, he'd be given a small breakfast before his chores. Then a mid-day meal, and lessons with Uncle Romain while he tried to stay awake. Then home again. All in all, he relished these Thursdays; they afforded a change of scenery for his restless eyes, as well as intriguing subjects for thought. He loved to imagine the conversations of the inscrutable Jesuit superiors, behind their oaken doors.

On this morning, he swung along in the waning darkness, humming and worrying the bushes with the occasional whack, sending up sprays of startled birds. The village appeared suddenly as always, shadowy but lit on the rooftops with delicate gold—the rising sun. Garamond slowed to watch the pale light touch the college, define it and give it color. Color emerged all around him, and he felt the energy rising up in his own body, an incredible optimism and feeling of strength. He longed to grasp the buildings of La Flèche, fling them in the air, and catch them again. He chuckled at the absurd thought, then folded the energy back inside. I must aim true today, he thought. No misses, no stray words. Before him, the village was waking: a door banged open, and a dog raced down the street, while roosters began to give voice. Garamond made for the college, humming again.

Brother Romain also loved these Thursdays, for he was given the whole day, even though he only instructed his nephew in the afternoon. This left him free to pursue his "famous essay," as he called it, his own philosophical treatise, his life's work. On every other day, he was obliged to teach Latin and letters to the real students: the sons of nobles and *bourgeois*, and the secret sons of priests. True, there were a handful of talented sons of farmers, and it was barely possible that Garamond could join them in their studies at La Flèche, but Romain was not enthusiastic at the prospect. He shook his head, *Mon Dieu*—the work that would take! He still had not broached the subject with Father Marcel. He knew it would not do to slight Andrée's son, who at that very moment, emerged from the kitchens heading for the well with a yoke of pails to fill.

"I will not think about it as yet," Romain said aloud. He rose slowly, fighting arthritis and the pain in his distended belly, and began to assemble his papers. It would be light enough to work shortly—he needed the cheerfulness of daylight. Outside, the spring warblers were already singing. How lovely, he thought. Soon enough he was ensconced at his desk and reciting his ritual Thursday questions: "How does one reconcile the sublime beauty of Nature with her unspeakable evil? What is Nature to God?" He addressed these queries to the four walls, and scanned the neat piles of papers before him, each of which bore a heading scratched ornately in ink. He took out a clean sheet of paper. He stared out the window. The answers to his questions fled, as usual, to the farthest, murkiest corners of his room.

Resolutely, he read the heading on the first pile of papers—Nature is Evil—and considered the ancient venerability of that claim. Really, it is comforting, he thought, in its tradition of *us* versus *them*. How many thousands of years has Nature sent her lawless, supernatural powers against us? Does not temptation dwell in the wilderness? Surely, we are obliged to rise above Nature. But he was troubled by the mention of "temptation," acutely aware of his lack of resolve in that department, and so quickly moved to the next stack of papers: Nature is Good.

Ah no, he thought. Nature is Glorious! Think of the breathtaking beauty, the sheer abundance she throws at our feet, like a careless gift. There can only be the hand of God in such goodness. Did not God create nature? Did He not create it for us?

He gazed at the sunlight bathing the edge of his desk in blinding white. He wondered briefly if he should go outside, perhaps amble along the pleasant path to the river, feel the soft spring breeze on his face. But he realized the light on the edge of his desk signified time passing. None to spare, he thought, and reached for the third pile: Nature is Our Servant.

He screwed up his face, concentrating. His most recent notes on this subject concerned the notion that to attempt understanding of Nature was a Christian's duty, both for the sake of human edification and in order to harness Nature for economic progress—another typically coarse English idea.

"I must not waste time on child's play such as these," he said aloud, and moved the three piles—Nature is Evil, Nature is Good, Nature is Our Servant—to a stool near his desk. With some ceremony, he laid out the last two stacks; on the left, God is Nature, and on the right, Nature is Indifferent. This last heading was written below several others, crossed out: Nature is Merciless, Nature is Neutral, Nature is Just, Nature is Unjust. For several moments, he sat motionless, noticing the ache in his hips and spine, the sudden hunger in his belly. Then, he set these distractions aside, as well.

"God is Nature," he whispered and delicately lifted the first sheet in that pile. He read the words of Pierre Bayle:

> . . . Nature is nothing else than God himself acting by certain laws which he has established of his own free will. So that the works of Nature are not less the effect of the power of God than miracles, and suppose as great a power as miracles, it being altogether as difficult to form a man by natural laws of generation as to raise him from the dead.

"*En garde*, Monsieur," Romain murmured, "Did the comet put that in your head?

There were also, carefully noted in this pile, a collection of the voices of Deists, Unitarians, and heretic philosophers, all variously contending that God and Nature are identical, completely alive, and consumed in one harmonious whole. Father Marcel had been unwilling to allow access to these works, but Romain had pestered shamelessly until he gave in.

"You are well aware, Brother Romain, of the risk involved in obtaining these documents? They are, of course, controversial, if not banned outright. While I applaud your philosophical endeavors, please, do not allow your soul to be contaminated in the process."

"Have no fear, Father. I am quite safe." And he *was* safe from these ideas, at least in the sense that they did not disturb him. It was only the last pile and its hideous corollary that threatened his equilibrium. That is, if God is Nature, and Nature is Indifferent, then . . .

In a burst of energy, he began to flip through the papers in the last pile. Each sheet bore a description of some particularly poignant natural tragedy: a nightingale's plundered nest; the long, long death of a boar in the woods, gnawed by hounds; the tortures of Romain's own body. He turned more pages, then lingered on the description of maggots in the corpse of a lamb, and the luxuriant green grass that grew in the spot the next year. He wrote: "The sheep that grazed the spot were killed for mutton over the winter; I ate of it as did we all. How close a kin are we to maggots? In the eyes of God, are we any different? Do maggots have souls?" Of course that was heresy.

He came then to the words of the notorious Dutch Jew, Spinoza:

> So when something in Nature appears to us as ridiculous, absurd, or evil, this is due to the fact that our knowledge is only partial, that we are largely ignorant of the order and coherence of the whole of Nature and

want all things to be arranged to suit our reason. Yet that which our reason declares to be evil is not evil in respect of the order and laws of universal Nature, but only in respect of the laws of our own nature.

God is Nature. Nature is Indifferent. Romain skipped to the last page to read the plaintive words of Blaise Pascal, heretic Jansenist and political arch-enemy of all good Jesuits:

This is what I see and what troubles me. I look around in every direction and all I see is darkness. Nature has nothing to offer me that does not give rise to doubt and anxiety. If I saw no sign there of a Divinity I should decide on a negative solution: if I saw signs of a Creator everywhere I should peacefully settle down in the faith. But, seeing too much to deny and not enough to affirm, I am in a pitiful state, where I have wished a hundred times over that, if there is a God supporting nature, she should unequivocally proclaim him, and that, if the signs in nature are deceptive, they should be completely erased; that nature should say all or nothing so that I could see what course I ought to follow.

"I cannot help you, my friend," Romain said. Instead, he chose a clean sheet and wrote: "Beauty in the corruption of the flesh?" He placed the sheet on top of the pile. At that moment, there was a tap on his door. Startled, he bumped the pile of papers, which slumped and scattered across his desk.

"Yes?"

The door opened partway and Garamond stuck his head inside. "If it pleases you, Uncle, I'm done early with my chores."

"So? I am not ready." Romain scrutinized his nephew. "Are you really finished?"

"Well, almost so."

"Mmm. Off you go."

The youth slowly closed the door, then quickly reopened it. "My parents would like to come Saturday, if it pleases you, Uncle."

Romain let out an exasperated, "Ehh—" and flapping his hands, shooed away his annoying student, this time, with success.

By then, the sun was approaching its zenith, its harshest rays falling on the disorder of his desk. He rose and began to shuffle around the room.

Pitiful, pitiful, he thought. I am sure I could vanquish these mysteries if I had only half the vigor of my nephew. Such injustice! The bitter irony of it!

He knew he should eat, but he didn't want to waste time. He sat again and without regrouping his notes, seized another blank sheet, and began to write furiously: "Has such as my nephew grown strong at the expense of poor souls such as me?"

His thoughts abruptly switched to the orchard where his own father had once tended peaches, pears, cherries, and apples. His father had said to him, "Some will wither and die, but that is good, for the others shall have more light and more good soil in which to grow—*merci de Dieu*." These words, forever branded in Romain's mind, offered him no comfort.

He continued to write, more methodically: "It is clear that my natural body has betrayed me, and that being so, one must own that Nature has shown her treacherous face, and because one cannot be both good and treacherous, on balance, Nature must be evil, and is only good in a capricious way, and we, as Christians, must strive, not to subdue or understand her, but to be wary of her and avoid her snares." Satisfied, he set down the quill and thought, God willing, my robust nephew will bring me something to eat.

Like a prayer answered, there was another tap on his door.

"Yes?"

But of all people, it was Father Marcel.

Romain flushed, thinking of his sister's plea for Garamond. Why not now? he thought recklessly. Why not get it over?

Before he could speak, Father Marcel said, "I've been observing your nephew, Brother Romain. How is he coming along?"

"Oh! Very well indeed, he is an excellent student!"

"Another Descartes, eh? We could use another distinguished alumnus! Ha! In all seriousness, I have a proposal for you." He put on his most friendly, confidential air. "As you know, one of our faithful *donnés* has died in Canada."

"Was it *les sauvages*, Father?"

"Mmm. Of course, we carry on, but we need lay helpers, there is no way around it. It is all very well to convert the heathen, but who will build our chapels? Who will cook our meals? We need to replace the fallen, Brother Romain."

"Yes, we do."

"It happens that our kind benefactor, de Fancamp, has just granted my request for help in this matter." Father Marcel beamed and rubbed his hands together. "He is willing to pay the passage for a new *donné* to the Montréal mission. Isn't that wonderful!"

"Wonderful!"

"I have in mind your nephew."

"Oh!" Romain gulped, smiling desperately, thrilled by this perfect solution to the problem of Garamond. God forgive me, he thought, but I could use the time! Then he checked himself.

"My sister may object. The danger—"

"I myself will talk to them. It is not so dangerous for a strong young man. He is the younger brother, is he not?"

"Yes, regrettably."

"Ah! But he will serve God and reap a greater reward than ever could be earned on a little farm here. When will you see his family again?"

"Saturday next."

"*Formidable*! It is all but settled." Father Marcel stood up and straightened his sleeves. He eyed Romain. "I see you are deep in your studies again. Shall I just mention it to the young man for you? And have food brought?"

"You are so kind, Father."

"No, no; leave everything to me."

They rose and bowed, and Father Marcel left to find Garamond.

Romain remained standing by his desk, gripping the back of his chair. I'm sure it is for the best, he thought. Canada would temper my nephew, challenge him—he needs that, even though it *is* a windfall for *me*. He smiled and sat down to wait for his food. Then he chuckled softly and, still all alone in his room, recited a favorite line of Dryden's—I am as free as nature first made man—!

Father Marcel let out a long sigh when he closed the door on Romain's room. "Thank Heavens," he muttered and strode down the corridor. Like most Jesuits, he was ambitious, astute, and physically strong; he could not help contrasting himself with Brother Romain. What a pathetic thing, he thought. That stick body with the bulging belly, the alarming gassiness. In such a state, he will never succeed in joining the Order. And that treatise is killing him! Bah, what a waste—he could have been a master linguist! Marcel shook it off and turned into the courtyard.

There, in the hot spring sun, was the young man, Garamond, pitching pebbles and eating bread he'd pilfered from the kitchens. Chewing hastily, Garamond stood to let the Jesuit superior pass, but the man stopped and addressed him. When Father Marcel asked him if he'd like to go to Canada and work at the Jesuit mission, Garamond's face lit up like a torch.

8.

Fort Atkinson, Wisconsin

July 1, 1992

I SPENT MY childhood summer days, the ones heavy with sweat, writing in my diary on top of a hill by our house. There was an open space, a field usually in clover, and a fringe of tall trees singing, in their raspy way, in the wind that always blew there. It was my dad who got me started on the diary. The whole idea was to get me to focus, to practice the skills I so woefully lacked in school, because I was really pissing away my grade school years. My parents worried I was some kind of proto-juvenile delinquent. So they made me write about everything that happened or that I noticed on the long rambles and hunting trips that Dad and I took. I wrote all kinds of stuff in that diary, small, wonderful, terrible things that could have been lost, or, on the other hand, obtusely stuck in my head like gum. There'd been a squirrel sprawled on a railing, sunbathing, and then in March, maybe the same squirrel, licking sap from our sugar maple tree. There were suicidal frogs leaping into our campfire, sparrows feasting on dandelions, and the ominous chanting of locusts.

After days of sodden heat, there would always come either a storm or a fresh hard breeze, and we'd wake in relief to an overcast sky, striped ivory and blue. By noon, the sun would burn through and colors would magically appear, all in crisp silhouette. My mother would point out the resemblance to a painting, say, one of Van Gogh's, with green, leafy branches stretched up to a turquoise sky. "Sublime!" she would say. This is how I remember the early summers in Fort, the sky and the woods and fields, and the serene brown river that flowed through the town. Sweet Jefferson County.

It was Grandma Beth's fault that my mother was so wrapped up in art. She had my mother going at an early age with watercolors and chalk because skill in art was still thought to be an "accomplishment" in grander circles. When my mother was small, she was given a book of Chagall prints—those colors!—and it was all over. I'll admit, Chagall's animals are something else. Whether natural or supernatural, they're everywhere with their friendly, knowing eyes, on a par with their human masters. Embarrassing to some of us, I suppose. My mother absolutely loved them, and this love of hers formed her own art: meticulously, almost photographically correct paintings of animals, especially domestic animals gone wild. Or at least way more powerful than they should be. By the time I was ten, these pictures were all over the house and bursting from cupboards, portfolios, and of course, her studio. My own favorite was the saddlebred show horse, drop-dead handsome, sparks flashing from his hooves, his rider a mere doll, a prop, a ticket to the show.

In 1961, Mrs. Hoard, wife of the *Hoard's Dairyman* magnate and town patroness, founded the annual Hoard Art Show and my mother immediately entered her picture, *The Insurgent*, which figured a dry Holstein cow, an old cow gone to seed, prancing through a primeval forest. The cow looks eagerly ahead. No one knew what to make of it, but it ended up in the "General Amateur" category and drew small, curious crowds (it did not sell). Grandma's equanimity was at last shaken. "Janet," she admonished, "Why should you enter such a frightful thing? You must try very hard to paint something appropriate for next year."

Well, my mother did try and eventually sold pictures, but not her best ones, at least in my opinion. But my mother was practical. She didn't need my approval, or anyone's. She did what she thought was right for herself as an artist. She was and is a quiet, no-nonsense woman with a keen eye and her own agenda.

Smack in the middle of all those pushy animals, on a calm wall in the living room, floated the old print of *Canoes in a Fog, Lake Superior*. It is so familiar to me, if I could draw, I could easily reproduce it from my heart's memory. The print had been handed down from Great-Grandma Marjorie, that faithful, hopeless student of Frances Anne Hopkins, and through Grandma to Janet, had ended up in our house. There, on the sofa beneath *Canoes in a Fog*, Grandma and I would sit in the evening and she would tell me all the stories. I would always ask, "Did it really happen?" and she would say, "Well it might have. And it might be just a tall tale, too."

I would cuddle next to her, her warm scent around me, and listen with every atom of my body to the story of how long, long ago the little girl Frances was born—not Frances Anne Hopkins, but the earlier Frances, the wild one.

"This is how I heard it from my mother," Grandma would begin. "And she heard it from Mrs. Hopkins, a famous lady artist who went canoeing with her husband in Canada. And she heard it from wild Indians who passed the story down from parent to child for years and years."

"Was she born with the Indians?"

"No, she was born with her mama and papa on a cold, windy, rainy, lonely old night. The wind was a-raging and the people all huddled together by the fire. Her mama wrapped her up to keep her warm and her grandma made a cake to celebrate her granddaughter's birthday."

"Why did they name her after me?"

Grandma Beth would smile and say, "No, they didn't name her after you, my dear. But after hundreds of years, you were born and your mother named you Frances after that little child, and also for the lady artist your great grandma knew. Your mother's an artist, too, you know."

"How did the Indians know about the baby?"

Oh, that's too long a story for tonight. And a very important story that you'll find out all about, I promise."

"Does Mom know any Indians, Grandma?"

"Heaven only knows but she might." She would stand me up carefully then, and lead me upstairs to my room. Little did she know what she'd started.

Before there was real hunting with Dad, there were my mother's famous treasure hunts that drew every last kid in our neighborhood. I mean these were thrilling events; we had tantalizing posters to announce the particulars and cunningly wrapped, illustrated instructions for each player. The path to the treasure was strewn with surprises, like tiaras and new packs of cards, and the final prize was always some fabulous, grown-up thing, the kind of thing a kid would never think of. Once I found the treasure and it was a fitting for a costume—any costume—at Mr. Johnson's Tailoring and Alterations. I chose to be a fiery dragon. My mother started all this as a way to keep me, the Action Girl, occupied and/or out of trouble, but she can hardly be blamed that the hunts became epic; it was in her nature, or rather her talent, to make them so. It got so that my best opportunities to run amok occurred *during* the treasure hunts. All those clues! They simply drove me wild.

But there couldn't be epics every day, and on any day for quite a few years, I would not sit still. Sing like a meadowlark, leap like a deer—yes. Sit still and listen? Never. My poor, harassed mother tried to interest me in art—"Who wouldn't be interested?" I'm sure she thought—and bought, at great trouble and probably expense, a book of Chagall's one hundred etchings of the *Fables of La Fontaine*. I was indifferent. She gave me paint set after paint set and deluxe edition crayons, and these were wonderful, but they only held my attention for, say, half an hour. I think it was when I was nine, in fourth grade, that her own attention waned. She handed me over to Dad, "She's your daughter, too," and disappeared into her studio.

I looked up at my dad and he, arms crossed on his chest, looked down at me. We were both perplexed I think; our respective worlds were evidently on different planets. What would we do without Mom? We would have no interpreter. I remember my neck started to cramp looking up at him like that—he was nearly six feet tall—and I started finally to drift away, the way kids do. Then his low, ragged voice broke the spell; he said, "You want to go look around?" This was family code for hunting, that is, the hunting of deer, ruffed grouse, and pheasants.

"Yes!"

"Well then," he sighed. "Go get your boots on and your raincoat. We'll give it a try."

That first day, all we did was walk through the fields on the edge of town. Dad said he was scouting for pheasants, though I'm sure he knew the prospects of that place inside and out already. I remember joyfully stomping through every low, muddy spot I could find. It was late in a good, wet summer, and though the farmers cursed all that rain before harvest, the weeds and the wildflowers rejoiced. Chicory, wild carrot, goldenrod, Joe-pye weed. My dad knew them all and made me repeat their names. I picked a spray of blue chicory to take home, and that evening my mother showed me how to press it flat in the dictionary between sheets of waxed paper.

"Here's the start of your collection," she said, with a note of satisfaction, at last, in her voice. "You can paste them in your scrapbook for something to show at school."

"Okay," I said. And so it began.

We went on the weekends and in the soft, early evenings, and were occasionally rewarded with the blur of a fleeing deer or the whir of wings. After I'd collected the common flowers for my scrapbook, Dad came up with another idea, which he didn't disclose right away. We packed lunches one Saturday morning and drove far out in the country to a completely new place (so he said), wild to my eyes and full of mystery. As we set out, he handed me a small notebook and a pencil, saying casually, "I want you to write down where we go on this hike, okay Franny? Because I don't know my way around here and I don't want to get lost. I'm counting on you because I'll be looking for signs of deer."

"Okay." Charged with this responsibility, I noted our every move. "Turn left at the white post and follow the row of bushes—"

"Those are dogwood bushes."

I squeezed in "dogwood" and continued to scribble. I barely had time to add "right at big tree" before Dad picked up the pace and almost vanished into the woods. "Wait!" I yelled. It was truly an amazing reversal of roles—I was hooked.

The scrapbook and the diary saved my life in school that fall. I walked and watched and wrote all through September, and proudly took my treasures and new skills to class. The weeks sped by and then Dad and I started scouting for deer stands in earnest. This was different; he would find a likely spot, using all the clues that he'd found and showed me (I furiously wrote them down), and then we'd sit there quietly for about an hour and just watch. This was Dad's crowning achievement; he got me to do this voluntarily. I sat there, sometimes motionless, always attentive, and recording everything on paper.

But I was a girl and this was 1960, after all, and so when it came down to actually hunting, I was left behind. Dad took off with Pete Schiller and Pete's dogs, Old Lady One and Old Lady Two, and they went grouse hunting without me. I sulked—oh, did I sulk—but I realized that would get me nowhere. So I pleaded relentlessly, as only kids can plead.

"Herb," my mother said one night, "look what she's written in her diary."

He picked up the diary, frowning, while I beamed from the doorway. He read in a man's weary voice, "Dear Diary it's almost time for Dad to take me hunting with Pete and the Old Ladies." I'd written the same entry each day for the last two weeks.

That diary ploy had come back to haunt him, all right. He rubbed his eyes in exasperation and could think of no way out. Thank God that he couldn't, because those hunting trips are the best memories I have.

Pete had a trailer up in Marathon County he and Dad used when they went hunting for grouse. After much negotiation, it was decided that we would drive up on a Friday night in October—me, Dad, Pete, and the dogs—and we would hunt all weekend, and I would do my homework without fail after supper or even in the car if need be. I started packing immediately. Eons later, the appointed day arrived.

The first night up there I slept on the saggy couch with Old Ladies One and Two, and woke at dawn to bacon and biscuits in a cast-iron pan, and orange juice, cocoa and eggs. I had to go to the bathroom outdoors, in the frozen, clear morning air, but I kind of liked it. A shivering film of mist hung on the edge of the woods; the Old Ladies danced with delight. Silently, Dad and Pete assembled their shotguns and ammo, and as we were ready to hit the trail, I could not help but let out a squeal of joy. Oops! I clasped my hands over my mouth, but it was too late; the dogs were already barking and whining. Pete chewed hard on his toothpick, while Dad tried to hide a quick scowl, unsuccessfully. They conferred, and the upshot was that Pete and the dogs went one way, and Dad and I went another. I was seriously chastened, but Dad didn't seem to mind, after all. I think he took it as a strange sort of adventure, not really hunting so much, and tolerated my foolishness with grace.

We set off on a nice, wide trail, wading through knee-high, wet grass. I was commanded to walk several steps behind, and to never, ever run out in front. Also, and this was surprising, I was not to be writing.

"Just keep your eyes on me, I don't need you stumbling around with your head down, understand? You can write it all down later."

"Okay."

We advanced single-file, oh so slowly, with me watching my dad's back, my own puffs of breath, and the little woods from the corners of my eyes. Every once in a while, Dad would pause and stare, listening, I guess, and then move on again. The sky turned electric blue and the smell of fallen poplar leaves rose around us sharp and energizing. The suspense was delicious, but I was still unprepared for the shocking leap of the grouse. A feathered whirlwind, it burst straight up from the brush and then angled giddily off toward the deep cover on our left. Unnoticed by me, my dad had raised the shotgun, following the flight of the grouse as it crossed a clearing, and then he fired with a stunningly loud bang, and the bird plummeted down.

"There, we got one," he said and glanced back at me. "Are you okay Franny?"

"Uh huh."

I remember my heart was hammering as if I'd been running for blocks. We retrieved the grouse, which was not quite dead. Dad scooped it up and did something, I could not tell what, and then it was dead, and he held it out for me to see. Its small, neat head was flopped over to one side and a thin spray of blood lingered on the palm of Dad's hand and the bird's neck. Its feathers, intricately dappled, soft and tawny, were irresistible and I touched them, lightly. I wished it were still alive, and felt a stab of guilt for admiring it so closely, without its consent, you might say, but I could not help myself. "What do we do now?" I asked, half afraid the death of the grouse meant we were done.

"Just keep going down this trail. See, there's alders down there where it's wet. Grouse like places like that, and these little balsams? And the popple, they like that too."

He tucked the dead bird into a pocket on the back of his jacket, and we continued on as before. My eyes were glued to the bulge on his back. We flushed several grouse that morning, but Dad only took two more shots, killing one especially unwary bird, and let the others fly. "Nope, nope," he would say as they spun away through a screen of trees. By lunchtime, I was almost used to the sight of my slow-talking, slow-walking dad transforming himself in an instant into, well, a big two-legged predator; let's call it what it is. The last flush was the best because we heard the rustling in the tall grass by the trail, and Dad swiftly shouldered the gun, and crept stealthily and hunched over with tension, toward the sound. He did not get a good shot, but I will never forget that change, from Dad to hunter right in front of my eyes, like catching the exact moment of sunrise.

We hiked back to the trailer for cheese sandwiches, apples, and cookies. Pete showed up with his limit of three grouse, but of course, he had the dogs. And then, oh Lord, the skinning began and I didn't know whether to cry or gape. Dad laid the first bird on its back, then stood with a boot on each wing, and grasped the legs and pulled, gently, but steadily.

"Oh no, Dad!"

"Why don't you take the dogs for a walk?"

The dogs looked on soberly. I did not move. When he was done, the feathers and legs and guts dangled from his hands, and between his feet on the ground lay two mounds of pink, glistening flesh. Dad clipped off the wings and head with his heavy shears and washed the meat in a pan of water. His hands were bright red with the cold. He gave me a quick glance while wrapping the grouse meat in paper, then he stashed it in the cooler, and looked at me again. He was not used to explaining such things.

"We always have to respect wildlife, Franny, but just think if nothing ever died? Some have to die to make room for the others, don't you think?"

"I don't know."

"Well, tonight we'll fix this for supper. Don't worry, someday the birds'll be eating us."

I had no idea what he meant, but I thought it sounded like justice.

We hunted all the rest of the afternoon, without much success until dusk. We savored the grouse, pan-fried in bacon fat, and Dad and Pete talked and drank, first beer, then coffee, while I did home-work. It all seemed very homey and exotic at the same time. Again I curled up with the Old Ladies. But it rained like the dickens the next day, so we drove home early.

I went hunting just one more time that fall, for squirrels in the woods near our house. That was enough to get me an honorable seat with Mom and Dad at the annual Fort Wisconservation Club dinner, and it gave me enough to think about for a long, long time. I remember my mother fixed the squirrels like so: quarter and brown, stew with tomatoes and onions all afternoon, bone and serve over rice. I had informed her at the beginning that the heart and lungs had been in the vicinity of the ribcage, in case she hadn't known. "Yes," she replied. That night, we ate the squirrels, respectfully, and then forgetfully. That was how I learned about the glory of the October woods, hunting and dying, and what it really means to eat the flesh of animals.

I think my experiences that year had an influence on my mother's painting, because in the spring, she started a new cycle she called *Seasons of the Deer*. She was fed up with selling her pictures as novelty items in gift shops and truck stops, and decided instead to do ironing to bring in a little money, and to concentrate on making real pictures. She had earned about $250 over the holidays on the *Speak to a Cow as You Would a Lady* series. The quote was from old W. D. Hoard, of course, and the pictures were indigestibly cute and sold like mad. But she was fed up, as I say, by January. The new cycle was to have five large paintings; she had it all planned out in advance with thumbnails and sketches to scale. The five were to be called: Fat Time (Summer), Killing Time (Fall), Snow Time (Winter), Starving Time (Late Winter), and Birthing Time (Spring). She started with Starving Time, a hair-raising picture that I was not allowed to study, and then in May, she did Birthing Time, also pretty realistic. Her great concern was to catch the tender, glowing green of the southern Wisconsin trees in May, that saturated gold and green that, when it happens each year, seems like a brand new color. My mother spent hours outside, especially in the early mornings and just before sunset, trying to get that color. "Just look how perfect," she'd say, bringing in a spray of foliage, which she placed in a jar of water against a white sheet.

It took a year and a half for her to complete *Seasons of the Deer*, and then she was firmly resolved on her course and plunged ahead into another series, and then another, year after year. My mother did not get her own show until 1981, when a branch of the Madison library displayed a dozen original Janet Bookstaffs, mistakenly, in the children's section. It was better than nothing, I guess. But that happened long after I'd grown up.

I went hunting with Dad all through my schooldays, but the pinnacle was the time he brought me along on a deer hunt. We'd found a place, thick with signs of deer, and hunkered down in the pre-dawn, crystal-cold stillness of the woods. We waited without speaking for three hours. Dad saw the deer first, of course. It was a small buck climbing the far side of a ravine. The animal saw us and stopped, staring, so motionless that its brown body blended into the dry November woods until it disappeared. Occasionally, it flicked an ear or twitched its tail, and so we would see it again. Sometimes, when I didn't expect it, the deer's image would suddenly resolve out of the tangle of branches and brush and I would see it again. If I shifted my gaze or moved my head just a hair, I would see it briefly. My dad just kept his eyes on the spot and waited. Eventually, halt-ingly, the deer began to move off. Dad carefully sighted and killed it with a shot.

I remember gazing down in a kind of reverence at the animal on the ground, and then, switching gears to help with the field dressing. I suppose it was a weird thing for a high school girl to be doing back then, but it seemed normal to me. By then, I felt comfortable, too comfortable, out in the woods. In fact, now I re-member another thing that happened; I got a little careless once and got lost. I guess that was in my sophomore year. I was scared to death but found my way back at last, and to a pretty severe scolding by my elders, as I recall. They still let me go when I wanted, only I was forced to learn how to use a compass and topo map. My dad was strict all right, but he wanted me to understand that the natural world was not benign, and as it happens, I've put that knowledge to good use.

Someone once told me, "Franny, you're a smart, feisty gal. Don't ever lose your edge, okay?" Now, who was that? I just can't pair the voice with a face, but I do remember being fascinated with the concept of "my edge" and wanting at all costs to keep it. I was instinctively drawn to the word; sometimes I even dreamed of my edge as a physical thing, though never really describable. Kind of like a sword or a cliff? No, it wasn't a scary thing, but rather, a valuable thing. I would lie in the grass, just watching the trees move in the wind, letting everything flood my senses, while I thought about my edge. I can see now it was the wild girl, the legendary Frances, making herself known. That's when I acquired a taste for taking odd ways home, down fence rows, alleys, ditches, places forsaken by everybody else and their vehicles. I had this idea I could feel my edge better there, that I could hear, smell, see more. In high school, I felt aimless, yet keenly aware. But you know, I gave all that up to raise my boys.

For me, everything converged in the year 1968, my senior year at Fort. Martin Luther King was killed, the war continued, college students were everywhere in revolt. My mother started to paint her very own *Homage to Chagall*, and my dad turned off the TV. It was the year I got to know Jerry, and to the strains of "Stoned Soul Picnic," I lost my virginity. It was clumsy, hot, and a bit funny; I wish I could remember more, but the details have fled and mingled with everything else that was happening then. I am sure we made love several times that spring, until, as you know, consequences ensued. And that, my friends, was that.

9.

The Three Voyageurs

Spring 1689

ALL THROUGH APRIL, the gentle month of hope, Andrée refused to accept the fact of her son's leaving. The planning went on around her, sometimes silently, but incessantly all the same. She set her face and ignored it. "He is not going. He is staying here," she would remark in a conversational tone, as if just in passing to a neighbor. But the days advanced until, at last, Garamond began to pack his town clothes.

She said no more about it for a time, only followed him with her hungry, sorrowful eyes. One morning, when he returned from the fields for rope—the plough had fouled in mud—she pulled him aside. "I must talk to you now."

He cursed under his breath. "*Maman*, I have to get back right away—"

"No, no. They can wait."

The way she said "they" alerted him; this was to be a discussion between a mother and her natural son—there would be no argument. Still he had to try.

"*Merde, maman*! Shit! Why can't you support me? I want to go!"

"Hush and listen to me." She grasped his shoulders and stared up at his face. "How long before I forget his face," she thought with a flash of desperation, which she thrust aside.

"I know you will go, I know it." She felt his arms begin to relax, though his eyes stayed hard. "But you will promise me one thing. You will study at the mission—" she raised her voice as he started to squirm— "and you will join the Order there just as Father Marcel has proposed. I know you can do this if you try. And you must write to Uncle, so we may know you are well. So I may know you are alive!"

He rolled his eyes. "All right." Then he softened and wrapped his arms around her. "*Ma belle mère*," he said and squeezed her tight.

She squeezed back. "Do you promise?"

"Yes I promise."

"You will have twenty years soon."

"Yes! An old man, eh *maman*?"

They both knew he would do what he pleased, but Andrée was satisfied. She knew he was canny and strong. He would do what was necessary, and, she hoped, what was good. So she drew his head down to kiss his cheek, and released him to his work. With utter concentration, she watched his figure recede, memorizing his walk and the tousling of his hair in the wind.

It was decided that Jean and Claude, another student from the college, would walk with Garamond. The *Sainte Anne* would sail from La Rochelle, the great port on the Atlantic, in the second week of May, so they would need to leave home soon after the feast of Saint Marc. They would take the colt to sell at the marsh works at Marais Poitevin, which they would reach just north of La Rochelle. They reckoned ten days of solid travel on the small roads heading southwest over the Hauteurs de Gâtine, and down to the marshes and the coast. After selling the colt, Garamond would go on to La Rochelle, and Jean and Claude would return home directly, stopping only in Angers to redeem the bill of sale.

"And no adventures on the side! I need you here, my Jean. Watch out for the cursed Huguenots and the gypsies. And hide from the soldiers, *d'accord?*" Auguste warned again and again.

They had a feast for Garamond on the night before departure, and the cottage was crowded with their neighbors and relatives from the village. Even Father Marcel deigned to visit and was instantly plied with food and attention.

"How delicious, Demoiselle Michon," he intoned as only a Jesuit could.

Andrée glowed at the praise, for she'd gone all out for the feast: dried pears from the fall soaked in wine and baked in honey. A magnificent stew of herbs and the salt pork they'd stored since Christmas in the big stone jar. This one evening would relieve them of all their reserves until the new year's first fruits came to harvest.

"Yes, yes! My wife is the best cook in Anjou!"

"*Fou*, Auguste— As you all can see, my husband can drink the most wine in Anjou."

Everyone laughed gaily. It was almost enough to make her forget that tomorrow she would lose her son.

Claude arrived at the farm promptly at dawn. He was thin and brash, and younger than Jean and Garamond, but even so, commendably cautious in his acts. On return from this business errand of Father Marcel's, Claude would enter his novitiate at the college, so he was keen that all should go well. He had not been allowed to attend the feast, so he lost no time in rousting Jean and Garamond out of bed. "Off we go, pilgrims!" he shouted in their pounding ears.

They dragged themselves from sleep. The sun swelled above the horizon, and suddenly everyone was dressed and bustling.

Garamond called on his way out the door, "I'll get the colt!"

By the time he'd led Little Ugly from the barn, Annebette was serving up cold porridge and leftover stew. They ate standing, Claude, too, then the bundles were assembled and strapped to the colt's broad back.

Auguste said, "Good luck to you, old Garamond. Perhaps you'll become famous in New France, eh? The famous Father Garamond!"

He gave his stepson a bear hug and kissed him on both cheeks. Then he turned to Jean. "Remember all I told you and make sure the colt is rested before you sell. You must be back for tilling, mark me."

"*Oui, papa.*"

They shared a round of embraces and murmured "good bye" and "good luck." Andrée lifted her chin, smiling encouragement and revealing no hint of sadness to hinder her son on his journey. Gratefully, he smiled back at her. Then the three pilgrims and the colt set off for the track by the river that would lead them to Angers. They were all in the highest of spirits.

They traded insults all morning to the pleasant sounds of birds, breeze, and the colt's muffled hoofbeats. They left the homely, twisted church spires on the horizon and the fields of their neighbors. Garamond thought he should examine this passing landscape that he would never see again, but he couldn't concentrate on the task. It was better to look ahead, to the unfolding road before him. Soon they reached the village of Durtal and crossed the bridge over the river. They paused to drink and wolf down a loaf of rye.

"*Sans blague*," said Jean, tossing a stick in the river. "That will get to the sea before we will."

"Farewell little dormouse," Garamond said to the river, for they were leaving its course to head straight overland to Angers. There, Claude would deliver a letter at the Cathédrale St.-Maurice. But for all their eagerness, there were still eight leagues to walk before that, so they were obliged to camp in a field that night. They walked the next day in rain, finally reaching the gates of the city at mid-day, and with the colt following tranquilly, they entered and climbed to the cathedral.

Claude was about to disappear with the letter, but he stopped short and said, "Tie the colt, Garamond. Your Uncle made me promise you would come in to pray. Come on, at least it's out of the rain."

It would be no good to protest, for Claude held the purse strings on this trip, backed mercilessly by the authority of Father Marcel.

"*Oui*, Sister Claudette," Garamond simpered. Jean was easing back down the steps, but Garamond grabbed him and hauled him in. "You too, my sinning brother."

Inside it was dark and cool enough that they could see their breaths. They crossed themselves, genuflected, and made their way to the glorious rose window, unfortunately dimmed by the rain outside.

"This is where my Uncle Romain had his great revelation."

"It must have been a sunny day, eh? You know, Garamond, I must check on the colt."

"I know." He sighed, then kneeled, listening to Jean's retreating steps echo on the stone floor. "What could Uncle have seen here? Was it just that he was sickly and needed refuge, or did he truly have a vision, some sort of miracle?" Garamond squeezed his eyes shut and tried to pray, but it was no use; the smell of cold smoke distracted him. Once, he'd been to Mass in the church of La Flèche and there'd been a choir of novices from the college, singing. The sun had streamed through the narrow, stained-glass windows in transparent rivers of color. He had been perhaps ten or eleven. He remembered being overcome by emotion, by the possibility of heavenly transport. But now, no matter how he tried, there was only impatience. At last, with relief, he felt Claude's tap on his shoulder.

"Time to go, pilgrim."

Outside, Jean and Little Ugly waited. A little wind had blown up and begun to scatter the clouds above. South they went, past the brooding, striped walls of the *château*. Then they left Angers and followed *la rivière* Maine a long league to its union with the Loire, muscular with high water. It would be too difficult to swim the colt, so they spent precious sols on a ferry. At last, their turn came and they led the colt on. Everything was fine until the ferry moved out in the current, and then the colt began to shake its ponderous head and longingly eye the receding shore.

"Watch it, watch it!" All three pilgrims held the colt's harness. The colt took a step toward the shore. "Hold up, hold up!"

So the ferry returned to shore. The ferryman, grinning broadly, said, "It will cost you."

But Garamond knew horses, and he especially knew the Poitevin colt. "Just stay here a moment," he directed. "Just let him get his legs under him." Claude passed a bottle of wine to the ferryman, who drank deeply and nodded.

Garamond took off his shirt and wrapped it around the colt's head, shielding its eyes. They stayed quietly for several more minutes. "All right," he said at last. The ferryman cast off and they eased back into the current. The colt stood stock still, listening to Garamond's voice. There was one restless moment far out in the middle of the river, but their luck held and then they were across. As the ferry touched the south shore, they unwrapped the colt's eyes and led him back onto sweet solid earth. Without a backward glance, Little Ugly headed up the bank, Garamond, Claude, and Jean scrambling after.

"Wait, wait, I haven't thanked you for your business—" the ferryman called after them, laughing and blowing them kisses. "*Merci beaucoup, au revoir mes petits!*"

"*Merde!*" Sprinting ahead, Jean caught up with the colt and grabbed its halter. "This beast is too strong for us!"

"At least he's headed for the right road, eh?"

"*Merde! Quel monstre stupide.*"

Calmly, the colt started to nibble the delicious spring grass, but his young masters had no time to lose. Garamond swatted the colt's hulking flank and they set out again, southwest on the old road, into the westering sun.

Thus began their real journey, beyond the familiar terrain of La Flèche, Angers, and the Loire, and on into strange lands. They would cross a new river, the Layon, and discover a new village, Chemillé, where they stopped to drink in a tavern. Then there were the headwaters of the Èvre, where they raided birds' nests for eggs and slept in a farmer's shed. They took turns riding the Poitevin colt and singing at the tops of their lungs. In Cholet, they bought excellent cheese and bread, but were swindled on wine. The countryside turned brilliant green as they advanced. They stopped for an afternoon to mend their shoes. When they weren't ravenous, they were having a fabulous time.

At first, in the cold, spring nights, they made campfires of twigs that warmed their hands and lit their faces, while the eyes of the colt glistened in the darkness beyond. As they traveled farther from the Loire Valley, they became more cautious and eventually made no fires, but rather hid themselves at night, folded into ravines or screened behind newly leafed hedges. They crossed the Sèvre and began to climb the Hauteurs de Gâtine to Pouzanges, where the people they met seemed to look on the pilgrims and their colt with thoughtful, jaded eyes. No one was willing to sell food and no one was willing to say how much farther were the marshes. It was just a matter of time before the three young men helped themselves.

Early one evening, they passed a rambling farm perched on a hillside with a wagon making for it, bearing a small girl, her father, and a cageful of panting, terrified chickens. As the wagon passed, the girl stared back at them and waved, taking care her father didn't see.

After a moment, Jean said, "Let us steal one of those chickens."

"Too risky, jackass. Forget it!"

The brothers howled in mock dismay. "Claude, Claude, don't you want to make some trouble before the Jesuits lock up your *queue*? You're the one whose growling belly keeps us up all night."

Claude frowned, shaking his head. "All right, they were plump. But I can't! If Father Marcel should hear—"

The brothers were already backtracking. They set a watch on the farm from the cover of a thicket, while Claude, jittery as a doomed chicken himself, stayed on the road with the colt. Occasionally, the cackles and chirps of the fowl could be heard from a shed adjacent the barn. So Jean and Garamond knew where they were. Soon the sun set, casting the farm in shadow and then in the darkness of night. It was time. Like hunters after quarry, they sneaked down the slope to the shed. Eased the door open. Waited for their eyes to find the shapes of chickens. There they were: herky-jerky shapes emitting heat and nervous clucks.

At this point, a shrill, resounding scream interrupted them. Whipping around, they saw the little girl standing there in bare feet, holding a bucket. She was taking a deep breath in order to scream again.

"Shh! Hush! We're leaving—"

Too late, for next they heard shouts and the sound of pounding boots, and soon an ominous crowd filled the yard. They were cornered. The father strode forward with a lantern, brandishing a poker. Then a woman, shrieking with rage, pushed through and fell on the would-be thieves, raining blows on their heads as hard and fast as she could. Then others joined her, until they were pleading for their lives.

There was a muffled crash, and a massive shape appeared at the edge of light—it was Claude astride the colt. "Hold!" he cried, which noise caused Little Ugly to rear. Now, for a beast as massive as the Poitevin colt to rear is a thunderous affair. For a moment, all were speechless. The father raised the lantern, squinting. Uncertainly, he asked, *"Monsieur le Duc?"*

"Allez, allez!" Jean yelled. "Run!"

The brothers bolted—two scoundrels seemingly pursued by a mounted avenger. Little Ugly, caught up in the excitement, broke into a bone-crushing trot. Behind them, the farmers watched their retreat with raised fists and curses, and a few guffaws, swiftly cut off. So the guilty escaped with their hides and the precious colt intact.

But they weren't finished. The next day, at another farm, they spied a little hen tied up in a pen, temporarily unwatched, her keepers having repaired to a mid-day meal. The three *voyageurs* moved fast, grabbed the hen, wrung her neck, and ran away all in the space of five minutes. They kept running, overland and dodging down fencerows and deep-set lanes until they were sure they weren't followed. At last, they crept behind a jumbled outcrop of rocks, where they roasted their prize and devoured it down to the bones. After that, they kept to the road.

Their first view of the Poitou occurred late of an afternoon, quite suddenly, as they turned down a switchback in the road. The lowlands were spread like a soft green cape before them, suffused with deep, hazy gold. They stopped, exclaiming, and pointed speculatively to the various indistinct landmarks.

By evening, they'd left the Hauteurs de Gâtine behind. The very air had changed, now rich and musky, moistly cool and racked by the cries of water-loving birds. A gossamer sheet of mist had fallen with the dusk, grazing the tips of reeds and grasses. When they led the colt to drink, they clove the mist like ships, leaving trailing, dissipating swirls of white, and soaking their legs in the wet. They camped on a hillock, but barely slept, and with morning, they rose and set off smartly to warm their chilled bones.

The road turned due south that day, undulating high and low, but mostly low and passing through marshes, wooded swamps, and a few drowning fields. Small farms clung to higher ground.

Soon they could see evidence of the marsh works: vaguely straight, muddy berms and sky-reflecting ditches of water. They stopped at a farm to ask directions to the roving camps of men, horses, and oxen laying waste to the opulent marshes. "Just west of that copse," they were told. They'd walked over eight leagues that day.

Jean decreed a day of rest for the colt. They bided their time at the camp, drinking and swapping stories and jibes with the men as if only passing through, but actually taking close note of the patterns of command and execution of the works. It was a wonder to the three *Anjevins*. They waited for the end of the day's labor, for they knew their colt's freshness and strength would show best when the crews came straggling back, driving their poor spent beasts before them.

Jean had already identified the man of authority, the foreman of the camp, and so they approached him and offered him a sale. He paced slowly around the colt, appraising it with exhausted eyes. He looked at its teeth and grunted approval, for it was a young beast. He ran his hands over the rough coat and down each leg to round, platter-sized hooves. "Bred for the marshes, this one," he remarked. They all smiled. He sent word to another man of authority, and they waited, idly chatting for half an hour as the sun sank.

At last the summoned man—the man of accounts—hailed them. He carried a book and a sheaf of papers, and while he made out the bill of sale, Jean kept a tight hold on the colt's halter, scrutinizing every scratch of the quill. The man finished, blew carefully on the ink and held the document for Jean to see— seventy livres. Jean nodded. The man folded the bill and handed it over, and at once the foreman led away the Poitevin colt. "Hup, hup," he said as the camp swallowed them.

"Little Ugly!" cried Garamond, "*Adieu* my old friend—"

Claude chimed in, "Eh, Ugly, give them a good stomp if they work you too hard!"

But the colt was already gone, and the three pilgrims were left standing forlornly in the midst of the darkening camp. They glanced at each other, at the scene around them, at their hands, their feet. Garamond wondered then if there was nothing left but for them to part as well. He was amazed to feel heat and welling tears in his eyes. "Good, good!" he said, "It's all settled, eh?" He punched Jean's shoulder, softly. Jean punched him back hard and began to laugh.

"What do you think, Rosamonde? Do you think we're going to leave you here all alone? *Quel petit con*! I may never be this close to the ocean again! Do you think I'd miss this chance? Claude, what do you care if we waste a couple days?"

"*Moi*? I care not. But we may have to steal another chicken, unless Rosamonde can catch us a ducky. Can you do that for us, *mon petit*?"

"You beggars! You think I didn't figure it out? I'll catch you a ducky—"

They laughed crazily, pounding each other's backs, and soon fell into an impromptu shoving match only extinguished when all three ran out of breath. Then they gathered their various bundles and resolved to walk on. In the last fading light, Jean examined the bill of sale again, then tucked it back in his shirt. "Which way to La Rochelle?" he shouted to the nearest man he could see.

On the tenth day of their journey, they caught a first breath of sea air and witnessed a flock of seagulls whirling and squealing above. They noted the change in the earth beneath them; there was sand, now, in the soil. The roadbed was raised and intermittently filled with *voyageurs* of all types—peasants, merchants, pilgrims, the destitute and the rich—all drawn to or propelled from the ports of La Rochelle, Rochefort, and Bordeaux farther down the coast. The three young men from Anjou, their blisters forgotten, fell in with the crowd bearing south, quarreling with some folk and joking with others. They amused themselves with fantastic stories they would tell Auguste and Father Marcel. These started plausibly enough:

"We couldn't sell the colt right away."

"We took the wrong road—no, no—we were given the wrong *directions*."

"We were converted by Huguenots!" Claude whispered and they broke down laughing.

"We had to rescue the colt from highway men!"

"No, we rescued a countess! Then, we were robbed—let us spend Annebette's dowry, what do you say?"

At that moment, a carriage overtook them, pulled by two tired horses and driven by a baby-faced man with a whip. A small girl poked her head out the window; her long pale hair flew around her face like an aureole as she stared at them.

"*Voilà la comtesse!*" Garamond yelled as the carriage rumbled past.

The girl twisted to watch them, then disappeared, then reappeared and let fall a wispy, white object; it was a feather. From inside the carriage, a faint shout: "Frances! *S'il te plaît!* Sit down!

Garamond picked up the feather and stuck it behind his ear.

"Oh Garamond, you have such a way with little girls, eh? But you'll be too old to do anything about it by the time that one's grown—"

"No, you are wrong, my brothers! My *grandpère* had a hundred years when he married the last time—"

He stopped short for they had crested a small hill, which had hidden the city of La Rochelle. "There it is," said Claude. A stiff wind blew back their hair and plastered their clothes to their bodies. Surrounded by people and carts, they stood in the road and looked long at the view before them. The city bristled with the energy of righteous commerce. There was a blazing afternoon sun and they imagined they could hear flags and pennants cracking in the wind. There in the harbor, with its squat white towers, was a strange floating forest of ships' masts, and the Atlantic, arching away to Canada.

"You've got your wish for the sea after all, old Garamond," said Jean. Then, as one, the three stepped forward and descended into the city.

10.

Marinette, Wisconsin

1991-92

The day I chose to leave Fort Atkinson was a full-moon day in August. Why full moon? Purely for the hell of it. Or rather—I couldn't help myself—it seemed like a good sign in a lunar kind of way, not to say a lunatic way. I kept all this to myself. It was sweltering in southern Wisconsin, and the air suffocatingly moist, so to be moving north at highway speed was so great a release as to induce instant euphoria. I took the 151/55 route—me at the wheel of a humble Ford Escort gone gray with winters parked on the street. Oh, for a green, open-souled T-Bird convertible on a day such as that, but that's okay. Flipping through radio stations, I remember I was brought to a full stop on a classical station broadcasting glorious waves of Vivaldi and Debussy. The music merged with the lush, summer landscape, more beautiful than I could ever remember, as if to kiss me goodbye.

Soon, glimpses of Lake Winnebago appeared on my left, dissolved in a liquid blue haze. I knew that Lake Michigan lay thirty miles to my right, so I imagined a maritime tinge on the strawberry fields I passed and the distant views east. The humidity began to dissipate. The Escort flew along like my own little *Chariot of Fire*, past small towns and the long shore of Green Bay, and suddenly, I found myself in Marinette, Wisconsin, bumping up hard against Michigan.

My cousin Chris was renting the ground floor of a tiny house on Oak Street, dingy white and circled by a sun-drenched yard. One lone pine tree guarded the northeast corner; kids' toys were scattered at random among dandelions. The house was for sale, so Chris was on a month-to-month lease, but, inveterate gardener that she was, she had still managed to sneak in half a dozen plots for veggies and flowers. At 6 P.M. sharp, we ate a celebratory supper of burgers, mega-salad, ice cream, and for the ladies, lite beer. I admit, I was reserving judgment that first night, as I slept or tried to sleep in an unfamiliar bed. Chris's, actually; she'd gallantly taken the couch.

"You're tuckered," she said sympathetically. "Don't worry, though. Tomorrow, I'll call the realtor and see if we can get you upstairs."

"Okay," I said with forced brightness, and commenced to lay staring and shivering for hours. I did get to sleep, but sunrise startled me awake at five. So I wrote a note to Chris and slipped out for a little early-bird reconnaissance. Amazed, I caught sight of a ghost of my breath in the cold still air as I climbed in the car. What a place! I thought, with the greatest of expectations.

The Escort and I prowled all over town that morning, a phone-book map on my lap while I juggled a cup of convenience-store coffee. I checked out the strip and the downtown and the Menominee River, the cemeteries, schools, and churches. I crossed the river into Michigan, and rambled around. Believe it or not, but it felt definitely foreign there, so I came back. Then I wandered down to the docks where I, in all my land-locked Fort Atkinson innocence, gaped at the huge, rusting ships floating casually by an actual drawbridge over the river. I'm sure I must have been smiling by then—my world had opened wide, possibilities ran rampant. I refueled on sweet rolls and drove around for another half hour, but I kept coming back to the bay, like a sailor to a siren, and at last pulled in to the parking lot at the mouth of the Little River, just on the south side of town. It felt good to get out of the car and stand under tall silver poplars. I gazed across the water to what I knew was the Door peninsula, a glowing blue streak on the horizon. At the mouth of the creek, an egret, snowy white, paced haltingly through brilliant green reeds; pausing, it bent ever so slowly toward the surface of the water, then struck like a dart, swallowed, and resumed pacing. The water glittered in the cold breeze. Right then, I decided to stay.

I returned to the little white house where Chris informed me that the realtor had okayed my moving in upstairs.

"Great," I said, but I had another idea. "How much is he asking for this dump?"

Chris's eyes widened. Then, all business, she said, "$38,000, last time I heard. The porch is collapsing and the stairs," she laughed out loud, "you have to go up the left side of the stairs, *only*, or you'll end up in the basement, *which* smells very, very bad." She waited, smiling, bright blue eyes in a round face. Chris was a woman used to disappointment, yet nothing, so family legend had it, fazed her for long. I had a feeling she would test me when I least expected it. I knew she'd be an excellent ally.

"What do I need for a down payment?"

"Don't know."

"If I bought this place, would you stay and kick in money for house payments every month?"

"Yeah, but—"

"I have a little money of my own, God knows I've been working my butt off, and don't forget, I have a son who's a bona fide carpenter, and, okay, I don't have a job yet. But something'll come up. Maybe Dad would co-sign."

Chris sent me a long, patronizing stare. "You're going to look around first, right? I mean, maybe you won't like it here. Then again," she chuckled, "*I* stayed after Cora was born. It does kinda grows on ya."

"Show me the basement," I said.

Chris, that is, Christine Kinney, my Uncle Samuel's third daughter, was an unwed, unrepentant, single mother of two. She was eleven years younger than me, a blond bundle of energy absolutely devoted to her children, Cora and John, and to any old cause that came along, but particularly those with a social justice slant. She was plump and did not care. She worked for a pittance at a daycare center that was bursting with about a dozen kids, including her own. But both the fathers of her children paid their share, so somehow she got by. Right from the start, she and I were a team, driving each other here and there, sharing the chores and the children. After supper, we'd go down to the park a couple blocks away, and sit at one of the picnic tables, just watching the waves and the kids chasing gulls. God, we talked and talked. I couldn't believe how at home I felt in Marinette, especially sitting there at the park with the bay and the red light house, the beach grass, the goldenrod, and purple milkweed. It seemed there was always a clean, cool breeze blowing there, and under its influence, I hatched more ideas and more plans than I'd had in all the years since Jerry and the divorce. I wrapped up everything in Fort, selling this, storing that, and settled into my new "apartment."

Well, there was still a recession on, so I didn't find a good job right away. I worked though; I did books part-time for a copy shop and took up waitressing again. I was working twelve hours a day sometimes, but I had a new purpose in life; I wanted to work because I wanted that house. The story there was that, if you wanted to avoid the mortgage insurance, the down-payment would be $7,600, and the payments would be $250 per month for, well, forever, and even with Dad's co-signing—he knew I'd never let him down, and besides, he said, "If you fix it up, it's a good investment"—I still needed fifteen hundred bucks. So yes, I worked twelve-hour days and kept looking for that job.

To console myself in the meantime, I did a little varnishing upstairs and sent away for as many prints of Frances Anne Hopkins's pictures as I could find. You had to search through gift shop and frame store catalogs, and I also enlisted my mother's help from afar. We found quite a few, and as they arrived in the mail, rolled snugly in cardboard tubes, I started getting other ideas. I suppose that was when I started looking at Marinette both as my new home base, and as a jumping off point for visits north. By then, my new outlook, my new energy had taken on the strength of new habit, and I thought, Why not? Had I not regained my edge? I had the pictures framed cheaply and deliberated at length where to put them. Soon the walls were hung in splendor.

The waitressing job, which was fast and relatively fun, was a necessary counter-weight to the copy shop job, which was boring or aggravating, depending on who else was working. The Homestyle Restaurant was down-home all right, old-fashioned and decked out with ceiling fans and comfy, green booths. The prices were fair; there was pie on the menu and Packer memorabilia for sale. I jumped at the chance to work there. I just knew the tips would be good—small but steady, and lots of them. It helped that I had experience, of course, good balance, and long legs; I could cover a lot of territory pretty quickly. So I will say with confidence that I did very well for myself. The restaurant pulled in a pretty mixed crowd: workmen, families, travelers, retired couples, women in pairs.

One extremely busy Friday night—we did a fabulous fish-fry—a group of kayakers came in. I'd seen them before and had already found out about their boats; "sea kayaks" they called them. Well, the place was packed except for one booth for four people, and here they were seven. I don't know how they did it, but they squeezed into that booth before anyone could stop them.

"Have fun," said Stevie, the night manager, to me as I girded myself with pen and pad.

But they weren't so bad, kind of frugal maybe, and reasonably polite. There was a silver-haired guy built like a brick, two young women, one svelte, the other chunky, and four guys of varying age and appearance. They gave off an interesting vibe, somewhat college kid, somewhat weekend warrior, but better than either of those. I guess I'd describe them as unfettered. They were on their way up the lakeshore to camp and paddle their kayaks all weekend; they were in high spirits; they made me jealous as hell. The funny thing is that I recognized their mood, because it matched mine exactly.

"Sounds fun," I said, "maybe I'll stow away in one of your boats." Of this, they heartily approved and began speculating on how they could fit me in. It was all very light and friendly. I took their orders—oh yeah, they wanted separate checks.

Get this: the guy on the outside orders chili, banana cream pie, and breakfast.

"How do you want your eggs?" I asked, trying hard not to react.

"As scrambled as possible, please."

What a smart ass, I thought. Oh he was cute all right, late twenties, with tight little blond curls. Lean as a racehorse.

I dropped the pen and, in swooping to retrieve it, I couldn't help noticing his mis-matched socks, one blue, the other plaid. I must have smirked.

"Hey," he said with a *faux* aggrieved air, "waste not, want not."

"Right."

"I save my matching socks for good, okay?"

"Right."

Then he winked at me, and, God help me, I rewarded him with a big, toothy grin. I made a hasty retreat to the kitchen.

"Seven orders, sorry," I called to the cook. She rolled her patient eyes. Damn, I thought, I need to get out more. I took a quick glance out the window at the multi-colored kayaks tied on the cars: red, orange, yellow, blue. Double-bladed paddles were lashed to the sides of the racks. I sighed pretty loud and wondered how many other things were out there, in the world outside my door, that I'd never even known to exist.

Well, I knocked off at 9:30 and walked home (home!) in the semi-dark, thinking about paddling, not motoring, but paddling a boat on any of the Great Lakes. And, blond guys who winked, or any guys really. When I got home, the kids were asleep and Chris was taking a bath, so I walked slowly from picture to picture, imagining how it would be to paddle a birch bark canoe. Pretty out there, I guess. It didn't take long before those pictures became a presence of their own in the house, magically creating a wilderness in our midst. They made the lonely pine tree in our yard sway in the wind, and the bay just down the street, flash with impatience. When will you come? it demanded. But these were just daydreams.

September became October, and Halloween came and went (we contributed a vampire and a bum), and finally, I found that decent job—bookkeeping, filing, and answering phones for St. Joseph's, the Catholic high school. It was only temporary while their regular gal was out on maternity leave, but I had high hopes. I kept on waitressing, just in case.

I broke down and bought the house. I was, how you say? delirious, drunk with the power of home ownership. Son Mike came up for a week at Thanksgiving and fixed the stairs. The porch fell down, but so what. We did what we could in the basement. It was mine, it was all mine, no matter what they thought at the bank; it was my little acorn on Oak Street. Chris and I made some subtle adjustments, mostly in our heads, and continued to live in the configuration with which we'd started: me in the two rooms upstairs; Chris and Cora in the bedroom downstairs; John in the study, or closet, or whatever it was; and we all shared the one bathroom downstairs, and the kitchen and the weird, U-shaped living room. I acquired a white kitten called Boris after Yeltsin, and gave it to the kids. Life had become positively exciting, but there was more to come, because my other son, Walt, the one at UW-Madison, had convinced me to go back to *school*. Gradually, of course; such a radical departure even I, in my current fearlessness, had to work up to.

"Just take one class, Mom," he cajoled me over the phone. "You're so smart, you'll do great." God I loved my kids. How could I go wrong with kids like that backing me?

So I drove by the UW-Marinette campus a couple times, just to check it out. I was intrigued, even tempted. There it was, set alluringly on the shore of the bay, a handful of cream-colored brick buildings under stately, soaring pines. I parked and walked in, stepping carefully around the inlaid *Numen Lumen* on the floor. What the hell does that mean, I wondered; it sounds religious. I swallowed and advanced to the information desk where I was directed to admissions, down the hall. Once there, I boldly asked for the actual forms, which were freely given, and then, with an air of knowing what I was doing, I assembled an armful of supplementary brochures, catalogs, maps, *et cetera*, and walked proudly off, straight over the *Numen Lumen*. I stopped to read the plaque about sifting and winnowing knowledge. I felt exhilarated, a feeling I was almost used to since leaving Fort, and even a little hallowed. The halls of academe, by God—bring it on.

At home, I spread everything out in the kitchen and took stock. There were so many choices! I laid out an entire two-year associate degree program in, I don't know, I think it was Bioscience. Then I threw that away and re-read the info on entrance exams. I could see right away I'd have to be coached. But you know, it was all possible. I went back to the campus and got advice from the deans, or the counselors, or whoever they were—they were angling to get another "returning adult student"—and I began to study. Walt coached me over the phone; I took the exam in December; I passed. Just in case I lost my nerve, there was a tuition check in my Christmas card from Grandma Beth, and a note in her precise but frail writing, gently demanding that I accept my fate. All right, then. I decided to take one class for the spring semester and see how it went.

Oh, and I went out on a few experimental dates. For the first time ever, probably, I took these seriously, and even though they all fizzled, at least I was out there, seeing what it really took to be a player on the frontier of love. I began to see, after all those bitter years, that my distrust of the male half was going to be a significant obstacle to happiness, because, you see, I definitely wanted to be with a man. So, I must have been paying attention. One day after the holidays, I was goofing around with the kids—they had new sleds—when a couple of lycra-clad men on skis went zooming by. I caught a glimpse of tight blond curls.

"Look at that guy," I muttered.

"What guy? Look at that guy!" This from Cora.

I shushed her, but had to laugh because the greyhounds were already out of sight. Oh yeah, I was itching to give chase.

I meant to start out with a modest subject like English or Intro Geography, but of course, when it came down to it, I chose a bear of a class for my college initiation. "Environmental Ethics" was described as (and I quote): "Philosophical examination of both traditional and recent concepts and values which structure human attitudes towards the natural environment." Why fool around, I thought. Let's see how deep it can get. It was worth three credits and they held it in the evenings, which clinched it for me. But I had no idea what to expect.

We started in mid-January, on a coal-black, zero-degree night, and not surprisingly, the first thing that happened was that I was crushed with the feeling of being excruciatingly old. I thought, Why oh why do I still have my hair this way? The room filled with twenty-somethings while the professor stood off to the side, gazing noncommittally over our heads. I felt like a bumbling elf.

But I stuck it out, the first fifteen minutes, that is, and then the ideas, opinions, and personalities started taking off like rockets. I mean, this was a motivated group of people. And when I listened to the voices, I picked out several that must have belonged to grown-ups like me, or anyway working stiffs, and in fact it turned out to be a pretty good mix.

"Why do we as a society value developed space and cultural achievement *over* untouched natural space?" our now beady-eyed leader demanded.

Throats cleared. Silence, and then a tentative chorus of response. "Wow," I said, apparently out loud because the young woman beside me threw me a glance. It was really amazing. Without trying hard at all, I forgot about my age and my hair and my *naiveté*, and let myself be carried away for two hours on the "winds of inquiry," as the brochure called it. At the end of the class, the prof socked us with an astounding amount of homework—the dues-paying—which brought me plummeting back to earth. It would be mostly readings at first, but then came the papers, one for every section for a total of six. I was forced to admit there would be no more waitressing on weeknights.

"That'll teach ya," Chris said later that night. She said she'd rather die than go back to school, but this was more her rebellious nature speaking than any aversion to ideas. Actually, she loved to grill me on the goings-on of my class, and never hesitated to add her two cents. "Ask why gardens aren't as important as department stores. That's what I want to know, God damn it. Why do people look down their noses at people who raise their own food?"

"Okay, okay, I'll bring it up."

Chris was the kind of person who took everything to heart, especially matters horticultural. This was her favorite cause. Maybe she was spurred on by me taking the ethics class, I don't know, but as soon as seed catalogs began showing up in the mail, she hatched a grand plan to start a community garden. "Like the one in Escanaba," she explained. "I'm going to call all the churches, all the do-gooders first, *before* I talk to the *city*." So we each had our little renaissance going, which was fun. And whenever I let things go to my head, it was Chris who kept me honest. You know, I would try to play the scholar even though I couldn't quite pull it off—it's so damned easy to get pompous when you don't really know what you mean.

Chris would say, "Are you trying to sound like Grandma Beth?"

"Uh, no."

"Because it doesn't work if you're not English, Franny."

"Hey, that's Frances to you, Christine." But then I would tone it down. Like I said, Chris and I made an excellent team.

There were other night classes at UW-Marinette of course, one of which was calculus, and from the room in which that was taught, issued, one night, the man with the tight blond curls. I caught his eye; he hesitated; we went our separate ways. But the next time, he appeared at my side and walked down the hall with me, and said, "Hey, aren't you a waitress at Homestyle?"

"That's me. And you're the kayaker."

His name was Irv, short for Irving. Irv Klein; it was a difficult name to pronounce and I stumbled over it when I told Chris. He was taking the math class, which he abhorred, to fill in the last missing requirement for grad school in Madison. He'd grown up in Marinette, gone two years to school there and most of two more in Madison, but then he'd defected to the National Park Service, The Nature Conservancy, the Forest Service, and then to a stint in the Peace Corps. Now he was back at college, obviously older, but still so, well, trim, and apparently determined to get a real degree and a real job as a field biologist. So he said.

"What's your area of study?" I had learned this much of the vocabulary.

"Fungi and their allies," he answered. "I'm into decomposition. It's the key to everything."

Allies—can you imagine?

So began our little dance. During the day, he helped teach a seminar on tropical ecology, drawing on his Peace Corps experiences, and he did a little work at Sears, too. In the evenings, after our respective classes, we would repair to a local establishment to talk and drink and flirt. We were each exotic to the other, and inevitably wound up in bed. I remember being surprised at the polished fairness of his skin. He was certainly experienced, but not so much that he controlled everything, and in fact, as we slept together more and more through February, March, April, *et cetera*, we developed a kind of sexual symbiosis. Two unlikes in perfect accord. But I'm slipping in that word, "symbiosis," too early. That's getting ahead.

When we weren't getting physical, we were talking passionately about the issues of the day, especially environmental issues. What with my class and his trajectory, these were uppermost in our minds. Irv read or had already read everything assigned in Environmental Ethics, and we discussed it all. I told him about my dad, the hunter, and my mother, the artist, and the gorgeous abundance of the southern Wisconsin landscape. He told me about all the places he had seen, too many to tell, actually. And the idea of wilderness, the necessity, the glory of wilderness.

I called in sick one day, and we spent the whole time wandering in the woods in the snow. I blurted out my desire—just formed that moment, at least with any coherence—to follow the trail of Frances Anne Hopkins, just to see what she had seen. And even—and this was the kind of thing you would only say to a stranger or a new lover—I even wanted to see what the other Frances—the wild one—had seen. So I told him all about that. Irv was entranced, to my joy, and said, "Oh man, that sounds great—take me with you, okay?"

We'd have to take my car, of course. He didn't have one, and although he acknowledged their utility, he could get around everywhere, even in winter, on a mountain bike. He really did do things like wear mismatched socks because he refused to waste resources on "artificially manufactured vanity." This was all very amusing, as Grandma Beth would say. But I respected his stance. Even now, I think Irv's great strength is that he truly is a minimalist. He examines every material thing and rejects most, but he's so resourceful that he doesn't seem to want for anything. Almost everything he does has purpose: he pursues the things he loves, and he lives in the way he thinks will most benefit the natural world in which he lives.

"Not that I'll get any thanks," he would laugh. "The wilderness really is implacable, just like Abbey says." He was always name-dropping. Because I was dying to catch up, I ran right out to buy *Desert*

Solitaire and read it straight through. But every once in a while, I'd catch him off balance, I think, just because I had a few years on him; I could see things coming that he couldn't, and then—oh so gratifying—he followed me around like a pet. Yes, the sex was splendid, almost always, and afterwards, we never ran out of conversation; sleep was for later. I was—how you say?—having the time of my life.

We were watching the Olympics on TV one night, each rooting for our favorites: speed skater Bonnie Blair for me, and Vegard Ulvang, champion cross-country skier ("*Nordic* skier," I was corrected) for Irv. We were at my house, and all of us—the kids, Chris with Boris on-board, me, and Irv—had crowded in one end of the U-shaped living room.

"Athletes are crazy," said Chris.

"No, they're not," said I, "they're passionate." I realized with a start that I'd just forgiven all athletes for including Jerry in their number.

"They're crazy!" This from Cora.

John requested for the tenth time a pair of black speed skates.

"What size does he wear?" I asked. "Maybe Mike's old skates would fit him."

Irv said, "I wish it was spring. I want to go paddling."

I met all the Marinette and Menominee paddlers, and quite a few from Green Bay, too, through Irv. Whether by canoe or kayak, whitewater or quiet water, they were every one as passionate as any Olympian, and their company was simply intoxicating. In winter, everyone, at one time or another, made an appearance at Du Nord's, our bar, where stories were swapped, gear analyzed, and liaisons—romantic or otherwise—were arranged. Du Nord's had the most eclectic selection of music; you never knew if you'd hear bluegrass, Hendrix, or Sousa. I was partial to the sultry stuff then, my sensual revival showing through, I suppose, and so I was always playing Chris Isaak and old blues. I noticed Irv kept his eye on me in the bar.

More gratification. I didn't have any clear idea of what they meant when they talked about paddling, of course. I'd only been in a fishing boat a couple times when I was a kid and all I remember is the smell of the engine, the clanking of metal on metal, and wind.

I was having so much fun that spring break kind of snuck up on me. Well, "spring." In March, there is no spring up here, although there is more light. I drove down to, not Florida, but Fort Atkinson for a weekend, and boy was that a shock. I felt like an alien, like a child. It was extremely uncomfortable because I was so anxious that everyone realize how different things were, that I was different, adventurous, in control. I even wanted to brag about getting regularly laid. I suspect Grandma Beth knew. Well, everyone kind of gave me a wide emotional berth, waiting to see how I'd act. I gave them the *spiel*, related Chris's news (How's Chrissy doing?), and gradually, we all calmed down, and everything was fine. It's strange how people can see you as you always were to them, and at the same time, see and accept you in a new incarnation. It's a schizophrenic thing, but maybe well advised. Maybe we want to be prepared for everything.

On Saturday night, son Walt took me to see the movie, *Black Robe*, in Madison. He'd been saving this as a special treat; I could sense his anticipation but I didn't understand why until they—the Indians and the missionaries—took to the birch bark canoes. Real birch bark canoes, paddled on real water. My jaw actually dropped. When the aerial shots of the canoes, arrowing across spacious blue water, came up on the screen, I had to exclaim, "Oh look!" It was transfixing; it was the Saguenay fjord, as we read in the credits. When we left the theater for the concrete of sidewalks and streets, what remained was the beauty of Quebec and the history come to life. There seemed to focus something in me, and notwithstanding the awful violence and the backwardness of religion, oh, and the sex—we, an embarrassed mother and son, slunk down in our seats—despite all that, I thought I saw something in that movie, a treasure, an answer. I don't know yet what it was.

When I returned to Marinette, I brought with me a history book with a Frances Anne Hopkins picture on the cover and the story of the French-Canadian voyageurs inside. I showed it to Irv and told him about the movie.

"Frances, you want to get out on the water?" he teased. "Well don't worry, if it's warm this weekend, we're going out for a little spin, because I fixed the tandem. The ice blew out yesterday." He ran his hands up my arms—what did he think, that I needed encouragement? "You have to come," he said, "I'll teach you everything."

Irv had his own sea kayak, but he also shared with a friend an old tank of a tandem, all brittle, yellowed fiberglass, and weighing over a hundred pounds. I found myself in the bow of this boat on a cold sunny day, the day of the spring equinox. After a barrage of instructions and safety admonitions from Irv, we were floating quietly over glass-clear water. It was pleasantly disorienting to be out *there* and looking *back* at the shore, where I'd stood many times, gazing out *here*. I would take a few strokes, be distracted, then take a few more. Irv paddled on through my pauses and occasional thrashing, counter-balancing my moves so deftly as to seem invisible himself, and not just because he was in back. All I could hear was the regular dip of his paddle and the cry of gulls; it was wonderful, but I knew it would be. The bliss outweighed all the negatives—the numbing cold, the strange little cramps, the reek of the borrowed wetsuit. All that was added embellishment, as far as I was concerned, just part of the mystique, the newly discovered groove of this sport. We came around a point and encountered waves, jolly rollicking waves tipped with light.

"Naw, too cold and you're too new at this," Irv's presence materialized from the stern. "We're turning around, remember how to turn? You do a sweep on the left when I tell you—"

"Can't we just back up?"

"Well yeah, okay. Back-paddle then."

This was interesting; the little waves heaved and hissed. Maybe

I was nervous, but not much. I was already thinking about getting my own boat.

We went out almost every weekend after that, except for very cold days, when, in any event, the bay temporarily refroze. Irv and company knew where the sheltered spots were, and there we went while I learned all about bracing, reading waves, turning, and leaning. Irv still had the rudder, which he didn't quite want to give up, so my progress, in my opinion, was limited. But I gave him hell in bed.

So there was a lot going on: the ethics class; the bookkeeping job; waitressing, although only rarely now, when someone else wanted time off on the weekend; the affair with my golden guy; the house; cousin Chris, and the kids. Even little Boris had his piece of my attention, and now there was kayaking. Really, something had to give—but nothing did. It all just continued to accelerate in a mad, thrilling kind of way.

In April, the existence of the "humongous fungus" was announced to the world, to the great joy of Irv. This fungus, *Armillaria bulbosa*, was living apparently very nearby on the Wisconsin and Michigan border, an underground filamentous blob spread over—under?—thirty-seven acres of forest. The thing was supposed to be fifteen hundred years old. Some of Irv's biology buddies came up from Madison and they all went merrily off on an expedition "to see what we can see" or to party, more likely, in the border bars. Thank God, because I really needed a break. My big paper—the second to the last but the most important—was shortly due. So I shut out all distractions and worked like a fiend for four days. I even took the draft to work with me and wrote surreptitiously in my top desk drawer.

My topic was hunting and killing. I mean, why waste time on frills? Chris was having her troubles then with the community garden planning ("friggin' bureaucracy!") and so she had a lot of frustration energy going. We had some intense conversations about food and food chains, (sending Cora to watch TV when things got gory) and how growing food to eat was a direct connection between land and people, and how eating hunted food was the same, without intermediaries. "It's the intermediaries that cause all the problems!" This from Chris. And how hunting and killing were the same as eating and living. On paper, this was all pretty breathless and disorganized, and I would only get a "C."

"Not enough structure," the beady-eyed prof wrote on the cover sheet, and disconcertingly, "How much of this paper is your work, Frances?" You see, I'd acknowledged Chris's input. I could not understand what was wrong with that. So I was a little embittered with the class, but I jumped through the remaining hoops and got a final "B." Not bad for a first effort, I guess.

"Screw that guy," Chris advised. "Didn't I tell you school was a waste of time?"

Well it was and it wasn't. My verdict is still out.

Anyway, with the class out of the way, there was more time to spend paddling. It was May and warm enough and light enough to go after work as well as on weekends. I did buy a new wetsuit and a ghastly green, used life jacket. Irv finally deemed me ready to solo—that was just some futile little power trip, Where does that come from? I wondered—and he let me take out his boat, a plastic orange Hydra, while he and various friends coached from the tandem. It was too cold to learn Eskimo rolls, so we just put in miles along safe shorelines and calm bays. We did a couple short crossings. I learned very quickly and Irv had to shut up about skills, although he still had me on weather and experience, I'll give him that. I learned to surf waves right away. I was foolish until the Juttner stretch thrashed me soundly one day; I dumped and had to swim to shore, pummeled all the way by the boat and my paddle, *et cetera*. But it didn't really slow me down. Waves just don't bother me, I don't know why. Well, I *do* have good balance, and I'm strong, and I'm good at visualizing where I am, you know, in relation to up and down and where it's okay to breathe. That's just luck, I suppose, so I can't take credit for being particularly brave.

I like waves even better when the sun clouds over. They stand out in relief, looking more heinous, even, than they really are. That slurping whoosh as a wave goes by, and the fizz of foam after that. And I love to drift over still water, to stare deep down to where the bottom is strewn with mysterious shadows and tree trunks like pickup sticks. And then, over shallows where the sun makes a mosaic of light on the sand. I love it all.

In June, I turned forty-one. Irv presented me with a fabulous, light-weight paddle, one I could break down to stow if necessary. This was better than passing the ethics class. In all that time, Irv and I had not discussed the fact that the semester, and also the summer, would end, and off he'd go to Madison. This conversation was scrupulously avoided. But then an excuse came along, an excellent excuse, a way to, if not prolong our pleasure, to intensify it. Irv had been on campus, tying up the loose ends for his seminar, and he came across an old flier that had been buried beneath maybe a hundred others on the "Extracurricular Events & Activities" bulletin board.

HEY!
**Do you want to take part in
world-class research in a pristine wilderness setting?
Join the Interdisciplinary Project on Lichen Indicators of
Air Pollutants in the Upper Great Lakes Region!**

**June-July, 1992
CONTACT Nicolette Poggi, UW-Stevens Point
poggn@debotsp.wisc**

"Lichen—oh man that's perfect!" he said, eyes sparkling, when we met at Du Nord's that night. "I already e-mailed from my prof's computer. Can you get vacation time, I hope, I hope? Please say they'll give you some vacation—"

"I could ask. It *is* summer, so everything's slow." I studied the dilapidated flier. "Would I have to declare a biology major? I'm not sure about that." Still, *a pristine wilderness setting* somewhere on the Great Lakes. Michigan? Superior? "What do you think we'd have to do?"

"Probably field samples. Who cares? They wouldn't have a flier here unless they're willing to teach you what to do. Just wait 'til I hear back from her," he tapped his finger on the name, Nicolette Poggi.

Via e-mail and phone, an interview was quickly arranged. We were to drive down to Stevens Point and meet with Ms. Poggi, who "seems okay," according to Irv. We would have to decide "as soon as possible." So, the next Saturday, we set out in the Escort, Irv explaining the weird world of lichens to me, all the way.

But when we got there, we discovered that our contact was just another lowly grad student, her tiny desk crammed into a roomful of similar, half of which were occupied that morning with other grad students, working dolefully through the weekend.

"Sure you want to live like this?" I whispered to Irv. He pretended not to hear.

Nicolette rounded up two other chairs and gestured for us to sit down. I knew right away there was a problem. I thought, Well who cares about lichen. She was a big young woman with wavy hair, and large expressive eyes, very dark brown. "Ah . . ." she began. "You must not have got my e-mail last night." I thought, You could have called.

"What happened is, for the time being, we don't have funding. We have a project, but no cash."

"Not enough cash," put in the student at the next desk.

"Exactly, not enough. I'm sorry, but everything's up in the air."

"She's sorry all right," said a woman in the back.

"We're all sorry; we're *disconsolate*." This from another guy and everybody laughed like crazy.

"It's the room of doom," he said with a straight face, and people laughed 'til they gasped. I had the feeling they'd been up all night.

"Okay," said Irv, trying to be nice, "tell us about the project anyways."

"Well, we were all going to different places, but my part is sampling the northern Lake Michigan islands and the Straits area, and I had hoped, the Soo. The terrestrial parts are no problem, but we need boats and gas, lots of gas, to get to all those islands; there's a lot of space that needs to be covered." She rubbed her hands on her knees in a stressed-out kind of way. "But I have to think about cutting back now. I still have to do something. Potentially, we'd be part of a really comprehensive project, with colleges from all over the U.S. and Canada. We were even talking to USGS." She sighed and everyone sort of quieted down. "So, what's your interest, Irving? And Frances?"

"You can't call me Irving, okay? It's Irv."

We launched into our respective backgrounds and credentials or the lack thereof. "Uh huh, uh huh," Nicolette listened and nodded while her eyes kind of glazed over. In the end, she promised to let us know if anything changed, and then she ushered us out of the room of doom.

So we drove home. I had thought about sea kayaks as soon as she'd said "we need boats and gas," but since Irv didn't say anything, I assumed there was no solution in that direction. Well, damned if he didn't call Nicolette as soon as we got back, from my phone, no less.

"Listen," he said into the receiver, "I have access to as many sea kayaks as we'd need for three people and gear. All we'd need is a ride out and back with the big stuff. We could set up a base camp. You can get to all kinds of places in kayaks that you can't in a motorboat. We could do your scaled-down trip." He nodded as he talked, pacing the length of the cord, avoiding my gaze.

I was furious that he hadn't discussed any of this with me in the car. Goddamnit, I thought, I want a say in this. Irv took one glance at my face as he responded to Nicolette's questions, and read my mind.

"Uh, can you hold on for a minute?" he said to the phone, then covering the receiver he asked me, all innocent, "Do you have any input?"

"Yeah. I won't go unless it's Lake Superior."

"Lake Superior?"

"Yeah." Okay, now I knew where I was going with this. "Eastern Lake Superior."

He relayed the new criteria, not bothering to ask me why or to argue. Oh, he knew he was walking a fine line.

"Okay! Great! Call anytime if you work it out, okay? This summer is a perfect time slot for me. I don't have access to e-mail all the time, so just call, okay? Great! Okay, 'bye."

That was how the strangest summer vacation I have ever had got started. Two long weeks passed after our visit to UW-Stevens Point, and then a flurry of phone calls and a weekend down there sorting potions and paraphernalia into waterproof containers. Nicolette took half a stipend, and Irv and I took none, except for *vita* material for him and potential course credit for me. We did our own food. The project was scaled back all right, all the way back to being only one of several reconnaissance surveys for an Orientation Study for the Primary Study of one small piece of the longed-for Big One; I don't know what all. It turned out that Pukaskwa National Park, in the northeast corner of Lake Superior, had already been on the lichenologists' radar, and so when Parks Canada gave their blessing with the caveat that we share our findings, I mean, the game was on. That the coast was regularly cruised by park patrols, as well as a ferry for campers and paddlers and sightseers, was the deciding factor for Nicolette's advisor. Strings were pulled; signatures affixed. Miraculously, St. Joseph's gave me time off without pay—ten days. They were not willing, but I promised on a stack of Bibles I'd work weekends to catch up, so they let me go.

The night of departure, down to the wire, and I should have been packing like mad. But I couldn't stop wondering, How can this all be happening? A year ago I'd been hating the wind in the trees in my old home town, and now I was about to see a small bit of the world of Frances Anne Hopkins. Great-Grandma Marjorie must have been smiling down on me. Outside in the driveway, the Escort was bulging with gear and crowned with sea kayaks—that old beater tandem and the orange Hydra. Where would we sit? Thank God Nicolette was already up in Canada.

It was pretty late by the time we left and headed north along the bay. We drove until midnight, when we could no longer stand our blurry eyes and cottony tongues. Time to stop. Irv knew of a strip of Lake Michigan beach, screened from the highway by pines; we found it, pulled in, and set up our tent. We'd have to be gone by sunrise to avoid getting hassled, less than four hours away, but it was better than nothing. In the dark, we could only sense the looming presence of the lake.

But dawn revealed what night had concealed. I woke up and unzipped the thin skin of our tent, letting cool air stream inside. In the east, the sun was just rising, directly across the water lapping white sand a few feet from our bed. Small waves curled up the beach and back down, as if to coax. I admired the contrast of white foam on dark water—I wasn't sure if I was really awake. A gull slid into view and hovered briefly before me. We were eye to eye, and for a moment I was shaken by the realization that this enormous world had been right outside the tiny eggshell world of our tent, all night long. I looked back at Irv. He was awake and smiling a beautiful, slow smile. I turned back to the lake, the sunrise, and the breeze, and thought, This is worth it, no matter what else happens, this is worth it.

11.

The Ocean Dreams

"All the rivers run into the sea; yet the sea is not full; unto the place from whence the rivers come, thither they return again."

— Ecclesiastes 1:7

IT IS NOT so very long ago in the rich scheme of time. *Diomedea exulans*, the Great Gull, slides silently over the face of the ocean. He is albatross, long-winged, a fragment of white on a band of blue on the glowing eastern horizon. There, the sun rises, underlining dark clouds with scarlet, then pink, then gold. *Diomedea exulans* slides and listens to the tale of the ocean's dream:

"I am dreaming of the rivers that send their waters to me. What lush gifts they bring! I smell the flowers of the plains and the pines of the uplands, the dark earth in low places, and the smoke of a million campfires. The sweetwater inland seas! Come back to me! Let me whisper in your heart, let me lure you; I shall take you in that you begin again."

The long wings of albatross are tipped with gold as he slides on the face of the ocean. The wind stirs the lambent, lowering sky, drawing foam from the water, while far away in the mountains, the glaciers drip, and far away in the forests, the springs rise, called by the longing inside.

12.

A Sea Journey

Spring and Summer 1689

THERE WAS A tradition in the seafaring towns of Europe to fix a plant or branch to the bowstem of a ship under construction. It was thought to bring good luck on the high seas. The *Sainte Anne*, so beautiful and brave, had borne such a talisman, long years ago. The sea had tested her time after time; still she returned safely to land. In the spring of the year 1689, she and two like her waited in the harbor of La Rochelle, on the verge of the great Atlantic, drowsing and filling with cargo and the dreams of a new mission. She was the ship that would carry Bernard Cornet and his new family to Canada, for he was returning there to the profitable and exhilarating trade he'd set up these many years. He was a practical man, tough but well meaning, and not past his prime. La Rochelle had been good to him and provided a bride within the allotted time—one short winter. The bride came of an excellent family of local merchants, and moreover, brought with her English connections, relations of her late husband. This, an intriguing fillip to Bernard Cornet's prospects, though not to be explored just yet. War was coming, after all, and who knew how matters would stand in a year?

The bride whom Cornet had just married was called Pauline,

black-haired and anxious, but putting on her brave face. The prospect of Nouvelle France filled her not with hope but fluttering dread. A wild land of wild people and horrifying beasts in monstrous, swelling forests. Once again, Pauline was bidding goodbye to her parents and everything she knew. But there was duty, and this steeled her. She held tightly to the hand of her daughter, Frances, the Englishman's daughter, who was all too apt to fly from her side on a whim. Eleven years old, watchful, and as pale as her mother was dark, Frances waited in judgment of her new father. She was willing to tolerate him for the sake of a chance to see swelling forests full of beasts and naked, brown people. For where her mother quailed, Frances yearned. As a bribe, Bernard Cornet had given her to read his own copy of Father Hennepin's book, *Description de la Louisiane*, the Recollet priest's harrowing account of his journey deep in the western wilderness of New France. She had read it twice through already, but had not softened to the new *papa*.

In the port city of La Rochelle, there were no clear-cut lines between public, private, and Godly endeavor. It was, rather, a tangle of government officials, over-zealous clergy, and a claustrophobic inter-relatedness of merchant families watching each other. Of necessity, for every merchant was both a debtor and a creditor; it was but good sense to keep informed. That year, the atmosphere in the city was sharpened by the Sun King's dire, foolish plans for those souls he deemed heretic. All Huguenots, Jews, and Protestant foreigners who had lingered were now leaving in haste. This was a shame, but it opened a well of opportunity for good Catholic merchants, like Bernard Cornet. At present, however, he was bent on avoiding payment of a particular debt, one inconveniently overdue, for a previous shipment of trade goods. These items—cloth, knives, kettles, and the like—were now in Indian hands, but not yet recompensed in furs. Such were the long logistics of the fur trade! But Bernard Cornet did not hesitate to do or not do whatever was required.

The Cornets had taken lodgings in a small inn, hard by the Jesuit houses where Garamond of Anjou was employed. They knew each other by sight already; they would all climb aboard *Sainte Anne* for Canada.

The eve of departure was fair but breezy, and, as Bernard Cornet wished to smoke, he was obliged to duck into a doorway to light his pipe. "Good evening," he said to Garamond, who brushed by him on his way out.

"Good evening, Monsieur," said Garamond. The young man stepped into the street and stretched his sore muscles, for he'd been loading cargo all day. "*Zut*," he muttered, "I forgot my sack." He turned to go back inside, but was prevented by a man barring his way. This man, finely dressed and coifed, stank of righteousness, for he was a debt collector.

"I am looking for someone," the man said. "Do you know a certain Bernard Cornet, a merchant who is said to be here with his family?"

Garamond noted with irritation the imperiousness of this question that seemed to say, "You, peasant, tell me what I want to know."

He could sense Cornet in the doorway just beyond. "Oh well, Monsieur, let me think for a moment." He gazed around noncommittally. For a second, his gaze registered Cornet's face, tense with warning. "You know, Monsieur, I think I may have seen that man leaving yesterday. His ship was bound for Nantes, for more cargo. Yes, I think there was a wife and a fair-haired girl. You know, Monsieur, I am sure of it."

The man studied the peasant's face, but found nothing suspicious there, for Garamond was expert at feigning innocence.

"You are quite sure?"

The peasant shrugged. The collector drew himself up, turned, and stalked off without wasting another word. Garamond watched him leave, wrinkling his nose with dislike.

"Young man," Bernard stepped toward him and said in his low, gruff voice, "I am indebted to you."

"*Non, non. Ça ne fait rien.* It was good to put him on the wrong track, I think. I am only a poor *Anjevin*, but I know that type, what do you say?"

Bernard chuckled. "*Bien sûr.* For myself, he is only a meddler, that one." He frowned and then smiled, and said, "Come, have you had your supper? You shall eat with me and my family."

"Oh, *merci beaucoup, merci Monsieur!*"

In fact, Garamond had just eaten a skimpy supper and was still hungry. He had no doubt of the excellence and plenitude of a merchant's table. His mouth watered as he followed Bernard Cornet to his lodgings down a well-lit, orderly side-street, where, with delight, he partook of a hearty second meal. He feasted his eyes on Cornet's wife and teased the daughter, the same, he could swear, who'd passed him and Jean and Claude on the road, and dropped a white feather. He answered all inquiries about the products of Anjou and of his plans to be a *donné* to the Jesuits, and to, perhaps, study for the Order. Then Pauline brought him a packet of cheese and bread to fortify his breakfast next morning.

"*Mais oui!*" She crossed herself piously. "You must study and serve Jesus and the Church! And make your poor *maman* so proud!"

He refrained from mentioning his schemes to run off with the fishing boats. He had cooled on this idea, anyway, when he realized how long was the reach of the Jesuits. He'd learned much in this short stay in the port of La Rochelle. Throughout that last congenial evening in France, he was aware of Bernard Cornet's appraising eyes, and parried his shrewd questions with what skill he could, and hoped that good luck would come of it. He thought, Yes, it is good to do favors for *les bourgeois*. This Cornet will remember me.

He left them around midnight and retired to his tiny pallet in the Jesuit granary, shared with a servant, who was already wrapped tight in the blanket. For a few hours, Garamond slept the deep, blameless sleep of fatigue. Long before daybreak, he was brusquely awakened and summoned to the ship with the rest of the crew. Passengers followed, and by mid-morning, a fine wind had arisen to fill *Sainte Anne's* sails and whisk her swiftly from France.

Just a week into the voyage, the girl Frances came down with ship fever. It had started with a strange wakefulness at night. She was simply not tired and lay staring into the blackness of their berth. Pauline slept by her side, while all around them folk snored and murmured. Frances imagined the immensity of the ocean pressing on the creaking timbers of the hull of *Sainte Anne*. She laid her hand on the wall to feel if it was damp. She felt very warm.

She fell asleep at last and dreamed of a bed of white lace. An exquisitely kind and beautiful woman in a frothy pink gown served her tea in a Chinese porcelain cup, like a gem in the hand. Frances smiled in her sleep, but gradually her face crumpled into a frown, then she woke crying, for the sea had burst into her dream, furiously sweeping the cup, the woman, and the lace into oblivion. "Leave me alone!" she cried. But no one awoke.

"Hush, hush, *petite*," she whispered, hugging herself in the darkness. She did not go back to sleep, but considered instead how insolently the waves slapped the hull of the ship. By morning, she'd passed out and passed into a watery world, awash in the dreams of illness.

So began a most trying voyage for the Cornets. Ship fever, a hodgepodge of dreadful symptoms, manifested itself in Frances as heat and thirst, and alternating periods of lucidity and dreams verging on hallucination. She would not eat, could not sleep. She refused all offers of familiar, homespun remedies, but—discriminating child!—drank all the costly tea she could get. It seemed to help, so Bernard ordered Pauline to drink a cup daily as preventative. After tea, Frances would earnestly tell them her dreams: fantastic fishes and birds, *Sainte Anne* soaring in the sky—"Don't you see, *maman*, how the sky has pulled us up?"— and dreams of wrapping herself in waves, or diving into the deepest heart of the ocean. They listened patiently, taking turns bathing her face in cold sea water before she would leave them again, like a bird on an errand.

To sail west on the Atlantic from France, it is necessary to first steer north, past Ireland and farther, riding improbably tropical wind and waves, until westward-bearing currents are found. The westward currents are cold, not so very far south of winter's grip, and when *Sainte Anne* found them, Frances's fever kept her warm while all others shivered. By this time, another child had fallen ill and quickly died, and then an elderly man with rheumy eyes also died. Frances stayed alive on broth, nibbles of biscuit, and the last of the tea.

Four weeks from departing the calm harbor of La Rochelle, they were battling tumultuous seas off the tip of Greenland, which violence caused panic in some, veiled anxiety in others, but, miraculously, a cure in the ravaged body of Frances Cornet. In the midst of a freezing gale, she ate a little biscuit, then some more, then a wrinkled apple, dried meat, cheese, and a crust of moldy bread before Pauline could stop her. For days, she ate and slept peacefully, and as the jagged black cliffs of Newfoundland drew in sight, she gathered her new strength and ascended to the pitching deck to see land again.

There was no one so glad of the sight of land as the young man, Garamond. Just as Frances had been cured of ship fever, he'd been cured of his wish for the sea. The monotony! The bad food, foul water, the brutish crew and snarling master and greedy, sniveling passengers! And, to his shame and surprise, he found himself hating the ocean, the all-encompassing horizon of water, which was either maddeningly flat or rumpled by shrieking wind and rain. He hated the incessant moaning of *Sainte Anne's* timbers, her recalcitrant, flapping sails, and tangled ropes. To crown his misery, he never could shake the sea-sickness. After the retching had passed, he was told, he would have his sea-legs. "Patience," they'd told him. It never happened, and, though he carefully hid this weakness, he was shaky and queasy for the whole trip. And how galling to see the dandified, land-lubber passengers striding about as confidently as if on solid earth. But his bitterness softened at last, for a continent appeared on the edge of the sea, as if born, and the little girl Frances as well, and there were the friendly, ribald cries of birds, filling him again with delight.

South they rode the coast of the island of Newfoundland, a forbidding line of soaring, fog-bearing rock and thin bristles of trees. Many days the fogs and mist denied them a view of the land they'd come so far to see. Then they could only listen to the birds, the surf, and ice popping and hissing in the water.

At last the land turned west and *Sainte Anne* followed. There, they found fishing boats crewed by wild-eyed, long-haired, laughing men who clung to the rigging like leaves to a tree. And sweet fortune!—these men informed them that yes, *Sainte Anne* was likely the first ship from France that year. Spirits took flight at the news.

The cliffs, fjords, and tundra-draped granite sped by ever faster, past Cap Sainte Marie, Baye de Plaisance, and Île St Pierre with its deep-hewed Baye de Fortune beyond. Thence to Cap de Raye and out to the open sea again, north to great Anticosti, floating in the flood of the Saint-Laurent.

Though a week of hard sailing remained, the decks and quarters of *Sainte Anne* soon swarmed with cleaning, repacking, and loud, cheerful talk. Another fishing boat hailed them, and then, wonder of wonders, they saw Indians in canoes—tiny, graceful crafts of bark—skimming the water like birds, straight and true from the shore to the ship.

"They are Montagnais," Bernard Cornet informed his companions as they stood rapt at the deck.

The Indians drew up below, thoughtfully noting the demeanor of the newcomers and the condition of the ship.

"*Bonjour mes amis!*" a crewman shouted.

An Indian man waved and shouted back in strangely accented French, "Will you trade with us, brother?"

"*Oui, oui!*" Master Chaviteau of *Sainte Anne* called out from his perch.

They anchored there for the day, lowered a boat with the master and two crewmen from which to trade ritual pleasantries and sundry goods with the astute native merchants of Canada. Fresh, red meat and glossy pelts changed hands for copper kettles, iron awls, chains and hooks, and strings of Venice beads. Words of ceremony for obligations to honor. The passengers of the ship watched these transactions silently, reverently, hardly daring to breathe for fear of distracting the Indians. How dramatic the appearance of the Montagnais! Their luxurious furs, their exotic adornments, their jewel-like canoes! All this, eyed hungrily by the French, and effortlessly incorporated into the dreams of Frances Cornet. The Indians, already familiar with the weird but persistent *Français*, politely but deliberately monitored the ship for signs of threat. There were none, and before dusk, the canoes departed in peace, leaving the enthralled *Sainte Anne* in their wake. Soon, bright blazing campfires appeared on the heretofore desolate shore.

"An auspicious beginning," remarked the master to the first mate.

But in the morning, there were no traces of Indians. In their place, a bright breeze had sprung from the east, so *Sainte Anne* raised anchor and departed. Everyone, crew and passengers alike, kept a sharp lookout, for their appetite for wonders had been thoroughly whetted. Continual discussion ensued. Would the Indians come back? What did they love best to trade? How perilous to travel by canoe! How brave they must be, or how careless?

To Garamond, these questions seemed crucial. He never concentrated so hard as he did then, listening to conversations among the seasoned veterans of Canada—Cornet, the ship's master, and a handful of others. Even in the midst of his eavesdropping and his work—coiling, reefing, hauling; oiling rusty winches—he could barely look away from the coast to starboard, dancing in and out of mist and sun. This coast shot up in wave-lashed cliffs, then mellowed to coves and beaches, then hardened again, and all darkly furred with forest. How magnificent! But best of all were the rivers, pure and foaming, that issued from a secret, beckoning interior. Slivers of white cleaving rock, pouring endlessly into the sea. Garamond noted each one. He already knew then, as *Sainte Anne* advanced west into the mouth of the great river, Saint-Laurent, that come what may, he would spend his life following the courses of rivers.

13.

A Nudge from Kitchi Gami

Summer 1869

"OH THE POOR children!" Mrs. Hopkins exclaimed. "Poor, innocent ones, burning with fever, all alone in the dark hold of that beastly ship!"

"But they were never alone, my dear." Edward gave her a measured glance, then said in a low voice, "Pray, calm yourself."

She subsided at once. Xavier, from his perch in the stern of the Hopkins's canoe, waited to see if the Englishwoman's mood would change, if the dismal cloud would lift just a little. He thought, There it is, I have reached her! But the silence lengthened and there were no signs.

They'd been four leisurely days on the lake, and though the initial late start had been pleasant enough, they found themselves rising earlier and earlier, falling into the familiar rhythm of a journey by canoe. The big lake was notorious for afternoon wind—*La Vieille*, it was called—the old woman. She slept late, so the voyageurs did not. They struck camp by dawn and paddled away to the red rising sun, cheered by the company of loons. So far, they'd had fog and showers, and long interludes of benevolent sun. Moderate waves, just enough to cause the bark canoes to twist and wallow in the troughs, but one got used to that. The *canots de maître* were extraordinarily stable, but they had a weakness—taking water over the sides—for even these in the Hopkins's party were loaded to within seven inches of freeboard. Light boats were expensive boats.

Since leaving Silver Islet with its new-discovered lode, Edward had been diligently searching for signs of minerals. He'd always noted interesting formations in the way of landmarks, but never beyond that, and now he was baffled by the range of inscrutable variations that constituted ordinary, homely, work-a-day rock. There were smooth, dark brown tumbled chunks of rock, warm from the sun and speckled with white crystallizations. There were rocks with green nodules, black specks, inch-long fibrous crystals; there were wrinkled gray and burnished gold rocks, and beautiful pink and coral ones at the place called Les Ecrits. There were rocks of multi-colored layers pressed together—bronze, black, gray, orange, and skeins of veins of white quartz. It all looked vaguely promising, but he soon gave it up. He would always be a trader, a Hudson's Bay man. It seemed easy then to foresee his life in London: reminiscing with old cronies over port. Well, he thought, That won't be so bad.

They'd had no mishaps on the trip and no incidents of note, save Baker's rather dramatic announcement that he planned to quit the Company that year, which statement he retracted after another mile had passed. They met a large party of Ojibway Indians camped on the long white beach on St. Ignace Island. Otherwise, no one. Xavier's storytelling, in his soft, mellow voice, wandered as they did, on past islands of all sorts—some park-like, one with an arch—and fine sheltered coves, but also exposed stretches of heavily wooded coast. The Slates became visible as faint blue shadows and then drew near and remained seemingly parallel for miles and miles. Cape Victoria, wicked as usual, kicked up her dancing, glittering, watery peaks, negotiated with skill by the steersman. But it was Denis, their blue-coated *avant*, who saved them in the surf at the mouth of the Steel River.

By consensus, all had decided the best campsite so far had been the snug, sandy beach at the foot of a purling stream, perhaps a hundred miles east of Fort William. Mr. Marsh, the younger clerk, had shot a partridge there in the woods, and there were fish at the mouth of the stream. For sunset, they had delicate, lilac-rimmed pink clouds in an aqua-blue sky, all graced by zooming dragonflies and before long, a full moon. Mrs. Hopkins had stayed a long while to study the scene, but she was unable or unwilling to recreate it on paper. That night in a dream, her nurse's voice woke her, as if from long ago, "Miss Frances, wake up, get up." Obediently, she rose and peeped out the flap of the tent, but there was only the white moon beaming down on their camp like daylight.

Xavier had observed Mrs. Hopkins as closely as he dared, searching for clues to her malaise. Of course, he knew all about the dead children and the strange English custom of mourning in black. But what of this prolonged, stubborn sadness? This, he felt, was akin to illness, and so amenable to curing if only he had the skill. His mother's people, the illustrious Cranes of the Sault Ojibway, were rife with healers and conjurers of all sorts, and once he'd been a candidate for learning those arts. But this and that happened and the chance was lost. So he picked up what he could from any source he could find—white doctors, old Indians, mothers. "Like cures like," he'd heard somewhere and never forgot. Thus his choice of the old tale, Frances and Garamond—an experiment to cure Mrs. Hopkins. To be safe, he told no one. He was sure there were ways to counter one ill with another, and thus cancel out both. So far, however, she'd shown no improvement.

On the fifth night, a curiously still, humid night, Xavier lay musing and swatting mosquitoes under his overturned canoe. He and all his companions were restless in the heat; they muttered and squirmed, and did not sleep. Xavier was thinking how pretty Mrs. Hopkins was in her hat and lace, even despite the somberness of her gown. How, he wondered, did she move so well over cobbles and sand in those dainty pointed shoes? She was a mystery to be both scorned and admired. He tried to imagine her stark naked, which was amusing but futile, so his thoughts turned to his own affairs—the two pestering

Yankees back in Red River. They were swine—*cochons*. They wanted trees of course; they would "help" him clear his little strip of land, should he, as a half-blood Ojibway, apply for it. Xavier rolled over irritably, eliciting "Eh, *gouvernail!*" from the sweating man by his side. He thought, Times are hard; perhaps I could use that money.

Morning was still and mild, and men began wagering on when the weather would break.

"By noon," said Denis.

"*Ce soir*," decreed their oldest, most canny voyageur.

"No, not 'til tomorrow." This, from Baker.

They set out in mists like wavering ribbons of gauze. Islands disappeared and reappeared like apparitions, and clouds of midges whirled above deep, humid cracks in the rock. There were hurried flights of ducks and the lusty cries of unseen ravens. Above it all shone the unrelenting sun, and soon, the mist and suspense melted away. The lake remained flat as a pond as the heat built. In an hour, they'd approached a series of crossings, which, after some deliberation, they decided to take if only to find a breeze. They did, lulled as they were by that point, and, though the breeze they found was only a small, sullen one, it was better than nothing. Better still, it was going their way, and so there was plenty of time to smoke.

Frances had resolved that morning to think cheerful thoughts, but the best she could manage, stewing gently there inside of her dress, was to think aimless ones. Why, she wondered, had Edna, their cook for two years, stolen a pair of earrings last fall? They'd had to let her go of course, and there'd been no suitable replacement, and so the holiday dinners were dull, and they'd dared not invite anyone. Olive, their little girl, would no doubt throw a tantrum on their return—she always did—while Manley would be a perfect angel. Frances yearned for them all, but she did not want to see them yet. With a glow of pride, she thought of her triumph at the Royal Academy. I shall do another painting, even better! she thought, and cast about in her mind for a subject. Canoes, yes, she loved the canoes and the north, but what exactly? Her glance fell on the surface of the water—that was it, she knew. The delicious, hypnotizing movement of water, if only she could capture it. She had not done it yet. At some point she realized she was falling asleep to the rhythm of paddle strokes.

"Pay attention!" she murmured out loud, then blushed as the conversations around her paused. She tried to watch the slick waves drifting past, but soon found her gaze sinking down through the water to the rocks below, which rose and descended in deep, green chasms as the canoe advanced above. Occasional shafts of sunlight played across this submerged chaos of huge boulders, caverns, and ledges just like, she thought, light on a rumpled heap of green satin. She thought of her mother's gown, so many years ago, and sighed. She wished that Xavier would go on with his tale.

Edward was reading her mind. He'd decided to head off Xavier's story with another, one of Baker's perhaps, which were at least pleasant, though boring. Carefully, he broke off the end of his pipe, for the clay had become clogged with tar.

"Ah, Mr. Baker—" he began.

But as the clerk turned around, his eyes rested, not on Edward Hopkins, but on the sky astern, dark blue and forbidding, and Mr. Baker's eyes grew round.

"I say! We've a squall coming, sir!"

Everyone turned. They were three miles into the crossing and somewhat more than a mile from shore.

"Plenty of time, plenty of time," Edward called out in his most authoritative, calming voice. But every mind was doing its own calculations. Without discussion, both bow-men resumed paddling, albeit at a blistering pace, matched stroke for stroke by every voyageur. Short, quick, mile-eating strokes, the blades snatched from the water and swept forward like lightning. Perhaps a quarter of an hour passed as the breeze grew into a wind, and the following waves surged higher until they began slopping over the gunwales. The sun disappeared, but they were not dismayed, for the shore was now in reach. They headed for a well-known cove and it seemed they would make it, but the water grew shallow before they were quite ready.

"Steady!" Baker cried. In an instant, the waves steepened around them, then started to break in long, savage curls. The stern of the Hopkins's canoe rose behind them, threatening to veer out of line, but Xavier fought it with all his strength. He prevailed! From somewhere came the sound of a woman's laughter, peals of laughter, and with a start, Xavier realized it was Mrs. Hopkins, apparently enthralled by their ride. He would have crossed himself if he could.

Perhaps it was the charge in the air before the approaching storm, or perhaps it was simply time. She felt, as they lurched toward shore, as if the film that had enveloped her for weeks had burst open, and let in the world and engaged all her senses. The curling of the waves combined with the wet on her face, the struggling crew, the sounds of pounding and froth. But really it was the canoe itself—climbing the waves like a live thing, lifting her, bearing her forward, and dropping her down—that delighted her so. She knew somewhere inside that here was peril, but what of that? The important thing was the joy! The stern rose again; they coasted swiftly forward; a twist of Xavier's paddle and they were safe in the water of the cove. Edward turned half around, beaming.

"Bravo, *gouvernail!*"

Xavier laughed; he and everyone knew that praise from Hopkins was a rare thing.

"Eh, Xavier! *Tu es un homme*, eh?"

"*Mais oui! Je suis un homme!*"

All began talking at once, shouting, clowning with relief. The *milieux* leaped out to steady the boats lest they rub on the rocks. Edward, in his excitement, got out to help his wife to shore. He lifted her tenderly and asked, "Were you frightened my dear?" It was at this moment that the squall broke and unleashed its torrent of rain; within minutes, they were soaked to the skin. But the rain, however so hard it might pour, could not wash the smile from Mrs. Hopkins's face.

14.

The Nebaunaubaewuk

AMONG THE LESSONS of the Ojibway elders are the tales of the *nebaunaubaewuk*, the mermen, and the *nebaunaubaequaewuk*, the mermaids. These are the sirens of deep water, and many the piteous mortal who has succumbed to their tricks. The *nebaunaubae* beings live unending lives in lakes and seas and rivers, in form like both fish and human. They play in the deeps and feast in caverns of stone. They are of the world of *manitous*, and as such, apart from our world—except when the fancy takes them. There are tales of coveted young men and young women snared by the merfolk and drowned, but they do not die. Perhaps they sleep for a while. In due time, the victims are healed and metamorphose, it is said, and take up new lives underwater where they dwell in peace with their captors, forever.

The lessons tell also of the *pau-eehnssiwuk*, the little *manitous* of water's edge, who warn the unwary of the *nebaunaubae* beings' designs. Especially at night, for night and dark water are a dangerous brew. But the *pau-eehnssiwuk* cannot be everywhere, and water in daylight seems lovely and safe. There are the mysteries of chance and there are mortals whose passions run deeper than they know. There is the din of surf and wind and beating blood in the veins, all of which may conspire so that small voices are never heard at all.

15.

The Honorable Men

June 1689

LATE IN THE day of the summer solstice, Bernard Cornet and Jean Garamond stood sentinel on the deck of *Sainte Anne* and watched sunset gild the cliffs of Canada. They'd not gone below deck all that day, for they did not want to miss an inch of the passing shore. Cornet's billowing, black greatcoat snapped in the wind.

"We are lucky," he said. "Only six weeks to Canada this time."

"And you, Monsieur—your little girl has recovered."

"Yes. I spent twenty livres of tea for her, and for my wife and myself. But I am sure it made all the difference." Bernard made a wry smile. "Though the dreams haven't left her—she's a strange little thing. But alive, *merci de Dieu.*"

"Yes, thanks be to God."

"Pray our luck holds! We're the first ship to New France this year—indeed, we shall make a bundle. And you, Jean Garamond, are you yet resolved on your course?"

"I think I'll be slaving for the Jesuits to pay my passage, Monsieur. But I *wish* to make a bundle of money, like you! I want to make my own way, you see?"

Cornet grunted, and after a short silence, he glanced sideways at his companion, then held his gaze.

"Perhaps I can help you out," said the merchant. "As you know, I am set up anew in Montréal, taking on my partner's profession—an outfitter in the trade for Canadian furs. He retires to France this very year. It is a new venture for me—an old import man, eh? Of course, Charles has left me all his *engagés* and the ongoing contracts, but I also wish to bring in new blood of my own choosing. Experienced men, yes, but also there is room for one or two untested, should they show promise. I believe you do, *Anjevin*, if I am a judge. Perhaps you even have the makings of an *homme honnête*, eh?"

Garamond looked mystified.

"It signifies a man of honor," Bernard explained. "An *homme honnête* keeps his word and strives to be astute, useful, and steady in all his endeavors that he may nurture his family and his fortune in this uncertain world. You must do the same, my young friend. How would you like to start as a crewman for my traders? You shall be a brave *coureur de bois* to go in my stead to the Indians of the North-west, barter for furs, and bring those furs back to me, that I may sell them to the *Ferme* for an excellent price. Which I would share accordingly. It could be a most beneficial arrangement—what do you say?"

Ruefully, Garamond kept silent. How he would love to be Cornet's man! But he did not wish to be a criminal on the run from the clergy.

Bernard smiled. "It would not do to cheat the Jesuits, but we may be able, over the course of this summer, to recruit someone in your place, because, Garamond, I think you are trustworthy and I know you are strong. And ambitious."

"*Oui*, Monsieur," Garamond beamed with pleasure, "I am all that!"

The merchant chuckled, enjoying the gathering dark and the glow of successful negotiation. The land of Canada had temporarily disappeared, but they could feel the push of the tide on *Sainte Anne's* hull, bearing them closer all the same. They watched the golden lights of a fishing boat drift past, heading in from sea.

Cornet said, "If I spring you from the Jesuits, you must give us the standard term, three years, *oui*?"

"*Bien sûr*! You have my word, Monsieur."

16.

Seventeenth Century Canada

Winter 2020

Gentle Reader,

IT IS FRUSTRATING to delve into the doings of the sixteenth and seventeenth centuries. Before one truly looks into the matter, it's easy to judge the history of North America as an inexorable slide into an abyss of imperialism, materialism, and environmental ruin. Bitter remorse. But with a little knowledge—only a little!—it becomes difficult to shake the feeling that things could have been different. Maybe, just maybe there was a stray chance that it could have worked: Indians and Europeans could have lived in some sort of harmony within a vast, sustaining wilderness; each culture borrowing the best from the other. If only this, if only that.

Because there *was* a stirring of tolerance in those days, inspired by the unwinding of time and the eye-opening Experience of seeing new lands, new peoples, and different ways. There could have been sweet fruit from that tree, at least in some places, among some peoples. Canada was such a place, because it is possible to imagine what the French traders in Canada wanted. They wanted prosperity of course, but prosperity in the context of the fur trade. This presented certain constraints, which, if honored, could have wrought a paradise of sorts. Without wilderness, Indians, and sustainable populations of fur-bearing animals, there could be no fur trade and therefore, no profits. So the traders wanted a wilderness intact (but sprinkled with trading posts), and free traffic with the Indians, unhindered by bureaucracy or war. They wanted the little colony of New France to thrive, that it may supply a middle market for their furs and a depot for trade goods desired by the Indians. It should be a reserve pool of young men, new money, and commercial alliances—whether by unspoken agreement or carefully arranged marriage. It should be a haven in which to indulge in the charms, but not the horrors, of old France. But it should not expand beyond the St. Lawrence.

Because mostly, the traders wanted to ramble in the wilderness and partake of the beautiful life and, unavoidably, the dreadful feuds of their Indian kin. But few get what they want on this earth, and so things turned out as they did.

Was it fate that forced Champlain in 1609 to take sides? He chose the northern Indians, with their higher-quality furs: the Algonquins, Montagnais, Ottawas, and the Hurons. With regret, he joined them against the Iroquois, and thus lost the love of the Five Nations forever.

And what terrible fate was it that Champlain and each soul who sailed from Europe harbored in their bodies an ocean of virulent disease? Wave after wave, for many hundreds of years, swept through the villages and cities of the native peoples, these people who seemed to be of legend, so perfect, straight, and tall they appeared to the Europeans of that time, and maybe to some in these days. As for the mournful question—How many millions died?—who shall ever tell? What is certain is that Europe was full and full ready to repopulate the lands of America.

When Cartier first came to Canada in the 1530s, he found Indians at Stadacona, which place became Québec, and at Hochelaga, which became Montréal. Those Indians were gone by the days of Champlain. Then, in the earliest years of the seventeenth century, the little colony grasped hold and grew from nubs of outposts into populous settlements with all the accoutrements of European civilization, but colored by the surrounding wilderness and the cachet of the Indians. To the north, the boreal forest marched to the arctic; to the south, the hardwood forest beckoned from a rich, mellow interior. But the end of the west had not yet been found, and in that direction were excellent furs and a possible route to Cathay.

Hard on the heels of the traders and fishermen, the religious orders, especially the Jesuits, arrived and dispersed into the wilderness. Some of them lost their lives and some of them found souls to save. They lived in the Huron villages and witnessed the massacres there, first by the Iroquois, then by disease, until the Hurons dispersed in their turn and the Jesuits moved on. All the effects of the journeys of these unfathomable men may never be known. Most of the black gowns were resented, even hated, but some were loved. Interestingly, there were no Salem witch trials in either the eastern settlements, or the hinterland outposts. There were some Indians who willingly converted to Christianity. Not many, but some. And the Jesuit missionaries needed the fur trade to get where they wanted to go.

In the summer of 1689, the colony of New France lay stretched on the banks of the great St. Lawrence River for near three hundred miles, from its confluence with the Ottawa River at the village of Montréal, down past strips of farms and forts and mills, the village of Three Rivers, and the city of Québec, on down to the old trading post, Tadoussac, at the mouth of deep Saguenay fjord. And thence into the sea. On the sea, there was cod fishing and whaling to be done. Between Montréal and Québec, neat, lonely farmsteads lined the banks of the river, each one set down there as if uncoiled from its strip of land reaching back to the mountains. Each farmstead was a grant from a *seigneur*, who in turn held his *seigneury* on a grant from His Majesty, Louis XIV, the Sun King of France.

What with land for the asking and all manner of royal monetary incentive, there were born in Canada many more children than in

France. The King sent many hundreds of soldiers, servants, and young women, as well. So, some eleven thousands of colonists lived there by then. They had survived fire, earthquake, the occasional starving winter, epidemic, and war. But no matter the hardships. There were a few who took ship with their riches, back to France, but most were not rich, and they could not bring themselves to return to misery. They hung on like wildcats.

Now, King Louis and his minister de Seignelay, successor of the great Colbert, did what they thought was right. They wanted a colony like the English had, one that would provide markets, profits, and resources with which to fight the wars of Europe. So they tried to mold New France into a colony blessed as if by the geography and climate of lands to the south. Which could not be done in the end. Rather, Louis and his minister ensnared the colony and the Indians in war, for they had not tasted the delights that their traders knew. Thus the powers of France did evil, whether they knew it or not.

Listen to the fantastic names: Jean Bochart de Champigny, Intendant of New France; Jacques Réné de Brisay, Marquis de Denonville and his successor, Louis de Buade, Comte de Frontenac et de Palluau, Governors General; Chevalier Louis-Hector de Callières, Governor of Montréal; Jean-Baptiste de la Croix de St. Vallier, Bishop.

These were the notables of the summer of 1689. What could they not do with names like that? But the merchants were the real dealmakers in Canada. The wealth and reach of La Rochelle and of the Dutch and all the pan-European merchant web was so great that, despite all odds, the trade survived.

Above everything, the King and his ministers desired order and a generous share of the profits of trade, and to achieve these aims, they set stringent regulations on the fur trade. It was therefore necessary for the merchants to buy a license to trade from the Crown, and also, to sell their furs to the Crown, and within New France and nowhere else. And some furs were taxed, a rare burden in Canada. The entire procedure was leavened with fraud, favoritism, and ineptitude, but there were enough agents of the Crown who were competent and ruthless, and they did crimp the style of the traders somewhat.

Think now for a moment of the young men who took to canoes and journeyed west to trade with the Indians. These were the *coureurs de bois*, that is, woods runners, or rangers, or rovers of the deep wilderness. The epithet, *coureurs de bois*, is somewhat untranslatable, but perhaps you get the drift. They were, to say the least, free spirits. Bankrolled and supplied by the merchants of Europe, they risked everything for the chance of a journey, for the adventure, for the company of Indians and other traders. Licenses to trade were neither here nor there. Imagine the extraordinary appearance of these men—clad in buckskins, fringes, beads, and the odd bits of outrageous French finery. Their hair was long and braided or bound with bright scarves. They were arrogant, perhaps filthy, highly skilled, and toughened by travel. Some were impoverished nobles or untitled gentlemen; many were peasants. They were, for the most part, happy.

There were attempts to keep these young men in the colony—in the fields or mills, and the beds of the young French women who would be brides. Notably, fairs were held at Montréal to lure the Indians in with their furs, thus obviating the reason for French men to go to the woods. The fairs were great fun, but ineffective in regulating trade. It proved impossible to keep the young men at home; when they wanted to, they simply disappeared into the forest. In truth, the authorities never pressed them too hard lest the young men grow frustrated and—horrors!—go over to the English.

These were some who wandered farthest: Daniel Greysolon du Lhut; Pierre Esprit Radisson and Médard Chouart des Groseilliers; Jacques de Noyon; Robert Cavalier de La Salle; Jean Péré; Louis Jolliet. How far had they gone by 1689? As far as the mouth of the Mississippi, and to Hudson's Bay, and the Rainy Lake, and the near reaches of the great interior prairie. And everywhere, they gathered all kinds of furs, though mostly beaver, and they brought these back and sold them to licensed traders on the sly. And then the Crown bought the furs at guaranteed prices. It was an endless river of fur pouring into the bulging warehouses of Europe, where the market was saturated and the furs could not be sold. Economic disaster awaiting.

About then the great Iroquois confederacy made its move. The Five Nations—Mohawk, Oneida, Onondaga, Cayuga, and Seneca—had lain quiet for near twenty years, biding their time and studying their foes, both traditional and exotic. The French they would never trust. The English they would use as best they could. Long had the Iroquois gazed at the rich lands of their westward neighbors, the Illinois. And they grew tired at last of the incursions of traders in lands that Iroquois should have milked. By then, they needed the Europeans' guns to survive against their enemies. To have guns, they must have furs to trade. They thought to strengthen themselves first in the west, and drive out the Illinois, then to eliminate, perhaps, the fur-trading tribes to the north, close-tied to the French, and then the French themselves. In response, the French rallied under the Marquis de Denonville, and drove against the Seneca, utterly destroying the villages and fields of corn, and thus the Iroquois were thwarted. So, in the summer of 1689, all of New France expected the arrival of an Iroquois delegation to ratify the treaty Denonville had made with them the preceding summer. For the French powers held the Iroquois as essential parts in a delicately balanced game of trade: the Iroquois must never be completely defeated lest the allies—the northern Indians—have no southern detriment to trading for cheap English goods.

Triumph in this far-flung game of chess would assure not only survival and control of the fur trade, but also control of the ancient net of trade routes that crisscrossed the continent. This net of rivers, lakes, and trails linked peoples of all kindreds without prejudice. From time beyond memory, this net had borne native products—from corn, to copper, to cowry shells from the southern sea—to every obscure corner, in the same comprehensive way that the web of the European merchants encompassed the land across the Atlantic. But there was an immense difference. The commerce of the Indians was not based on unlimited desire, but on delight or need, ceremony, friendship, and the building of alliances. Lust for material wealth did not afflict them; rather they desired above all else, honor, and to gain it they would give away their possessions without a second thought. And so, after much error, the Europeans discovered that the key to getting the Indians to trade, was to invoke, not greed, but ceremony symbolic of larger concerns.

The principle Indian nations concerned with New France dwelt in these lands: about the great St. Lawrence were the Algonquin, Montagnais, and Naskapi to the north, and Abenaki to the south; farther south and west were the Iroquois and Illinois; farther north and west by the upper lakes were the Huron, Ottawa, Ojibway, Potawatomie, Menominee, Miami, Winnebago, and Dakota Sioux; and farther north were the Cree and the Assiniboine; and farther south were the Osage, the Choctaw, and the descendants of great cities, emptied by disease.

Throughout all these lands were the marks of long habitation, for the Indians had always used the wilderness and its creatures for their own ends. This they did in good faith, for they loved the land and their place in it. And even with the arrival of the fair-skinned people of Europe with their insatiable appetite for the skins of animals, the Indians still asked these animals for permission, still thanked them for giving their lives, and honored them to ensure their goodwill, that they would continue to sustain the people who killed them. And so a typical June night in the year 1689 would still be characterized by cool darkness under the fierce light of stars. There would be the warm panting breaths of animals gliding through lush vegetation, and, like pin-pricks in the dark, the bright burning fires of the Indians. This state of affairs would continue for perhaps one hundred more years.

17.

Settling Accounts

Summer 1689

WHEN, AT LONG last, the faithful *Sainte Anne* swept up to moor at the docks of Québec, Jean Garamond debarked in haste, kissed the ground, and resolved to never again go to sea. Before him, the city rose up in stony tiers: the houses of the merchants near the water and the houses of their betters near the sky. At once he felt the keen air of possibility that infused all that land. Greedily, he took in the scene: the clattering and jostling of trade, the press of these people, these bright-eyed *Canadiens*. He breathed deep of the smell of muddy water and laughed.

"I am here, I am yours for the taking, *mes amis!*" he cried to God, the saints, and the entire populace of New France.

But it was only another crewman who heard and clapped him on the shoulder, saying, "Back to work, *Anjevin*."

Immediately upon arrival, Bernard Cornet went in search of his agent in Canada, the rotund Monsieur Dubois. They found each other at a shared warehouse that climbed in four stories from the wharf to the street above. One corner of the warehouse was stacked with animal pelts, dried, flattened, and baled. Most of the space was empty, awaiting its share of *Sainte Anne's* cargo. Cornet wasted no words.

"So. Have the Iroquois come? Have they ratified Denonville's treaty? Eh? It is crucial, *n'est-ce pas?*"

"Yes, it is crucial, and it has not come to pass, Monsieur. They have not come, they send no word." Dubois pursed his lips in his round face and frowned at the merchant. "On the surface, all seems well, all seems safe, yet we know nothing for certain. And you, Monsieur, what is your news? Are we at war?"

"Not yet."

Dubois said, "The Iroquois will side with the English colony, *bien sûr*—we must trade our wares with all speed, before the storm."

"Yes! But there is much to do. I cannot hope to be ready to send canoes before summer's end." Cornet sucked in his breath, calculating logistics and politics and the temperaments of his employees. "Do you hear from Charles?" he asked. "Are we full-crewed for the September run?"

Dubois took a long time to answer, for it was a tricky question, and he had no wish to say more than was necessary. Finally, he said, "It would be well to make provisional arrangements, Monsieur, just in case."

"Ah. I have at least one in mind, a young peasant from La Flèche who came over on *Sainte Anne*. I will have all I can manage to extricate him from the Jesuits. He is of course busy with the cargo for now. I shall ascend to that rarified air," Cornet gestured sarcastically, alluding to the Jesuit houses in upper Québec, "day after next to bargain for him. Yes, yes I know. But I have a feeling it will be worth the trouble. He seems the perfect *engagé* for us—strong and willing and unjaded. And besides, he has done me a good turn."

"He will learn quickly; they all do of that sort."

"Yes, he will. He will find out everything soon enough. But say nothing to *ma femme* of these difficult matters. She is wary enough of the country, though the daughter seems willing." He laughed. "The daughter has said she would go to the woods herself to trade if

I asked—oh she is stranger than ever, since her fever."

The extrication of Garamond was, to the annoyance of Bernard Cornet, only accomplished with great effort, for there were not enough able-bodied men to go around in New France that year. So many had left for the woods; so many had died in skirmishes with the Iroquois. And so very many had died from a recent infestation of disease. The estimable Father Phillippe of the Jesuit college was loth to release Garamond, a known quantity, and quite adequate for a *donné*. He smiled politely and said, "But Monsieur Cornet, we have such great, great need of him. Oh, such great need. What could induce us to give him up? I can think of nothing."

"Perhaps someone in his place?"

The Jesuit only raised his eyebrows. He patted the documents spread before him. "Do you see, Monsieur, here is his contract. Here is the receipt for his passage. Here are affidavits attesting to his abilities. And loyalty." He sighed. "So much paper work to run the world, eh?"

"I have in mind a young *Rochelais*, a crewman for *Sainte Anne*, very healthy, skilled in carpentry. I am sure Master Chaviteau would recommend him."

"Oh, well, really? A good Catholic? I am skeptical of all *Rochelais*, of course."

Bernard stifled impatience and said, "In fact, he may even have been helpful in the recent, ah, purges."

"Oh, well. Nevertheless."

"Perhaps, with your indulgence, I may arrange an interview?"

Father Phillippe chuckled and gazed at the ceiling. "I am engaged in so many urgent matters this week. You may ask me again tomorrow."

"*Merci* Monseigneur. I am most grateful." Bernard got up to go, resigned but seething.

As he reached the door, Father Phillippe called after him, "Oh, and Jean Garamond's passage is sixty-five livres. Payable to me."

It took a solid week to close and notarize the deal: release of Jean Garamond from his contract with the Jesuit college; payment in the amount of his passage by Cornet, Dubois, and Charles Laverdure to Father Phillippe; affidavit and contract drawn up for the hapless *Rochelais* sailor; and Garamond's three-year contract with his new masters, and his debt to them for passage. And the notary's bill for six livres. Lest anyone think to question this arrangement, it was decided that Garamond would leave at once with Cornet and his family, and journey to the island of Montréal, a five-day voyage upstream.

The weather on their trip succeeded too well in confirming Pauline's fears. There was a succession of gales, sheets of rain, and fierce, glowering clouds. It was cold, and then hot, and Bernard Cornet was hard put to convince his new wife of the glories of Canada. But the girl Frances had to be restrained more than once from leaning perilously over the rail, just to trail her hands in the water, or to leap to the woods the moment they stepped on shore. In three days, they arrived at the village of Trois Rivières, where the inflowing stream St Maurice split into three and the tide disappeared. There, they stayed the night with Monsieur Le Maître, canoe builder and fur trader, and Bernard opened negotiations for Garamond's expedition west. Le Maître invited them to his wedding, and in fact, he would join their party to Montréal, for his *fiancée* awaited him there with her family.

Mid-day of the ninth of July, they sighted at last the great island of Montréal, its downstream tip bounded by the Saint-Laurent and Rivière des Prairies, deep in the land of New France. Six leagues farther and they reached the settlement of Ville Marie, where they would live with perhaps five hundred others. A large, three-peaked hill, which everyone called *la Montagne*, rose to the west; the Saint-Laurent flowed past on the east. Within an hour, the girl Frances disappeared and did not return to her poor *maman* until dusk. What could they do? The child came back smeared with earth and crowned with wild, ragged flowers like some fairy of ancient days.

21 juillet, 1689
Journal du Bernard Cornet

We are situated nicely here, just west of the village in an adequate house we shall rent from Callières, our *gouverneur* in Montréal. It seems he is in France this past year, pleading our cause with King Louis— good luck to him— and in his place is one Vaudreuil. I had never met the man. He is rather dour, but all right in his way. He made a point of greeting us at Le Maître's wedding. My wife and the daughter are supremely content, I am sure.

On Sunday, more *Québecois* arrived with rumors of war between England and Louis. We have all expected it, however, the summer here continues serenely, so we hope for the best. When more ships come from France, we shall know all. As for business, we have made the usual arrangements. The return cargo will be quite light, I'm afraid. The brigades from up-country have not dared to come down with their furs— the danger was very great last year— and the colony has produced little else. But our preparations go on apace— I relish this task!

Our plan is quite brave, for we are determined to search out the Nadouessioux and establish trade with them directly, circumventing our good Ottawas. Of course, we have no license and I cannot compete in any case with the big men— Le Moyne, Leber, *et cetera*. They are too well connected. However, I have arranged things with Mathurin Cadot, and so I shall have a license, twice removed, so to speak. Our *engagés* will go up with perhaps a dozen others with the Ottawas as usual. But at Missilimackinac, they will slip off to the Sault Sainte Marie and thence west along the southern shore of Lac Tracy, or Supérieur, where they will find the Nadouessioux— or just "Sioux" as we say— past the place called Chegouwameeagan and even farther. I have the greatest confidence in this venture, for Charles and I have studied Cadot's map carefully and confided at length with him and certain others. The Sioux— they are a market virtually untapped. Of course, Father Hennepin had great trial of them, as he tells in his marvelous book. Their customs do seem perplexing, if not alarming. But a priest does not go as well as a trader, in my experience.

For supplies, we shall have victuals, arms and ammunition, materiel for repairing the canoes, blankets, moccasins, snow-shoes, coats and breeches, stockings. Tobacco and brandy for the Indians. Of course our traders shall help themselves and nothing can prevent it. For goods to trade, we shall have axes and knives, kettles, fish hooks, needles and threads, vermilion and Venice beads, cloth of all sorts, and muskets with a quantity of powder, shot, and fuse. Luckily, all these items arrived safely in the hold of *Sainte Anne* and are now tucked away in our warehouse— None are to be had for purchase here, for the colony is quite "out" this summer. Our expedition will be, of necessity, an exploratory one, in the sense that no one really knows what the Sioux may desire. Perhaps they detest the color blue, perhaps they will love India cotton, but not wool, and so on. It is difficult to rest with all this to think of! I am impatient to see Le Maître's canoe come gliding up to Montréal, but that shall not occur for at least another fortnight.

That same morning found Garamond procrastinating in Cornet's little house west of the village. He knew perfectly well he shouldn't be mooning after Cornet's wife, but he couldn't help himself. And the girl Frances was mooning after him. Half an hour of this and Pauline threw him out.

"Off with you!" she admonished, "make yourself useful."

"*Oui, oui,* I'm going."

Usually at that early hour, he would have been working in the fields of the Sulpicians, digging himself out of debt. The Sulpicians, cashless like everyone else, paid him in playing-card money, but Cornet took it, so it was all right. So far, Cornet had never failed to find him work, if not with the Sulpicians, then down at the river helping to dig the new canal. So Garamond was rarely idle. But today was set aside for, as Charles Laverdure mockingly said, "polishing your accomplishments." This amounted to learning how to handle a canoe—which task Garamond loved and excelled at—or more often, practicing with the musket, which he dreaded. He was terrified of mixing up the steps—pack powder, *then* ball down the muzzle with ramrod, aim, fire, clear the barrel, reload—lest the thing blow up in his face. And he was a terrible shot.

So, unwillingly, he collected the gear and made his way to the makeshift shooting range at the end of the field. He could not help but feel guilty, as he picked out the target and fired off the first wayward shot. For it was an excellent firearm, a flintlock with a rifled barrel. An expert could get off five or six shots for each one from an older gun. Supposedly. He took another shot, wincing at the report and the kick against his shoulder. Waving away the bitter blue smoke, he could see the target was not even grazed.

"*Putain de merde.*"

"*Putain de merde!*" It was Frances, standing close behind him.

"Oh, you should not sneak up on me like that! What if you get hurt? And watch what you say, eh? Little smarty."

She didn't answer, but puckered her invisible eyebrows, looking earnestly up at him. She was yet a child then, tow-headed, thin, and, some would say, homely. She was clutching Father Hennepin's book, for she was charged with reading to Garamond about the Nadouessioux in odd moments while he worked, as no one else had the time. She was thrilled to have this responsibility. She loved Hennepin's book, and also the *Fables of La Fontaine* with their wise animals, and she was enchanted by dark-haired Garamond. He smiled down at her, for he was fond of her—strange little girl—and asked, "My lady *Comtesse*, what do you think I'm doing wrong, eh?"

"I bet you're aiming with the wrong eye."

"Probably." He sighed. The wayward eye was of course the problem. Such a small thing, but no matter how he tried, he could not place the target in its true position. "But what can I do?" he complained. "Likely I'll starve on this journey, or learn to eat rocks, eh?"

"Just don't believe it, what that eye shows you. Pretend you see something else! That's easy to do, you don't even have to practice!" She became quite excited by this idea and danced around him, waving the book.

He laughed. "How can I do that?"

"Just aim for somewhere else!"

Without any real hope, but just to please her, he raised the musket and aimed to each side of the target, as if shooting the air beside it. Then he carefully cleaned the barrel and reloaded, and took aim a finger's width to the left. He pulled the trigger, the gun roared, and before he could stop her, Frances raced to examine the target. There was a hole on one side of it. She came running back, whooping, "Again, again! Now you must marry me for sure!"

He took another shot, then another, closing in on his line. It was ridiculous firing at thin air, but it worked.

"*Oh là, là, ma Comtesse*, we make a fine team, eh? When you grow up I'll marry you, what do you say?" Or someone better, he thought.

"*Mais oui! Je t'adore*, Garamond!"

After the breakthrough, which he always attributed to Frances—he pronounced it Fransezz—Garamond became an enthusiastic marksman. And in the evenings, he was allowed to go up to the village to practice paddling canoe. He was good-natured and strong, so he'd made many friends—Le Clerc, Gerbault, Louvet,

Miron, and others. They helped him learn, more or less. Often enough with a good dunking, but he only laughed at his blunders and so progressed easily. After these lessons, they would all repair to the taverns, numerous to be sure, and discuss each tiny detail of his education and the relative merits of the *demoiselles* of Montréal. They would tell him harrowing tales of life in the interior: heat and insects that would drive him mad, back-breaking toil, ferocious rapids, winters that would freeze a man to the trail. But they were all going back and he could not wait to go with them. He learned also the names of the famous *coureurs de bois* and their exploits, especially Daniel Greysolon, Sieur du Lhut, the most loved and respected of all. And, as the great man was actually in the colony that summer, Garamond would wander back to the Cornet's, bleary with talk and liquor, and imagine what he would say or do should he ever meet Du Lhut.

He would wake the next day hung over, and try to look repentant or at least serious. Pauline would upbraid him and command him again to write to his "sweet *maman* in France." Then off he went to the Sulpicians' fields, where, very often, Frances would follow behind him as he worked, reading aloud from Hennepin's book, well seasoned with the words of La Fontaine. It was a curious but agreeable life.

There came a morning in early August, after a long night of thunder and rain, when Garamond, like many others of those who dwelt on the island of Montréal, did not want to wake up. He laid in his bed and rejected unequivocally the over-bright sun and the call of chores. He dreamed instead of payment for all his life's worth of debt—he would be a free man at last! In the dream, he piled sol after sol in towering stacks, lined up on a polished counter of marble. The marble, however, was strangely hot, blazing hot, and so he shifted uneasily in his dream. Long moments passed as the marble started to smoke, and then, from some far place outside all dreams, he heard a thin, wailing shriek. His eyes snapped open—

the very wall by his bed was in flames! For there was a price for living in the land of Canada, apart from all contracts and debts. It was a price exacted by deep-held wrongs: the Iroquois had come in force.

The Fish and the Cormorant

A Fable by Jean de la Fontaine

Nowhere in the region could a single pool be found
Where a Cormorant didn't collect his tax,
Reservoirs, ponds brought meals in stacks,
A diet most hearty. But when old age made its round
  And the poor bird felt its chill,
  This diet went from good to ill.
Every Cormorant functions as his very own supplier;
Ours, a bit too old to see all the way down to the riverbed,
  With no traps, no nets to spread,
  Now suffered from hunger quite dire.
What to do? Necessity, doctor of stratagems, applier
Of schemes, provided this one: at pond's edge one day
  Cormorant saw a Crayfish come by.
"Neighbor," he said, "go this instant, don't delay,
  With this important news, I pray,
  To those folks: every one of them must die.
The owner of this place is coming to fish, in a week."
  Crayfish swam in haste to seek
  The others. In great consternation
  They met, sent the Bird a deputation.
  "Sir Cormorant, about our duress:

Whence comes your information? What proof do you possess?
    Are you sure all this is true?
Don't you know any way out? What's a good thing to do?"
"Move away from here," he said. "Just how can that be done?"
"Don't worry about a thing. I'll transport you, every one
    In order, straight off to my den.
None but God and I know how to get there through the lands;
    No dwelling's more hidden from men.
A fishpond there, hollowed out by Nature's hands,
    Unknown to faithless human bands,
    Saves you all with this stroke."
    They believed him. The aquatic folk
    Were taken, one by one with no snag,
    And placed beneath his lonely crag.
    Cormorant, good apostle and brother,
    Having put them in the spot to keep,
    A limpid pool, long and narrow but not deep,
Caught them with no trouble; one day one, the next day another.
    He taught them, at a cost they bore,
That one must never be so foolish, or so blind,
    As to put one's trust in a carnivore.
Yet what had they really to lose, inasmuch as humankind
Too would have munched its fair share of this prey?

What matter who eats you? Man, wolf, all bellies large or small
    To me seem alike in that way.
    A day's advance, a day's further delay.
    The difference isn't great at all.

The Complete Fables of Jean de la Fontaine (Book Ten). Edited and translated by Norman B. Spector. 1988. Northwestern University Press, Evanston, IL.

18.

A Great Adventure

Summer and Fall 1689

THE ATTACK BROUGHT all preparations for Garamond's journey to an abrupt halt, except that he had many more than one occasion to aim one finger's width to the left, and fire. *Les habitants* of Montréal fled to the forts and the village, and remained therein while the Iroquois burned their farms. It was supposed, and rightly, that the Iroquois had crossed the river under cover of the hailstorm in the night and then hid themselves, and struck Lachine, a settlement west of Ville Marie, at dawn. By the end of that bloody day, over a hundred *Français* were killed or taken prisoner, and hundreds more had hid in the woods. Then the Iroquois made a leisurely retreat back to the far shore and lit fires of torment for their captives and for the benefit of those who watched in dismay from the palisades. It was long before all that had passed was known, for all information that day was confused by grief and dread.

In the thick of the turmoil, it was Denonville, *Gouverneur Général* of the colony, still haggard from the previous year's campaign, who rallied the colonists. Striding through the streets of Ville Marie, he seemed to exude reason and purpose, and with the force of his will held the line against unbridled panic. He sent forth his officers and they did their best, each according to his merits, until a semblance of order was restored. It was necessary to post armed guards around each farmer who dared tend his fields that summer, for the Iroquois did not leave, but lay in ambush, first here, then there. Again and again the alarms would sound: drums, cannon shots, shouts, screams. Folk remained behind palisade walls at night.

In all those weeks of siege, the ships from France did not arrive. These ships would bring supplies and trade goods, news and dispatches from the Court, as well as Denonville's replacement, the Comte de Frontenac. Though news of Europe was hardly necessary anymore; everyone had decided that England and France must be at war, and thus the Iroquois were emboldened by their allies—the *Bastonnais*, the English colonists—to attack Montréal. Yet the colonists of New France continued to yearn for the ships, especially Denonville, for he feared his body would not hold out much longer.

There was one great miracle that summer—though it would not seem so in the eyes of the Iroquois—and that was the return of 150 *coureurs de bois* and their Indian allies from the northwest, their canoes groaning with three years' worth of furs. All the Montréalers left their work to gather along the portage road and watch the procession—and cheer—for there would be little use in staving off enemies if there were no furs to sell in Europe.

"*Mon Dieu*, there must be hundreds of thousands of livres here—and to come all that way in bark canoes, such frail vessels," Bernard had remarked, shaking his head, "I will never get used to it." He and Garamond had joined the crowd in the village to view the spectacle of countless bales of fur unloading. "Somehow we must contrive to get you out there, my friend— are you still willing?" He chuckled, watching the young man from the corner of his eye, for Bernard already knew the answer to his question.

"I am willing," Garamond said gruffly, his heart kindled with greed. "They say the Iroquois will go back to their country when the leaves fall. When they can no longer hide in wait. There will be time yet, Monsieur."

All the while the warriors of the Five Nations held Montréal hostage, Cornet and his partner, Charles Laverdure, and his friend, Mathurin Cadot, studied their maps and thought ardently of the Sioux to the west. If the brigade had got through, they reasoned, why not send the September run, heavily fortified, of course? Though the risk was incalculable, the profits could be staggeringly high. But who among their *engagés* would go? These would have to be chosen—and perhaps convinced—with great care.

Deep into the nights, in a small room of the warehouse, the merchants deliberated and pondered and drank, wasting precious candles. Summer ripened to fall and they came to their decision: for the sake of stealth, it would be a small party, lightly loaded with small, high-value goods. Only two men would go on to the Sioux, a mere feint perhaps, but more than that they would not venture. It would be enough if the main party slipped by the Iroquois.

20 septembre, 1689
Journal du Bernard Cornet

We have decided that Garamond and Cadot's man—
one Michel Miron— shall deliver two casks of powder
to another of Cadot's associates in Missilimackinac,
and then make for the Sault Sainte Marie as if to winter
there. But no, they will continue west until they find
the Sioux encampment. It is risky. But Garamond is
strong as a bull, and intelligent in the way of a peasant,
and he shall follow Miron's lead. I have met
Miron— He is a big, somewhat grimy man, but very
capable, and he gets on well with the *Anjevin*. It is all
coming together at last— may God grant us good fortune!

Only two days later, the party of traders was ready to leave Montréal. A waxing moon glowed overhead like a lamp, lighting the village and river in silver. The village still slept. Garamond and the others moved silently to load the carts for the portage road to Lachine, some three and a half leagues distant. The moon caused their shadows to ripple in confusion over the bundles and gear, creating odd angles of dark and light so that it was easier to pack by feel than by sight.

In the stillness, a small clear voice said, "I have come to say *au revoir*."

Garamond reached for another bundle and smiled. "Don't let your *papa* catch you down here, little rascal."

Frances squatted beside him. She was wrapped in a cloak, but wore only her shift underneath. Her head was bare and her eyes, pale in daylight, now seemed dark and huge.

"You'll take cold, you know," he said. "What if your *maman* were here? How she'd scold—"

"I have decided to let you go."

"*Ah bon. Merci.*"

"But it would be better if I came with you!"

"No, it would not be better."

"I know Father Hennepin's book by heart. You'll forget everything without me!"

"Ssh! We're trying to be quiet here."

"Please take me, Garamond."

He sighed and glanced around. Miron was grinning at him and two of the Ottawa men nudged each other, laughing softly.

"Frances, I promise I will come back, eh?"

She didn't move at all, only continued to watch him. "I will be twelve this winter."

"I know, you are always telling me."

"When you come back, King Louis will pay you twenty livres to marry me."

"Oh—"

"Do you swear to come back in the spring? Swear it."

He hesitated. To swear an oath, even to a child, was not a trivial thing. What would she do if he refused? Likely raise a commotion, he thought, or even try to follow from shore. What a bothersome girl—like a yellow-haired mosquito.

"I swear I'll come back in the spring. By the light of the moon, I swear it. Does that satisfy you?"

"Leave her, Garamond," Miron lifted one end of a canoe. "We are ready to go."

But Frances had already jumped up and gone running back to the village. Garamond watched her go for a moment, then took up his pack and the other end of the canoe, and started down the road round the great rapids of Sault Saint Louis.

Soon the sun rose, painting all the *voyageurs* in pink and lighting the dust of the road. Garamond felt the familiar joy of his own strength and his mood rising to meet the day. He had to restrain himself from whistling as he trundled along, smelling the spicy autumn leaves and grass, his breath blowing white. He understood well how vulnerable they were, Cornet's guards on their flanks notwithstanding, but he could not feel the fear that day, not yet.

They could not avoid being seen, for there were numerous farms near Lachine and the west end of Montréal. Folk stared as they set out for their fields, burdened with as many firearms as tools. The traders didn't stop to answer questions—the canoes and loaded carts told the story anyway. They reached the landing at the river, and there they transferred the gear to the canoes, all their movements marvelously quiet and swift, for they imagined the eyes of the Iroquois upon them. At last, Garamond waded into the water and carefully took his place in the middle of Le Maître's canoe.

The first thing that happened was that the Ottawa man in the bow of Garamond's canoe cast a small amount of perfectly good tobacco onto the surface of the river, and uttered what sounded like a prayer in his own tongue. This man allowed the *Français* to call him Frère

Bouleau, that is, Brother Birch, for his legendary prowess with the making and handling of canoes. He was the principal member of the Ottawa party. Frère Bouleau, Garamond, and Miron formed the crew of one canoe; the other three Ottawa paddled together; and the other five *coureurs de bois* paddled in two more canoes, making a company of four canoes and eleven men. These were men chosen for experience, spirit, or strength, and though they knew their danger, their optimism ran high. Yet, the tobacco was cast on the water for the sake of grace. Then they turned and began to labor upstream.

Immediately, Garamond found there was a startling, sobering difference in the effort required to paddle a fully loaded canoe against the Saint Laurent compared to one light and empty in the slack water before Ville Marie. With every stroke, he felt the pull on each muscle of his back, his arms and shoulders, belly, and even his legs. The four canoes fell into line, following a path of least current still deep enough to float. There was no noise save the susurration of bark hull against water and the liquid thunk of plunging paddle blades. After perhaps one million strokes, Garamond glanced over his shoulder and, with a thrill of triumph, saw that the landing had disappeared. Behind him, Miron chuckled.

The current diminished where the river widened into Lac Saint Louis, and they made good time. Then they slipped between Montréal and Île Perot, lined the Rapide de Brussi, and passed into the Lac des Deux Montagnes and beyond the settlements of the *Français*. By the end of that first day, they had gained the mouth of the Ottawa, the Rivière Outaouais, and there they camped, twelve long leagues from Ville Marie.

So began the routine of a wilderness journey. The days, grueling and exhilarating. The nights a flurry of minute inspection of the hides of the birch bark canoes, and ravenous eating. Then sleeping like dead men on soothingly mentholated beds of pine needles and crushed cones. The food was cold, for they made no cooking fires to draw the attention of any loitering Iroquois. They were cautious when they went to the bushes, and drew lots for the nightly watch. When it rained, the forest did not drink, so the river rose for a day or two. One night bristled with frost, and the mosquitoes and flies vanished. Garamond grew stronger and surer every day, as if he had found a world made for his particular delight. He felt absolutely stupendous. It would take forty-five days to paddle from Montréal to Missilimackinac, some three hundred sixty leagues, and most of it upstream on the Ottawa and Mattawa rivers. Then across the length of the Lac Nipissing, and down the Rivière Français with its perilous rapids to great Lac Huron. There would be thirty-six portages on the journey.

On still days, when no wind or rapids muffled the sound of their passage, they kept silent, and so each man thought his own thoughts. Frère Bouleau, from his seat in the bow, thought long on the weakness of the *Français* and their shameful thrashing at the hands of the Iroquois. He would now return to his people at Missilimackinac and tell them everything. Then the elders would decide what to do. Perhaps they already know, he thought, and are deciding even now. Should we hold to our alliance with the *Français* weaklings and forego trade with the *Bastonnais*? If we hold and the *Français* fail, the Iroquois will scour us all from the face of the earth. The Five Nations are old foes—yes. But the world has changed. Would it not therefore be better to make alliance with them? Have they not made overtures to the Odawa already? These are questions of life and death!

His gaze automatically registered the dimple of a large submerged rock and, with a subtle gesture, indicated which direction Miron should steer. Behind him, he heard a small grunt of frustration as the newcomer, Jean Garamond, held back a question. Frère Bouleau smiled. So eager, this Garamond—he wants to know everything about our canoes. But he does not listen when I tell him about the Odawa and our relatives, the Ojibwa, and the Potawatomie. These are important matters that he ignores. So self-absorbed are the *Français*.

A few moments later, they came to the mouth of Gatineau's river, and here, all the *coureurs de bois* paused and crossed themselves. Just six years before, one of their number—it was Nicolas Gatineau—had vanished from this area. Without discussion, they ferried to the far shore of the wide Ottawa and continued upstream. No one looked back. But at the next turn of the river, the bow-man of the first canoe held up his hand in alarm, for he had seen the unmistakable form of an Iroquois craft—low, flat, fast—disappearing around the bend of an island. The traders drifted back in the current, angling to shore. Then they drew their weapons and waited, hearts pounding, but the Iroquois did not turn back. Even so, after a whispered debate, the traders decided to stay put for the rest of the day, and the night as well, and to send scouts upstream on foot. Two of the Ottawa and one *coureur de bois*, armed extravagantly with knives, muskets, bows and arrows, took off through the woods. They were grateful for the morning's drizzle, which had quieted the fallen leaves. The remaining eight men nervously made the canoes fast and took what defensive positions they could; then they waited and watched.

"*Putain*, it is bad luck, so close to Gatineau," the man Doucette blurted in a low voice.

The others glared at him—*be quiet!*—their eyes screamed.

Frère Bouleau shook his head. These *Français*, he thought, are so superstitious.

They held a tenuous vigil for several hours, and finally, as the sky clouded over again in the afternoon, the scouts returned.

"They've gone on far ahead. It does not seem as if they ever knew we were there." It was the young Ottawa man, Little Owl, who spoke. "They were talking about their women," he said in disgust. Everyone laughed as if he'd made a great joke, and so he laughed, too. "They are anxious to finish their hunting, I guess!" More peals of relieved laughter.

"Come let us camp here. We'll let them be, eh?" Miron stretched, and cracked his knuckles. "But we should have double watch tonight."

"I wish I could have seen them," Garamond said as they started unpacking the canoes. He was both wound up and famished. He felt he hadn't talked above whispers in days. Then he stubbed his toe on a rock. "*Merde!* I miss my boots!"

"Don't be a fool, *mon petit*," Louvet admonished. "No one wants to see them."

"Just their canoe, you know? They are said to be made of elm bark. They are said to be perfectly silent in the water, and—"

"You are childish, *Français*," Little Owl broke in. "The Iroquois canoes are evil, like their owners. They sneak like snakes."

"Oh, *petit hibou*, don't get excited, eh?" Garamond flicked a bunch of leaves at the young Ottawa man and raised his arms in mock menace. "Woo, woo, woo!" Little Owl did not deign to answer, but Garamond, with the unerring instinct of the boisterous to seek out and annoy the sensitive, continued to flap his arms and cry, "woo, woo!" until Louvet silenced him. But it proved an irresistible entertainment, and, by the end of the evening, several others had taken up the game. Little Owl only seemed to bear it with indifference, and Garamond was not forgiven.

It turned out that the sighting of the Iroquois canoe was the closest they came to disaster. Only once, Miron was frightened by a thin, deadly flight past his ear. He thought it was an arrow, but later, he thought it may have been a bird. They ribbed him unmercifully to cover their fear, and labored on against the implacable current of the river.

Everyday, they felt the season advancing around them. The leaves colored and fell, first the bright yellow of aspen and birch, then maples and poplar, and last the orange feathers of the larches. The flowering plants were all gone to seed, yet ferns remained, green as summer, in the deep woods, as did the sphagnum mosses, which gave up, when trod upon, a sharp smell like varnish. There followed a string of dim, cloudy days, during which hard paddling seemed the only way to stay warm. Garamond kept his head down, digging and pulling, and lost himself in reverie. He would study Frère Bouleau's back and his curious fringe of standing hair. Then he'd study the angle of his paddle blade, first, as it gripped the water, then as it sliced through the air. Suddenly he'd see a flash of gold and think, "The sun has come out!" But it would only be a late-turning birch in some sheltered place.

Some twenty-five leagues past Gatineau's river, the Ottawa commenced to twist in great loops and to split around large wooded islands. Keeping to the west bank, the traders came into view of several smaller islands choking the current. Here, their way narrowed to two violent chutes, and so they were forced to portage. Garamond had already scented the whitewater from far downstream. As always, he felt his spirits rise, whether or not the rapids were marked with crosses for the dead. To Garamond, the atmosphere of rapids seemed charged somehow, akin to lightning, or the new-born air in the wake of a storm. Happily, he leaped from the canoe to unload, bustling to help everyone else as well—including Little Owl, who spurned him—and then ran down the path to admire the chutes. The waves of the rapids, capped in white foam, stood in strangely immobile rows, a phenomenon he still puzzled over. Why did they not move downstream? As he wondered, Frère Bouleau, loaded with bundles, caught up with him and paused for a moment at his side.

Though the young man had acquitted himself well so far, Frère Bouleau was sure he could already discern in him the telltale signs of greed, so characteristic of both the *Français* and the *Bastonnais.*

"Not far from this place," said the elder, "we shall pass the mouth of the Petawawa. There is a lake in the headwaters of that river, which is the lair of the wendigo, a demon."

Garamond nodded politely, still gazing at the rapids. He thought, "The *sauvages* are always talking about their sprites and their demons. They are so superstitious—"

Mildly, Frère Bouleau continued. "The wendigo is a monster of greed. It is born in the starving depths of winter. Once, it made a terrible mistake. To slake its hunger, it ate another human being."

Garamond frowned and looked at the Ottawa man, checking to see if he was serious. "That would be a mortal sin, if anything would, Monsieur."

Frère Bouleau smiled. "Once he made his terrible mistake, the wendigo could not stop eating human flesh, and grew into a giant ravening beast, consumed forever by his greed."

"Greed? I don't understand you, Frère Bouleau. Greed for what?"

"For life, for anything. It does not matter what it is for— it is the greed itself that consumes."

They could hear Miron and Doucette, then, conversing loudly as they trudged up the trail. They passed and Frère Bouleau turned to follow them.

"Where is this demon river, Frère Bouleau?"

"Just upstream. You will hear it."

Frère Bouleau said nothing later that day when, just at sunset, they passed the mouth of Petawawa, noisily disgorging its haunted waters in rapids and falls into the Ottawa. Garamond could not help but notice that the plunging water was red. It is just the late sunlight, he thought, but he was glad to leave that place behind. They paddled on, for the Ottawa was broad and slack here, and they made four more miles before camping.

The weather cleared and stilled that night, revealing an expanse of stardust, thicker it seemed, than the blackness beyond. The cold tightened its fingers on the camp until they awoke in the morning shivering and covered with frost.

"Let's be moving, *mes amis*," Miron urged them. He kicked at the nearest grumbling, blanketed form. "There are countless thousands of leagues between us and the hot fires of Missilimackinac, eh? Up, up!"

Paddling was easy that day and the next, past rock walls that shot straight from the water. Then more rapids appeared, some they could pole or line their way up, some they portaged gladly. In due time, they came on a wide stretch that howled with wind, and passed the mouth of the river to the Ki-we-gama, and then the Ottawa flowed toward them directly from the west. Frère Bouleau informed them that they had come far enough into the lands of their allies, so that they might risk a fire that night.

This lighting of the fire was attended by all with religious intensity. Every man was cold to his marrow, skin chafed from the constantly wet rags and buckskins they wore, and desperate for any sort of food that was not cold dry jerky or biscuit. Miron brought forth his fire kit, wrapped the charcloth over his knuckles, struck firesteel against flint and swiftly produced a shower of magic glowing sparks. Some of these, encouraged by eleven pairs of eyes, lit on the charcloth and smoldered there gently until Miron laid them in the bed he'd prepared—a fragrant nest of the shredded inner bark of cedar. He blew, as soft as if on a baby's cheek, and the sparks bloomed into fire.

"Ah!" they all cried.

A brass kettle filled with water appeared, then an iron tripod on which to hang it. Twigs and tinder and small branches were arranged by several eager hands beneath, and the burning nest set inside. Then everyone went off to dig through their provisions for their most longed-for victuals: peas, corn, dried berries, nutmeats, maple sugar—all were contributed and thrown into the kettle with the dried meat. There it all simmered while they told stories and heated packets of pitch to repair the accumulated hurts of their precious canoes. And when they could no longer wait, they dipped their bowls in the stew, and ate every morsel, and licked every drop. Then they made another batch and pulled out the liquor.

It was by far the latest they'd stayed up on any night of the trip. The flames of their fire, like bright gothic curls, entranced their eyes and loosened their tongues. They lay on blankets and bundles, or leaned against the canoes, and talked of everything: the river, the game in the woods they'd dared not pursue, the Iroquois, the allies, and the Sun King of France. They described in loving detail every *demoiselle*—French and Indian alike—they'd ever desired, and also the ones they'd escaped. They spoke of their homes, and their relatives, and all their long, long journeys, and by the time they fell asleep at last, every man had told what he wanted to tell. Except that Garamond and Miron did not speak of their plans to visit the Sioux.

Early the next day, they came suddenly to the long-awaited Mattawa River. Here the great Ottawa veered, flowing from the north, while the Mattawa opened directly from the west. Thither they would go, by stream, pond, and portage to the Lac Huron, sweetwater sea that washed the beach at Missilimackinac, their destination. One by one, the canoes slipped sideways into the Mattawa, and then struck upstream on new water. To Garamond, it seemed a mysterious transition, as if full of an import he could sense but not grasp. He let out a wild, joyful whoop and dug hard into the current. Then even the seasoned traders couldn't resist a holler and whoop of their own— dignity be damned.

It took three days to paddle the length of the pine-clad Mattawa, much of the way beset by irkingly shallow rapids. It was, Miron said, the hardest stretch of their route, and that they must take extra care to save the canoe's skin from the countless jagged rocks. Too often, they found themselves walking the river, twisting ankles, wrenching knees, and cutting their wrinkled, soggy feet right through their moccasins. And the October cold grew inexorably deeper. There was a place where they turned sharply south, and there, while portaging the falls called Paresseux, a heavy bundle of trade goods—they knew not what it contained—tumbled into the water and was lost. It was put down to malicious spirits, and so they grew even more wary than they'd been in the Iroquois' hunting grounds.

On they toiled, between sixteen-fathom cliffs on both shores, and not long after that, they gratefully left the Mattawa to embark on a chain of small lakes. After one last portage, they gained the Lac Nipissing, the highest reach of their journey. Here, they encamped for a day with a party of hunters of the Nipissing band—

the Matawasibi—who were fast allies. One of these men, an old acquaintance, Frère Bouleau drew aside to relate the story of the Iroquois attack on Montréal.

"We have heard a rumor of this disaster," said the Nipissing hunter when he'd heard it all. "But you saw it with your own eyes, and so it is true. I fear the consequences will reach very far."

"Yes, everything changes."

They glanced covertly at the *coureurs de bois* lingering near the fire, and the hunter continued, "The strife shall become unbearable someday. It is already turning the animals against us. We have called and called for moose, and none have come."

Frère Bouleau had no answer for this. He had hoped to spend a day hunting along the shore of the lake, for in other years, the alders had been thick with grouse. Now, he thought, perhaps it would be wise to let them be. He said, "We shall depart early tomorrow, before the wind comes up. Good luck in your hunting, my friend."

The Lac Nipissing stretched sixteen leagues from east to west, and was wont to gather the west wind in a gale. This was common knowledge. The traders rose in the dark, packed, and paddled three leagues by the time the sun came up. By mid-day, the swells began to rise and slyly spill into each heavily laden canoe. A teaspoon here, a bucketful there. A swamped canoe was stubborn at best, but worst of all to the traders was the thought of the wet penetrating their goods. Still, if only they could go on, they would put Nipissing behind them.

"I think it is shifting," Louvet called out. "It may not get worse after all— Should we keep on? What do you think?"

"Yes! This may be the worst." Frère Bouleau gestured ahead to the others. "Keep on, keep on!"

"Garamond, *mon petit*," Miron said, "we are going to quarter the waves, so you must lean into them just a little, eh? Do not lean away—"

"But why do we quarter them?"

"We don't take as much water that way— Look now, how the bow slides up and over! Ah *oui*, that's good, that's good."

The wind peaked and then began to subside, but slowly, so that they paddled the heaving lake for the rest of the afternoon. They bailed as best they could and held close to the south shore, which offered the effect of a small lee, but far out enough to avoid the wave-pounded shore. After hours, the sun sank and the stars appeared, and only then, at last, Frère Bouleau pointed to the far end of a shadowy bay, and said, "The outlet of this lake lies there—the river that brings the *Français*. Two more days to the Lac Huron."

"*Formidable!*" Garamond stared ahead eagerly. "We can float at our ease for once, eh Monsieur?"

Frère Bouleau chuckled. "Yes, we will float, but not restfully, *Français*. There are three falls to carry, and also, merely rough water. You must pay close attention."

"Oh, I cannot wait!"

Miron put in, "You must paddle backwards with all your might when I command it, eh? I'm sorry to disappoint you, but we must always try to go slower than the current."

"Oh, but why? I think we should go faster to leap right over—"

"But no one asks you, *petit Anjevin*."

Frère Bouleau stopped paddling and, turning sideways, draped his leg over the side of the boat so he could massage his knee. Soon, the other canoes glided up and drifted, too, while the traders smoked and stretched their cramped muscles.

Little Owl said, "Now do you see how inferior are the Iroquois craft, *Français*? They are too low! They would have foundered in those waves that our canoes took so easily." He smiled broadly, confident that this would pay Garamond for his insolence.

"That is true," said Doucette, "but I think the Iroquois craft has its uses. You know how they slip under branches? In small streams, they may be better."

"Of course, they are good enough for skulking!"

Garamond hunched his shoulders comically, his eyes wide and

mouth open in an "O." It was a perfect parody of the taunts he'd aimed at Little Owl back on the Ottawa, and everyone burst out laughing. Little Owl froze, then attempted to laugh also, but—poor young man—he failed and sat silently while they mimicked Garamond. Frère Bouleau and Miron exchanged a glance.

It is a pity, thought Frère Bouleau, but there's nothing to be done. Besides, it was apparent that Little Owl thought too often of himself, a potentially grave error. Better for the *Français* to torment him than the wind or the rapids. Then Frère Bouleau had to stifle his own laughter, for he'd just caught how well the *Anjevin* was doing a *real* little owl, all puffed with alarm.

Garamond did not let up, so by the next day, the friction had turned to jostling on the portage trails and petty sabotage in camp. This was entertaining enough for the others, but Miron warned that whoever next lost a bundle of merchandise would pay dearly indeed, which chastened them a little. Finally, it was the first snowfall of the year that cooled the feud, for they woke covered in cold white. The snow fell thickly all morning, obscuring the rocks and rapids, and, though it melted quickly on the ground, it clung like paste to the bare trees and packs. Garamond was astonished to find his paddle filmed over in ice. "Winter, winter," whispered the snow, so they redoubled their pace and did not stop at all that day.

Near dusk, the sky cleared, and with joy, they felt a warm breeze flowing from downstream. This breeze melted the snow in a wink, and grew stronger as they advanced, and soon they heard the rolling chant of surf, for they'd reached the Lac Huron, at last. It opened before them, vast and full of light, as if they were paddling off the river and into the sky. Far to the south and west, on the edge of sight, vague undulations indicated great Manitoulin Island, ancient home of the Odawa, as Frère Bouleau said pointedly to Garamond. The traders, collecting themselves beyond the surf, set out due west along the strand. On their right, the shore unwound in pines and bare birch trees, beaches, and humped, white rock. On their left, the lake glittered under a rinsed, autumn sky. Manitoulin and its covey of islets arced away to Missilimackinac. It would be a two-day journey in fine weather.

They paddled long after dark, for the waves stilled as night drew on, and an icy moon lit their way. Then they slept on freezing sand for a scant few hours, and rose again before dawn to make all the miles they could before old woman wind, *La Vieille*, took notice. They would cheat her as best they could in the days on the lake, weaving their way among islands and deep bays, working south and west until they struck a spur from the mainland, a western continuation of Manitoulin's arc. When they got there, Miron nudged Garamond and said, "Look back and mark this place. If you take the north shore of the peninsula, you enter the river of Sainte Marie, eh? We will be coming back this way very soon."

19.

The Conspirators

Fall and Winter 1689

I T WAS THE fourth of November, of a crystalline cold morning, when they smelled the campfires of Missilimackinac, perched on the north coast of the straits between the Lac Huron and the Lac des Illinois. Glorious, homely whiffs of wood smoke and savory stew! They gave a cheer, and rounding a point, came into view of the Algonquin village, farthest outlier of the settlement. The traders waved to the few people near shore, who waved and called back in amazement, "Well done, brothers! You have cheated the Iroquois as well as *La Vieille*! Come tell us of your journey—"

The four canoes swept by in a rush, spurred by longing to see their kin and friends. They arrived next at the Ottawa village, a gathering of longhouses inside a stout palisade, which soon emitted a stream of relatives. Here, Frère Bouleau and the three young Ottawa drew in to shore and began unloading their gear. "A fortunate return, my friends," Frère Bouleau said to Miron and Garamond. "We shall celebrate with a feast tonight."

They left him with his people, and hurried to catch up with the other *coureurs de bois*. They came to a small, protected bay, like a notch in the shoreline at the foot of steep wooded hills. Immediately, they passed the Huron village, and then paddled up to the new fort, Fort de Buade, after Frontenac, the new *Gouverneur Général*. Their companions had already pulled their canoes on the bank, and were shouting greetings to traders coming down from the settlement. Above them, tucked up against the hill, the mission of St. Ignace let peal her bells in welcome. Even to Garamond, it felt like a homecoming.

"Mercier, Mercier!" Miron was beckoning to a tall man with a gigantic sandy beard, who was descending the path toward them.

"Heh, Miron, old comrade— Who would have thought it? Oh, you look well! What news is there? Did the brigade get through? What do you have for me, eh?" The two men bear-hugged, jabbering and laughing while they unloaded bundles and packs.

"I have for you two casks of powder, some bars of lead, *quelques choses* for fixing your musket. And this young fool is called Jean Garamond. He has come all the way from Anjou to get drunk with you."

Garamond unwrapped the casks of powder, miraculously dry, and handed them up to Mercier.

"My angel!" Mercier cried. He bent down to cradle Garamond's face in his hands and planted a long thorough kiss on his lips. Flabbergasted, Garamond pulled away and abruptly fell on his butt while Miron gasped with laughter.

"Oh Mercier, I have missed you!"

"And I you! Come, come, my angel! Let us sample your charms, eh? Oh don't be wary—"

Mercier had a hut in the French settlement, between the fort and the mission, and there the three traders packed all the bundles and kegs of goods. They spent the afternoon talking, drinking, and gorging on venison roasted on a fire behind the hut. A Huron girl, also called My Angel, who shared Mercier's bed, attended them and laughed at their jokes.

"But what is that she calls you, old *coquin*?" Miron asked.

"Oh, I fear she does not take me seriously. It is something to do with 'tall' and 'buffoon.' Such impudence." Mercier smiled benevolently.

She left as the dusk fell, and so Miron judged it was time to divulge their plans.

"Mercier," he said. "I have some news for you. Those packs out there are not for Missilimackinac."

"Eh? What do you mean?" Mercier wiped his beard and leaned forward. "Cadot is sending you on?"

"*Oui.*"

"South? There are others going south, of course."

"North and west. We are going to the Nadouessioux."

Mercier narrowed his eyes and peered hard at them. "Oh, our Indians will not like that. They already feel put out, you know. We do not protect them from the Iroquois and yet they are called upon to defend New France. We French are piss-poor allies! And now the disaster on Montréal! They long to make a truce with the Five Nations. It is already in the works! And the *Bastonnais* will jump, you know. They have already been nosing around, even here." Mercier sucked in his breath, remembering.

"Still, we go on, eh? Garamond has been learning about the Sioux. Did you know that priest, that Hennepin? He wrote a book, and your angel," Miron nodded to Garamond, "has learned from the book. Isn't that right, *mon petit?*"

"It was Cornet's little girl who read it to me. I can read very well! But she read to me while I worked." Garamond tapped his forehead. "*Oui, oui,* it's all in here."

Miron winked at Mercier. "Our *Anjevin* is pledged, you know, to the little girl." He laughed and gave Garamond a brotherly shove. "Anyway, think of the furs they must have. They cannot remain forever beyond our reach. Why not us, eh? We will be the first to trade with the Sioux."

"Not the first. Not at all, my starry-eyed friend."

"Oh well, who cares? We are going, even before dawn. But if you think it's impossible, we can make a story for the Montréalers. What do you say, Jules?"

Mercier took a long drink of brandy. He glared at the table and drummed his fingers, then sighed. He got up to light a candle. Anxiously, Garamond looked from Mercier to Miron and back to Mercier.

"Well, if you must, you must go soon. Winter is coming, *mes amis*, and so is the freeze. But you cannot go tomorrow. The hunters of the Kiskagon Ottawa are going north. They have been delayed because their best tracker fell ill, oh, several weeks ago. He recovered, and they were going to leave this very day. But they will stay tonight to feast with Frère Bouleau. *Alors*, I think they will go tomorrow."

"Where are they going to hunt?"

"Tahquamenon country. You will have to pass right by there."

Miron nodded. "We will give them a day, and then keep our distance."

"We can do that! It is the same as when the Iroquois were in front of us—"

"Oh, listen to him," Miron smiled. "Mercier, you know best, eh?"

Mercier crossed himself. "I will say you have gone to the Sault Sainte Marie, which of course you must. But be very careful."

"I was thinking, if we have trouble, we could say we're looking for the Ojibwa hunters."

"That would go well. That's a good idea, Miron. Now, let us prepare for the feast."

By the time they left Mercier's hut to go down to the Ottawa feast, it had started to snow. They brought with them liquor and a large basket of cured, smoked fish. Doucette came down with them, and several young Huron men, too. Though the path was veiled by falling snow, it was not hard to know where the party was, for the noise and the delicious smell of it were strong indeed. The other *coureurs de bois* were already there, and a smattering of French soldiers, and the whole of the Ottawa encampment. Everywhere, fires and cooking pots drew clusters of laughing, arguing people, and hungry dogs. The atmosphere was so warm and convivial that the snow seemed to melt and vanish in the air, far above. And every man was decked in his best bits of finery: strings of beads and shells and polished bone, and fringes, and feathers, so that Garamond felt very plain indeed.

"*Regard*," Miron whispered and nodded toward an imposing group seated nearby. It was Frère Bouleau, the Ottawa elders, and the commandant of the French post, Olivier Morel de la Durantaye."Give them a wide berth, eh? We don't need Durantaye to notice us, nor the priest, de Carheil. He is here somewhere, I'll wager."

Garamond was disappointed at this, for he dearly wanted to study these important personages, and perhaps, to impress them. But he saw the wisdom in Miron's words, and together, they faded into the background. They made their way through the crowd, following familiar voices from fire to fire. They watched a game of dice and sampled as many kettles as they could find. The place was so brimming with comely, vivacious Indian women, that Garamond did not know where to look first. At one point, he was sure he'd found a partner, and shared with her one tantalizing embrace, but she eluded him. Then he stopped to watch a game of cat-and-mouse—a roar went up as one man was bested. There were calls for Garamond and Little Owl to play, but as no one could find Little Owl, they let it go.

"Little Owl," someone said, "is going with the Kiskagon tomorrow, for he is a fine hunter, after all." At this, Garamond and Miron exchanged a glance and discreetly withdrew from the circle.

Such sobriety, however, became less and less necessary. By midnight, the party had degenerated into a fog of liquor. The important personages retired for the evening and the food disappeared, and music and dancing replaced conversation, and even brawling gave way to stupor. It was hours later, when the drunkenness had reached and passed its zenith, that Mercier grabbed Miron and Garamond by their sagging shoulders and dragged them back to his hut.

Garamond woke to the stabbing sounds of ladle against kettle and a glinting needle of sunlight in his eye. He could not feel his hands or feet, but was only vaguely alarmed. "Mmmm," was all he could muster before falling back asleep. A while later, he awoke again to

Miron's loud snores. Gingerly, he rose to sit, then staggered out to the bushes. The settlement was dead quiet, save for the calling of crows in the trees and a gentle wind. From inside the hut, he heard a thud and Miron cursing, "*Fils de pute!*"

"Heh, Miron, where is everybody?"

There was no answer, so Garamond wandered round to the back and sat down in a sunny patch to wait. Mindlessly, he gazed at the transparent flickering of the fire. Then he heard Mercier's voice coming up the path, saying, "Tell him My Angel, they are probably still asleep."

"They must arise now, for my uncle is here to trade," a feminine voice answered. Garamond stood up and peeked around to the front. There were Mercier, My Angel, and a stocky Huron man advancing up the path. The man was carrying a bundle of furs. "He desires tobacco, lead balls, and cloth for his *femme*," My Angel said firmly.

"Uh, *un moment*. Wait here."

Garamond ducked back and, pressing his ear to the wall of the hut, heard Mercier and Miron murmuring. Then, "*Non, non,*" Miron said, "We cannot trade here. Only a little! One bar of lead, eh? Whatever he wants to give, but that's all." There was more murmuring, then Mercier went back out.

"*Alors*, everything is still packed. But here is some lead for your trouble. You must come back later, Monsieur, *oui*? Tell him My Angel. What does he give?"

The girl, speaking rapidly in her Huron tongue, related this information to her uncle; his answering tone, polite but disappointed. There was a rustling as the exchange was made, then the retreating footsteps of the Indians. Garamond sneaked around from the back and vanished inside with Mercier.

"What did he give?"

"Eh? Why, marten skins, quite good enough. But there will be others coming. You two must lay low today, though I daresay, you cannot do otherwise. Hah!" Mercier beamed at Miron's painfully wrinkled face.

Garamond was stroking the marten fur. "Our first trade, Miron! Heh, Mercier, what about breakfast? I could eat an ox."

"*Nom de Dieu*. Feed him, Mercier," Miron groaned. "I beg you, get him out of here."

Luckily, Mercier knew well what to do with the likes of the young *Anjevin*—fill him with food and tales. Thus Garamond spent the whole blissful day listening with rapt attention and eating all he could hold—a prodigious amount—for the hospitality of the tall trader was boundless. There was squash baked in maple sugar, and wild rice stewed with dried blueberries, raspberries, strawberries, currants, and grapes. In the afternoon, My Angel brought a string of whitefish, and together, she and Mercier prepared a *sagamité* of the creamy fish, cornmeal, and wild onion. Even Miron got up and ate heartily of this.

"When shall they trade?" My Angel kept asking.

"Tomorrow, tomorrow," said Mercier, and sent her home early. Regretfully, he watched her go, then sat down to smoke with his guests. "You two must set out before the sun, you know."

"Don't worry, old *coquin*."

"Your canoe is worthy? Big water up north, you know."

"*Oui, oui.*"

"Good thing it's Cadot's. The Indians are getting three hundred livres for a canoe this year."

Garamond whistled and said, "Maybe I could learn how to build one someday."

"To learn that art, you would have no time to go trading, *mon petit*."

They smoked and chatted into the evening, occasionally dozing off until the fire smoldered down to coals. At last, Mercier sent them to bed. It seemed as if they'd just closed their eyes, and he was shaking them awake again. Before they knew it, they were gulping hot tea and loading their canoe on the deserted shore of the bay. Low, smooth swells of water lapped the beach, leaving the rocks and pebbles slicked over with ice. It was difficult to walk, but they managed with the help of Mercier's lamp, and by the time the eastern horizon emerged, they were ready. Mercier extinguished his lamp.

"Do not get too friendly with the Sioux, *mes amis*," came his voice in the dark. "Du Lhut's treaty may not last, and then it would not do for the Ottawa or their Ojibwa brothers to find you in the ranks of their old enemies, trade or no trade. Return to me in the spring, as soon as the ice breaks, eh? *Au revoir.*"

"Oh Garamond, kiss him good-bye, you know you want to."

"He'll miss my cooking at least, eh?"

Garamond eased into the bow, grateful to escape a kiss. They floated gently from shore with only a few liquid ripples to betray their going. All that day and part of the next, they retraced their route north to the Rivière Sainte Marie. They saw no one but an old Algonquin woman, fishing. She marked the two traders, but did not hail them. The wind came up from the south, which only helped them on their way up the river.

"But it won't last, *mon petit*," said Miron as they camped for the night. "We must break our butts to get to the Sault."

They woke at sunrise on a bed of glowing copper leaves beneath bare trees, with the water rippling gold past their camp. As they packed, Miron told Garamond what they'd encounter that day—rapids and portages and people—for the Sault Sainte Marie was inhabited by many hundreds of people. "Let me talk to them," he said, "and follow my lead always. I shall say we are going to the Ottawa hunters. Then I shall say we are going to trade with the bands north and *east*. Then I shall say we are going to pray with Father Nouvel—that will send them scampering. Do you see? We can't help leaving a trail, but let it be a confused one. *Alors*, it will be a long day, but we shall camp on the Lac Supérieur tonight."

Miron, luckily, was an expert at dodging direct conversation without seeming to mean to. They would crisscross the river as if to retrieve some item blown away, or to go to the bushes, or to avoid a difficult ferry. When confronted, Miron would ask passers-by bogus questions, like, "Which way to Bowating?" and, "Have you said your prayers today, my brother?" Then he would hurry by, nodding pleasantly or calling out some Latin gibberish to Garamond. Most people shrugged and let them go, as if to say, "Well, it's none of our concern."

There was only one instance of serious questioning, and that was when a party of Ojibwa fishers, who'd been working the foot of the rapids, returned to shore just as the two traders happened by, up to their eyebrows with gear.

"Let us help you carry your goods," one man offered, "Perhaps we will carry it home with us in exchange for these beautiful whitefish! What say you? Stop and see our catch—"

"Oh, *non, non,* Monsieur, it is all for the mission, you know." Miron ducked his head and kept walking, but the Ojibwa man followed alongside.

"But what, if I may ask, is that watery sound in your bundle?" He rapped speculatively on a small keg strapped on top of Miron's load.

"Wine for the sacraments. Have you said your prayers today—"

The man turned to walk backwards and asked Garamond, "What is that you're carrying, young *Français*? It seems very heavy."

Garamond only looked blankly ahead, and Miron chuckled. "Take no notice, he is simple."

But the Ojibwa man followed them back and forth on their portage, even taking an end of the canoe as the late afternoon deepened to dusk. "What are you called, *Français*?" he insisted.

Miron pretended a sneezing fit and pulled out his best trick. "I fear I am taking ill, my friend, the same as the poor folk at Missilimackinac. Eh shoo!" It was a master performance, complete with fluids and wan face.

They reached the end of the portage, and Miron went to thank the man, who prudently backed away. Then while Miron swayed on the bank, Garamond threw the bundles in the canoe. They clambered in and waved to the Ojibwa man, swiftly paddled out in the river and picked their way to the other side. Garamond kept glancing back; the man remained where they'd left him, watching, then gesturing to others of his party as they came up. But they did not try to follow.

Nevertheless, Garamond and Miron decided to stay on the far shore. They pulled the canoe into an eddy overhung with the green and rusty fans of a great cedar, and bided their time, chewing on Mercier's jerky and keeping watch for curious *Saulteurs*. When they felt sufficiently hidden by darkness, they continued upstream, stealthily poling, lining, and paddling, until they drew away from the twinkling campfires of the settlement. But this was the most miserable and risky of tasks, for, by then, they were hopelessly chilled and the starless dark not only hid them, but their way forward, as well. Several times, Garamond wondered aloud, "Should we not wait for morning?" But Miron would not rest.

"Almost there, *mon petit*."

"*Merci de Dieu*, you crazy sot."

At last, the rapids smoothed and the water spread out in a wide sheet of black, yet still moving and gathering itself in a mass to plunge downstream. They paddled out strongly, well above the rapids, and then turned to cross to the westward shore. And still they pressed on, until their arms were lead, and their feet, long past feeling, seemed like useless chunks of ice. The clouds blew away and revealed a brilliant array of stars. By contrast, it seemed bright as day, and looking off to their left, they could see a pale crescent of beach. Without comment, they gave up for the night and paddled to shore.

Garamond could think only of his warm, dry fur robe, safely encased in oil cloth, and of hot soup, for he would build a small fire, whether Miron sanctioned it or not. Weary and quivering with cold, they unloaded their gear, made the canoe fast, and set up a hasty, hidden camp. They barely spoke as they supped, concentrating only on warmth and filling their bellies. Soon they were done.

Then Miron said, "We'll see Gros Cap in the morning, *mon petit*. It is over there, on the other shore, for we are in a small bay above the Sault. Gros Cap is a landmark— you should fix it in your mind."

Sure enough, when Garamond woke at the first peep of the sun, there was Gros Cap, its shadowy bulk reared from the opposite shore. To its south was a pine-shrouded peninsula. On his own side, he could see a low point of land marking their route. And beyond, he knew, was another point, thrusting eastward as if to join with Gros Cap on the other side of the bay. These were the very portals of the Lac Supérieur, of which he had heard so much! In an instant he was wide awake and packing his gear.

But Miron had beaten him; he was already up and hurrying to the canoe. "*Vite, vite, Anjevin!*" he cried, "The wind is early today!"

Attentively watching from the foil of a cedar glade were Little Owl and his party of Kiskagon Ottawa hunters. One of their number, a scout, had come on the traders at night, and, in the morning, the whole group had gathered in the glade to consider what to do. They cast lots as to whether the pair would make it around the great point, Nadoueuigoning, the place of Iroquois bones, two and a half leagues farther north, and into the vast bay beyond. The wind would be whistling there, they knew. Chuckling, they watched the traders struggle past the small point near the beach. How the waves did buffet the little *Français*! Yet they continued and passed the spot where the Ottawa had hidden their canoes, and on out of sight.

"Knowing them as I do," said Little Owl, "there is only one reason why they'd come to this place. They are going to the Sioux." He spat. "It is too late for them to think of going to the Cree, and no one of any account is at Chegouwameeagan this winter. They do not have enough supplies to over-winter at Chegouwameeagan in that small canoe."

"They mean to evade us, in any case," agreed the gaunt man who led the hunt. "It is time we made a stand. Let us teach them a lesson."

"Yes, let us lighten their load," said the scout.

But Little Owl was loth to confront Garamond. The *Anjevin* was so clever! Grimacing, he had a fleeting vision of being ridiculed in front of his companions. Garamond hunching his shoulders in that ludicrous way, baiting him. What if the others laughed?

"Let us take their canoe when they sleep," said the scout, warming to his idea. "That will curtail their adventure and force them to return to Bowating. And there, they will have to explain themselves. Perhaps we may be there to enjoy their chastisement when this guilty errand is exposed. And yet, the *Français* could not blame us."

"Ah!" his companions, all smiles, nodded in agreement.

"That is a good idea," said the gaunt man. "We could easily get their canoe tonight. You and I, and two others will go." He clapped his arm around the beaming young man, and turning to Little Owl, said, "What is your opinion, kinsman?"

Little Owl stared down at his hands, frowning, while he grappled with his dislike of Jean Garamond. He knew a man should rise above such things. So his uncles had taught him. He thought of Frère Bouleau. Then he said, "We should not harm the *Français*. Leave them be."

Having never known their peril, the traders escaped the ill will of the Ottawa hunters, and went on their way all puffed up with pride. Miron made his estimates each night, adjusting for all that befell them in the ways of weather and chance and their store of provisions. The breath of the Lac Supérieur blew dank and bitter cold, and *La Vieille* seemed ever wrathful or nearly so. They were forced to paddle whenever they could, whether under starlight or in clinging, icy fog, until what notions they'd had of the time for sleep and the time for waking were utterly confused. Always, they looked to the shore, evaluating with wary eyes all escapes should Kitchi Gami arise. They spent countless long hours high up on beaches or tucked into small, desperate coves, waiting and listening to the roaring seas. In their hearts, they were oftentimes daunted by these desolate shores, bereft of people—though to each other, they showed only casual strength, *bien sûr*. Miron would pace down the pounding beaches, threading through lines of dry grasses curled over by wind. Garamond tended fire after fire, flickering lights on red sand. The red sand beaches were skimmed with ice and scabbed with frozen, oozing, wave-sculpted mounds. He would watch waves pick up the sand

and roll it around, turning the water dark and nasty red, and think long on all of his debts.

Still they progressed, past towering dunes and colored cliffs and great forested heights. With joy, they found the passage through the great Kianon peninsula, deep cleft and calm, and at last, as November sank to its end, over one hundred fifty leagues from the Sault Sainte Marie, they beheld the Chegouwameeagan, with its tiny settlement on the tip of a long sandy point. They came at night and hurried by, unremarked, they hoped. Just a handful of *Français*, Ojibwa, and Cree were there, but the rumor of a ghostly canoe rippled among them and was talked of for weeks.

Two days farther west, Miron made a critical decision: to pass the mouth of Du Lhut's river and the long, southern way to the Sioux.

"There is another way, *Anjevin*," he said as they drew past, well out from the surf. "It lies at the farthest corner of this *lac terrible*. It is the Rivière du Fond du Lac. *Mon Dieu*, the portage is horrendous, but I think, overall, it is the shorter way. We will come to the Sioux from the north and a little east."

Garamond was quiet as he studied the route before them. Far off in blue shadows, he could see the northern coast of the lake as it ran southwestward to meet the south shore. It looked like another ten leagues of paddling and he was already hungry. And he longed to stretch out and sleep by a fire for days.

"*Quel mauvais*, let us get off this lake, Miron. I am sick to death of it. Before God and Cornet and all of you, I admit it."

Miron laughed. "So tender, all you farmers. Don't cry, eh? We'll get there tonight."

But *La Vieille* had other ideas. She was offended and, within an hour, let loose her icy breath in a gale. They struggled to shore. There, on a narrow, wave-beaten strand, they made one last camp on the lake and watched the sun fall on the western horizon, so far out of reach. To console themselves, they made a ripping hot fire.

After long paddling, Miron loved to bathe his feet in hot water, for otherwise he could never warm them enough to sleep. That night, after they'd cooked and devoured their stew, he took a small kettle to get water for his soak. Though the sand was frozen, its texture gave good walking, so he paid little attention to where he set down his feet. He did not see the slick, icy stone at the waterline, for the edge of a wave washed over it just as he glanced down. He slipped on it and fell with a splash and a sharp, cracking thud.

"Heh, Miron—" There was no answer, so Garamond, mildly alarmed, got up and walked down to the shore. "Heh, Miron, are you hurt?"

There came a groggy moan. Garamond helped the big man to his feet and guided his shaky steps to the campfire. "You are soaked all right, and you're soaking me, too. Good thing you still had your old coat on! Miron are you all right?"

"*Oui, oui. Merde!* Let me sit here, eh?"

"I'll get your dry things. I'll make you some tea. Then we can sleep, what do you say?"

"*Oui*, that's good."

"Heh, you're bleeding, you must have hit your head." Swiftly, Garamond set the kettle to boil and pulled out herbs for the tea. He made Miron strip off his wet clothes and bundled him in furs. Then he did the same for himself, and built up the fire. "We're going to get warmed up, my friend."

"Don't worry so much, *Anjevin*," said Miron. He clenched the cup of hot tea to his chest, inhaling the steam, until, in a while, he began to revive. He stuck his feet in the hot bath Garamond had made, though it made his head pound like a hammer. Yet his thoughts were clear. As he did every night, he went over all that had happened that day, and estimated how far they could get in the next. He said nothing to Garamond, but he was worried about the lateness of their journey. According to Cadot's map, the Sioux could not be far west, perhaps another fortnight. He held the cup to his mouth, blowing white steam into the fire. At least, he thought, once we leave the lake, the old bitch wind can't stop us.

When Garamond awoke, he realized it was late, for the sun was strong enough to light up the inside of his fur cocoon. He unwrapped his face, squinting, and looked anxiously around. All was still. He rubbed his eyes and stared hard at the water. It was frozen like a fine sheet of glass from the shoreline on out, as far as he could see. Just a skim of ice, he thought. The smallest breeze will break it right up. Or our paddles.

"Wake up, Miron. Heh, it's pretty cold." Garamond got up and walked down to the shore. An experimental tap caused the skim of ice to disintegrate. He grunted in approval, went off to relieve himself, and started to root around in the packs. Miron was still motionless under his furs.

"Lazy old man, get up," said Garamond and tossed a handful of pebbles at him. There was no response, so heaving a sigh to cover his sudden fear, Garamond leaned over and gave him a shove, then pulled back the fur and saw Miron's still face, the forehead marred by a vivid black bruise.

"Michel?" Garamond shook him again gently, but he knew very well Miron was dead.

For an hour, he sat near the body, alternately grieving and considering the choices he faced. A cold breeze sprang up, riffling the trees and dispersing the ice. The sun rose higher, and still Garamond could not decide what to do. Should he take Miron back to Chegouwameeagan? And what then? Give up on the Sioux and trade there as best he could. Perhaps join with others in the spring, who would wonder, of course, about his original plans. He would make up some story. Or journey back to Missilimackinac, the more appealing course. Then he thought again of poor Miron. A man in the prime of his life! May God grant him peace and forgive his sins—

But he couldn't quite shake the prospect of another course, one which, he was sure, Miron, not to mention Monsieur Cornet and his partner and his pretty wife, and even little Frances, would approve. Go on to the Sioux! They are not very far!

He got up to pace, all at once realizing how hungry he was. He dug out some dried salted fish and a handful of dry currants. Then he drank long of the limpid water of the Lac Supérieur. Turning back to the body, he made his decision and set about the burial. He unwrapped Miron and dragged him into the woods. He laid him out on a low level spot and spent the rest of the morning carrying stones to cover him. He made a bargain with himself: If *La Vieille* allowed him to leave, then he would go west by himself. If she found him, he would go back to Chegouwameeagan and see what developed.

"To be fair," he said piously, "I shall not avoid discovery." So he let the stones fall as noisily as they would on poor Miron, and did not try to stay out of sight. But the old woman wind held her peace.

It was near noon when he finished and said a farewell prayer for Miron. Then, resolutely, he banished his grief and doubt. He packed the canoe, arranging the gear so that he could sit just back of the middle, and paddled out. His excitement was such, at that point, that he didn't feel the cold at all, nor hunger, nor shock at the death of his friend, for he was impelled now, on this journey, and could not turn back. It was strange, paddling by himself! With every tremulous stroke, the canoe nudged to his left, farther and farther, until he was forced to make a clumsy, overdone steering stroke, and thus he zigzagged away, sometimes switching sides to paddle, otherwise ruddering hard to one side until he slowed to a crawl.

"*Alors*, I am not so good at this," he muttered.

As if summoned, the wind bent suddenly to tickle the lake. Within perhaps half an hour, she'd blown small waves into tall ones, and soon, Garamond was battling the canoe, the lake, the wind, and fear. Gritting his teeth, he dug into an oncoming wave and pulled. "*Lean into the waves on a lake, mon petit.*"

"For you, Miron!" he shouted defiantly.

The canoe, though still heavy, floated higher with only one man, which helped shed the waves, but caught more of the wind. He was forced to make every stroke a correction. With dismay, he measured his slow progress against landmarks on shore: that boulder, that leaning pine, that lonely stand of slender, bare trees. Cobalt waves, as far as he could see, marched toward him, crowned with bright white caps. Their spray wetted him and froze in his beard until he had to claw the ice from his mustaches. And then he lost all momentum. Once, he put in to rest and walk out the cramps in his calves, but it was so difficult to get safely to shore, and then again to launch in the surf, that he resolved to stay out for the rest of the afternoon in one long, unbroken stretch. By the time he reached the gap between two sand points at the *fond du lac*, he was paddling in late afternoon shadow. Here, the waves broke in confusion, casting him first one way, then another. He drove on with strength born of fear until he crept through the gap, straight into the glare of the setting sun. "*Putain!*" he cried, and made a wobbly turn to shore. As he drew near, the waves began to break in the shallows until one of them whipped the canoe sideways and dashed him toward the beach. With only instinct to go on, he vaulted from the boat, fell to his knees in the water, but somehow managed to keep the canoe from capsizing. Then towing it between swells, he lurched into a small cove and at last found a spot calm enough to unload. Every bundle was encased in ice.

"*Ah*! I have wrenched my hand!"

Wincing he pulled up the canoe and sat down in a heap, relieved to be alive. He had made the mouth of the river.

When Garamond rolled up in his furs that night, sheltered beneath the canoe, a tide of exhaustion washed over him, a summation, not only of his harrowing, thrilling afternoon and the dreadful morning of grief, loneliness, and agonizing decision, but also of his whole journey from Montréal, so long ago it seemed, in a distant past. His body demanded payment: deep, long, rejuvenating sleep. For he would surely need it. As he lay there on the beach, he listened to Miron's words, now engraved in his memory: "*We follow the Rivière du Fond du Lac twenty odd leagues. We shall pole up the rapids or carry around them or paddle against the current, even if our hearts should burst. We shall work, mon petit! Where the river turns north, we will find a small stream and go west. Then a long portage. Then the Messipi—at last—shall bear us into their country, the country of the Nadouessioux."*

He woke to the sound of cold drizzle tapping the hull of the canoe. It would be a chill, slippery day, but he was not dissuaded. Grimly now, he bulled his way upstream, forging into the broad current of the river while he mastered the stroke of a solo paddler. Soon there were rapids to contend with, but he cut a sapling for a pole and proceeded to learn that art as well. He had some near calls. Then he heard the deep growl of a falls up ahead, louder than the sound of the rapids around him, and he knew he'd reached the first portage. But, try as he might, he could not find the trail. He fought to subdue a sudden, fierce anger at delay, lost the skirmish and shouted, "Where is it, Miron? Heh? I have no time to lose, damn you!"

Exasperated, he pulled in to where at least there was a sort of track, a deer track at best. He unloaded the packs, then gingerly hefted the canoe onto shore. He cast about for something to cushion the hull, for he realized he'd have to drag the delicate birch bark craft—it was far too heavy to carry, soaked as it was with water. Soon, he'd fashioned a cradle out of soft evergreens and set out up the track, stopping often to lift the ends of the canoe over rocks. As the tedium set in, his frustration mounted to fantastic heights. Meanwhile, the river filled his head with thunder and he could not help but stare at the water pouring over wickedly sharp rocks, only several arm-lengths away. Unexpectedly, the track dead-ended at the brink of a cascade.

"*Merde!* Pile of shit!"

Peering upstream, he could just spy a stretch of calm water. He thought, I am not going back! I will tow the canoe from the shore and then pull it out again! He knew that was foolish. He could only take the canoe back to the packs and look again for the portage trail that had to be there. He started to haul the boat back the way he'd come; immediately, it tangled in low-hanging branches. In a fit of irritation, he kicked the bow, which spun around so that the stern now teetered over the water. The canoe groaned as all its weight fell on the middle of the hull. Garamond did not mean to let go of the bow; he only wished to take some of that weight. But he could not reach in two directions at once, and the canoe began to slide. How it yearned for the water! He could not keep his footing and he could not keep hold, for the canoe pivoted out of his grasp, wrenching the same hand he'd injured in the surf. The canoe fell and whirled noiselessly into the rapids, then leapt up as if in play, then disappeared. The sun chose that moment to burst from the clouds, illuminating the scene in cruel detail. With horror, Garamond could only watch as his world crashed into bits.

20.

Dégradé

Summer 1869

IMAGINE, IF YOU will, the dancing, several-hued folds of the northern lights, set in a pitch black sky. They are scarcely there, yet the observer's gaze is fixed upon them—there, no they are *there*—until the night no longer seems dark at all. The fragile forms of the aurorae—rays and waves of rose, palest green, and glowing white frost—share the same distant quality as scenes seen through water. They are the manifestations of forces *un*seen, electromagnetism and the stuff of spirits, tied all mysteriously to the eleven-year cycles of spots on the sun.

It happened that the peak of one cycle encompassed the year 1869, which was therefore extravagantly blessed by aurorae. And further, that the pure air of Canada offered a splendid view. In the wee, early hours of a night in July, Edward Hopkins, captain emeritus of the H. B. Co., stood agape on the shore of Lake Superior, staring up at the lights. He was, strangely enough, more panicky than awed, for he greatly feared he would never again see such a thing. Not in London, at least. Then, feeling foolish, he gave himself a shake, inside as it were, and thought, I shall wake Frances. He turned toward the tent, stumbling, for he couldn't tear his eyes from the sky.

She was instantly awake when he touched her, and eager to come out for the show. They moved silently, husband and wife, gathering cloaks and blankets, and, taking care not to disturb their sleeping voyageurs, found a place to settle themselves out of the breeze.

"They are said to make sounds," Edward whispered, "similar to crackling or hissing. Hearn himself wrote the sound is like a flag snapping in a gale."

Mrs. Hopkins listened as hard as she could, but the wind and surf drowned out all else. She had no wish to paint the lights, nor unravel the secrets of their rippling waves. She was content as she nestled there in companionable peace with her husband. She gave herself up to watching, and thought, I bear witness; tonight that is all I have to do.

There was a moment when the lights went rolling and twisting from the zenith to every horizon, and the man and woman could not help but sigh, "Oh!" Predictably, however, they could not pay attention for long. It was warm in the blankets; the air, pleasantly cool. First Edward fell asleep, then Frances, her mind slowly emptied by the flaring and fading above. Oblivious, the lights played on without them.

They woke hours later to spatters of rain on their faces, sprang up and ran to the tent. The noise of the lake, pounding the beach now, could be heard above the wind and rain, and soon it was light enough to see the size of the surf. Clearly, it would be a day for staying onshore.

"*Dégradé!*" Edward announced, after precious little thought, "We are wind-bound; everyone go back to sleep."

No one argued, for the luxury of *un jour dégradé* was a thing to be savored. It was marvelous—even the cook slept in. By mid-morning, the rain dribbled to a stop and, drawing on all of their skills, they built a roaring fire that dried the air and surrounding white pebbles for several feet. Everyone huddled near for a hot breakfast while Edward regaled them with tales of the northern lights. He made it sound so heroic—that he and his wife slept under the sky—the voyageurs had to hide their smiles.

The wind gradually swung round from the north and northwest to the west and southwest, accelerating as it spun. Rain clouds remained, lowering gray-blue and casting black shadows on the lake. But the water was of that odd green color, accented by white froth, that hints at imminent sun. And sure enough, sometime before noon, the sun blazed out in a glory above huge whitecaps as far as the eye could see. It would be a perfect afternoon for drying wet clothes, wet gear, and most importantly, the supplies and goods they carried down-lake. Soon, all the rocks and whitened logs and driftwood round the camp were festooned with cargo and clothes. It made a comic sight, for more than one voyageur ran scurrying to rescue an item from the clutches of the stiff, southwest wind. When all was secured, they settled down to lazing or wandering about, as each soul fancied, until the Iroquois from Québec decided to get up a game. It was a new game, involving nets and sticks and small leather pouches filled with whatever was handy to give the right heft. The rules seemed to still be evolving. Before long, the voyageurs were taught what was deemed they should know, and all went cavorting down the beach. At which Mr. Marsh, the younger clerk, could only look with envy, for his ambition did not allow sport with the common *engagés*. Morosely, he watched them, and seeing this, Edward took him aside for instruction. Edward felt it was his duty to do so, which opportunity gave his wife Frances leave to go off by herself.

She was wearing, of necessity, the "lighter" black dress with broad gray stripes round the hem, while her full mourning gown dried on the rocks like a bedraggled crow. She felt light as a cloud, and unaccountably happy, a long neglected emotion on this trip. She thought, I shall just explore for a bit.

There was so much to see! The fantastic energy of the waves as they broke on the shore, the gulls hunkered down on their rocks, all facing into the wind. There were mountain ash in fruit, fragrant juniper, alders, blueberries, yarrow, and larch. Spruce and fir and birch. The water, translucent green in the shallows. She was not worried about painting at all, only taking it in, witnessing. She clambered over the cobbles, teetering often, a smile curving her lips. She was obliged several times to pour sand from her shoes, discreetly out of sight, and in a moment of abandon, to recline on a flat, sloping rock. At length, she made her way back to camp and the shouting voyageurs—I shall watch the game—she decided, but she was brought up quite short by the sight of the black dress, laying there like an admonition.

"Frightful thing!" she said through clenched teeth. But she burned only briefly with resentment, and then guilt swept in as the dear, lost faces of her children invaded her mind's eye. She stood indecisively, looking this way and that.

"Hallo, my dear, where have you been?" Edward called out with affection.

She forced a bright smile. "I've been on a bit of a ramble. So lovely here."

"Come and join me then, I've missed you."

She pushed away the faces in her memory. "Yes, Edward," she said, "I'm coming."

They very nearly had a party that night, what with the nibbling and sipping, and feeding the fire. Edward was compelled to open a small keg of spirits, which was drained forthwith by thirsty voyageurs. They had a violet sunset before them and a velvety green forest behind. As the alcohol worked, they created riotous renditions of old French songs, Yankee doggerel, and prim, proper fables of all origins, only slightly hindered by the presence of a lady. "Xavier, go on with your tale!" they cried. "What happened to old Garamond and his *petite fille sauvage*?" But Xavier declined. Mr. Baker recited several dull jokes, received with derision, before he gave up. The moon swiftly rose, bathing them in light and providing a convivial counterpoint to the light from the fire. It was many hours before the festivities wound down, in fits and starts, toward bedtime. When Mrs. Hopkins retired, talk was somewhat more free for a while, but the liquor was gone, and so the tone changed from mirth to sobriety. Eventually, all who were left at the fire were Edward, Mr. Marsh, Xavier, and Denis the passionate young *avant*.

Denis said, "*Messieurs*, I make you a vow tonight, all right? This very night. I, Denis Montclair, vow I will never, never put these hands on the plough, all right? Never!" He held his callused hands to the fire, as if he'd rather burn them up than sully them with a plough, or anything, really, that was not a canoe paddle. "I belong to the *pays sauvage*, all right? All of this—" he swept an arm in the general direction of the darkness, the northern wilderness, so threatened by change, by Dominion.

"The brigades are finished, my friend." Xavier calmly lit his pipe, regarding the youngster. "What will you do? You'll have to pay, what do they say, the *taxes*, isn't that so, Monsieur?"

"I admit I'm not clear on that score," Edward answered. "I should think it may be harder to live on hares and fishes in the coming years. It would be well for all of you to diversify your interests."

There was a pained silence.

"The Company, of course, can no longer—"

"But Monsieur! It makes no sense!" Denis interrupted. "You will talk all you want to these people, these muddy *fermiers*, and all right, they are so disrespecting! So ignorant, so—"

"Self-righteous," Mr. Marsh put in.

Mutters of agreement. Xavier got to his feet, his pipe glowing as he took a deep pull. "They think all this is evil, *comprenez?* It stands in the way of their towns and fields and churches. It is difficult to understand, but we must." He spat into the fire and started to walk away. "They had nothing, so now they want everything. Good night to you," he called over his shoulder before melting into the dark.

Edward said, "Yes, they think anything that cannot be controlled is the work of the devil, ultimately, and so must be destroyed. An absurd philosophy, yes, but there's nothing to be done about it. In any case, however, where are we to put all those people?" He felt suddenly very tired. Where indeed? And thought, It is really not my affair anymore. He stood up, noting the wind had gone, though the waves still broke in the shallows.

"I am planning an early start tomorrow, come what may. Best get some sleep, *avant*." He clapped Denis on the shoulder. "You too, Mr. Marsh. Never fear for your place in the Company. We shall manage somehow."

Edward and Marsh discussed for a few moments longer more neutral subjects, as gentlemen would do in order to end the evening on a seemly note. Edward was already thinking about Frances. She had seemed almost happy that day. He calculated the distance between their tent and the nearest sleeping man. Perhaps he could risk an *amour* this evening. Probably not, however. He bid the young men good night and ambled off hopefully. Then, Mr. Marsh, rubbing the smoke and fatigue from his eyes, nodded *bonne nuit* and disappeared also, leaving poor Denis to glower at the fire.

But morning dawned clear and tranquil, and free of sad regrets. The Hopkinses and their party were more than ready to move on; such is the nature of canoeing, a certain restlessness after even one day ashore.

Mrs. Hopkins was not so willing to don the big, black dress that morning, but she did so, not out of duty or sadness or even obstinacy, but out of that frustrating sense that one must stay a disagreeable course because there is no other way to save face. The dress felt far heavier than before. She was determined, however, to be cheerful, and Edward, without comment, laced her corset rather loose. It was the way he usually did when they went camping, an unspoken concession to comfort. It was one of their small bonds, which he'd missed so far on this trip. Perhaps it shall go well, now, he thought. In fact, romance had eluded him the night before, but his expectations were high for the near future. There would be the post at Michipicoten with their own private room, thank Heavens.

"Look, Edward," Frances had put on white lace cuffs. She held out her hands for him to see. "My skin has turned brown in the sun!"

21.

The Northern Forest

Winter 2020

Gentle Reader,

THE NORTHERN FOREST in certain weather seems to emit its own light, a luminosity that softens the darkest days. Perhaps it is the contrast between the glowing green of deciduous trees against the dark of the conifers. Yet, they are all photosynthesizing for all they are worth, from bud-out to leaf-drop, and the doughty dark conifers persevere in this work even in winter, whenever there is enough of a thaw to provide water. The essential ingredients for photosynthesis are twelve molecules of water and six molecules of carbon dioxide. Add the radiant energy of the sun. Here, the cook steps in, that is, chlorophyll—such a magical word. This most fortuitous of chemical compounds is found in all green plants in the world. Chlorophyll uses sunlight to break the bonds between atoms of water and carbon dioxide, and to rearrange them, and *voilà*! When the cook is done, there is one molecule of glucose—precious energy stored as food—as well as windfalls of oxygen and water. The magic is that nothing has been lost or gained in the cooking; one may carefully count up the elements at the beginning and end, and find there are always six carbons, twenty-four oxygens, twenty-four hydrogens, and either a chemical or a radiant manifestation of energy. And chlorophyll remains, a little older and grayer one suspects, but never fear, for the glucose will fuel the creation of new chlorophyll cooks, as well as the doings of metabolism and maturation. At night the cooks sleep—even those that reside in the needles of northern conifers—serene in the knowledge of a job well done. The net effect of all this is an abundance of atmospheric oxygen, for more is produced in photosynthesis than is used to burn glucose. Thus the magnanimous nature of green plants, the Mother Theresas of the biome that is Earth.

But, what form will the plant or the tree or the alga assume once it has satisfied its sweet tooth for glucose? That depends on the environment in which it grows, as well as the history of all its forebears. We are speaking here of natural selection, the winnowing of individuals. It is a very personal procedure. Either a tree survives and thrives enough to produce viable offspring, or not. The question is, how appropriately adapted is a tree?

Let us think of *Abies balsamea*, the balsam fir of Christmas tree fame, needle-leaved and evergreen like most conifers. Its pleasing, pyramidal shape excels at shedding heavy snow. Its leaves are evergreen so that their chlorophyll cooks are always on call, an advantage in extending those short northern summers. Its aromatic resins help deter insects (but not people). And curiously, *A. balsamea's* tough needle leaves and thick bark are adaptations for conserving water, which would seem to be plentiful throughout its range. But not so, for in winter, the tree suffers drought when the soil freezes, and even in summer, its roots may be plunged in water too cold or too acidic to use, which is the situation in certain lowlands and bogs. These are the same adaptations that many *desert* plants use to contend with another set of adverse conditions: aridity, heat, abrasive wind. Indeed, it is climate that finally determines the configuration of ecosystems and the adaptations of the organisms therein.

Consider that the north shore of Lake Superior is brushed by the subarctic, but that most of the Great Lakes country lies within a humid continental climate zone. Ideal country for, say, hemlock

or white oak, important species of the northern and southern hardwood forests, respectively. They mingle in what ecologists call a
"tension zone," (grist for countless witticisms, one is sure) which
meanders in a generally northwest to southeast band from Minnesota to Ohio and Pennsylvania. It is perhaps eighty miles north of
Fort Atkinson, Wisconsin. The northern forest varies as the contours of the land do, so that, for example, higher, dryer ground is
the haven of pines, while streambanks are often fringed with alders.
The best land, with moist, rich soil and good drainage, is given over
to the sugar maples, *Acer saccharinum*. These are the "mesic" forests.
Here is John Curtis, in his landmark book, *Vegetation of Wisconsin*,
describing the northern mesic forests:

> The heavier soils were typically covered by mixed
> conifer-hardwoods, with white pine, hemlock, balsam
> fir, and white spruce as the conifers, and sugar maple,
> basswood, yellow birch, beech, American elm, red oak,
> and ironwood as the deciduous species.

Sugar maples are remarkable for the dense shade they cast, which
discourages all but the most shade-tolerant seedlings and saplings
struggling below. Sun-lovers must wait for a gap in the maple canopy, whether occasioned by disaster or the demise of their elders,
and then shoot for the sky. In the spring, before the maples leaf
out, there blooms an array of wildflowers on the forest floor—these
are the "spring ephemerals." Canada mayflower, trillium, wild oats,
toothwort, hepatica, bloodroot, twinflower (the famous *Linnaea borealis*), violets, trout lily, wild ginger, and many more. It is like walking through a forest ankle-deep in stars, but it's over in two or three
weeks.

And then there are the "xeric" forests.

> Curtis: The dry lands were dominated by pine, with
> jack and red pine on the lighter sands and white pine
> on the sandy loams.

They are still there, but reduced, for the glories of the north fell long ago to build Chicago, Milwaukee, and the Twin Cities, and a million Midwestern farmsteads and towns. One dreams of a comeback—a horizon of regal white pines; red pines clinging to cliffs, their candelabra arms stretched out to the wind; that dry, sweet scent. On the poorest, driest soils, jack pine still reigns, one of the few to endure the rigors and frequent fires. The branches of jack pine droop as if carrying the weight of the world, but they faithfully bear their crop of cones each year, small, pointed, baroque-looking cones sealed with resin. The fires melt the resin and release a million seeds to germinate in smoking ash; thus the pine barrens rise again like the phoenix.

And then there are the wetlands.

> Curtis: The wet lands contained either conifer swamps, dominated by tamarack, black spruce, and white cedar, or hardwood swamps with black ash and yellow birch.

These northern lowlands are troublesome in the extreme if one needs to cross them in any season but winter. They remain the bane of the traveler, though they make amends in other ways and we shall try to be objective. Northern wetlands occupy either sites delved by glaciers or winding streams in shallow, open valleys. These open wetlands—whether marshes or sedge meadows—harbor waterfowl, moose, beaver, and strong light in abundance, as well as mosquitoes. But mosquitoes are everywhere. One's best defenses against them are wind, cold, or hot sun—best of luck.

In the forest, the wetlands are hushed by startlingly chartreuse carpets of sphagnum moss and the general stillness that prevails within thickets of spruce, fir and cedar—these last beloved of deer. And in the deepest spots, one may discover the bizarre but charming sphagnum bog, a tightly-knit suite of strange vegetation that surrounds an opening of dark water. Here, the mosses and other plants have accumulated in a mat that may literally float on the water, gradually sinking under its weight and rebuilding itself on top, until the edges of the pond begin to fill with peat. The water is so acidic and cold as to hinder decomposition, and so the process is slow but amazingly steady, and a thousand years hence, the open water may disappear. Meanwhile, stunted black spruce, tamarack, and balsam fir make their stands on the outer edges, where the mat is thickest, while all manner of ericaceous shrubs like cranberry and Labrador tea, as well as orchids and iris cheerfully subsist on the sunny mat. Most of the common bog trees—tamarack, black spruce, white cedar—grow roots from their lower branches as they are buried in moss; these roots are called "adventitious." Everyday phenomena that crop up in unexpected places. Likewise, many plants have, of necessity in this nutrient-poor environment, assumed the carnivory habit—they trap insects in goo or innards or both, and digest them. Adventitious digestion. Anything goes in the bogs. One may even, on the Midsummer's eve, find a lingering slick of ice, hiding beneath an insulating layer of peat. It is not surprising that trees grow ever so slowly in places like this; a six-foot black spruce may be eighty years old. It is said that black spruce bogs are the most stable assemblages of vegetation in the north. And that the conifer swamps of the mixed hardwood forests are the closest in nature to the vast boreal forests farther north, maybe even their offspring, or their forebears, depending on which direction one is looking down the reaches of time.

And ultimately, there are the boreal forests; per Curtis, stands of spruce and fir in the coldest terrains. It is tempting to wonder, do they long for the days of the glacier, these valiants of the north? The boreal forests are of a type that circles the northern hemisphere between the approximate latitudes of fifty and seventy degrees. In Europe, the influence of the Gulf Stream holds these forests to the far north, but they have full rein in Siberia. On this continent, they stretch across Canada and southward on mountain heights. They maintain outposts on the south shore of Lake Superior and the tip of the Door Peninsula, Wisconsin. They are often hung with lichen and robed with moss, and in form, they range from impenetrable masses of vegetation to thin muskeg. The dominants here are white spruce on the somewhat drier soils, and our *A. balsamea*, on the somewhat wetter, though it doesn't matter much in the deep freeze of winter. But in summer, how beguiling the fragrance of balsam fir when mingled with ripe thimbleberries! There are mountain maples, black spruce, white pines, white cedars, and mountain ash—its crimson fruit devoured by thrushes, waxwings, grosbeaks. There are caribou, spruce grouse, and wolves.

Yet all these forests shade into each other, like so many things do—it seems there is not much black and white in this world. So let us think of continua in shades of green, which extend through both time and space, in scales of eons and continents, but also of human life spans, or the slopes of a local sledding hill.

It is convenient to describe common assemblages of plants as "ecological communities," such as bogs or pine barrens. The fortunes of ecological communities when tracked through time is known as "succession," for one community often succeeds another in a predictable sequence. A sledding hill may be carefully mown and tended, but when park budgets dwindle in hard times, the hill may be left to its own devices. Weediness is succeeded by shrubbiness—which makes for challenging sliding to be sure—and then appear small trees, and so on, until either the local economy improves and the hill is shaved bare again, or the local appreciation of hills stippled with trees grows strong. In which case, a woodland may take root, its composition dependent on the underlying soil, its exposure to sun and nearby seed sources, as well as other random or climatic factors. The community on the hill will be tending all this time toward a certain mix, more and more diverse and resilient as it proceeds. Every stage nurtures hangers-on from the past and harbingers of the future, thus the fuzzy nature of succession. Disturbance happens, as they say, perhaps in the form of a spring ice storm or a band of nostalgic sledders.

On a larger scale of time, one waits for the glacier's return. As it slowly approaches, the flora of the hill take on a boreal cast, until at last, the ice crushes all (but there is a spruce-fir forest on the *surface* of the Malaspina Glacier in Alaska!). Then the earth warms again, the glacier retreats, and waves of succeeding ecosystems ripple slowly forward.

At the same scale, but across geographic space, there is at any time a gradual change in vegetation from one regime to another. This change may be very subtle. For example, the northern mixed hardwood-conifer forest is perhaps either older or richer at the eastern end of its range, for there are more species there than in the Midwest. One can trace the relative abundance of, say, hemlock, yellow birch, and beech on a gradient of decreasing occurrence from east to west. Beech drops out just west of Lake Michigan, hemlock reaches the Mississippi River, and only yellow birch of the three braves the extremes of northern Minnesota. Beyond, are intimations of Prairie and West, the characteristic species of which gradually encroach on the forest.

Note, there are continua that reside *within* species as well as among communities. A cline in this sense is a gradual shift in certain characteristics of a species that inhabits a wide area. There is a species of meadow frog, for example, that ranges from Florida to Quebec. Each local population of frogs is nearly identical to its adjacent northern or southern neighbors, but the meadow frogs of Quebec are distinct from their tropical relatives, to the extent that they may become two species instead of one. It is the same process that has made Italian distinct from French; here is a cline that runs from Sicily to Normandy. There was a great leap when the French sailed to Canada and sowed the seeds of a new dialect there. In ecology, the outliers in clines are termed "exotics." The arrivals of exotics may serve as agents of disturbance, disaster, or rarely, enrichment of the local biodiversity.

One may think of ecological change in the northern forest, then, as a slow striving, punctuated by wind throw, fire, infestation, and flood. It is good sometimes to see these things with one's own eyes, and since *H. sapiens sapiens* is not so good at waiting, it becomes necessary to take to the road or the trail, or the river. All the gradations of nature are pertinent when ascertaining one's surroundings. What is here, that is redolent of there? This is the stuff of dreams and longing.

There is a tension zone between the northern mixed conifer-hardwood forest and the boreal forest, and one can experience it on the east shore of Kitchi Gami. Drive north on the main highway and watch for the change: it occurs somewhere near Lake Superior Provincial Park, Ontario. First the sugar maples go missing, and then the white pines. By Wawa, the boreal forest has enveloped all; from here, it extends seven or eight hundred miles northeast and northwest to the barren grounds of the arctic tundra.

22.

Pukaskwa

Summer 1992

THE FIRST THING I learned was that "Pukaskwa" is pronounced "**puck**asaw." The next thing I learned, or rather, had drilled into my inner-most being, was the all-encompassing importance of the Scientific Method, but I'll get to that later. First I must tell about the road trip up here, because it was truly marvelous.

Even though it had been calm when we woke up that morning somewhere north of Marinette, by the time we'd stopped for breakfast and were underway again, the bay was studded with whitecaps. The day would prove to be overcast and cool, rimmed dramatically with cloudbanks. It was perfect driving weather. I played all my Bonnie Raitt tapes and cranked it up for my favorites, "Luck of the Draw," *et cetera*. When Irv took the wheel, I pored over maps of the Upper Peninsula, the lake, and the deep unknown—to me—of northern Ontario. There, in a corner of blue water, south of Pukaskwa, hung Michipicoten Island like an earring on the Lake Superior wolf. I was determined to see it.

"Maybe we can ride out there somehow," I ventured, well, repeated, fishing for advice.

"Yeah, you never know. That'd be cool." Irv had already said this, but we both knew by then that Nicolette had every second of our "vacation" accounted for. Still.

Right away, I'd decided to keep a wildflower list for the trip. This was something I'd always done on vacations and camping trips, a little ritual I'd passed on to Walt and Mike. It was always entitled, "Wildflowers in Bloom," and we'd write down our finds with date and place in a small, dime-store notebook. "Nf" meant the plant was not flowering, but we'd been able to identify it anyway by the leaves—a special score. Birds, bugs, and wildlife were listed from the back, so that if it was a great trip, the wildflower list and the every-thing-else list would meet somewhere in the middle. On this trip, as we cruised through the U.P., the mid-summer daisies lay thick in the fields, together with flaming drifts of hawkweed. For the back of the notebook, there were already yellow swallowtail butterflies, swarms of mayflies, and, buzzing a puddle at a wayside, dragonflies. I wrote it all down.

It was interesting to go through customs for the first time in my life. I was so excited to show my birth certificate, maybe too excited, because the courteous but thorough gate-keeper ended up going through all our stuff, and that took a while. You have to realize a lot of our gear looked pretty suspect. I mean, pipettes? X-ACTO blades? Paraphenylenediamine? You bet they checked us out. But then, off we went, up and over the bridge; I looked down and my heart stopped for a beat—there below was a massive ship bearing the name, *Frontenac*. It was easing down to the maze of locks on the river. I felt absurdly pleased, as if the deep history of the voyageurs had touched my own. And then we were winding through the streets of another Sault Sainte Marie, where Irv said that visiting Canada was like visiting his brother's house: the same but different. I gaped at everything anyway as if we were in Timbuktu. Then we struck the highway north—how exotic it felt to go one hundred kilome-ters per hour. Soon there were ominous, moose-silhouetted signs on the side of the road—*Danger de Nuit!* Lake Superior appeared and stayed faithfully on our left. Somewhere around Batchawana

Bay, and again at Agawa Bay, we took a leg-stretching break during which I recorded pussy toes, hawkweed, yarrow, and vaccinium on dry rocky exposures; and twin-flower (*Linnaea borealis!*), shinleaf, Canada mayflower, and wild sarsaparilla in the woods. There were ravens and tiny lavender butterflies (I would look them up later) for the back of the book. For a joke I wrote, "40-ft birch bark canoe, western horizon, personnel unknown."

We left the lake behind for a while, gassed up, and forged ahead on our ribbon of Highway 17 into the amazing Canadian wilderness: the dense, dark back-country, all rugged and rocky. How different the northern forest is from our woodlots back home. The trees I grew up with float like puffs of green, going blue with distance. But here the deciduous forest is pinioned to bedrock by spruce and fir, and the forest covers everything except bogs and cliffs. The forest is what this place is.

Pukaskwa National Park headquarters is situated in a place called Hattie Cove, a safe little pocket on the northern edge of the coast. There is a campground, visitor's center, trailheads, and everything is clean. I was charmed, and fantasized about living there forever, forsaking my treasured house back on Oak Street. We found Nicolette first thing in the afternoon and set up camp.

That night, the team from Lakehead University, Thunder Bay hosted a campground potluck, and it was really a ball. They were basking in the glory of a just-published article on their 1987 lichen project on Isle Royale, and basically, they were calling the shots for the reconnaissance trips this time around. It was very exciting: the rapid-fire instructions, the plans, the banter, all in that crisp Canadian speech. Apparently, they'd already christened us the "kayak wranglers" from Wisconsin, which was flattering and put us in the best of spirits. While we worked the coast and quarter-mile transects inland, they would be in the back-country, as deep as they could get with their gear. They told us that Sault College and Lake Superior State with their Environment Canada advisors were already at Lake

Superior Provincial Park and that we must have passed them on the way up. Everyone was terribly concerned that we all use the same methods and controls, what with all the non-specialist volunteers (like me and Irv), and there was a lot of talk about ECODATA standards, and QA/QC, *et cetera.* I resolved to do whatever I was told because I had no idea about any of this. Irv was only slightly more informed. "Not to worry," Nicolette told us, "I'll verify everything. It's all on me." *That* was reassuring.

Then there was gossip and wishful thinking about a fall project on Isle Royale—federally funded no less, and there were UW–Superior and UM–Duluth eyeing the Apostle Islands, and maybe Michigan Tech and Marquette University claiming the Keweenaw and the Hurons. It sounded like a grand plan all right, but I don't think anyone had much hope of pulling it together. Yet, these lichenologists, both seasoned and budding, had the highest of aims. I mean, they were passionate, and as the potluck progressed, and the beer and the lichen lore flowed, I have to admit, by the time I turned in for the night, I wanted nothing better than to help record the fate of lichens with the most meticulous of care. This desire was only somewhat dimmed in the morning. The lake was too rough for the ferry, which meant we'd have a day to get oriented, relax, and to go through our mountain of stuff. By 9 A.M., the Lakehead folks had packed up and departed in a cloud of dust.

As soon as she'd seen my wildflower/fauna list, Nicolette made me the trip "phenologist." Phenology, she explained, is the recording of natural phenomena through the seasons.

"It's kind of like old-fashioned natural history," she said, "which is how everything got started. Hey Irv? How much distilled water did you bring?"

I was really beginning to like Nicolette. The lowdown on her was that she was married to a chemistry guy at UW–Stevens Point. They were both second-generation Italian Americans, which explained all the good food we'd brought. Our little reconnaissance was Nicolette's big chance to direct a project of her own and she wanted it to be perfect. She had a very quiet and deliberate way of moving and explaining, and I watched her pretty closely as she ran through the list of gear. She was, I thought, the quintessential scientist. I had no doubt she would check and double-check everything we did.

This was the plan: We would catch a ride on the ferry, weather permitting, and go directly to our first base camp at Oiseau Bay. From there, we would take the kayaks to points north and south, and five days later, again via ferry, move twenty miles down the coast to Otter Island. Depending on circumstances, we could ride farther south with the park warden stationed in Otter Cove, or simply use the same strategy with the kayaks as before. And then we'd be picked up for the return to Hattie Cove. We would be looking for four species of lichen, beginning at about a dozen points on the lakeshore and walking transects due east. The idea for this, our preliminary survey, was to note which general types of lichen were there in addition to the four species, and to think about logistics for the main studies to come. Everything had to be documented, every last detail, just as if this *were* the main study. These are the lichens, the curious hybrid creatures we sought:

- *Cladina rangiferina*
- *Evernia mesomorpha*
- *Hypogymnia physodes*
- *Parmelia sulcata*

Impressive names; humble bodies. *C. rangiferina*, rounded clumps of caribou "moss;" *E. mesomorpha*, like drooped lightning; *H. physodes* with its peculiarly skeletal look; and *P. sulcata*, a shield lichen, as if made of metal and beaten flat. Irv and I studied the photos in our Hale's dichotomous key and were thankful for Nicolette's presence. For her part, she spent rather a long time on the park service phone hashing things out with her advisor back in Point. After that she cleared off a picnic table and buried herself in books and stacks of journals, none of which would come with us. We left her alone.

In the late afternoon, Irv and I took a stroll toward the falls on the

White River. We would never make it so far as that, but it was good to move and not think and just take in the surroundings. I added rattlesnake plantain—strange name—to my list, and then what I thought was a Swainson's thrush. We turned a corner and came on a broad meadow, and wouldn't you know—there was a bull moose feeding there, far enough away to never-mind us. His antlers were about as big as his ears. One moose in a meadow of wild iris. Irv and I didn't say much, just looked and strolled, holding hands like kids and nodding quiet greetings to the hikers straggling back from the falls. Laughed at a red squirrel bounding down the trail with a huge mushroom clenched in its teeth. That night, I saw a long-legged hare in the campground. I put it all in the notebook.

The *Century*, our ferry, was a gallant, oddball thing, for all the world like an old bachelor's basement hide-away. By morning, I was thrilled to be setting out. We eased through a narrow slot in the rocks lining the shore. Hattie Cove disappeared, and before us Pulpwood Harbor opened wide to the lake. It seemed fairly calm, so I couldn't see why everyone was so tense, but as we advanced toward Campbell Point, the reality of Lake Superior's mood was revealed. There were swells coming in seemingly endless ranks from the west, all the way from Minnesota, I guess. The ferry began to rise and fall in sort of a spooky way, and then at the point, the waves turned big and surly and we could see how this trip would be.

"Hang on ya hosers," called out our captain. Nicolette's face carefully froze as she took up a post in an inner doorway, but she was hopeless at looking tough. Myself, I was watching the incoming horizon on the one hand, and the welling and pouring of water on rock on the other. The *Century* pounded around the point, bucking and groaning, and turned south, going for it. What would it be like to play in waves like this? I couldn't help wonder, and imagined bracing and surfing in the orange Hydra. Irv looked at me and just shook his head.

"You're crazy, Frances," he said. "These are hungry waves."

He was right; they were truly chaotic, hurried and worried with spray blowing off the crests. I glanced over at Nicolette; poor thing, she had a death grip on that doorway. We had three hours of this until we reached Oiseau Bay. The coast we passed was gorgeous: rosy brown rocks, a natural breakwater at the mouth of the White River, caves in Cave Harbor, and islands at Morrison, all passed by to the sounds of toiling engine and whooshing waves. We got somewhat used to the ferry's pitching, but never quite enough to relax. We took note of the beaches at Fish Harbor, for, with any luck, we'd be back there in the kayaks. The rocks on the shore turned gray and bleached, and then there was wide Oiseau Bay with its long lines of white sand. Beyond the beaches, the terrain roughened, stretching up and back, clothed in swatches of dark conifers and lighter deciduous trees. Here we unloaded all of the gear, which took only a fraction of the time it had taken to pack; we switched places in the ferry with a tired-out troop of backpacking boy scouts. They were at the end of their trail, all right. But we were at our first camp and we were really psyched.

Nicolette shook off the effects of the voyage and took charge without a trace of self-consciousness. She had us lugging and sorting and setting up tarps like mad; I had to sneak a bagel and peanut butter when I went off to pee. Clearly, there would be no more lounging that day, but that was okay—wasn't I the Action Girl? Within half an hour, we felt just a sprinkling of rain, then two or three brief bright showers. We continued working. I was given the task of re-checking Nicolette's project list, while she and Irv laid out the first transect. Here's what we had:

- reference materials
- two cameras
- hand lenses, microscopes, binoculars
- flashlights, hi-intensity lights, batteries
- the usual tools (hammers, chisels . . .)
- special tools for air monitoring
- four compasses (the Lakehead team had their own GPS)
- unbleached cloth bags; sturdy boxes, some waterproof

- pre-printed data sheets
- pencils, felt-tips
- basic set of meteorological instruments: thermometer, barometer, etc.
- basic chem tests: medicine droppers and pipettes, X-ACTO blades, reagents: bleach, K, P (paraphenylenediamine)
- distilled water
- pH meter/Litmus strips
- soil matrix fixative/glue
- rope/carabiners/duct tape
- radio/marine radio

Then we had one stupendous shower that forced us under the tarps. This is when I had a moment of doubt. "How are we going to pull this thing off?" I whispered to Irv. He shrugged with a skeptical smile.

But Nicolette never wavered, and the shower passed, and she announced in the sudden quiet, "Let's do a trial run."

What a strange, strange sight. There we were, creeping through the soaking forest, calling out cryptically to each other, and huddling in excitement around these obscure little plant-like entities. Mosquitoes rose in clouds but were foiled by our DEET, a luxury we would have to forego when collecting samples, for nothing would be allowed to sully the chemical composition of the lichens. Soon, we were coated in moist, rich forest debris. Everything smelled fabulous, cool and rested and full, like the world always is before dawn. I could easily have pushed farther and farther; a kind of mindless energy took hold of me, but my compadres reeled me back.

That night after supper, we built a campfire on the beach and talked about science. Although I could not imagine a more pure landscape than the one we were in, we were there looking for signs and patterns of air pollution. In this, as Nicolette informed us, we built on earlier work, especially Dodd's Isle Royale study in '83 and '84, and Averill's study at Thunder Bay; thus the Lakehead crew. This year, the reconnaissance teams were all looking for the same species, which had been chosen for their pollution tolerance, abundance, easy-to-recognize appearance, and use in previous work. Depending on how things went, the Orientation Study next year would focus on one or two of these species. Predictably, the Lakeheaders were rooting for *H. physodes*, but Nicolette was pushing *Cladina*, the reindeer lichens. Apparently, she cherished an unofficial hope that they could broaden the studies, to make them interdisciplinary and include wildlife biologists. She admitted it was a pipe dream. Anyway, our samples would be analyzed for heavy metals and sulfur, and everyone was sure that we'd find those things in our innocent little lichens, and that the results would provide baseline data for the future.

Nicolette said, "The inland teams will probably find the pollutants on the ridge tops, like in the other studies." She poked at the campfire thoughtfully; I could tell she was wide-awake, but then, so was I. Only Irv was stifling yawns, and soon he would be stumbling off to our tent.

"The ridge tops are where the lichens intercept the heaviest concentrations of pollution—it comes in on the wind, and the ridge tops are windiest. For us, there's also the question of the funnel-effect of the shoreline. So, essentially, that's another variable." Nicolette leaned back, sighing with anticipation. "We just have to make sure everything's in sync with the other groups so it can be a valid comparison." She eyed me for a moment, then without asking if I needed to be told all this, she launched into a quickie lecture on the absolute necessity of "rigorous methodology." So that our results should at all costs, be repeatable, that is, verifiable, accessible and standardized for the benefit of future studies.

I understood what she was talking about. I mean, you just basically have to compare apples to apples, right? "Yeah, I get it," I said.

"You have to be so picky because some of this stuff ends up in court, you know."

"I suppose."

"Oh yes. If point sources can be identified, well, it's possible to bring pressure to bear." Then she told me about the old iron-sintering plant at Wawa with its downwind deadly plume, and the industries—and jobs—at Terrace Bay and Marathon. Farther south, there were the Sault Sainte Maries, and farther west, Thunder Bay, Duluth-Superior, and the Minnesota north shore. There was stuff going on all over the shores of Lake Superior, some of which had resulted in actual lichen "deserts" and who-knows-what else.

"But there's so much that comes from even farther away; we may never know where it's all coming from. These might be the last days for baseline studies, Frances. We're already into damage control. Say," she brightened, "tomorrow I want to redo the transect we did today, first thing, okay? We need to get some samples in the bag."

"Sure, sure. Don't worry, I'll make sure we're up by eight?"

"How about seven?"

So much for sleeping in. "Sure, okay."

We went to bed. And, as I fell asleep next to Irv, who didn't even hear me come into the tent—I mean, he was *out*—I imagined the industrial infernos of the world, and the smell of sulfur, and by God—I'm a mother after all—I wanted to protect those defenseless lichens and everything that depended on them. Because by then, I kind of knew about the concepts of food chains and canaries in coal mines. These were things I'd extrapolated from living, in fact. Who hasn't by the time you hit forty?

Day two on Oiseau Bay, cool and sunny and us wrapped in bug nets, grappling data sheets. We worked our tails off all day. When the afternoon petered out, we suddenly had leisure to notice that the lake had gone flat as a sheet on a new-made bed. Irv said, "Should I check the marine radio for tomorrow?"

"Oh, good idea," Nicolette agreed, somewhat off-handedly, I thought. I could tell she wasn't thrilled about the sea kayaks.

Irv wandered down the beach for better reception; he paused for a long time with the thing up to his ear, then turned suddenly to us and yelled, "Hey! It's going to be good! Waves less than a meter." He trotted back happily. "We should go while we can, right?"

"We'll wait and see what it's like in the morning," said Nicolette, futzing with the stove. "It can totally change overnight, you know." Irv and I smiled behind her back. Too bad for our fearful leader— day three dawned dead calm and the forecast remained the same. So we packed for an overnight, secured the camp with excessive tarp- age, and floated out onto the bay.

How callous I am. I knew how nervous Nicolette felt, and how burdened Irv was, paddling her around in the tandem, instructing and soothing. So long as I was free to play in the Hydra, I sim- ply didn't care. I took off to explore here and there, gazing in little reveries down at the rocks jumbled below like an underwater field of huge cat's eye marbles. I figured I could always catch up with the tandem. But that was a mistake, because once Nicolette got a little used to the boat, she turned on the steam all right. I mean, she is one strong woman, and the combination of her strength and Irv's, and the long centerline of the tandem resulted very soon in me being left far behind. So much for foolish pride. Fortunately, Nicolette became nervous again when she realized how far behind I was—though Irv, the cad, seemed not to mind—so they stopped to wait for me to catch up. I took a breather; we continued; we sang "The Wreck of the Edmund Fitzgerald" with gusto; we arrived at Fish Harbor intact.

It was a good day, even with late afternoon rain showers, and we feasted that night, imprudently, I guess, and sipped on whiskey as the sun began to set. We were just chatting quietly, finishing up chores and all, when we realized we were in for a show. I mean, we were stopped cold. On our left, there appeared a rainbow, arched across a violet sky and ragged pink clouds. On our right, a glowing sunset, incandescent peach above, molten gold below; a ridge ser- rated with black trees. All this against openings of intense turquoise sky. I'm not kidding about any of this. It ended with deep rose over dark teal water. We watched a gull circle above us a couple times, then soar out to the lake, its tiny figure passing before that colossal, multi-colored sky like a landscape on another planet. We drank every drop of the whiskey. Day four, we rode a brisk north wind back to Oiseau, and south as far as the White Gravel River, sampling lichen all the way.

Yes, it was all going too well, so it came as no surprise when the weather turned to shit. Day five, we'd made it back to Oiseau just before the wind but not before the downpour. That's one reason for wetsuits, I guess. The *Century* was delayed. So we hunkered down, played cards and napped, read a little. Nicolette worked on her notes, so her tent was off-limits. The sky cleared but the wind was cold and mean; that was one churning Great Lake out there, and even I had sense enough to wait patiently onshore. Menacing breakers were soon rolling in from the west, and when each long curling wave met rock, it sounded like ten thousand ripping sheets over one deep, bass boom. Driftwood that had been white was now apricot-colored, bronze, even yellow. Our tents and tarps were jiggling like mad, so I wrapped myself up in rain gear and went 'round tightening every line I could find.

I'm sure it was the night of the big wind that I started to feel a little mixed up. Irv and I, of course, had learned plenty about each other's bodies by then. He had a way, when we made love, of running his hands over my skin, first just fingertips, then his whole hands, then fingertips again, in long, slow movements and the occasional tickle. Soft drift of fingers; intimate brush of wrist. It got so I could almost picture desire as a tangible thing, pushing upward to meet Irv's hands. That night, I could not separate this sensation, inflamed and subsiding by turns, from the wind pressing on the nylon walls of the tent, as if the tent were breathing, nor from the lichens in their bags, our boats tied up on the beach, the house in Marinette, the notions of environmental ethicists. Three woman-girls named "Frances." I remember closing my eyes, giving up and moving until at last there was climax and sounds—astonishing sounds—pulled from some deep sexual root in me. For once, we didn't talk about anything afterward, but plunged instead into sleep.

I was awakened just an hour later by a half moon so bright that it fooled one poor bird into singing, as if morning had come, though how could that be? These birds were used to the brightness of the moon. It was me who was not. I lay there, anticipating the regret I would feel when Irv should leave. Perhaps six more weeks. And I wondered, furious with myself, if I was falling in love with him. Had he fallen for me? It was folly. I turned to watch him for a moment as he slept; studied the curled, rumpled hair of this young man. And me, a damned matron, practically. I searched around in the dark for my camp towel, found it, and went out.

Day six, another rough ride on the *Century*. We arrived at the old light keeper's house, now uninhabited, on the north tip of Otter Island late in the afternoon. We had a smaller pile of gear by then, and not as much excellent Italian food—even dried and canned, it was excellent—and we sent all of the lichen samples we'd acquired back to Hattie Cove on the ferry. If everything went right, we'd have one day to get to the mouth of the Cascade River, two days to sample Otter Island, and another to move a bit south on the mainland. We crossed to the Cascade River first thing the next day; it was top priority, though none of us would admit it, because we were dying to bathe in the clear, warm falls at the mouth of the river. And yes, it was heavenly. We swam before, between, and after walking our transects, and returned very late to Otter. Time seemed to be passing quickly.

Maybe it was that consciousness of the end of the trip, but the three of us and the Otter Cove warden—he paid us a surprise visit that evening—had one of those extremely intense, melancholy conversations that spontaneously arise in a darkened room. We were lounging on the old musty couches in the house, a strangely indoor setting for talk of wilderness. The desperation, futility, and sadness of saving wilderness.

"It's a fight that can't be won in the long run." This from Steven, the warden.

"The problem is we don't have the resources to counter all the *interests* out there," Nicolette said. "You can win one fight, but they can afford to wait for the next one."

"Yeah, it's never-ending."

"But you try anyways." This from Irv. "You can never give up—it's not human nature to give up, ever." He kept coming back to this as we talked; he was very firm about it. There was a conviction in his voice that surprised me, or rather, reminded me of what he was. I hadn't heard that tone for a while, I guess; we'd been having such a good time. Still, how I loved to hear him talk. But the case against wilderness, against the places like Pukaskwa or even the humble county forest at home, seemed overwhelming, I mean, I thought we were lucky to have what we did.

"Well, when I'm really bummed out about it, I think about John Seed," said Irv. His voice was by then disembodied because the light was completely gone. "He wrote somewhere that we all share the same elements, the same molecules that have been here since the beginning. We're all the same—rocks, animals, trees—and all of us will continue to exist. Just in different forms."

Nicolette said, "That's interesting, Irv. I think I read something by that guy once. Didn't Leopold say something like that in *A Sand County Almanac*?"

So that got us started on the books we'd read, and the places we'd seen, and finally Steven got up to go.

"Hey, good talkin' to you guys," he said over his shoulder, "Probably see you again before you take off. Might be fair for another couple days, eh?"

After that, I had another little spell of being scared or mad about this thing I was doing with Irv. It was supposed to be a fling, as discussed with Chris, if not planned outright. What was I doing here really? To soothe myself, I avoided him that night, and sat by myself with my flashlight and my wildflower list, working hard to lose myself in the absorption of the collector. Listlessly I turned the pages—early blueberries, cinquefoil, butterwort, bluebead lilies gone to seed. *What the hell am I doing?* I gave up and went in search of the last of our liquor.

Everything seemed better in daylight, of course. It was a good day, actually, an alpine day with hot sun. Late in the afternoon, we were winding things up, thinking we were pros, in fact, when Steven pulled up in his launch.

"Well, Yanks," he said, "I'm off to Hattie in the morning. Wanted to let you know. Ah, you might reconsider about tomorrow. No good getting stuck off the island if you've got the ferry coming."

We gathered around to weigh our options. I spoke up about my hope of getting a little farther south, "where we might catch a glimpse of Michipicoten Island."

"What?" This from Nicolette.

"You already have," said Steven. "It's that way out there," he pointed to a dark patch on the horizon, "That's not part of the mainland; that's the island. It's quite big, but it must be, oh, thirty kilometers from here. You can't always see it."

How do people get out there, I wanted to ask, but Nicolette was discussing business already: logistics, spare food, and the need to finish up in good order. It was no time to bring in my absurd little schemes. I could feel Irv's eyes on me, but he said nothing.

I had an interesting dream that night, vivid enough to paint, and I thought of my mother—I would try to remember to describe it to her. In this dream I was traveling aboard a concert hall that was floating down a river. While gazing out from the stern of this thing, I saw two wolves leap into the water and swim after me. One was pale and the other was dark. Waves of color that I can only describe as fluorescent rippled across their fur, which stood up in electrified tufts. For a long time I was riveted by the energy of these animals and could not move. Eventually I broke it off and went in to the concert; it was a rock and roll band from the old days. But as the music played and we continued to float downstream, I could not forget the sparkly red eyes of the wolves, as hot as small suns, following behind. When I woke up in the morning, the sun was already baking the side of the tent facing east.

23.

Little Ice Age

Winter 2020

It has been estimated that the sun—not King Louis, but the sun around which the earth revolves—was one-quarter of 1 percent dimmer than "usual" during the period between roughly 1350 and 1850. There were little in the way of sunspots in those years, those cooler darker regions on the sun's burning surface that are visible through heavy filters. And so one must think, well, the sun would have been brighter, not dimmer. But sunspots are closely joined with much hotter regions, and it is this roiling of the sun's energy, this appalling tension, that erupts at intervals in the infernal bursts we call solar flares. If these go missing, we on Earth feel the consequences.

The larger Ice Age ended circa ten thousand years ago, long before Galileo watched the skies. It was followed by small warm-ups and cool-downs. We had an extraordinary warming between 900 and 1300, the Medieval Optimum, during which Vikings colonized Iceland and Greenland, and wine grapes flourished in England. But then the plunge into what we now call the Little Ice Age.

It affected especially the northern hemisphere—all that land giving up its heat (so much more readily than do oceans) to outer space. Summers were short and wet; winters severe, descending early and lingering late. The evidence is circumstantial but convincing, everything from records of grain prices and meteorological data, to tree rings, to landscape paintings of overcast skies, to ice cores drilled from glaciers. Mountain glaciers advanced worldwide. There were repeated famines in Europe and entire Alpine villages given over to ice. The Thames froze in winter and offered itself as a festival ground. The Dutch canals froze, as did the Baltic Sound, and the ancient orange groves of China succumbed. During these years, the native peoples of North America shifted around as best as they could, territory jostling territory. It is said that the League of the Iroquois was born in those days, a path to peace in hard times. The corn belt retreated south so that some peoples returned to hunting as their primary endeavor for food.

Most pitiful were the fates of the Norse colonists in the north Atlantic. Iceland was encased in snow and ice, such that open ocean could no longer be seen even from the highest heights. The population shrank by 50 percent. Greenland, even worse; the brave farmsteads, villages, and graveyards overrun by accumulating white, and buried. Even whaling declined, affecting not only colonists but the native Thule peoples, who were soon driven south; conflict ensued. Meanwhile the fist of cold tightened until all the Norse peoples there had died or fled, and then the colony was no more.

There were two periods of deepest cold in the Little Ice Age, one in the 1400s and another in the late 1600s. The first, perhaps thankfully, followed the depopulating effects of the great plague in Europe. But the seventeenth century nadir, dolefully called the Maunder Minimum, struck its hammer blows on the poor, who by then had again reached saturation numbers. With each miserable harvest came long, horrifying hunger, to be borne or not. The famines in Europe of the late 1640s, mid '60s, and '90s were more or less widespread, while others, liberally distributed throughout the seventy-year period were local in nature. The recovery began in the second decade of the eighteenth century.

It happens that sunspots and their attendant solar turmoil are the genesis of aurorae in the night skies. The Maunder Minimum was a period of exceptionally low sunspot activity and a corresponding dearth of aurorae. It is interesting to learn that the Ottawa people of Manitoulin Island regard the northern lights as a sign of goodwill from the manitou hero, Nanaboujou. He it was, who, with the help of one small muskrat, reassembled the land above a great flood, and so saved his people from ruin. But it begs the question: Did Nanaboujou abandon them in the Little Ice Age? Or more likely, perhaps—because he is a peculiarly human manitou—did his attention simply wander elsewhere?

24.

The Trials of Garamond

Winter 1689-90

NOT FAR FROM the waves of Kitchi Gami, on the shore of a ruthless river, Garamond of Anjou sits cross-legged and silent, in the exact middle of a circle of packs. He is wrapped in fur and cradles a musket on his lap. He is peering intently into the frigid heart of the forest.

What Little Owl and his comrades and perhaps most of the Indian peoples of that time would not have foreseen, was that an ignorant *Français* farmer, alone in the wild northwest, would choose other than to hike back to the nearest habitation—Chegouwameeagan. But how could they understand the soul of a seventeenth-century peasant, forged over centuries of marginal clinging to survival in the shadow of the overclass? Whereas Garamond, without even needing to picture it, remembered very clearly the poverty of a second son's future, which so easily could be his. He had come this far from his stepfather's farm—he did not want to fail. His pride burned at the thought. And, as the most random and frivolous chance of genetics would have it, it happened that this young *Français* was stubborn, wily, and imbued with great strength. In the circle of packs by the river, he closed his eyes and saw again the stream of carts rolling into Ville Marie. "Hundreds of thousands of livres," Cornet's voice rang in his head, like a bell, like a clarion call.

What would it feel like, he wondered—to be rich?

He opened his eyes; he did not see the forest, but rather, a sharply-etched vision of Cadot's map to the Sioux. There they lay in the west, on the shore of a lake, just beyond a featureless stretch of land, through which—Miron had said—the Rivière du Fond du Lac curved its way to a portage. Was this vision of Garamond's an accurate rendering of Cadot's map? Alas, the young *Français* did not care.

So it was with a kind of single-minded ferocity that he rose and began to tear down the packs. When he was done, he stepped back to survey their contents spread over the frozen ground: three muskets and ammunition, victuals from Missilimackinac, accoutrements of canoe travel and repair, fur robes and blankets, thick wool stockings, a shirt and two pairs of breeches, Miron's coat, moccasin leather and *raquettes* for walking on snow, twist tobacco, brandy and salt, axes, knives, fish hooks, a set of nesting kettles, needles, thread, and cloth, and for the adornment of the Sioux—vermilion and glowing strings of beads. He could not help himself then; he let out an unholy yowl. Immediately, the wind lifted a corner of precious cotton cloth and gave it a sly shake.

"*Sacre la Vieille!*"

But he would not waste more energy railing at fate. He proceeded to rapidly make decisions: leave the canoe gear, two muskets, the heavy bales of cloth, the largest and the smallest kettles. Take just the tea and all the tobacco, the fish hooks, wire for snares, several knives, needles, thread, beads, vermilion. Leave the axes and most of the brandy. He made a big mound of the victuals and items to take, and covered it with a fur robe. Then, gritting his teeth, he carried all the forsaken treasures into the woods, where he built a cairn to bury them, just as he'd done for poor Miron. He marked the cache by twisting the boughs of a spruce into a sort of flag. Then, he committed the place to memory.

He spent the rest of that day and the next methodically sorting the pile by the river and devising a capacious pack out of leather, a blanket, and lengths of thong. He waddled about on the snowshoes and doubted their worth, but decided to use them as pack frames. While he worked, he kept the middle-sized kettle filled and simmering with all the food he would not be able to take. He gorged on bacon and peas, smoked whitefish and cornmeal, wild rice sweetened with berries and maple sugar. He did not eat it all at once! But a mouthful here and several there, during every waking hour. It turned out to be more than he'd ever eaten in his life in the course of one day, which was no small comfort to a *Français* peasant.

He set out on the fifth of December, carrying three weeks' worth of food, gear for hunting and fishing, and enough trade goods to make an impression on the Sioux. He promised, I will turn back in a fortnight if I don't find them. I will make a notch in my spoon each day to keep track. He had every intention of coming back for the cache.

At first, he did not mind the weight of the pack and was surprised at how good it felt to stride along on his legs, after paddling so long. The air stung with cold, but he was perfectly warm as he walked, singing every dirty song and rhyme he could think of until—in spite of himself—he began to be happy again.

He trekked west along the river, slogging indifferently over boulders and ice and frozen undergrowth. The rapids roared incessantly and drowned the sound of his footsteps. Sudden cataracts poured in amber sheets and sent up a mist that sheathed every surface in ice. By the afternoon, he had to shift the pack again and again, for it chafed his shoulders and pressed in his back.

"At least it will get lighter as I go," he thought. "And I, stronger."

He camped at last on a rocky point above the river, under the frail brilliance of a winter sunset: the sky banded blue and pink, a crescent moon, and bare black branches etched thereon. From his perch, he could see the gorge of the river dropping down into shadow. He built his fire and cooked a frugal supper, and then made a notch on his spoon to mark the first day. In the morning, he took to the woods again and gloried in the rightness of his decision.

For the first time since he'd set foot in Canada, he focused on the trees, the shrubs, and the plants—now dried up and frozen—and their collective disposition on the land. He stood beneath a stand of magnificent white pines and gaped upward, as snow sifted down through the branches. He took note of hardwoods on the heights and hemlocks in the draws, and sunny pockets of brown bracken ferns. He learned to watch for the creases in the hills where water flowed. The little trails came and went, but he learned how to walk the bumpy terrain and not stumble.

There were times when he could not help but think of the treachery of the river and the obtuse flight of the canoe, but he forced himself to give up on that because there was no peace in it. Then he let his thoughts linger on Miron and all of his friends, and the girl at Missilimackinac. In the evening, when he built his small fire and cooked his food, he was lonely and wondered, half fearfully, if the Sioux could remedy that. At dawn, he found himself surrounded, not by men, but a flock of noisy, gaudy jays, gamboling round his camp. He lay as still as he could, trying to follow their antics and admiring their astounding plumage—bright blue, purple, black, gray, and pure white. Then he could not help but laugh, and they flew up and away, clowning as they went. Mightily cheered, he made himself a generous breakfast. Before leaving that place, he picked up two fallen blue feathers, and stuck them in his shirt. He thought of the white feather little Frances had dropped from the carriage, so long ago it seemed, and smiled.

By mid-morning, the wind had shifted to the east, bringing a fine rain of snow. Too soon, he found the river turning north and he wondered in alarm how that could be. Miron had clearly said, *twenty odd leagues*. He traipsed on while the merciless wind drove the snow in his eyes and coated the right half of his body. Soon, he gave up combing ice from his beard. At noon he stopped to rest.

"I need to go more west," he said aloud. He squinted against the pellets of snow and considered, I have no canoe—why should I follow the river? The Messipi is over there, no matter if I go a little more north or not. He stared westward over the low, wooded hills and open country between him and the Sioux. He longed to put his back to the wind. At last he said, "There are bound to be trails," and struck off to the west, leaving the river behind.

He had not gone far before the land descended and leveled out in lumpy marshes and cold, sucking mud. He was forced to post-hole through slush, soaking his moccasins and leggings. He kept on. After hours, it seemed that he had hardly advanced at all. The sharp snow did not let up, and, when the high ground behind him faded in early dusk, he decided to stop so he wouldn't lose his bearings. "I must always be sure of the sun," he reminded himself, and besides, he was famished again. He camped on a hillock with only bushes for shelter, ate some dried fruit and smoked fish and threw the bones into the reeds. He made a fire to dry his things and rolled up in his furs for a nap. Contentedly, he let out a long, luxurious belch.

But there in the marsh was a rustle and a snapping twig. Pulling his knife in alarm, he sprang away from the firelight and into the safety of darkness. He stared hard toward the noise, and soon saw two shiny eyes, low and sliding away, and then came the sound of a small beast galloping off in the snow. Relief, for a moment, made his legs wobble, but then he had an idea: he would set a snare by the fish bones. Almost as soon as he'd done that and returned to the fire, he was amazed to hear the irritated, then frantic struggles of an animal, caught. He let out a whoop and raced to kill his quarry. He was overjoyed to find it was a raccoon.

"Oh! There is not the likes of you in Anjou, *petite*! You will make me good mittens, eh? I'm going to skin you. I'm going to eat you! Right now!"

Hasty with greed, he killed the raccoon and cleaned out the guts. He should have taken the time to build up the fire then, but he did not, and made do with skinning and butchering in its dim light. It was a small enough creature, so before long, he had hunks of its meat ready to roast. For this, he made a crackling fire and raptly watched the meat color and the juices drip, although, he admitted, he was not very hungry. But when it was done, he set to with relish, thinking, "I'll eat the whole damned thing, *toutes les choses.*" He ate quickly at first, stuffing—and burning—his mouth, but slowed down after a few swallows. Slower and slower he chewed, until he stopped and spat out the meat. It was rank.

"Faugh! I should have cleaned off the fat!"

Compulsively, he took one more mouthful. It was undoubtedly the most bitter, foul, musty thing he'd ever tasted. In disgust, he gathered all of it up and hurled it into the marsh.

When he woke in the morning, he felt as if he'd not slept at all. Still, he set out and made fair progress, for there was high ground interspersed with low, and wooded places for good cover. Day followed day in like manner. But when clouds hid the sun or the stars, he could not find direction and was forced to tighten his belt and wait. He did not see any more game. Sometimes, he worked on the mittens, but they were only half cured by wood smoke, and starting to smell. And he grew to dread the nights, for it seemed that the country awoke between dusk and dawn and watched him in pregnant, malevolent silence. He did not remember feeling that way before.

One day, he traversed a clearing and looking up, was startled to see a weird, white roll of cloud stretched from one end of the northern horizon to the other. Yet above him, there was a bright blue strip of sky. He crossed himself in wonder, but walked on. Within an hour, snow was falling so thick that great chunks of it built up on his eyebrows and beard, and slid blurrily off his eyelashes. He was forced to stop and take shelter in a cedar grove. He watched it snow for three days straight. When the sky cleared and the sun returned, he emerged into a blinding haze of blue and white. Blinking and squinting, he trudged off, up to his knees in snow like a sea of down. He had to work like a beast to break trail, sinking jerkily to the ground with every step, and the huge pack like a hill on his shoulders. After some of this, he decided to try the *raquettes*. He disengaged them from the pack—replacing them with a framework of cut saplings—and fastened them on his feet. How awkward they were! He hopped around in a circle, testing them and tripping twice, but then he mastered the strange, straddling gait that was needed. Gamely, he resumed his course. Managing the snow, he found, was indeed easier with the *raquettes*, and the powdery, crystalline puffs shooting up through their webbing was a cheerful sight. Soon, he could walk without watching his feet, and that was even better.

He camped in another cedar glade, on a bed of boughs to keep out the wet. But he needn't have bothered as the temperature, that night, fell away into deepest, deathly cold. He woke in the earliest hours to the heart-stopping crack of a freezing, tortured tree. Unwillingly, he got up, dancing and hopping to get warm, and gobbled the last of Mercier's smoked whitefish. Then he set out again, plunging through the snow on his *raquettes*.

"*Merci de Dieu*," he muttered. "I must just keep going."

He was amazed that it hurt to breathe, and was compelled to shield his mouth and nose with a scrap of cloth. The hissing of reeds and grasses seemed unbearably crisp. He was swaddled in more white than he'd ever seen or imagined. The brightness of the snow hurt his eyes, just as the cold hurt his lungs and pinched his nose. Glittering shards of white assaulted his eyes until they throbbed and itched, and forced him to retreat behind a leather mask. From there, he would cautiously peep out through two slits and watch his white hell for signs of life.

There was never any sign of the Sioux, nor of any people whatsoever, in all those days. Nor animals, so he relied completely on the food he carried. One evening, he was shocked to realize he'd lost track of making notches on his spoon.

"Has it been a fortnight?" he wondered.

It was time, at least, to take stock, so he pulled out all of his food and calculated how long it would last. In dismay, he found he was down to mere handfuls of peas, beans, and wild black rice. He'd used all the cornmeal for thickening stews. There were still some raisins and half a flagon each of vinegar and brandy. But he'd skimped on Mercier's jerky, for it was compact and a sure source of endless soup, so there was plenty for a return journey. He heaved a sigh, thinking suddenly of the golden fruits of Anjou. He remembered sitting out on warm summer nights and watching the moon rise, its light smoothing the faces of his family. And then, he was surprised and frightened to feel tears seeping down his cheeks. He stood up quickly and rubbed them away.

"*Sacredieu!* I must go back—now. There are no Sioux, they are a dream!"

He started to repack the food, grimly measuring the weary way back to the cache and Miron's grave, and then Chegouwameeagan with its suspicious Indians and *Français* traders. But people, all the same. People to talk with, to drink with! He gave a bitter laugh. He felt suddenly exhausted, as if he could not even finish packing. His movements slowed; he paused, and stared blankly around. He felt he had never been so tired.

"But they are a dream," he mumbled, rubbing his eyes. "I have come all this way for nothing." He let out a mighty yawn, then, surrendering, rolled himself in his fur, and within moments, was sound asleep.

Studying this scene in wonder and great fascination was a small hungry fox, motionless in a thick copse of alders nearby. The little fox had never in its life smelled anything so tempting as Mercier's jerky. So patient, this creature, gazing first at the man, then at the strange mound of meat, fragrant inside a loose skin. The man was huge, terrifying, but asleep. Night gathered and hid the man and the food from sight, but not from smell. The little fox waited long, but not forever. When Garamond awoke suddenly at dawn, he stared around amazed, almost amused at his long sleep. Until he discovered the missing jerky, the one crucial item that had reassured him he would survive.

"Oh! Oh! Where is it?" was all he could cry. Frantically, he circled the camp, wider and wider, searching for tracks, for crumbs. He kept this up for a long time. Then at last, he went back to his pack, drew the half flagon of brandy, and drank until he was very drunk. It was a curious, pathetic sight: the bedraggled man, singing and babbling in the bushes, all alone with his pack and the winter woods stretching beyond view all around. When the brandy was gone, he smashed the precious glass bottle on the ground, and screeched to the sky — "I am a fool!"

Unbeknownst to the young *Français* trader, Christ's birthday arrived on schedule and was duly celebrated by millions of winter-worn people throughout Europe and New France. In Angers, there was high mass; at the palace of Versailles, pious prayers and murmurs of love in dark corners. In Québec, the venerable Comte de Frontenac, heavy and coarse with his lust for power, raised a glass of excellent wine; and in Missilimackinac, Father de Carheil waited patiently for morning. Somewhere far north, Garamond huddled in his camp, a miserable, freezing wreck, and thought longingly of mucking the Jesuit stables in La Flèche.

Of course, he knew that he would have to hunt or die. He tried his utmost. He set snares, cut fishing holes in the ice, waited hours on game trails that wound through the snow, his rifle in his hands. But he was only a farmer from Anjou, where hunting was reserved for the nobles. He did not know how to hunt, and he had no luck, save for a couple of bony fish. It did not help that he scared so easily now, that unwittingly, he warned away any animal that did come near. The steady noise of wind, and silence also, gnawed at his nerves until he took refuge for a while in some thicket. There, he would gradually calm down and satisfy his hunger with lewd thoughts of Cornet's wife. Then he would briefly fall asleep.

One day, he was following a low ridge, not knowing or caring whether it led east or west, or anywhere in particular, when he stumbled upon a carcass. He threw off his pack, fell to his knees, and thanked God and Mary and every saint he could remember, as well as his luck and all his wretched ancestors. He made soup from the bones and skin of the carcass, and what remnants of flesh were there, and, as his belly filled with hot liquid, his mind cleared and floated for a while above the ponderous weight of his plight. He was content. He was grateful. The sky colored as the sun set, transforming the nude forest around him into ranks of radiant, red wands. Watching this spectacle, he felt infused with energy. He had no more patience for misery—he would cast it off! He was sure there was something, just out of reach, that was waiting steadfastly for him. He looked and looked, but could not discover it. It was tempting, then, to give way to despair, but he resisted. As the light subsided, he made his bed, his motions as absent-minded as if he'd piled leaves and boughs into a nest on the ground every night of his life. When he slept, the only movement was the mist rising from his breath.

How many days had he wandered? He never made another notch in his spoon, so he did not know. He labored on, becoming thinner and finally, weaker. Experimentally, he chewed odds and ends of his own leather and sharp bits of the lichen, *tripe de roche*. He brewed a hopeful tea of white cedar, dry berries, and twigs. But one night he was horrified to find he could no longer lift a log to his fire. *In extremis*, he remembered a Jesuit hymn and gained enough strength to drag wood to coals.

At last, a day came when he too hungry and weak to do anything but lie on the ground and gaze at a small, frozen pond. He fell asleep and dreamed that the day was only cool and soft gray. There was a fitful breeze that played across the surface of the water, like fingers caressing skin. Reflections in the deep green water stretched and shimmered. Small white fluttering moths appeared and disappeared. He listened to the wind in the trees. He was warm.

And then, just by chance, a flock of jays descended on the dying form of the man by the pond.

"Jeeah! Jeeah! Jeeah!" they screamed.

Until he heard them, from ever so far away, and emerged from his trance. He gaped at his small saviors, their blue feathers flashing. Then he sat up. He smiled, heedlessly cracking his swollen, burnt lips, and said, *"Merci, les oiseaux,* my scoundrels, thank you, *mille fois, merci."*

There were, after all, crumbs to savor. He turned out all of the pouches and wrappings he could find and made a pitiful, unidentifiable mound and gulped it down. Stood up. Beneath his feet, he was shocked to see hoof prints of deer and diverse paw prints, claws stretched out to grip, all trapped in layers of ice. He studied this picture, the first sign of animals he'd seen in weeks. It was not long after that he found the antler of a gigantic deer. The antler was the color of dark ivory. Garamond did not know that a moose, and not a deer, had shed this glorious object.

When he first saw the animal standing motionless in a ravine, he thought it was Little Ugly, the Poitevin colt, regarding him with wise, ancient eyes. The eyes of the prey that knows it will not flee this predator. The figure of the colt resolved into a bull moose, massive, miraculous, and still. From its great height, it stared at Garamond. Was it injured? It did not move. Garamond ran his gaze over its body, and yes, he could see that its leg was broken. And then, he saw the evidence of its fall from above, for it had stepped all trustingly onto a delicate cornice of snow, and so tumbled down. Perhaps several days before. The bull moose, haughty and jet black, glared at the man, but did not move.

The man slowly lowered the pack he bore and drew out his musket. With shaking hands, he poured powder and rammed ball, cringing at the raucous sounds of cold, whiny metal. He raised his weapon, steadied himself, and aimed one finger-width to the left, and fired a killing shot.

The crack was surpassingly loud. The smoke bloomed in a choking blue cloud, and the man feared the moose would escape, but when his senses cleared, he saw that it was laid on its side with the base of its skull blasted away. He fell on the body, soaking in its warmth and embracing its fantastic store of energy and shelter. As the blood ran and the wind blew, the man cried out loud, so that his tears and snot ran freezing down his beard, and he whispered to the creature he'd slain, "Thank you, thank you, thank you, thank you."

He gutted the moose in a cloud of steam from its body, stopping every now and then to bolt a slice of raw flesh. He began to think very clearly about what must be done. Every morsel of meat must be saved, and every square inch of hide must be cured. And all else of the body must be put by for some future, unforeseen use. Somehow, all this sudden wealth must be kept from the hungry beasts of the forest. That is, those other than him. Garamond chuckled at this, and thought, I am a ravening beast, to be sure.

In the end, he built a small empire around the moose. With great difficulty, he chiseled and peeled the hide from the carcass, one side at a time. Then he butchered the meat, darkest red and dense as wood, and hoisted great joints and slabs of it from the limbs of white pines. To hide the smell of the offal, he hauled it to a lake in the valley, cut a hole in the ice, and sank it. For the first time in over a week, he moved his bowels, a shockingly painful event that wore on for hours. He recovered and proceeded with his work. On the far side of the lake, he piled the bones of the moose and left them to the beasts and the weather, for he thought he may use them yet. And then, with the greatest of care, he cleaned and scraped and smoked the hide. It took days to accomplish this task. Then he sewed it back together with sinew and made himself moccasins and a vast cloak. After that, he constructed a hut and arrayed his possessions around him, and did not budge again. He slept for twelve hours of every day, while his body renewed itself from within. He did not let his fire go out, but faithfully banked its coals before each long nap.

He grew stronger and began to venture out on short forays. It seemed to Garamond that everywhere he looked now, there were animal tracks in the snow. He found himself fascinated by the tracery of mice, the bounding indentations of squirrels, the right-left march of a grouse. Here was a furrow in the snow made by an otter, like an inlaid ribbon, footprints punched neatly down the center. Here were the flurrying impressions of the wings of an owl, stooping to its prey.

He wandered longer and longer, following trails through endless groves and over and around the pits and mounds of downed trees, hidden beneath the snow. He shot a hare and made a clumsy sled.

On a fine day, when his re-born body would no longer wait, he turned himself loose for the long trek east to Chegouwameea-gan. He pulled the sled, heavy with frozen red meat and gear, and daydreamed of joking and drinking with traders, of sleeping with women, and even, in odd moments, of confessing his sins. Steadily, he whittled away the miles before him, though it was all he could do to keep the sled, sidling along on bone runners, upright. Finally one day, weary of negotiating a sideways-slanting game trail, he abandoned it for a while, and climbed a small bluff for a look around. The horizon to the east was lined with dark blue and purple hills. The forest, both north and south, swathed the contours of the land in downy gray and brown, like the underfur of an animal. He turned to gaze west and could not believe his eyes. There, far down in a valley, was the figure of a human being, inching along a barely discernable path.

The old woman, a venerable member of the Mdewakanton band of the great nation of the Dakota Sioux, was bent nearly double under a heavy bundle of wood. She was concentrating on placing her snowshoes just so, and did not see or hear Garamond until he was quite near. When she looked up, she could not believe her eyes, for there, plunging down a hill, was a bellowing, black-bearded, wild-eyed monster. His arms stretched toward her, hands like claws. He fell and whirled to his feet without even touching the ground. She thought then that perhaps she would die of fright. But instead, she turned and ran for her life, the monster close behind.

25.

Gallantry

Summer 1869

"THAT WOMAN MUST have thought Garamond was a windigo, coming at her like that!" Xavier laughed from the stern of the Hopkins's canoe. "But he knew by then how to temper his desire, *comprenez?* That is the key, my friends. That was how he was purified of his greed, even if only to see another human being; it was the only way to survive the snows of winter, eh? Let alone the Sioux," and he added under his breath, "*les serpentes, Sioux diables!*"

"He was a very fortunate young man, after all," said Mrs. Hopkins, in her precise and feminine voice, so strange to hear in a bark canoe. "I fancy the Sioux took him in. They must have seemed like angels—"

"Madame, I don't know why he wanted so badly to go with the Sioux. They have always been the worst sort of people!" But at this, Xavier stopped short, for he remembered the massacre just seven years ago. The Sioux had been cruelly vanquished. Everyone knew this and no one doubted its implicit warning to Indians everywhere in the north. So to rail against traditional foes was surely the most empty of gestures. He thought bitterly of his mother's people, the Ojibway, loyal and brave, hanging on in a shrunken homeland. In silence, he fumed, and then, What do I care about it?

"You are indulging in generalizations, *gouvernail*. Just as the Sioux are not so bad, neither are the Iroquois who annoyed the French so in your tale." It was the White Shell, who spoke.

"Maybe."

"Don't forget, Messieurs et Madame, there were many hundreds of Iroquois who loved the Jesuits and came to live with them at Sault Saint Louis, and lived there as perfect Christians. Many of us," the White Shell glanced around, "are their descendants. Is that not so?"

Low murmurs of agreement answered from among the Iroquois of Québec.

Cautiously, Mr. Marsh asked, "So you fought *with* the French, *against* the Crown? I have always thought the Nations were our allies."

All of the Iroquois paddlers chuckled at this, to the discomfiture of the clerk.

"The English found my people to be formidable warriors, even against our own relatives. But that is all in the past, Monsieur."

Frances glanced curiously back at the *métis*, wondering if he'd go on with his tale. How taciturn he seemed, silhouetted against layers of wreathing clouds. She sighed, seeing that he was done for the time being.

They'd been making excellent time on this south-bound leg of the journey, aided by fair skies and light winds perfect for sailing the big canoes. They'd done their obligatory stop at Pic River, with its sandy, pine-strewn dunes and its rustic post. They'd had a day paddling smooth three-foot swells, benign as long as the horizon stayed flat, though they felt the rolling in their bodies all night long. Past bays and capes and treacherous shallows they'd advanced with no troubles. They'd surprised a dozen geese, rafted up at the mouth of a river, and shot one. Then on past wide Oiseau Bay, shaded so prettily in the morning.

Frances had tried now and then to draw, but she could not concentrate and finally left the sketchbook precariously perched on the gunwale beside her. They were nearing the White Gravel River where they hoped to camp. All around were cliffs and rocky islets washed bare on the lake side and prickled by struggling spruce toward land. Wave upon wave of forested ridges ascended east, receding in progressively paler shades of green. As usual, she noted all of this and even pointed out the occasional *picturesque* to her husband. He was happy to humor her, or so he thought, and made a special effort to describe the events and curiosities associated with that stretch of the coast. She listened attentively and asked pertinent questions. But her will waned as the afternoon lengthened, and at last she was quiet again. She could not help but notice how pitilessly the sun illuminated every contour of the bare, gnarled rocks that they passed. How time-worn, even care-worn are these rocks, she thought. Raked by storms and tormented, no doubt, by ice. She imagined soothing them, tracing her fingers down their old, lined faces. A sudden upwelling of tears caused her to hastily lower her veil. She knew perfectly well why the tears came and that they'd dry as fast as they'd come. She had only to wait, but that was difficult. She daren't let Edward see her cry; she knew how impatient he was by then, broiling away beneath a serene, pipe-smoking exterior.

They came into sight of the beach at the mouth of the river, a drift of fine white sand behind boulders. The waves became choppy, and as they drew near to unload at the shore, the forgotten sketchbook on the gunwale slid with a splash into the water.

"No!" was all she had time to exclaim, though it seemed enough time for years of regret to transpire.

At this, one of their voyageurs, young Patrice, leaped in after the sketchbook, which still floated, though with each wave it was jostled and dashed against boulders. He made a grab for it and missed; the white of the pages began to fade; it was sinking.

"Oh, I didn't mean to lose— It is my fault! Do be careful!"

Between the sloshing water and the creviced rocks beneath, poor Patrice could not keep his footing. Floundering noisily, he tried to orient himself; he inhaled a massive gulp of air, eyes bulging, and dived. By now, everyone was watching with some concern, for no one knew if Patrice could swim. Xavier stood ready to fish for him with the long, steersman's paddle, while Mr. Baker uncoiled a rope. They waited, staring into frigid blue water, for perhaps thirty seconds. Then Patrice exploded to the surface, the sodden, drooping sketchbook triumphantly waved in one hand.

"Excellent! Well done!" said Edward, taking the book. In a low voice, asked his wife, "Is it ruined, my dear?"

"Yes, and I have no other with me." She felt flustered in the extreme, like a spoiled, penitent child—to have acted so carelessly! And the young man so heroic for her sake! She bestowed her most ravishing smile on Patrice, who still clutched the side of the canoe. She thought, I shall make it up to all of them.

To Edward, she said, "Perhaps I shall dry some of the pages. They may still be of some service, after all." Then she turned to Patrice and said loudly enough for all to hear, "How may I thank you, young man?"

He beamed with joy, but he was, in fact, fearfully skinned up. His shirt was torn and he'd lost both moccasins. To Patrice, these were badges of honor, for he nurtured a secret hope, an unlikely, never-spoken hope—he wished to be an artist. Mrs. Hopkins's sketchbook, was therefore, to him, a sacred object and its rescue a pilgrimage. Where did it come from, this strange ambition? He was remarkably handsome, though so self-effacing as to negate any benefit to be gleaned thereby. His ancestry was obscure, even to him, but his face was one easily taken for native. That was enough, one day, for a white man to take him as a model for painting. The picture had turned out beautifully and Patrice never tired of examining it, and all the others the man kept in a portfolio in a rough little hut. The man had left all too soon. Afterward, Patrice remained entranced, not by the picture, but by the act of painting. He tried to do so himself with absurd results.

And then the wondrous chance of a canoe trip with Mr. Edward

Hopkins's wife, who, as everyone knew, was a paintress of great merit. Patrice wrangled a seat in the Hopkins's canoe and then boldly, a seat behind Edward. There, he had a perfect view of the English-woman's lap, on which settled—to no avail!—her sketchbook. Why did she wait? What magic would occur to unleash the lead pencil? He'd kept faithful watch for eleven days. And then, his great swan-dive. Now, Mrs. Hopkins herself sewed up his shirt, while he basked in glory beside her. The moccasins washed up on the shore. The cleanest papers from the sketchbook were cut from their binding and spread to dry, becoming hopelessly puckered in the process.

In the morning, Frances put away the black gown for good and brought forth the light one, so handsomely striped in gray. Kitchi Gami bestowed its blessings, also: cold water in which to bathe her face, crystalline air, and warm sun on the top of her head. They coasted twelve perfect miles before stopping at a beach with a tall frothing waterfall that plummeted directly into the lake. All the men, even Edward, ran to frolic in the stream, so distinctively split in two. A scene such as that should be remembered forever, she thought. She settled herself nearby and commanded, Simply begin. With no fuss at all, she began to sketch on a rumpled sheet of paper. A quarter hour passed in a moment. She became so absorbed, she did not even notice Patrice until he approached to offer her an opulent northern bouquet: wood lilies, yarrow, and deepest purple harebells.

"Patrice," she said, "they are charming! What a gentleman you are."

But he had already forgotten the flowers and was studying her sketch with an expression both reverent and eager.

Amused, she asked, "Would you like to see?" and handed him the sheet.

"How is it done, Madame? I would give my very soul to know."

She laughed, but kindly, and said, "There is no need for that. I can show you a little. Here is paper and here—" she rummaged for another pencil, but found none. So she gave him hers. "Don't concern yourself with how it looks at first. Don't think of anything at all."

He glanced at her doubtfully and tried in vain to place the sheet in what he thought was the proper position. Then he tested the point of the pencil. "What should I do?" he asked.

Edward's favorite hat, broad-brimmed and battered, lay close to hand, so she took it and placed it on a rock in full sun. "Do you see the shadow here? Draw the edge of the shadow."

Up went his eyebrows as high as they'd go; he drew a line, then another, and then looped them around in a sort of shaky crescent. Then he put down the pencil and frowned.

"Now the curve of the band, just the curve itself, nothing else."

They stayed thus on the beach, two artists—one accomplished and one brand new—for close to an hour. It almost seemed that two worlds were meeting in harmony there: the polish of the old world; the vibrancy of the new. But it was really not to be, not yet anyway. All too soon, Mr. Marsh and Mr. Baker strode up in a business-like way and put an end to the impromptu studio.

"That's enough bothering, *milieu*," said Baker. Off you go. My apologies, Mrs. Hopkins, if he took liberties; he can't understand, of course."

"No, no, it was my pleasure."

She gathered up her things, including Patrice's drawing, and handed them to young Marsh. Both clerks gave her their arms, and laughingly, she accepted. Then they trooped back to the canoe, trading pleasantries, never noticing the veiled, bitter gaze of Patrice.

But it was glorious to set out again on that fine, sun-drenched day. The canoes cut the water with flawless grace. The proud curves of the bows brought to Frances's mind the arched necks of stallions, flying on desert wind. She smiled at Edward, surprising him into a clumsy, "How lovely you are!" If anyone witnessed that small, fleeting intimacy, there was, of course, no sign. The voyageurs never missed a beat in their swift rhythm, and Frances found herself marveling that these exotic, half-wild men were held in check by the mere authority of her husband. She glanced his way; he gazed straight ahead; one fine, strong hand grasped his staff. Swathed in the rich fabric of her gown, she sat there at the right hand of her husband, scion of Empire, while the *canots de maître* skimmed across Lake Superior. She smiled again, just to herself, and for one long, delicious moment, was astounded by the beauty and grandeur of her life.

26.

The Dakota Sioux

Spring 1690

THE WOMAN WAS, after all, old, and so Garamond caught up with her and held her fast. She fought him ferociously, writhing, and jabbing at his face with a knife of splintered bone. She did not waste breath on screaming, but hissed and snarled so fearfully that he let her go.

"*Merci de Dieu, arrêtez! Sauvez-moi!*" In despair, he started to weep. He fell on his knees in the snow. "Have pity on me, I beg you!" he cried.

Startled, she clambered up and away from him, waving the knife. But when he only followed on his knees, pleading, she stopped and gave him a good, long look. They stayed so a little while, puffing and calming themselves. Garamond wiped his eyes and suddenly realized his pathetic display was exactly how Father Hennepin had described the peculiar greeting employed by the Sioux. The irony! He could not help but laugh, just a little, but he sobered when the old woman frowned.

"*Je m'appelle Jean Garamond,*" he told her. "I mean you no harm! I am lost! I am a trader seeking the Nadouessioux. Madame! Are you one, a Nadouessioux? I don't care—please take me with you!"

Her frown deepened at the odious word, "Nadouessioux."

Clearly, he was ignorant. Though the impertinence of the monster astounded her, she decided he was harmless, at least at present. And she could not deny her curiosity. She stared in fascination at his hairy face and noted the wayward gaze of one eye. His appearance signified that he was one of the *Français* of whom she had heard. Others of her people had met these foreigners and they would know what to do with this one. They would even, perhaps, honor her for bringing him in. She broke into a careful smile.

"*Êtes-vous* Nadouessioux, Madame?"

"No!" She spoke sharply in her own tongue and jabbed the air with her knife with all the menace she could muster. "There are no Nadouessioux! Dakota! I am Dakota!"

"Daquotot?" The word puzzled him, so he tried another of Hennepin's names. "Issati?" he asked.

"Aah," she nodded. "I am a respected grandmother from Issati, yes." She thought, He is not entirely ignorant.

She motioned down the path and made as if to herd him along. Thrilled, he quickly complied, but as he stooped to gather her bundle of wood, he remembered his sled piled with moose meat and abandoned on the ridge.

"Oh, *merde*! Wait here, *s'il vous plaît*! Wait here, wait here!" He raced back up the hill. But now, she did not want to lose him, and so, grunting with the effort it cost her old body, she tore after him, waving her knife. The snow on the hill was drifted deep and soft, and so their chase consumed long minutes of slow-motion wading, albeit with much vigorous shouting. At last, Garamond disappeared over the ridge, but soon reappeared with his sled, and bounded back to his captor.

"Heh! Aah!" she gasped for breath, holding her sides. Then, thoughtfully, she circled the sled, inspecting and poking. She even stopped to pat his arm. His relief was so intense that he began to cry again, at which she actually laughed. Then they set off together, a most incongruous pair.

The Dakota encampment lay just one valley over, and in fact, the old woman's absence had already set up a worried buzz. Someone had asked, "Where is my sister, Yellow Deer?" Another answered, "Yes, where is my mother?" Preparations were made and soon a small party went out to look. Their astonishment was very great, for they found her at once, striding proudly toward them and driving before her a strange fair-skinned man with a sled. A *Français* man!

Warily, the people formed a ring around Yellow Deer and the man, whose eyes were huge in his bearded face. There was silence, until the old woman chuckled, and spoke.

"Don't worry, my children, I have him under control."

At this, they all crowded 'round, talking at once, examining the *Français*, laughing and pounding poor Yellow Deer's shoulders. Then they formed a procession and advanced to the camp. Garamond, transfixed between apprehension and delight, hustled to keep their pace. As he hurried around a bend in the trail, he caught one heady whiff of wood smoke, and beheld a wondrous sight.

There, tucked up against a protective cliff, was an assemblage of tall cone-shaped tipis erected on a patch of level ground. The ground had been swept clear of snow. An open brook tumbled near the base of the cliff. Cooking fires smoked and crackled. People were tending the fires, conversing, working. Women, children, and men! Garamond stopped to stare, as if he would inhale the scene through his eyes. He would never forget this rapturous sight. But then all the people, as well as several large, barking dogs, streamed in a rush toward him. Some of the people seemed angry, others amazed, still others shouted back and forth until all seemed chaos. One woman grabbed her child and ran. Garamond was frightened, but he showed no sign, and then he heard the old woman chuckling again. He forced himself to smile.

"Eh... *bonjour*." He cleared his throat and quavered, "*Je m'appelle Jean Garamond*." What should I do? he thought. Then he noticed several pairs of eyes on his sled, and others on his pack, and he knew precisely what to do. Carefully, he pulled up the sled and unwrapped the meat. Then he wrapped it again and pushed the sled toward the Issatis.

A ripple of goodwill passed through the camp. The old woman, Yellow Deer, beamed. Then a small thin man issued from the crowd, walked up to Garamond, looked hard into his face, and said, "Frangseh?"

"*Oui, je suis Français!* Please accept my gift, Monsieur." Garamond bowed to the man. The man looked immediately to Garamond's pack, but made no move. He continued to study the captive. After long seconds had passed, he nodded and addressed the people. He pointed to the sled and a woman came up and hauled it away. Then he turned back to Garamond and smiled. "You are our guest," he said to the uncomprehending young man, "We shall have a feast of your moose meat."

The celebration commenced at once. They showed Garamond to a spot near a fire and there he remained, nodding and smiling with the Issati men of authority. Identity was soon established.

"Shining Heart, Shining Heart," the small thin man placed his hands on his breast. Then he tried to say "Garamond," but the sound was so outlandish, he could only laugh, but politely. Others of the men tried it with similar results. Soon, there were children racing through the camp, all shouting and giggling, "Kahwahmong!" in various permutations. Nearby, Yellow Deer chopped moose meat and told her tale to a wide-eyed audience of women.

Toward evening, a party of hunters returned to the camp with a yearling deer slung by its legs from a pole. Bows and arrows bristled from their winter garments. They were amazed to see a *Français* sitting before their fire, flanked by their smiling elders. When the commotion died down, Shining Heart signaled to one of the young men, who ran to fetch a beautifully wrought pipe of red stone and a pouch of tobacco. Shining Heart filled the pipe and lifted it in four directions. Garamond did not know the significance of these gestures, but apprehended well their solemnity. He remembered the tobacco in his pack and resolved to give it all away to these fabulous, magnanimous Sioux. Shining Heart lit the pipe and puffed gently. Then he exhaled through his nose, momentarily obscuring his face except for his deep brown eyes, enmeshed in fine lines. He gave the pipe to Garamond, who, as he inhaled, saw that every face was turned his way. It felt like taking communion in the church of La Flèche. Gravely, he exhaled and passed the beautiful pipe to the next man. He felt absolutely blessed.

After that, the pace of the ceremonies quickened. The old woman approached with a tray of glistening, fragrant, roasted meat, and fed to Garamond, with her own hands, three morsels. He was embarrassed by this act, but soon all the people were chatting and laughing as if it were the normal course of events, and so he was put at ease. They began to eat a fantastic quantity of meat: moose, venison, grouse. Tray after tray was consumed. The fires burned down and were built back up. More flesh was roasted, stewed, devoured. After he knew not how many hours, his stomach rebelled and he waved away the food, to the extreme merriment of his hosts. It seemed he had failed a good-natured test, so to redeem himself, he decided to give more gifts.

He went to retrieve his pack, marked closely by the entire company, and proceeded to unpack his pitiful store of trade goods. He spread everything out on the ground before the fire: the musket, tobacco, fish hooks, wire, knives, needles, thread, vermilion, and a small rainbow of Venice beads.

He motioned to Shining Heart, "I give it all to you, Monsieur, I do not care to haggle! You may give me whatever you have or nothing at all. You have saved me! *Merci bien, mille fois*! I am forever in your debt!"

The Issatis listened intently to the melodious speech of the *Français*. They exchanged glances and shrugged. Their attention returned to the array of exotic items on the ground. Every man gazed longingly at the musket, but Shining Heart picked a twist of tobacco, sniffed it, and nodded.

"My gift to you." Garamond closed Shining Heart's hands on the tobacco and smiled. An elderly man grasped the musket. He hefted it tentatively, aimed, set it back on the ground, and waited.

"*Bien sûr*, let me show you, old man," said Garamond. "It is a fine musket, indeed! *Regardez*—" He loaded the weapon, carried it to the edge of the camp, the people following, and fired it at the eastern stars. The report was deafening, of course, and, although the people had known what to expect, they were horrified just the same. Some could not help but duck when the *Français* turned back to join them, while others nervously cheered. Only Shining Heart dared to laugh out loud. He pressed the little powder horn and lead back into Garamond's arms, and Garamond, understanding, tucked it inside his coat for safe-keeping. Then he offered the musket to the elderly man, who accepted and disappeared with it into the crowd.

In a flash, all of the trade goods were passed through the camp, examined, admired, and distributed to whomever it seemed best. By the time the party wound down, long after Garamond had lost all pretense of understanding, the prevailing sentiment in the camp was that this particular *Français* was welcome.

But he awoke the next morning in a most perplexing state. He'd been laid to sleep inside one of the graceful Issati tipis, and nestled in a warm mass of fur and bodies. He slept deeply, without fear, and without the half-conscious vigilance that had characterized his nights for weeks. In fact, it took all the dignified efforts of Shining Heart to wake him. As he opened his eyes, the walls of the tipi opened to the sky and the sun, and to peals of women's laughter. They were dismantling the tipi around him! He started upright, and saw that his resting place was heaped with furs of all kinds. There were also a pair of tautly woven snowshoes, several bundles, and a heavy necklace of polished, sable stones. The musket and its accoutrements lay undisturbed by his side. He glanced around. Clearly, the Issatis were decamping. Were they leaving him? He had a nightmare vision of being alone again in the winter woods, with a pile of beautiful items that he could not move. He leapt up and bellowed, "Shining Heart! What is happening!"

In his panic, he did not hear the old woman's voice behind him. "What are you crying for now, *Français*? Help me secure your things.

We are leaving, don't you see?" He did not respond, but continued looking wildly around. Finally, she took his arm and smiled. "If you are good, I may adopt you into my family. You will take the place of my poor little son, dead so long ago!" She wiped away tears.

"*Pute*! Don't leave me, old hag!"

She sighed and frowned. So excitable, this foreigner! She beckoned to a girl who'd been lounging nearby, and together, they packed all of the furs and bundles onto a sled while Garamond fretted and raved. Then tenderly, Yellow Deer placed the sable necklace over his head and handed him the new snowshoes. She affixed her own and took up the traces of the sled. And then, she simply trudged away, following the trail beaten into the snow after her people. Garamond was dumbfounded. But, after a few desperate moments, he grabbed the snowshoes and ran after her, calling, "Wait, wait! I am coming!"

They journeyed for two days, during which Garamond basked in their indecipherable companionship. He did not care that they laughed at him, or growing impatient, tormented him. It did not matter, for he would have rather died at their hands than alone in the forest. He tried to remember words in their tongue from Father Hennepin's book, but failed when all he could think of was the shrill tone of little Frances's voice. He did mention "Chegouwameeagan" to Shining Heart and the old woman, but they did not seem interested. Finally when Garamond persisted, Shining Heart halted his march and waved to the east, saying in his own tongue, "It is far away. We go there rarely because we do not trust the Ojibwa. Sometimes we go. We may go in the summer when the *Français* traders come." It was as if their present trek and Garamond's question were entirely separate entities that could never be mixed, for Shining Heart was a man of the deepest concentration. Noticing the head shakes and stares around him, Garamond was abashed. He held his tongue and thought, *Eh bien*, it seems I will not see Chegouwameeagan for a while.

The new encampment lay by a long, frozen lake, surrounded by gentle hills. As more and more of the people arrived with their burdens, a tired, but cheerful communion arose. First the women cleared the site of snow and leveled the frozen ground as best they could with sharp sticks. Next they assembled the tipis and set up for cooking, and Garamond could only marvel at the speed and ease with which they did those things. By nightfall, the hunters arrived with only a brace of grouse and a hare, but also with news of the signs of deer all around the vicinity of the lake.

This was the routine of an Issati camp in winter. Early each morning, the chief of the hunt would summon the hunters and advise them in the intricacies of the day's venture. Together, they would decide who would hunt with whom, and where, and what strategy they should use. On the second morning, Shining Heart gestured to Garamond and gave him to understand that he might accompany two of the young men with his musket. Every morning, this same invitation was offered. At first, Garamond's agitation was extreme because he had never taken a shot at an animal on the move, and of course, except for the moose and one hare, his luck had been abysmal indeed. Right away, he was offered the use of a bow, but he ruefully waved it away, saying, "*Ah non*, I am sorry *Messieurs*. I cannot use that thing." They did not bother to hide their scorn. But he was to fire his musket, should the arrows of his companions miss.

These forays into the world of hunting, especially of hunting deer, fascinated Garamond of Anjou. He and the two young men ate nothing and spoke little from their leaving the camp in the morning until their return in the dark. Garamond watched them avidly, trying to copy their moves and follow their cues, but he could not hide his own blunders. They would exchange a sardonic glance, and later report all the ignorant *Français* had done to Shining Heart and the elders. Shining Heart would sigh, but again the next day he bade them take Garamond on the hunt.

Then late one day, in the pearly, whispery dusk that suffused a broad marsh, they surprised a doe. The Issati hunters drew and shot two arrows so swiftly that Garamond saw just a blur of singing tension let go; he turned to see the doe pierced. Away she bounded into a grove of small balsams and the hunters raced after. There was only a little daylight left by then, and the red of blood on the snow quickly faded to gray, but they did not lose the trail of the doe. Soon they found her, breathing her last on a deep drift of snow. Garamond caught up to them just as the creature died. He heard them speaking reverently to the body. Then they carried it back to the camp, nearly a league away in the night.

The Issatis' sojourn in that place lasted as long as it took for the half moon to wax full. Then they moved again, west, for they were returning to their summer home. The journey was sometimes very hard. In the wet of a winter thaw, the snow would sink into itself, opaque and deep white, and lay siege to their snowshoes and sleds. The heat turned straw-colored grasses to old gold and copper, and streaked the bark of trees with snowmelt. Soon the people were panting and sweating, though no one complained. Garamond watched the snow stick to the webbing of his *raquettes*, piling heavier and heavier until, with a grunt, he would pause to shake it off with a great snap. Before long, he mastered this snapping gait and, when climbing, the crucial reverse scoop, and then his progress improved. But the thongs binding his feet stretched endlessly and he had to tighten and re-tie them each hour. It was the same for everyone. Almost as soon as the sun turned west, Shining Heart gave the signal to camp.

The relief, the joy of stopping! The relief of bending one's will to the forces of nature! Their spirits rose and the camp materialized on high, piney ground. In a while, after all was arranged, the women set themselves to mend moccasins and mind the fires, while the men gathered to be taught the secrets of the *Français* musket. The children and even the dogs looked on with barely contained excitement. Garamond, proud of this chance to prove his worth, took the greatest of pains to explain—by gesture and unintelligible French—the operation and dangers of the musket.

He demonstrated once, then offered the weapon to Mamehnese, an expert archer and respected warrior. This man was truly great in the sense that, in spite of his skill and confidence, he was humble and allowed himself to be taught. He did exactly as Garamond and fired an experimental shot into the forest. To the great mirth of all, the kick of said shot knocked him unceremoniously on his butt. Mamehnese only laughed at himself and tried again. And so the afternoon passed pleasantly. The musket traded hands so many times that Garamond began to worry about his powder supply, so he caught Shining Heart's eye and tried to pantomime an empty horn. He needn't have bothered, for Shining Heart and all the Issatis understood the constraints of ammunition—so difficult to obtain. Now fate had given them this young *Français* man and his musket. They would not waste the powder, nor the lead, nor even the young man's patience, for they were resolved to save his gifts for more important concerns, such as war.

There followed a period of change, in which winter days alternated with days of warmth and melting, and so the season of hunting wound down. The band of Issatis and their guest worked their way west and then south, all the way to the villages of home, set like embers in a maze of woods, lakes, and wild rice marshes. West beyond the Issati villages stretched a windswept land of prairie, for they dwelt near the border of east and west.

Yellow Deer took Garamond to live with her in the village of Issati and treated him like a son. Shining Heart, her brother, lived nearby with his family and all the others. There were some sixty people in all. Garamond was assigned a mentor to instruct him in the Dakota language spoken by the Issatis and their close relations. This mentor was a severe young man, a relative of Yellow Deer's whom Garamond was taught to address as *Mitahansi*, "my cousin." It turned out the language lessons were fun, though difficult, and to his surprise, he established an excellent rapport with his teacher, as well as the children who followed him everywhere. They would stroll as a group through the village and along the paths in the woods and name everything that came to hand. "*Taketchiabihen?*" he would ask. "What is it called?" They would answer in a chorus, *canghasang*, "sugar maple;" *ona*, "campfire;" *chingcha*, "baby;" *mde*, "lake." Every day Garamond wished vainly for paper and ink, fearing his memory couldn't hold all the words. But they scorned him for worrying. Mitahansi would say, "You have need of devices, but we do not. Are you stupid? Or is it a characteristic of all the *Français?*" Although Garamond didn't understand all the words, he caught the gist well enough. So he would set the young man a difficult sentence in French. Mitahansi would try it bravely, and to Garamond's disgust, succeed in disentangling the best part.

Fortunately, Garamond could call up what skills he'd learned, so long ago it seemed, from his Uncle Romain. After all, the old Jesuit had pounded some Latin into his head, so he was not utterly at sea. He progressed in fits and starts, from vocabulary to common phrases to sentences. And, as Mitahansi was fascinated by the mysteries of French, they spurred each other on. Before anyone realized it was happening, the Issati children were shouting and joking in the pure accents of Anjou.

Sometimes Shining Heart and others of the people would sit in on the lessons. On one of these occasions, a warm drizzle had driven them inside a *cabane*, fragrantly strewn with cedar. Shining Heart sat to one side with his brothers and nodded encouragingly, so Garamond summoned all of his knowledge of Dakota to inquire, as best he could, about other *Français* traders. He started by dropping the name of the Sieur du Lhut.

"Yes, we have met him. He is a brave man, very sober. Yes, we love him very much. And you, do you love him, Garamond?"

"*Ah non*, I have never met him, though I am sure to someday. He is my countryman, you know, and so, you could say I love him." Garamond laughed at the unusual words. "Are there others who have come here to Issati?"

"Yes. There was D'noyon, Mahress, Puroh, and—" Shining Heart paused, trying to remember. No one mentioned Hennepin, and Garamond, unwilling to bring up the priest's difficulties, let it pass.

Shining Heart said, "I don't remember the others. They have all seemed very vigorous, but not as pretty as you."

Garamond flushed scarlet. He was not sure he had heard right, but the round of chuckling made him think he had. He thought, They are toying with me! He said in French, "Perhaps if you guide me to my countrymen, I could get more trade goods, eh? Would you like that?" Then he told them about the cache, and nodded to Mitahansi to translate.

"Mm," his young teacher listened to their answer. "They say we will talk about it sometime, perhaps this summer, before we go to hunt buffalo." He pantomimed the horns of a buffalo. "And then we will hunt our enemies!" Shining Heart and his brothers smiled. But Garamond did not understand the word for "enemies."

It seemed, in these last days of winter, that the whole village was at leisure. Men rested, women chatted, and all worked at sundry mellow tasks. It was the time between seasons when food—meat from the hunt and last year's rice and roots—was scarce, and all watched for signs of spring. They noted the shoots and limbs of willows turning bright gold and days growing ever longer. Just a half a league from the village, was a thick grove of sugar maples on high ground. There came at last a stretch of warm sunny days and freezing nights when the trees, like sleeping beauties, awoke. Many of the people moved up to the woods at once, for the sap would run for only, perhaps, a fortnight. One breezy morning, those left in the village awoke to the sound of ice out—a tinkling soup of ice fragments jangling pleasantly at the shore of the lake. The men took to the water again to spear for walleyed pike. The best marksmen stalked the hordes of returning ducks, and still others went trapping. Garamond, to his relief, went with these, for spearing or bow-hunting was too fine a work for his eyes. Instead, he trailed after Mitahansi's long-suffering grandfather and learned where to lay traps for muskrat and beaver. Much of the land of the Issatis was low and marshy and hard of access if one didn't know the trails, but Garamond's companion knew every inch.

Now in all this time, the old woman Yellow Deer had treated Garamond with loving care. "*Mitchinchi*" she called him. And he knew that meant "my son." But soon after the sugar camp, he discovered that this endearment was more than casual. The occasion was the arrival of a large group of Dakota who'd paddled up the Rivière de St. François from their homes in the south. In greeting these people, Shining Heart singled out Garamond, and announced, "Behold our good fortune; we have encountered a *Français* trader, and our beloved Yellow Deer wishes to adopt him as her own son." There ensued a round of congratulations, embraces, and tears.

Garamond bore it all with mounting alarm. He smiled and nodded, but as soon as he could get away, he ran to seek Mitahansi. "What do they mean, her actual son? That is absurd! You must tell me what all this means, *je t'en prie*!"

Mitahansi regarded him critically and said, "Yellow Deer saved you, *Français*. And the elders judged her worthy of adopting you. It is to ease her grief for her son who died tragically when she was young."

"But I do not want— I am a trader! I do not want—"

Mitahansi drilled him with his eyes. "You were lost, weren't you?"

"Yes, yes, but—"

"You should not be ungrateful."

"Oh yes, but I am a trader, and besides, I have my own *maman* at home in France." He crossed himself, then felt ridiculous, and said, "What if I don't agree?"

"Then you must leave, I suppose. And that may not be possible," Mitahansi glanced away, "so soon."

Garamond said nothing, but stared at the young man before him. He thought, There are many things going on here, and I must take care—great care. He asked, "How did the child die?"

"There was an illness and many of the people died. It was long ago, long before I was born." He shot Garamond a look. "Yellow Deer's grief was very great! You should be kind to her as she has been kind to you."

Garamond swore, then forced a smile. Bah! he thought, It cannot be helped.

After the elders had shared tobacco, everyone scattered to make ready for a night of dancing. Finery appeared from hidden corners and transformed the people into fantastic creatures of color and ornament. Men's hair sprouted feathers, and stars and moons of copper hung from their ears. Garamond wore his necklace of sable stones and, reluctantly at first, gave himself to the spirit of the party. He made himself embrace Yellow Deer, admitting silently that she was a fine old lady, after all. He even sat by her throughout the feast, sharing delicious morsels, for he was a prudent *Anjevin* peasant, and believed in hedging his bets. But when the dancing began, he edged away and stood in the back, all the better to study his saviors—his captors?—and to consider his fate.

The question was, how could he find his way to a trading post? To Chegouwameeagan, or the Sault, or even back to Missilimacki-nac? He had a small but real store of furs to send back to Cornet, and then of course, he should retrieve his cache and obtain more trade goods. And then he could proceed. That was the plan. But how could he get the plan back from the Dakota, who seemed to have plans of their own? What if they should keep him forever? Ga-ramond could not deny the attraction—they were superb—but he knew in his heart it would not do. Even as he stood there, watching the exuberant dancers of Issati, he felt the pull of journeying and riv-ers, and the company of the *coureurs de bois*. He thought, I must just bide my time and make myself useful here, and something is bound to come up. Then, feeling a measure of peace in this decision, his attention focused on the dancers. For he had learned to be patient and to set aside greed.

By then, the women were dancing, and he soon fell under their spell. Their movements, in complete contrast to the men, were subtle and slow. They appeared to be almost still, while the fringes of their dresses swept the ground in perfect rhythm to the Issati drums.

"*Mon Dieu*, they are beautiful," said Garamond to the man beside him. The man glanced at him sideways and smiled.

Later, Garamond caught the eye of one of the young woman dancers, not for the first time. She was elfin small with a slow, devastating smile. Far at the edge of the light of the fires, he took her hand and pulled her away. The night was deliciously cold and their breath made a sinuous cloud between them. She slipped a wafer of maple sugar between his lips, where it melted, and then there was really no good way to stop. They were lucky and their coupling went undiscovered. But after, to his chagrin, the girl never looked at him twice. In fact, if he ever again tried to catch her eye, her lovely face would simply freeze, save for the barest hint of panic, for the Dakota took the chastity of their women very seriously. So Garamond had to be satisfied with one night. So much, he thought, for the wanton ways of the *sauvages*.

The last of the snow did not melt away until the spring equinox was long gone. Then, in a matter of days, the forest floor bloomed in a deep layer of pink and white flowers, and the birds of summer returned. Soon the night marshes rang with the calls of diminutive, amorous frogs. Mitahansi taught all these things to Garamond: the name of each plant and each creature, their habits, and every mood of the weather. Then Garamond would tell of his step-father's farm in Anjou, of Little Ugly's journey to the Poitou, and the miseries of sea-faring, which last he exaggerated shamelessly. Their command of Dakota and French grew so quickly then that they and the *troupe* of children jabbered together quite easily in a loud *mélange* of the two tongues. Garamond never tired of hearing the Issatis speak of their travels; how they followed the plants and animals, each according to season in an endless cycle. He felt, when he listened to these tales, a stirring of memory, as if some ancient part of him recognized this life, and he wondered if he could ever again be a farmer.

Shining Heart one day took a hand in Garamond's instruction. He brought him into his own spacious *cabane*, and spent a morning explaining the Dakota world in which they lived: that they called themselves after the *mde wakan*, the sacred lake north of the village; that they were the forebears of all the Dakota; and that their close relatives were the Mantantonwan, the Wahpetonwan, the Wahpekute, the Sisetonwan, and that far away dwelt their Tinthonha relatives on the great prairie.

Then Shining Heart asked Garamond to explain the relations and origins of the *Français*. But poor Garamond did not know where to begin. He tried several tacks, always avoiding the controversies of religion and the vagaries of war, and he ended by saying that the Sun King had inherited his throne from an unbroken line of Sun Kings to the beginning of time, and that his own people had lived in Anjou forever.

"That is, Monsieur, so far as I know."

Shining Heart looked at him askance, apprehending well that this was a child's story, and waited.

After an uncomfortable moment, Garamond added, unwillingly, "But you know, there are very many of us, Monsieur, and the Sun King is very rich." He sighed, wondering how he could turn the conversation to trade, for of that, at least, he could offer some insight.

"Mm." Shining Heart regarded him and read his mind, and said, "Someday, you may return to the *Français* traders and procure for us some things."

"*Mais oui!* That is my great hope!"

"For our enemies lie on our north and our south and all of our east, and they are armed with *Français* weapons. I wish you to help us in these matters, Garamond, for we would take you into our family. You will fight with us. Tell me of your cache on the Rivière du Fond du Lac."

Garamond felt his mouth go dry. He could think of nothing to say and only continued to stare at Shining Heart. Mitahansi coughed at his side, and then Shining Heart smiled broadly and patted his arm.

"We will talk another time, I think. I can see that your teacher here," he nodded at Mitahansi, "is very strict. I must let you get back to your lessons."

Mitahansi rose casually and ushered Garamond from the *cabane*. They walked away in silence to Yellow Deer's fire. Then Mitahansi grabbed Garamond's arm and said, "You must get the muskets for us, *Français*! Then you and I will fight side by side as warriors!" His eyes gleamed with hope and with a will too fierce, Garamond thought, for so young a man.

For the better part of several days, Garamond thought of nothing but Shining Heart's request, the ramifications of which were pregnant with risk. If only Miron were here now! What would he say? What would he do? Garamond was quite sure that he, himself, did not want to be mired in the wars of the Indians. Had he not just barely escaped the Sun King's army? He had come here to be a trader!

But Miron's advice was gone forever, so Garamond knew he would have to set his own course. He thought, I am indebted to them! I am practically Yellow Deer's son, and as such, I must defend her and this village from enemies. It is only right! It is also right that the Dakota be armed as well as their enemies. They should not be slaughtered like dogs!

The crux of the matter, he knew, was that he himself was not a warrior, and he was not Dakota. And he did not want those things.

So he devised a practical plan. One evening, he approached Shining Heart and said, "Monsieur, I have been thinking, and I would like to talk with you."

Mitahansi was sent for, and the three withdrew to a quiet spot nearby.

Garamond began, "Monsieur, I have two more muskets hidden near the mouth of the Rivière du Fond du Lac, and I would get them for you, if you let me."

"Two muskets would help us very much, Garamond. We have need of many more."

"Some of my people would trade muskets for furs, although, although—" He paused a moment to choose his words. "Although it would have to be carefully done, Monsieur, so as not to be known by your enemies." Our allies, he thought grimly.

Shining Heart scrutinized Garamond's face. "You would go to the *Français* traders, and then you would return to us?"

"I do not know the way, but I could learn, Monsieur. I would come back to you once—"

Mitahansi's eyes grew wide, and Shining Heart smiled the barest smile.

"And then, Monsieur, I would return to my countrymen and set up as a trader. Perhaps there are many things the Dakota would trade for their furs. Things that are easier to get than muskets, eh?"

"Mm," Shining Heart nodded, "I will think about your idea. In the meantime, two of our young men will go to your cache for you, and bring it back here. For it is a difficult journey and we don't wish to lose you."

With that, the discussion ended. Three days later, Garamond watched as the Issati men paddled away for his cache, its location described with every detail he could remember. They would go and see if his word was true, and all he could do was wait.

"Don't worry, *Français*," Mitahansi said earnestly. "If they find it, Yellow Deer will adopt you and get you a wife."

About the time that the cattails came into new green, the men of Issati decided to hold an archery contest, and invited all the people in the villages nearby. The presence of the *Français* was explained again and again, and Garamond grew proficient in pretending to love Yellow Deer. It seemed that most were fooled. But there were some who spoke openly against him, muttering that he was a friend to their foes, likely a spy, or worse, a conjurer sent to plague them. One of these suspicious men was called Wasu, a broad-shouldered man of the village, who had never trusted Garamond. His *cabane* was far from Yellow Deer's, nearer the water. His young wife was called

Sitka Toh, and her younger sister lived with them. On the last day of the contest, Wasu taunted Garamond—again—for his miserable skill with the bow.

"What does that eye of yours see, *Français*? What good is a man who can't see his target?"

"Well you know, Monsieur, I just have to practice. Maybe I should practice on you, eh?" People laughed, but Garamond glanced around for a way out. He could not see Shining Heart or his brothers or any of Yellow Deer's relations. He thought, *Quel crétin.* But I am alone, I will have to put up with this brute. He smiled and said, "You never know when the lessons will take. It was the same when I learned the musket. I'm very good at that right now, Monsieur."

Wasu sneered. A man from the village of Ouadebaton laughed loudly, breaking the evil spell. People began to disperse. Garamond did not show his relief, but his gaze swept the scene, registering the face of each person. He was brought up short then, as he looked briefly into the eyes the young woman, Sitka Toh. It was not pity that he saw there, or admiration, or amusement, or dislike. It was rather, recognition, as if from some other life. Or, perhaps that was only his imagination. He turned to follow the contestants to the archery ground, but he glanced her way again, just once. She did not see him.

The visitors left for home the next morning, leaving a feeling of sudden quiet and intimacy in their wake. The village was, after all, very small. It seemed that, in the course of a day, Garamond saw Sitka Toh at every other turn, but of course they never spoke to each other. He could not help bending his thoughts toward her, willing her to look his way or to pass nearer. She could not help but to feel his will, and so she put her child between them, or stayed with the women. Soon, the women were aware of the new situation, and then Wasu, and finally, everyone in Issati was, too. First there were chuckles, then innuendo. Wasu put up a good show of scowling and stalking about, but really he was pleased that the famous *Français* guest should think his own wife so desirable. Garamond shrank into himself with embarrassment.

He was acutely aware that the bond between husband and wife was sacred, and that Wasu was a formidable man, and that all was hopeless. Shining Heart spoke to him of finding a suitable match—"Which maiden do you like, my son?"—but Garamond could think of none. When Mitahansi's grandfather offered to take him on a fishing trip to the upper creeks, Garamond leapt at the offer. But the trip lasted only two days.

Summer began in earnest then, so people stayed in the shade when they could, working steadily and telling tales. Hunting and fishing parties came and went, as ever, and Garamond did his best to help. He and Sitka Toh tried to avoid each other, in a sort of invisible dance, until, by chance, they met one day, down in the steaming marshes. Or was it by design that they put themselves in the way of chance? Who can say? Garamond took the chance and drew near her, and whispered, "Sitka Toh."

She looked away, and then she looked back.

Stepping close, he brushed her face lightly and said, "Sitka Toh is a beautiful name."

"You must not approach me," she said, very softly. But her eyes said otherwise.

He knew he should leave her alone. And yet, those eyes. He was sure he could feel the heat of her body. With great effort, he turned to go, but then—to his joy—her hand shot out and touched his arm. They embraced and kissed for the space of seven, sacred heartbeats. Hearing voices, they parted. But they were found standing in the trail, staring at each other with sheer longing. There was no hope of fooling anyone, and, in a matter of hours, every person in the village of Issati was discussing the shameful affair.

The elders quickly took over. That it was a special case was understood by all, but that didn't mean the rules of society could be cast off. Wasu, in a rage, threatened to kill Garamond and to disfigure his wife, though no one took him seriously. But he did beat her. All agreed it was a terrible misfortune for Sitka Toh. But it would not do to vex the young man either, for what of the muskets? The elders talked, and the lovers were chastised and kept far apart. As if weighing in, the weather turned hot and humid.

In the middle of everything and with great fanfare, the two young men returned with the contents of Garamond's cache heaped perilously in their canoe. They had found it! So amongst all the other emotions that strove within him, there was also relief, for his word was proved beyond doubt. In short order, Shining Heart arranged for Yellow Deer's formal adoption of the *Français*—they would have a feast of roast meats and stew and young *psinchincha*, dug from the shallow lake. Yellow Deer was arrayed in a generous length of Bernard Cornet's *écarlatine* cloth, just a little stained, and food and beautiful furs of all kinds were offered in exchange for Garamond's goods. Thus was the old woman's *cabane* enriched. Except that Wasu took the large kettle for only a few small pelts. Garamond could say nothing to that.

They pressed him now to choose a maiden for a wife and so tie all his new bonds to these people as tight as could be. Still he resisted. So Shining Heart offered two choices to Garamond of Anjou.

"Soon the people will go south to hunt buffalo," said the elder. "You may come with us, for we would not leave you here all alone. And when, as always, we encounter our enemies, perhaps you will fight bravely. Or perhaps we will encounter your countrymen, and then you may go with them. But remember," and Shining Heart paused to look gravely at Garamond, who chafed, but met his gaze, "Remember that Yellow Deer needs your help as you needed hers once. If you go with the *Français*, go to trade, and then come back to us with your goods. And your muskets."

Preparations for the move south began within days, for the Mdewakantonwan were already late. Garamond, however, had one other idea for his future. He had not forgotten Sitka Toh. He thought, Perhaps she would leave that man and come with me! I must speak with her soon, in private, and come to an agreement. Then, we'll be ready should we find the *coureurs de bois*. He clenched his fists with hope.

But, try as he might, he could not get near Sitka Toh. Finally, after failing to meet her when she went to the bushes—she was escorted even there—he enlisted the aid of one of the children of the little band of linguists. This boy idolized Garamond and—poor thing!—could not resist the *Français'* call for aid.

"Go to Sitka Toh and tell her to come before sunrise to the canoes, and we will paddle onto the lake, and," Garamond hesitated, "and we will talk." The little boy's eyes grew big, but he slowly nodded, his heart bursting with pride to be entrusted with this most secret, dangerous mission.

He succeeded. In the last hour before dawn, Garamond and Sitka Toh met again in the marshes by the lake. Stealthily they took a canoe and set it in the water. When they'd paddled far enough away from shore that they could speak without being heard, Garamond said, "Sitka Toh, that man doesn't treat you so well. Wouldn't you rather come with me? We could live at Missilimackinac. I will be a great trader and you will live like a queen."

She laid down her paddle and laughed quietly, then turned around so they faced each other from opposite ends of the canoe.

"What is a queen, *Français*?"

There were several arm-lengths between them. He knew that the deerskin dress she wore was velvety smooth, and that her skin was warm and soft, and that, if he were holding her, his fingers might not tell which was which. But he ached to try. She regarded him with eyes so wistful, that he already knew her answer.

They floated there and spoke little, but watched the sunrise and trailed their hands in the water. They watched snow-white pelicans hunting fish in the shallows. They witnessed the birth of a breeze out of nowhere that stirred the reeds and the rice, and gently rocked their canoe.

"Could you not come away with me?"

"No." She shook her head sadly.

As the light gathered, they could see that people had come to stand on the shore. Then two canoes put on to the lake. Garamond could tell at a glance that Shining Heart and Sitka Toh's uncle paddled in one of them. They began to move purposefully, but unhurriedly, toward the fugitives.

"We could go together to Missilimackinac—"

She was silent, as he knew by then she would be. She was already composing herself for the punishment to come. He ran his hands through his hair, sighing in frustration, then stared at the bottom of the canoe. So their last minutes together slid away. They waited for the canoes to come, and drifted, and watched the white pelicans fly up and spiral into the sky, out of reach.

27.

Grand Père Shows Up

Summer 1690

By the coming of the summer solstice and the long, long days, the Dakota were streaming south on their river, the Rivière des Issatis, embedded in marshes and swamps. They had a long way to go, farther than usual, to the very threshold of the Illinois, their enemies, for they wished to expand their summer hunting territories. This, their only recourse, for the northernmost reaches of the buffalo country became less friendly to the Dakota with each passing year.

Garamond paddled with Mamehnese and his brother, not among Shining Heart's people, but with the hundreds led by Ouasicondé, the great Pierced Pine, foremost of all the Mdewakanton Dakota. Garamond was relieved to be among people he did not know, save for Mamehnese, who treated him with kindness and a certain amount of sympathy. He was allowed to sit quietly, if he only paddled very well, and listen to the conversations around him. His thoughts drifted here and there, but always returned to Sitka Toh. He realized that Mamehnese and the others were trying to distract him with their talk of hunting and raiding. They would say in so many words, "We will find you a woman, *Français*, maybe more than one. Are you content?"

He ignored them. He was content to be paddling the canoe, anes-thetized in its rhythm. But at night, when all the people slept away their exhaustion, he would lie awake in a kind of anguish, thinking of her and all of his choices. Only once he said to Mamehnese, "I did not expect this—" and he stared, helpless for a moment, at the Dakota warrior. Mamehnese, in the prime of his life, had two wives and honor and skill in all things. He remembered how long ago, the only woman who existed in the world had despised him, and he embraced Garamond, and pressed his forehead against the young man's. But that only happened once.

The river passed out of the marshes and turned sharply east, then sharply south again. Some seventy leagues from the villages of Is-sati, they descended upon the broad Messipi, and here they stopped for a while to rest and to gather birch bark in the woods. It was the best season in which to harvest bark, for with care, the taking would not kill the tree, and so they hoped to obtain favor for their journey. The days turned cool, the sky dove gray, and soon rain sifted down on the luminous green forest. Garamond spent entire days in the woods, slicing the bark and carefully peeling it away, crisp and wet, and bearing it back to the camps. He was forced by fatigue, at last, to sleep. Then down they went on the river, a floating nation, heading south and southeast.

Not much farther on, they portaged around the great waterfall of which Father Hennepin had written, and after that, they kept to the islands and western shore. They set watch at night and sent forth their scouts in the day, and softened the noise of their passage as best they could. A great river joined them from the west, and some of the people went thither to hunt, but Garamond and Mamehnese and most of the others continued down the swollen Messipi east and south. Here, it seemed to Garamond that his companions grew ever more solicitous of his good will, and he wondered what lay ahead.

"Do you still love us, *Français?*" they would ask, and, "Have you forgotten your troubles?" and, "Will you stay with us and help us?" "Tell us," they insisted, "what is in your heart."

He put them off, not knowing, in truth, what was in his heart. In fact his confusion only deepened until all he could do was sit mute and glower. So they stopped asking, and he noticed that a space seemed more and more to appear between him and the people. It was about then that they encountered the old man.

First they saw his beard, immense and white. He was waiting in an eddy on the shore, at the point of the confluence between the Messipi and another great river from the north. He was waiting there in the eddy with Shining Heart and Ouasicondé and others of the Mdewakanton men. He was alone in a sprightly bark canoe.

"Look," Mamehnese exclaimed, "It is Tugan! Well, we did not foresee that, *Français*," and he slapped Garamond's shoulders. "You are saved, it seems."

"Who—!" Garamond almost stood in the canoe until they shouted and pulled him back. From across the water came the sound of the old man's laughter.

"Bonjour, Jean Garamond!"

"Bonjour! Bonjour Monsieur! Heh!"

Garamond dug his paddle in the water with all his might. They wheeled into the eddy as the old man beamed encouragement. He was, Garamond was amazed to see, resplendent in quillwork, intricate embroidery, and gorgeously dressed skins. His face was ancient, but his body was strong and barrel-shaped, and he held his canoe in place effortlessly. He said in elegant, courtly French, "We have been waiting for you, my young friend. We," he gestured to the eminent men of the Mdewakantonwan, "will now have a consultation on your behalf, in this very place, for you will not go south, after all. You will go north with me."

Garamond could only sputter. They all went ashore on the point of land and gathered in a stately circle to smoke. A young warrior tenderly rubbed the old man's legs with bear grease, and then a regal wife of Ouasicondé brought out and unwrapped a bundle. Inside were a Jesuit cassock and prayer book. The old man nodded pleasantly and patted her head. She rewrapped the items and disappeared. Garamond felt he would burst with the mystery of it all, but he closed his eyes, gulped, and stayed still. Everyone regarded him with amusement for a moment, and then Ouasicondé and the old man began to converse in a language Garamond did not know, but guessed was akin to Ottawa. They droned on and on, all while Dakota canoes passed by and pulled onto the banks at the confluence, until the camp stretched down both sides of the Messipi, like two ribbons of ivory beads. Garamond could only catch the name, "Chegouwameeagan," uttered thrice, and each time, his heart pounded with hope. By then, he knew quite well what was in his heart. He wanted more than anything to go north with the old man and forget all about the Dakota Sioux.

They were allowed to leave just as the sun set in an amber sky. Garamond's things were transferred to the old man's canoe, then they slipped into the eddy and rounded the point. The Dakota watched them go in silence, and very quickly the sprightly canoe disappeared in the dusk, angling upstream on the Rivière Saint Croix. The old man refused to speak, so they paddled until night fell thick and black. At last, Garamond jumped out and dragged the canoe and the old man to shore.

"Who are you, Monsieur?" he demanded, a little roughly, and then, "What happened back there!"

"*Calmez-vous.*" With a groan, the old man climbed up the bank, leaving Garamond to bring up the canoe and the gear.

"Well, Monsieur?"

"You may call me Grand Père, as everyone does in the north. No, no, don't thank me—thank our blessed Sainte Anne this day for your deliverance. Oh, my weary bones! Help me, my little child."

"Grand Père? But I have many grandfathers already, more than I can count. What is your real name? And what have you to do with the Jesuits?" Garamond felt a twinge of guilt and alarm. Incongruously, he saw his mother's face, but blinked it away.

"Grand Père is good enough for the likes of you. I have the privilege of calling myself old *barbon*, and the Dakota have the privilege of calling me Tugan, but you shall call me Grand Père like all the others. Besides, you know, I have outlived everyone who knew me by another name." He laughed, then winced. "Oh, my old bones."

"Well then, how did you arrange all this?"

"I have been trained in the art of diplomacy, of course."

"You are a Jesuit!"

"At one time. By the way, you are under a very dire obligation to procure armaments for the Dakota. And to provide for the old woman, one Yellow Deer, I believe. But don't worry, perhaps I can help you in these matters."

"Are we going to Chegouwameeagan?"

"Probably. The Lac Supérieur is many leagues north of here, but in good time, we shall grace its shore." Grand Père laughed again. "I knew you were here—we all heard of the young *Français* wendigo. You are famous, my son."

"Wendigo? Oh, you mean— But how did you know?"

"A few small parties of Sioux came down the rivers last month to trade with the Ojibwa while the truce holds. They brought tidings of a young *Français* called Garamond, whom was thought to have been lost—he and his partner." Grand Père looked sharply at his companion.

"May? They came down the rivers in May! To Chegouwameeagan?" Garamond smacked his fist on his knees.

"Perhaps they did not inform you."

"*Merde!*"

"And Michel Miron?"

Garamond took a deep breath. He could not see the old man's face in the dark. "Miron hit his head and died in his sleep. I buried him two days west of Chegouwameeagan. I lost the canoe in the Rivière du Fond du Lac and left most everything there."

Grand Père grunted. "And then you wandered, thinking to be a hero, to be rich, *n'est-ce pas?*"

"Yes, yes. I nearly starved, and then the Dakota found me and brought me to their villages. I had only a few things to trade when they found me, but they went back for my cache," Garamond made a wry face, "without me." He shrugged, and said, "Let us light a little fire, eh?"

"There is no need. You will grow used to the dark, and then we will only sleep for a while. We must move fast for a few days, at least until we pass the great falls, above. What else do you want to know?"

"Well, Monsieur, it still seems incredible that we found you."

"But the confluence is known to all. And if I had missed you, there are always the men at Perrot's little fort. You were only a day north of there—"

"What fort!"

"More than likely, they would have taken you under their protection. Perhaps no one informed you of the fort."

"Did not inform me—!" Garamond rose and viciously kicked at the bushes. Then he hurled a stone in the river and continued to seethe while the old man laughed.

"The Dakota are crazy! They thought I'd become one of them, you know. Marry some girl they would choose for me. Fight for them. Get muskets for them. Everything."

"Well, why not? What had they to lose by hoping?"

"And then you showed up. Why did you come all this way for me, Monsieur? I could have stayed at the fort, as you say."

"Well, first of all, it was my Christian duty, and then I admit I was curious. You see, my child, I have need of just such a one as you— strong and spirited, but perhaps wiser than you were a year ago, 'tempered,' shall we say?" The old man's beard glimmered whitely in the dark.

"And what do you need me for, old man?"

"You may address me as Grand Père. I believe I will die soon, perhaps within the year. I have built a thriving business in trade in this country, illegal, to be sure, but far more viable in the long run than most operations out here. I am looking for a successor. The candidate would accompany me this summer, very far north, to settle my affairs with the Cree. Tell me about your winter alone, young wendigo."

"Eh, what do you mean? Are you really dying?"

"Most likely."

Garamond peered into the gloom in the old man's direction. How can I trust him? he thought. All this talk of dying! But he has come for me and I should repay him.

He cleared his throat and said, "I must tell you I'm under contract with a merchant in Montréal. And, even though I have failed him miserably so far, I intend to fulfill my obligation. Eventually, that is." He laughed. "But I will prove to you all that I am an *homme honnête*, eh? Wait and see, Monsieur, I will not fail."

"I will help you if you will help me. If all goes well, God willing, in two years, your contract will be fulfilled and you may become my partner. What else would you like to know?"

"Countless things." Garamond leaned back against the broad trunk of a pine. He could feel his body relaxing. He heaved a huge sigh and closed his eyes for a moment. "You are well met, Monsieur Grand Père," he said.

They talked for hours that night, until the dew settled on their hair and their breath came in billows. Grand Père told of his winter trapping in the Cree lands, and how he'd pulled a sledge of the best furs to the trading post at Nipigon. And how in the spring, he'd sent them on to Missilimackinac with his associates from the east. Then, Garamond could only wonder how this man could be dying, but he said nothing. Grand Père went on to tell how he'd traded Cree medicines for corn and delicate, whorled shells from the sea, for he did not trade only for furs. Rather, he had joined the network of trade forged ages ago by the Indians, one that shared out the riches of the land, but did not seek to deplete it of any one thing. Grand Père's business was different—a finely wrought meld of Indian and *Français* concerns.

He said, "I am going now to Kitchi Gami, where I have left many bushels of beautiful corn and excellent English tobacco with some *coureurs de bois* whom I trust. We shall send your furs with them. But you and I shall take my goods to the Cree, and also retrieve my cache of all the furs I could not bring down to Nipigon. We will paddle a canoe, of course, for the entire way. And then we will come down to the Sault Sainte Marie, and then we will see what happens."

"You are a wonderful grandfather, Monsieur. I love the sound of all of it."

"So you consent?"

"*Bien sûr*. I can think of nothing better."

For a dying man, Grand Père proved to be a tireless *voyageur*. He was, in fact, impervious to fatigue or discomfort of any kind and would simply continue all day, and end the day as vigorously as he'd begun. He never stopped complaining of his aches and pains, and his imminent demise. "Oh my old bones!" he would say. "I creak, I rust!" Until Garamond rolled his eyes. But the old man kept up a steady patter of news for the benefit of his new *protégé*. He told of the eastern Indians and the Ottawas and the Hurons who all wished to make peace with the Iroquois, this in the wake of the disaster at Lachine, and how the French were hard-pressed to maintain their alliances. And how Joliet had, at great peril, journeyed from Missilimackinac to deliver similar tidings to the new *gouverneur* in Québec—the Comte de Frontenac. And how Frontenac had sent troops to Albany in the winter to stop the troubles at their source.

Grand Père knew all this from the far-flung traders, Indians, soldiers, and priests in the north, among whom news trickled like rain. Garamond would shout questions at intervals and try to digest it all. He was convinced the old man was just steering and lounging at his leisure in the stern of the canoe, and so, on a pretext, he would turn his head quickly to catch him, but never succeeded. Grand Père would always be paddling with gusto, smiling, and talking. So Garamond could not complain, but only continue toiling upstream. The Rivière Saint Croix was slow as a lake there, so they made good time.

On the third day, they came to a dark gorge of sheer pinnacles and walls of rock, where the river hurried and foamed, and here Grand Père decreed that they should stop early to climb the cliffs. "For the beautiful view," he said to Garamond's unvoiced question.

They made the canoe fast, and climbed through a fragrant forest of pine until they found a perch, high above the river. Here, the wind swept through the pines, and there were no bugs. The river glittered below, and to the west, the forest stretched all the way to the horizon, and melted there with the sky.

"What a fabulous land!" Grand Père exclaimed.

"It is like the Garden of Eden," said Garamond. Then he asked, "Monsieur, how did you come to be here? Here in this country?"

"I came as a missionary of course. Long ago, when Louis had just taken the reins of government, and the Society of Jesus was still very strong in New France. I journeyed west in much the same manner as you. Like you, I was lost in the forest. Quite near here, in fact. But it was summer. I believe I may have been delirious for a long time." Grand Père pitched a pebble off the cliff, and leaned forward, listening for the "ping."

"The Sioux found me, but unlike you, I did not stay with them. I was impelled by terrible dreams, perhaps for years. I lived like a wild man."

"*Mon Dieu*, Monsieur, I am sorry I asked."

Chuckling, the old man lay back on the rock, staring at the sky. "Do not be troubled, *mon ami*. But I was never the same after that. For one thing, I regained my strength. For another, I shed the machinations of my Order like the skin of a snake, though I am still a Christian man, despite everything. But my ideas of what that means—how to live—have changed."

"But how?"

"I do not know how to tell you, or perhaps I am lazy. Perhaps you will find out for yourself by watching what I do. Perhaps not." He turned, squinting at Garamond. "I must be honest with you; I was interested in your case specifically because of the winter you have just passed. I hope you will tell me about it. Tell me," he said with sudden intensity, "when you were alone all those weeks, did you see anything… odd? Devilish?"

"Well no." Garamond felt embarrassed and wary at the same time. "I admit I was scared as a *petite jeune fille*, sometimes!" He laughed. It all seemed so ridiculous now, but then he remembered a little more. "You know, Grand Père, there were times when it helped to sing hymns, eh? Maybe there were devils I didn't see."

Grand Père frowned, and looked back into the sky, so innocently blue. He said, "I know it is not in the nature of a young man like you to dwell on these things, but as a favor, I ask you to tell me, as it occurs to you, anything that seems pertinent. I still look everywhere for—" he paused, "for illumination, one could say. After all these years, it is still very confusing; perhaps none of it was real—"

"Eh, Grand Père, but your business is real enough, I hope."

"Don't worry, my child." Grand Père smiled and tossed another pebble off the cliff. "I deal in very real furs and real corn and what-not. You will see." He rose stiffly and, wheezing a little, started to pick his way down the cliff, not even looking to see if Garamond followed.

"But Grand Père, have you never thought to return to France? Or at least to Montréal? To Québec?"

"Never!" the old man shouted without looking up, "Never!"

"Is there nothing you miss?"

"Well—" The old man stopped to think for a moment. "Yes, I miss the music."

"What?"

"Did you never hear Mass at Angers?"

"How did you know—"

"From your accent, of course. I passed my novitiate at La Flèche. Were you ever there?"

So Garamond had to tell about his Uncle Romain and the never-ending essay on Nature, the farm, his family, and all the rest. They made camp by the river and built a sparkling fire, and talked the night away again. This plenitude of conversation was delicious to Garamond, despite the old man's strange questions. How exquisite to share all he'd been through with a countryman! At last, as they stretched out to sleep, he said, "Grand Père, I feel the same as you; I can never go back to what I was."

"No, none of us will ever be the same," came Grand Père's voice, rough with sleep. "The French, the English, all of the Indians. Everything has changed forever. Good night."

More than sixty leagues and ten days above its union with the Messipi, the Saint Croix rose in the lakes and marshes of its headwaters, and there they passed a miserable cabin, its timbers stained with wet, which Du Lhut had built seven years before. Nearby, they found the rutted portage trail ascending a steep ridge, and Grand Père and Garamond prepared to cross from the realm of the Messipi to that of the Lac Supérieur. In one trip, they carried their bundles and most of Garamond's furs, and left them in a pile half-way. Then they returned for the rest and the canoe, raised upon their shoulders. The trail was cut by ravines, and paralleled on their left by a long, open wetland, very beautiful and twinkling with springs.

When they reached the halfway point again, they carefully laid down their burdens and threw themselves down on the trail.

"I have been saving this," Grand Père announced, and he pulled from his bundles a flask of wine. With just the slightest expression of wickedness, he held out the flask to Garamond, but just beyond reach.

Garamond, eyes narrowed, ignored the flask and studied the old man. They held each other's stare a moment longer, Garamond thinking, You old bastard. What do you really want from me?

"Perhaps that wandering eye of yours does not see my flask of wine?"

Garamond smiled and stood up, towering over Grand Père's upturned, now guileless face. He reached down and swept the flask from the old Jesuit's hand. They both started to chuckle, low, and at last, comradely. Grand Père patted the ground beside him and Garamond sat back down. The moment was broken and they proceeded to drain the flask.

"A toast to you, old man."

"And to you, young oaf! Look, do you see that small lake? It drains to both rivers. From here on, everything flows to the Atlantic, think of that. Another toast, my young friend, to the Rivière aux Aunages, may it bear us safely these next few days."

"You know, Grand Père, I am sure that must be the river that Miron and I passed in the winter—it is the Nemissakouat to the Dakota."

"Yes it is the same. It is fair enough, but the very devil to paddle. There are numerous rapids, especially farther down. We shall have to work in concert."

"Oh, *formidable*! I love the rapids! You know, coming west with the Ottawa, they only put me in the middle. I could do nothing but paddle straight forward or backward, or take orders from Miron: 'Lean this way, lean that way, *mon petit!*'" Garamond frowned, wiped a trickle of wine from his beard, and said, "Still, he was a good man, Miron."

"No doubt." Grand Père took for himself the last swallow. "Come, let us finish the portage. We shall camp and start early tomorrow."

When Garamond thought next of Miron, it was to imagine his approval, for he and Grand Père were dancing down the Nemissakouat, mile after flawless mile. There were long, narrow lakes and beaver dams to haul over, but also mild rapids and windings in which to practice the strokes a bow paddler should know. He learned how to lean his body and the canoe, and to use the current instead of fighting it. Grand Père would ask, "What is the best route in this place?" Garamond would scrutinize the chutes and waves and mysterious frothing holes, and hazard a guess. Sometimes he was right, but more often Grand Père would correct him and say, "But see how the current will push us away from your route?" or, "It is too shallow in that channel to take a good stroke." Garamond longed to plunge through the wildest waves, but he knew that always their aim should be to stay dry and to save the fragile bark shell of the canoe.

In the afternoon, they paddled a long, twisting stretch of calm water, sheltered from the wind by thick forest. Families of ducks and mergansers hurried before them, until the mothers could stand no more and flew up and away, while their babies huddled in the reeds. The two men ignored them and swept by. Then the rapids began again and for almost a league they picked their way through continuous delights.

They camped above a large rapids that fell away in four stony ledges. As they cooked their supper that night, Grand Père said, "We have done well today, but the real test lies ahead. Be assured that if our canoe were filled with goods, we would be obliged to portage much of the rapids tomorrow. But we don't carry much on this trip and your furs are well covered, and so we shall chance it. I confess that I love to find the *fil d'eau*, safe but close to disaster, and to slide by harmlessly while the waves thunder there. It gives me a little thrill."

"You are full of surprises, old man."

"Who is not?" Grand Père smiled broadly and sipped his broth. "You must see that our paddles are like wings," he said. "Tomorrow I will teach you how to use them to make the canoe bank and hover in the water like a bird in the air. What do you say to that, *Anjevin*?"

"I think this is Heaven, of course."

And it seemed so, in the morning, as they ran the first rapids with exuberance and inspired skill. It seemed that all they did was perfect. Grand Père would shout instructions to Garamond, all while guiding the stern in deft, delicate counterpoint.

"Draw the bow left!" he would cry. "Now slow, slow! Wait for me to line up! Now drive into the eddy as I taught you!"

So Garamond dug in and leaned and felt with joy how the blade of his paddle stuck there in the water as if in earth, and the canoe spun round behind him until they were floating safely in the lee of a boulder and gazing upstream. He shook the spray from his eyes, amazed by the change of perspective. Then Grand Père called out, "Now, forward hard! Yes, just so! Now pull us around and back into the current— Lean into your turn— Ah! Well done!" And off they flew down the river.

Only a little ways on, there was another, larger set of ledges, and here Garamond paddled with all his might into the thick of the maelstrom. Perhaps he did not hear Grand Père's shouts. But after they'd shot through the waves, he found he could not turn the bow so easily, and in astonishment realized the canoe was flooded with clear, cold water, up to his seat. He could feel the old man's baleful eyes on his back, and so he labored to shore and leaped out to hold the bark from the rocks. Silently, they pulled out the soaking bundles and turned the canoe to empty it.

"Please, please, no damage," Garamond murmured. There was none that could not be easily fixed, and so he felt it was a miracle. But as he crossed himself and raised his sorry eyes to heaven, Grand Père aimed him a hard cuff and yelled, "*Imbécile*!" in his ear.

"Oh all right, I'm sorry old man, but there's no harm done—"

"No harm!" Grand Père was still for a moment, his outrage overpowering his speech, then he renewed his blows and drove his young apprentice into the woods. "May the flies and the bears devour you!" he yelled after the retreating form. Garamond did not dare to return for an hour.

He was more cautious after that and the rest of the day went well. The rapids gentled, and steep red banks rose on either side of them, and the water grew cloudy with clay. Grand Père lectured and complained of his aching bones, but would not allow any stopping.

"We will dry your things on the beach at the mouth of the river," he said gruffly. "You have some good pelts there. Besides, my associates will be waiting." He snorted. "Wait until they see what a careless brute I've brought with me. Oh they will laugh!"

Prudently, Garamond did not reply.

As dusk approached, they turned a bend in the river and felt the first breeze from the lake. There was no fragrance in it, but rather a clarity as if blown over snow. The shadows deepened to blue and they heard the whisper of surf, and then they turned a last corner and the Lac Supérieur opened before them. Carefully, they maneuvered through the turbulence at the mouth of the river, and turning east along the shore, they spied a campfire, like a bright star on the beach.

"Eh! Giroux, Saint Pierre! Eh!" Grand Père bellowed, causing Garamond to nearly drop his paddle.

"You have healthy lungs for an old goat," he muttered, but his spirits rose as answering shouts floated over the water.

The associates had wintered in the south and journeyed to Chegouwameeagan to meet the old man in the spring. Then, hearing of the lost *Français*, they'd all three gone to the Rivière aux Aunages. Giroux, a burly Frenchman from Brittany, and Saint Pierre, a French-Huron *métis*, had waited there on the beach for twenty-two days, trading with passing canoes and fishing in the river. It had been very fine, they informed Grand Père and Garamond after introductions were exchanged. But now they were anxious to be off, for they'd received news of a large convoy of canoes gathering at Missilimackinac to go down to Montréal in force, and thus make their way through the Iroquois gauntlet. Everyone in the west was starved for French trade goods and glutted with fur—some pelts two or even three years old, and some sure to go to waste. And though they were three hundred leagues away, everyone heard in their heads the clamoring of the eastern merchants.

"The new *gouverneur* has sent Louvigny to take over the post from our good Durantaye, and so he and anyone who can make it in time shall go down," Giroux explained. "We did not want to wait for you, Grand Père, when we heard. Of course we stayed to watch your goods. Will you go on to the Cree or come down in the convoy with us?"

"As you know, I have no use for the settlements. I shall go to the

Cree as planned, but you shall take down my best pelts from Chegouwameeagan. *D'accord?*"

"Yes, we can do that in the usual way. But what about the *Anjevin?* He goes with you?"

They all looked at Garamond, his face, like theirs, lit up by the fire and the talk. He cleared his throat nervously. "*Eh bien*, I'm not sure—" He was thinking of his pile of sopping furs and the certain wrath with which Cornet would greet him. He said, "I've agreed to help Grand Père—"

"Oh yes, you shall be a great help, no doubt."

Giroux and Saint Pierre smirked.

"Do not fear," the old man continued, "You may still accompany me, and if you acquit yourself well, or at least better, you shall have something more to send down, perhaps before winter. Of course, I shall cut you in on the profits from my furs. But you must promise to learn everything I have to teach you, for you will not be familiar with my arrangements. I am no merchant's *engagé.*"

They decided that Garamond and Grand Père would go north to the Cree, and Giroux and Saint Pierre would go east, taking Grand Père's furs, and also Garamond's. As soon as they had access to pen and paper, a letter to Bernard Cornet would be composed with the following message: that Michel Miron had died in an accident and that Jean Garamond had endured many troubles, but he had found the Sioux (so to speak), and that he was safe and diligently pursuing Monsieur Cornet's interests; that said Jean Garamond has sent these furs as an advance return on Monsieur Cornet's investment, and that the balance shall be sent forthwith; *et cetera.* Or words to that effect. Giroux and Saint Pierre were to return north as soon as they could, their canoe replenished with French wares.

Garamond spent that night feeding an array of hot driftwood fires in an attempt to dry his furs, all while the others slept like babes. He had some success, and as Grand Père's associates packed their canoe in the dark of pre-dawn, Garamond made them promise to air the pelts whenever the wind should keep them on shore. To this, they agreed, for there was a measure of honor among *coureurs de bois*, and besides, they loved Grand Père well. And so, Giroux and Saint Pierre paddled away to the sunrise, leaving the old man and the young on the beach. Garamond turned his gaze west then, to the deep bay of the Rivière Saint Louis, his nemesis.

Grand Père said, "As always, the lake is most often calm in the evening and early morning, so we shall rise every day in the dark, and perhaps we shall paddle very late, and cook our food in the middle of the night. We stay or go by God's choosing, here. Do you understand?"

"I understand completely, *bien sûr*. I remember the Lac Supérieur very well."

"Well then, you shall load the canoe, *n'est-ce pas?* And do exactly as I say."

28.

Lichen

Summer 1992

I KNOW A thing or two about lichen by now, beyond the basics of what Irv had told me on the drive up to Pukaskwa. In fact, between our reference books and Nicolette's expertise, and not to mention all that crawling through the woods, I've picked up quite a bit for a middle-aged ex-housewife, waitress, and office gal.

Definition: a lichen is an association between a fungus and a photosynthesizing partner, usually an alga, but often a cyanobacterium. Or both. A lichen is alive—it can certainly be killed—but it is not an organism. It is classified, if anywhere, within the Kingdom of Fungi (the land of Irv), because the fungal partner is the distinguishing element in the concept that is lichen. Each "species" of lichen is therefore named after its fungal component, which comprises up to 80 percent of the whole. The photosynthesizing partner is known as the "photobiont" and usually hails from only a few different tribes: the *Trebouxia*, the *Nostoc*, the *Trentepohlia*. The fact that a lichen is an association and not an organism has caused serious consternation in the halls of taxonomy for over one hundred years.

It is, as they say today, a "miniature ecosystem." Or a perfect symbiosis. Or a state of "controlled parasitism." This last invites you to weigh the costs and benefits experienced by each partner. The fungus provides a comfortable, stable matrix in which the little photobionts may live. In return, they supply carbohydrates and sometimes nitrogen for the benefit of the fungus. The photobionts in their natural form are usually aquatic, i.e., algae, so in lichens, they can see the world, so to speak, albeit as captives of a fungus (what a fate!).

So, parasitism or symbiosis? You decide. I myself, after giving the matter considerable thought, have come to the conclusion that a lichen is not anything so much as a small but Bohemian party. And I have not even mentioned the gang of party-crashers, the various and diminutive members of the Kingdoms of Protista and Animalia; let us not name names. There may even be a moss or two hanging around. (But we ourselves are a party, too, as Nicolette gently informed me, with our "gut fauna" and our parasites. For example, the tiny fleas that we all have, scampering through our eyelashes at night. I can hear Grandma Beth: "How perfectly appalling!" Frankly, I prefer not to acknowledge that particular party.)

Lichen: It is in fact a shifting/dispersing/reorganizing party of organisms. If you don't quite believe that, consider this:

The union of a fungus and a photobiont results in a body—the thallus—that is completely different in form from its individual constituents on their own. The lichen thallus can range from a simple mass of fungal filaments and algae to exotic growth forms that are highly differentiated into cortex, medulla, "fruiting bodies,"—love that term—*et cetera*. Sometimes thalli fuse and sometimes they divide.

Two different fungi can share the same photobiont partner, when it suits them, and perhaps trade later. Sometimes they trade photobionts according to geographical or other environmental factors, or even reproductive stage. For example, photomorphs are lichens that contain either algae or cyanobacteria as photosynthesizing partners, depending on, for example, conditions of light and humidity. The two forms are radically different in appearance, but gradually blend together as their micro-environment changes. You see, lichens seem to be capable of reorganizing themselves as the need arises, like a lizard that grows a new tail, or a right-handed person who has learned to write left-handed.

And let's not leave the Mineral Kingdom out of the party. Many lichens, of course, grow on rocks, and they do this by sending their extremely strong and persistent rhizines and hyphae into the outermost millimeters of cold, hard rock. They get a firm hold and nutrients, too. If you should see one of those scanning electron photographs of the hyphae in the rock, you may wonder just where the lichen ends and the rock begins. There are also the parties called "cryptoendoliths" in Antarctica and places like that, and these lichens lie completely entombed, entangled in the pores between translucent grains of rock just below the surface. There, they are protected from the desiccating cold. Now, would you say that rock is alive or only a good place to party?

And what goes on in the back rooms is just what you'd think—reproduction, either sexual or vegetative or even "mechanical," as in hybridization. The favorite strategy seems to be vegetative, in which a lichen emits fragments of itself to colonize the great unknown. As for sex, no one has actually seen it occur, as it does with, say, flowering plants, with the pollen and eggs and all. With lichens, it's a mystery, still.

So with all its inventiveness, it turns out that lichen is one of the most widespread, successful forms of life—make that associations of—no, let's just say festive events—on the planet. Apparently the "lichen habit," as they say, has evolved several times on this old earth. A typical lichen may only grow one-tenth of an inch per year, but they grow everywhere except the deeps of the oceans. They are sources of food, soil builders, and carbon sinks. They are foliose (leafy), crustose (crusty), fruticose (shrubby). We have beard lichens, pin lichens, coral, script, and flask lichens. We have pixie cups, and of course, reindeer "moss," that is, our beloved *Cladina rangiferina* and *C. stellaris*.

The reason *we* are here, that is, me, Irv, Nicolette, and our multi-striped gang of lichenologists, is to collect evidence of air pollution from the tissues of four selected species of lichen. That it is an issue at all is due to the peculiar way in which lichens take in the water they need to survive. You see, they have no real skin. They get what they need through what they do have, a flimsy, permeable, sponge-like covering of cortex (and poor *Cladina* has not even this; it is naked to the elements). Lichens drink straight out of the air, from fog or mist or simple high humidity. Rain is nice but not necessary. How ingenious you think, but the hitch is that they cannot regulate themselves, and must helplessly absorb whatever is there: moisture, nutrients, trace elements. Also pollutants of every kind, including radioactivity, and how lichens react to these insults varies. Some sicken, some die—the absence of lichens is a very good indication of bad air—and some are unaffected except that they accumulate the toxins, year in and year out. These contaminated lichens may die eventually by slow poisoning, or by the usual natural causes: flood, fire, or, an encounter with some hungry creature, which all unknowingly consumes a load of toxins with its meal.

Or, one of these contaminated lichens could be collected by a hapless field grunt like me, and then live briefly in the glory of the lab as a bona fide biomonitor. Some exemplary samples may even be enshrined forever in herbaria. These, we call "vouchers."

People don't eat much lichen, it seems, although it's feasible—fried, boiled, thrown into soup. *Umbilicaria*, that is, rock tripe—*tripe de roche*—has been devoured by starving people on countless, desperate occasions. I would not be tempted on this trip, thank God, but I would try an antibiotic made from lichen if I were sick, or a perfume or a dye, all these and others derived from the prosaically named "lichen substances." But really, what I would most love to use lichens for, is to fall in ecstasy into a soft, cool, dewy bed of *C. stellaris*. This would be frowned upon by the official set, but Irv and I are just the hired help and we did once give in to temptation.

"Yah, I'm likin' lichen." This from Irv.

"Don't get smart," said I, "or they'll sit up and bite you on the ass."

He chuckled, but we both knew it was just bravado; things were changing between us.

Irv is subject to what you might call scientific hubris. He's the kind of guy who is way too sure about things. From his point of view, everything can be explained, rectified, or dismissed via science. He has no patience for shades of gray, but this I think is a function of his youth, and I still wonder what will happen when he is forced one day to admit ambiguity. I can't see him wearing matching socks or anything, but his is such a definite personality, I must think he would change, respond somehow, and probably with purpose. But for now, he is reckless and proud, and infectiously sure of himself.

On the other hand, Nicolette. Her great strength is her native caution, her careful weighing of each matter on its own merits. I have seen how she recognizes the hubris not only in Irv, but in others. I have seen her smile when she sees it. She loves nature and wilderness, I think, because it is beautiful and satisfies her intellectual curiosity, and because it reminds her of larger issues that may or may not be accessible through science. I get the feeling Nicolette is wise beyond her years, far wiser than me, and I find myself wishing, absurdly, that I could be her best friend. My favorite memory of Nicolette is the day she braved her fears of Lake Superior for the sake of lichen.

And me? I like that delicate place where mystery and objective inquiry meet. I am drawn to that place, that particular party. Lichen, such a fabulous example; it is a natural phenomenon that can't be pinned down. How fond I am of lichen! But I suppose I've missed the boat on science. I mean, I'm starting to grasp the elegance of it, the exhilaration of the clear eye and the curious mind, but I believe I'm too old to really get on board, to join that community. I feel a little left out, truth be known, a little sad that I gave up so much before I even left high school. So, like every parent in the world, I look to my kids and Chris's; maybe they'll go further than us. I think of Cora and John raptly listening to Irv's detailed and vivid tales of slime mold. I think of my two sons, the exact number of sons that Frances Anne Hopkins lost so long ago, and I feel a quick, piercing fear. The need to hang on to what I love versus the need to let everything go, and I think of the little girl Frances, skipping down the beach, reciting Hennepin. This morning, I had an unexpected crying jag. I can't imagine where I'll be at this time next year.

But one of the best things about lichen is its miraculous ability to quicken, with even just a little moisture, from a drought-stricken, seemingly lifeless state. Before the storm, the forest had been so parched under that hot sun that lichens crumbled underfoot; even the duff was dry as powder. One breath of rain-laden air was enough to revive them, so that they could drink their fill in the rain. If they can do it, so can I.

Nicolette told me that the day she was hooked on science was the day she looked through a microscope for the first time. She was in third grade, and the complexities and mysteries of cells would command her attention for the next seventeen years. That is in fact how she met her husband, the Italian cooking wizard, the chemistry man. I imagine the two of them trading hot, cellular passwords, chemical formulae of their own brand of love potion, *et cetera*. I find myself feeling jealous. What kind of bond must they have?

The day of our last transect on Otter Island. I am high on a hillside, on my hands and knees squinting through a hand lens at the landscape that is the surface of *P. sulcata*. It is a small specimen on a stump, half-buried by moss, embellished with all the usual miniature glories of the floor of the boreal forest. The view through the hand lens, I know, is infinitely expandable in the direction of the smallest things, and this is amusing until I look up, stare blankly at the immense presence of Kitchi Gami, itself blending into the sky, and am blown backward on my butt, not laughing, as if I'd been punched by a giant silent fist.

29.

The Prize

Summer 1690

WHEN THEY WERE ready, Grand Père brought forth the tobacco. He cast a generous offering to the Lac Supérieur and began, "*Nostre pater in celis . . .*"

Garamond chimed in and together they recited the Lord's Prayer as the tobacco dispersed and then whirled away in their wake.

They set out due west, keeping to the shore. It was good to watch the wide horizon after journeying so long in the forest. They passed Miron's grave, crossed themselves, but went on. All remained still, the sky clear and the lake unperturbed, so they made a great distance that day, and camped just short of the *fond du lac*. In the morning, they decided to cross the rest of the bay, perhaps one long league, all at once. They set out. Gradually, the water spread round them like shimmering blue crepe—but so very cold! And with all of Grand Père's corn and tobacco, the canoe was heavy-laden and riding almost to the gunwales. It would not be possible to take waves of any size, so they paddled for the north shore as swiftly as they could.

"I should tell you, my little child, of how I was once caught in just such a crossing as this," Grand Père suddenly broke the silence.

"*Crisse*, old man. Do you have to talk about that now?"

"I find it exhilarating to discuss such things when one is most sensitive to them."

"You are crazy, all right."

Grand Père was delighted to hear it. "It was a squall from the east and we paddled west before it. The waves grew instantly to enormous heights, which of course, we could not weather. So we cast everything over except our ammunition, and with this we loaded the bow, in order, do you see? to raise the stern from the following seas. It almost worked. Do you know how to swim, *Anjevin*?"

"Yes, I do."

"Well, I do not." The old man burst out in a guffaw that trailed off into chuckles, lasting, it seemed to Garamond, forever. "Our canoe was utterly swamped, but we were driven onto the rocks by pure luck! Then the canoe splintered and we were left clinging there for hours and hours. I have never been so cold. My partner and I both lost consciousness, I am sure, many times before it was over."

"All right, Monsieur, that's enough of your mischief. *Merci de Dieu*, we are almost there, but there is a fog on the shore. Do you see it?"

"Yes, it is a common occurrence here. Inconvenient."

It was the beginning of a plague of fogs. What wind there was, was light and blew from the west, so they paddled safely in the lee of the land. Each day began and ended in icy mists, dampening their campfires, and afflicting them with uncontrollable shivers and chattering teeth. They knew that cliffs loomed to their left, and they could hear the descents of great cataracts; but they saw very little, except a glimpse now and then when the sun grew hot, far above, and melted the fog for a while.

One night, Garamond dreamed of glorious music swelling the cathedral of Angers. He woke up, but the music did not stop. He stared open-mouthed around him, realizing with a shock that the music was the howling of wolves. Perhaps far, perhaps close, he could not tell. It was a sound he had only heard of in tales, though he'd seen the pelts of wolves and he knew they'd come close to him in the winter. He listened now with all his attention. It seemed that they sang together, deliberately, but in the strangest of chords. There were solos, choruses, and descants as if directed by some unknown plan. The music did not strike him as sad or eerie—for so he'd heard it described—but rather as thoughtful, as if the animals pondered great mysteries. He became aware of a sound behind him and turned to see Grand Père muttering by the coals of their fire. The old man was gathering kindling, and soon blew the flames back to life. He began to say his rosary.

"Eh, Grand Père, are you afraid of the wolves?" Garamond came to join him and sat down. The howling wavered on from somewhere in the interior.

"The Indians revere them, you know. It is most curious." The old priest returned to his rosary as Garamond eyed him. They stayed long by the fire, listening to the music and praying by turns, holding the mist at bay.

But morning brought a stiff breeze from the south that shredded the fog and sped them forward. Shadows and sunlight marbled the surface of the water as they went. When the sun came out in full, Grand Père gazed out at the lake with relief, saying only, "Look, it is God's own mirror."

They were tireless that day and did not think of stopping at all, for they would reach the fires of the Grand Portage by evening. The little breeze kicked up enough of a surf to prevent their landing, in any case. They mopped the seepage and splash and carried on with confidence, as if they'd paddled together for years, for they'd found the timeless, rhythmic symmetry of the tandem canoe. Even as they turned in to the round, mellow bay of the portage, with its wooded, hilly, welcoming arms, they paddled as strongly as they'd done a dozen hours before.

On that particular evening, the encampment comprised a mix of Ojibwa, Cree, and Assiniboine Indians, men, women, and children, and all of them traders and bringers of news. Grand Père was known to many of these people and word of his arrival spread in a cheerful wave through the camp. Garamond, the *Français* wendigo and Sioux-friend to boot, was greeted rather more coolly, but with enough curiosity to keep him busy. A fair number of these Indians spoke French, some fluently, some only passably, and so with Grand Père's command of Ojibwa and a smattering of all the others, the conversations flowed freely all night and the next day. There was trade and gossip and flirting, and hunters coming in from the woods. Cooking fires burned incessantly, as well as smudge fires to drive the mosquitoes away and to melt pitch for repairing canoes. There was something happening in every quarter and a constant inquiry about who would be leaving or arriving, and whether by lake or by trail.

"The trail," said Grand Père, "is nearly four leagues over horrible terrain. The journey is necessary to avoid the falls and the rapids on the lower Nantaouagan. We shall pass the mouth of that river tomorrow."

"They say the pelts are fantastic up there." Garamond was intent on patching his moccasins, worn to shreds on the trails he'd already hiked. He could sense when Grand Père had more on his mind, so he glanced up at the old priest and waited.

"That could be your country, someday. I will never get there now..." Grand Père puffed solemnly on his pipe, then he smiled. "But yes, the pelts are of the highest quality. De Noyon is up there already. He went looking for the Lake of the Cree and the Lake of the Assiniboines. People here are saying he reached them."

"Do you know him?"

"I met him, yes. He went by way of the Kaministiquia River, not the Nantaouagan. We shall pass the fort at Kaministiquia, but we shall not go in, for it is deep in a bay of the lake, far from our route. In due time, we shall make De Noyon a partner." Grand Père rose and stretched. "Oh, I am old, *mon Dieu*! Tomorrow is the feast of Saint Bonaventure, and that is auspicious. We shall go at dawn."

They were accompanied by many of the Cree traders, who wished to return to their country in the north. Each canoe paused at the far point of the bay to pay homage to a small wizened cedar tree growing from the bare rock. It was the sacred *Manitou Geezhigaynce* of the Ojibwa, revered by all who journeyed on the Lac Supérieur. Tobacco floated there in speckled clouds, and then they embarked one by one, paddling in a long, strung-out mass. The Île Minong stretched purple for miles on their right, and cormorants wheeled in the sky like silent black crosses.

They paddled with a family of Cree Indians, the father, called Snow-in-his-Hair and the mother, Singing Woman. The hours passed pleasantly, with speechifying or companionable chatting in broken French and Cree. The children giggled at Garamond's strange *Français* jokes, while Snow-in-his-Hair and Grand Père struck a deal to exchange Cree medicine for corn and tobacco. They spoke of the trading post at Nipigon, manned then by Du Lhut's brother, which they would pass on their way north, and they wondered who would be there. When Snow-in-his-Hair mentioned that his brother was a hunting steward near the post, Garamond was intrigued, and asked what it meant.

"My brother is responsible for the hunting ground and the animals therein," Snow-in-his-Hair replied.

"Does he protect the animals, Monsieur? Does he pray for them?"

"It is something like that."

"You know, Monsieur, I learned some things about animals when I was lost in the forest. I was starving, as everyone knows."

"Did you abuse the animal spirits?"

"I may have, out of ignorance. There was a little raccoon, a gift, and I threw him away, like a fool. But there came a time when my bad luck turned. It was God or the animals, or both, that saved me. I found a great bull moose, for all the world, like a miracle. I wonder, Monsieur, how does one become a steward like your brother—"

Grand Père interrupted, "*Anjevin*, did you see the devils before or after that happened?"

The Indians listened with interest. Garamond was definitely alarmed for he could see a weird glint in the old man's eyes that had not been there before when he spoke of devils.

"Grand Père," he said with studied calm, "I am still not so sure I saw devils." Then he added, "But I am sorry."

"Eh? Oh well, it is all right that you did not see them. They are often hidden." Grand Père passed his hands over his eyes, then stared out at the blue infinity of the lake.

They let the subject drop.

The flotilla covered forty leagues of the Lac Supérieur's shore in the days to come, drawing slowly past a spectacular coastline of pinnacles and rock. After a treacherous crossing of more than two leagues, they paddled beneath the hulking gray walls of a peninsula, over a hundred fathoms high, and then another crossing and another peninsula, this one with hills like the breasts of a woman. The Île Minong was visible for a long time, but at last it fell from sight, and they wove their way through sweet, secret passages between islands. Above, there was heaven, and below, shafts of light in emerald water, like sun streaming through the stained-glass of a church window. They turned north and paddled onto the restless water of the bay of the Rivière Nipigon, and thence upstream to the great, spreading Lac Nipigon. And there was the post, Fort La Tourette, with Claude Greysolon in command.

As far as the Nipigon traders were concerned, the first business to be settled was whether the newcomers brought brandy, for the post was fresh out. However, Grand Père carried only his Jesuit prejudices against liquor, which he shared freely, inciting first disappointment, then suspicion, and a surly crowding 'round of unwashed, ill-tempered *coureurs de bois*.

"You had better hope our supplies come soon, old *barbon*," growled one man, his hair bedecked with beads and tattered ribbons. He leaned forward with menace. But then Garamond stepped in, grinning with recognition, and planted a kiss on the man's cheek.

"Is it you Doucette? Don't you remember me?"

"Eh? Garamond! Jean Garamond! Why, we all thought you were dead! Mercier would say nothing, you little scamp—" He wrapped the young man in a bear hug, then held him off to look at him. "You have come a long way from Ville Marie, *Anjevin*." Then the other traders demanded to be introduced, as well as the Cree and Nipissing Indians gathered to greet their relatives. Then Greysolon himself came down and, with reverence, kissed Grand Père's hand, and so the party commenced, brandy or no.

They stayed at the post for the better part of a week, for it was too pleasant to mingle with the Indians there and the *coureurs de bois*. Doucette had taken a Nipissing wife and dwelt nearby, having eschewed altogether the *Français* in the east. Greysolon, Sieur de la Tourette, was loved by all and carried himself with the same honor and stamina as his brother, Du Lhut. The fishing was good, the women, congenial; it was summer in the north woods. One evening, the kinfolk of Snow-in-his-Hair came to the post and reported that swift-burning fires were ravaging the north, for it had been very dry in all of that country, and this also persuaded Grand Père and Garamond to linger at Nipigon.

"Wait for rain," Doucette advised them, "and then you can go to your cache in safety. Eh, by the way, where is it you're going? Otoskwin? Attawapiskat? Rivière Péré? You may run into the English if you're not careful—"

Snow-in-his-Hair glanced at his brother, but said nothing, for their own plans were to journey to the great bay of the northern ocean to join their relations and to trade with the English for cheap English goods. They would go soon, in fact, and not wait for rain. Snow-in-his-Hair had already traded his wife's medicines for Grand Père's goods, and now that his brother's family had come, all was ready.

Grand Père nodded amiably to Doucette, but said nothing as to the whereabouts of his cache. He said, "Have I ever told you of the time when I and my Jesuit brothers tricked the Iroquois? Oh it was masterfully done!"

"Of course, everyone has heard that story. But what about your cache?"

"You know, Doucette, he will never tell you a thing," Garamond put in. "People are always asking."

"He is a crafty old priest, I guess."

"Yes, but his stories are good!" Then several *coureurs* called out for the familiar tale of how, long ago in the east, the French had been held captive in their own fort by the Iroquois warriors. Grand Père closed his eyes, inhaled, then exhaled in a noisy whoosh, while everyone waited for him to start and all the children nearby squeezed into the circle to listen.

"Young Radisson was there, and Dablon, and my superior, and also Frémin," he began. "We were running out of time; our ammunition was almost gone; and any day more Iroquois would come to overpower us with sheer numbers. But God inspired us with a plan! In secret, we built a fleet of barks with which to escape. How did we build them in secret?" He stared around at them with bulging eyes, while half the traders chuckled and the others shouted what rude suggestions came into their heads.

"We built them in the attic! One by one, and then we disassembled them so we could sneak them down the stairs. Now, Radisson was a favorite of these Iroquois—he'd been captured by them once before—and so was able to gain their trust, poor foolish Iroquois!" Everyone yelled their approval. "He told them he'd dreamed he would die unless they held a great feast, in which every last morsel must be consumed, according to custom. The Iroquois thought they would humor him, since they planned to kill all of us anyway, and so they came to the feast. They ate until their stomachs groaned and their heads swam in misery. Then our good *pierrot* tuned up his fiddle and played the sleepiest tunes that he knew, and finally Radisson declared the feast a success, and gave them leave to stop eating. At once, they fell fast asleep."

"What happened next, Grand Père?" asked the boldest child, eyes wide with delight.

"Why then, we carried the barks from the attic in pieces and put them together in the dark. Then we all escaped down the river, chopping ice as we went! In the morning, the Iroquois burst into the fort and conquered—" he paused and raised his eyes to heaven, "our chickens!"

Hearing the applause, more people were drawn to the circle. Soon they'd embarked on a story-telling marathon that went into the night. There were more tales of trickery, many of valor, and of duels with demons. Garamond was asked how it felt to be a *Français* wendigo, and he tried to meet expectations. Late at night, there were tragic tales of love, and so finally he had to escape. Away from the fires and the talk, he wandered near the water and let thoughts of the young woman, Sitka Toh, fill his head. He listened to the music of loons, unseen in the dark, like a soulful, avian echo of wolves. He listened and found it difficult to contain his sadness. For the first time in many weeks, he could not sleep that night.

In the morning, Grand Père said, "What is wrong with you *Anjevin*, you look dreadful."

"That is not your concern, old man."

"No? But it most certainly is. Please do not tell me you're still lusting for the Sioux girl."

Garamond jabbed viciously at the little campfire. It was windy and sparks flew off in a shower with each poke. He was feeling very mean. "Yes," he said, "All right, I will make confession then; I've had impure thoughts about an Issati whore. So what?"

Grand Père shook his head and smiled. "There is no such thing, of course. Ah! The Sioux are so very strict. All you can have are your thoughts, no doubt. What a pity!"

"You know Grand Père, some of them had two, or even three wives—not all of them happy, you know? That husband of hers was a monster, I am sure."

"Still, one must not pine over these things. There are other tribes with different traditions, and you shall have illicit relations with many women, I am sure."

"Do not play with me."

Grand Père sighed. "Women are all the same, like glistening flowers. You do not have to choose."

So far, however, there was not one woman who could take the place of Sitka Tóh in Garamond's heart. Two days later, Snow-in-his-Hair and his family left for home, taking with them Grand Père's corn and tobacco. The rains came soon after, but also six canoes loaded with trade goods, including a large quantity of brandy. From out of nowhere, it seemed, piles of magnificent furs—beaver, otter, fox, bear—appeared in exchange for the hot fire of *Français* liquor. Every one of the adult population of Fort la Tourette proceeded to get very drunk, save the old Jesuit priest and his frustrated partner. Greysolon, to his credit, tried to temper the excess, but in vain, for he was only one man, after all, and very far from home.

"Oh please, Grand Père," Garamond begged, "We should celebrate with the others! We may not taste brandy for months, for years, who knows! Come to your senses, old man!"

But Grand Père was unmoved. "We must leave immediately, *Anjevin*. Do you see? I am leaving. Do you come with me, my child? We shall return, never fear."

"*Merde!* Pig's arse, you stubborn old—"

Grand Père was already taking his place in the stern of the canoe. He gracefully sculled the blade of his paddle over the surface of the silky water, just as if, Garamond thought with anguish, the old man caressed a woman's skin. And so they left in the middle of the day, their departure unnoticed by any of the forty-odd revelers, and made with all speed for the upper country.

After a long silence, Grand Père said, "I cannot help but pity them."

"But why! It is only in fun and look at all the furs, old man! They are worth a fortune—"

"Greed," Grand Père went on unperturbed, "is the only protection, the only armor that some of them have."

Garamond scoffed. "What armor?"

"Their armor, their security, their safe passage in this wild country. Otherwise they would be devoured. Surely you must realize by now how vulnerable is your soul in a place like this. The Jesuits, for all their care, do not understand this. They think they're invincible, but as we all know, they are not."

"What in the name of the Virgin are you talking about?"

"Greed is all right in that it serves the purpose as well as anything. But it is better for one's soul to employ something more useful, for example, hunting for food, or exploring to some purpose; even simple camaraderie is better than greed."

Garamond stopped paddling and turned to stare at the old priest. "Did we not just leave all of our comrades?" he shouted.

"Ha, ha! Good point! You are not so dull, *Anjevin*, as one would think. It never pays to underestimate a peasant, my superior always said."

"I am not dull! And you, with your great Jesuit learning, you are the one afraid of your shadow in the forest, you and your devils! Or is your own armor not so good, eh?"

"Ah! My armor is full of holes."

"Yes, but what are these holes, Monsieur, tell me that."

"You are shrewd indeed, *Anjevin*." Grand Père stifled an impulse to splash Garamond with his paddle, then laughed out loud at himself.

Garamond sighed and demanded to know what was funny.

"I believe now that I am subject to the sin of pride. When I was in the Order, I hid it well enough, but of course subterfuge does not fix the hole. I shall always battle pride, my weakness, the entrance by which the devils approach."

They passed then around a windy point and gave all their attention to the waves.

The canoe was lightly burdened with only the two men, the Cree medicines, and provisions, and so it bounded alarmingly in the chop. "Steady," Grand Père called out. "Paddle forward with authority. Good! We shall keep our momentum and go right around."

Soon they gained the lee of the point and floated there peacefully, letting the diminished breeze push them on by itself. Grand Père said, "That is why you and I make a good team, you know. My knowledge and your mysterious ability to withstand the assaults of the devils."

Garamond was about to retort how easy it was to withstand something that didn't exist, but then he stopped to consider. "Maybe you're right," he said, "We are a good team. Still, I would throw you to the devils for a sip of strong brandy."

With so little to hinder them, they made fast time and soon left the Lac Nipigon behind. The country they traveled was a winding patchwork of rivers, waterfalls, and lakes, the mainland so fractured as to be indistinguishable from the islands. But Grand Père never faltered, so his companion could not help but to trust and admire him.

The trees of that forest were smaller than in the south. There were blueberries ripening in the sunny spots, and pickerel, homely but delicious, swarming below cascades in the rivers. Grand Père and Garamond ate well and had little need to tap their provisions.

One day, they passed a burnt region, oppressive and tangled with blackened trees. The fires had been so hot that the bare bones of rock were exposed, which seemed indecent somehow. The two men hurried on. Not long after, with great relief, they found themselves paddling in the midst of a forest burned long ago, but now springing to life again with wildflowers and saplings. It was just past there that Grand Père exclaimed, "At last! Here is the creek!"

With renewed energy, they turned up the creek and wound their way half a league through a broad marsh. A harrier skimmed and banked a scant few feet above the reeds, while crowds of fingerling fish darted through the water, fleeing the canoe and a giant hunting pike. The water spread out until it was very shallow and just a hand's width remained above the dark liquid sediment forming the bottom of the creek. The sediment offered hardly more resistance than water, and in the wake of each paddle stroke, clouds of it bloomed in all directions, releasing bubbles of malodorous gas like a thousand sizzling farts.

"Faugh! What a stench!" Garamond cried.

The old man smiled.

At a certain point, they disembarked and splashed over a portage in a meadow laced with rivulets and springs. Then they floated again on a swift twisting stream, its water transparent, slipping through overhanging tangles of alder and downed trees. They were obliged to maneuver gently over numerous beaver dams, for which they were grateful, for it meant the animals were abundant in that country. Once they spotted a beaver swimming below the canoe, its eyes, Garamond was sure, smoldering with resentment.

They came at last to a dam that had ponded the stream at the foot of a bare hill. Here they brought the canoe to rest and unloaded it on the bank. Grand Père started up the hill without a word, Garamond behind hiding his eagerness. They followed a steep trail up the hill through berry bushes and bracken fern. Garamond's heart labored with the effort, blood pounding in his ears with a force he could feel on the top of his head, and he wondered again at his partner's strength. Finally they reached the crest of the hill and paused to catch breath. There was a curiously gnarled birch and the marks of old campfires, and an expansive view of the marsh below, prickled with the trunks of drowned trees. The stream reflected the late sun like a winding glass, and the forest of spruce and birch lay beyond.

"Ah. Here we are."

"I don't see any cache, old man." Garamond had a sudden fear he'd been duped. The old Jesuit was crazy, wasn't he? What if the cache was some spiritual, devilish nonsense? "You hid it very well, I guess!" He laughed nervously.

"Look up, *Anjevin*."

He looked up. High in the gnarled birch were five large bundles hanging from branches in nets.

"Oh! *Merci de Dieu*, Grand Père!" he cried, pounding the old man on his back until he staggered from the blows.

"Have a care, villain! I am too old for such foolishness!" Grand Père pushed him roughly away. "Look, you have injured me! Now, go get our things up that damnable hill."

Garamond ran down the hill, and soon returned puffing with an armload of gear. Then he climbed the birch, but gingerly, for he didn't trust its limbs, and cut the nets. Bundles cascaded to the ground.

"Still sound," Grand Père remarked with satisfaction as he unwrapped and inspected. "Leave me a while, my child, so I may count in peace. Go and kill our supper while there's still light."

By the end of that culminating day, the triumphant traders sat at their ease on the hill, roasting a pair of ducks and laying their plans for the future.

Grand Père said, "Turn and turn about, my young partner. We shall now go to the Sault, and then to Missilimackinac for the goods from the east that are sure to arrive. It will be good to meet some old friends, *n'est-ce pas?*"

"Yes." Garamond looked out over the marsh, filling with mist in the cool of night. "But you know, I will not stay long at Missilimackinac."

Grand Père waited for him to go on. They could see the edge of the moon floating slowly up from the trees, and in a few moments, it had kindled the mist in the valley to white.

"*Mon Dieu, c'est belle.*" Garamond lit his pipe, drew deep, and luxuriously blew smoke to the moon. He smiled, thinking how easy it was to make promises by that soft, lovely light. "I am going back to the Issatis," he said. "I will look after the old woman for a while and help them with the rice." He looked at Grand Père. "I will see Sitka Toh again, yes. And maybe, Monsieur, I will take her away this time."

30.

Montréal

1690-92

THE GIRL, FRANCES Cornet, stood under the eaves of the lean-to where she and the cattle had gone to wait out the rain. The sun had just emerged. Frances was hypnotized by the sight before her; a row of dark spruce trees pierced by rays of light; each needle, shiny with rain. The water, shed first in bright streams and then in long dripping streaks, made an intermittent net of light against dark. She was so fair and plain that she seemed to have no eyebrows nor eyelashes. Only when she squinted at the net of light, then her brows appeared, faint ridges beneath quizzical, vertical furrows. Perhaps her eyesight was only fair. She was tall, like her mother, and that made her seem much older than she really was, which was twelve. It was the summer of 1690, and Frances Cornet was yet innocent and open, and plain as dust.

20 août, 1690
Journal du Bernard Cornet

Well. They have come at last. Fifty-five canoes full of fur. And where, exactly is our Jean Garamond? A curious question, that. Here, in my hands is a very tattered and filthy letter from our young man. Excuses. But do not forget this pile of foul-smelling skins. He has sent us that! But the risks in this country are very great indeed. Our troubles mount ever higher. For the time being, I shall have to content myself with this abject little harvest. Fauconnet will take it with all the others and send it on for further seasoning in the ghastly hold of his ship. The skins are good enough for the Russian felt market and so a little return will go a very long way in these desperate days. Even trifles are wept over with joy.

With the demise of Michel Miron, it seems that our Garamond has taken up with the two characters who brought down his furs. I made inquiries to ascertain their reputations, and so I am willing to try them. Giroux, Saint Pierre, and Company— they are not exactly in the official accounts. I sent up what I could with them for Garamond. We shall see what comes of it.

My wife slowly reconciles herself to— what I cannot hide— this dreadful fate. I am sure she dreams of returning to France. She must not. For one thing, I want an heir, and not some other man's strange spawn, for such is the girl, the Englishman's daughter. She will bring the clergy on us yet, for she thinks only of joining the *sauvages*, or of Jean Garamond, or of running like a deer in the woods.

In December, Frances turned thirteen and stole away with Marc, her great friend, to celebrate and explore each other's bodies. Their favorite spot was the farthest corner of Monsieur de Chesnaye's warehouse. It was always dark, so their discoveries were made in their tingling fingertips and skin. Later, they could only try to imagine how those strange shapes and textures really looked, but they were sure they would find out. These carnal investigations were a blessing, for they took their minds off the cold and their empty bellies. There was famine on Montréal that winter, for the Iroquois had thwarted the harvest, and Admiral Phips's invasion of Québec, though unsuccessful, had tapped all the colonists' energy at the wrong time, and now they could only endure. When Frances and Marc could not disappear together, they would wander the streets of the village, run the odd errand for their elders, and scrounge what bits of food they could find. Marc would regale her with stories of the Montagnais and their kin, the Naskapi, far to the north at the edge of the forest. Marc knew all kinds of stories, but he always came back to the Montagnais, for that was what Frances liked best.

"Tell me again of the deer in the north. Tell me of the Montagnais hunters!"

Marc laughed. She was the only girl he could fascinate. A pity she was so plain. Still, he wondered how far she would let his caresses go.

"The *curé* says they hunt reindeer. Those are like whitish deer, I guess. The Montagnais make magic jackets out of the skins. Then they paint the reindeer trails on the jackets, like maps. So they can always find them."

"But then they wouldn't be starving."

"No, I guess not."

"Let us do the divination. Show me again!"

"But there are no reindeer around here, stupid."

She smiled at him with pity. "I want to hunt Jean Garamond, of course, not reindeer."

"Oh! So you refuse to break your engagement? What about me?"

"Come, Marc, let us do the divination. You know how things stand." She pulled him to his feet. "You are my best friend. What would I do without you?"

He let her lead him from one refuse pile to another until they found a few boiled and bleached bones left from someone's poor soup. These they spirited away to a back garden, desolate beneath gray, crusty snow. They cleared a space, and Marc set a tiny fire of leaves and twigs, just enough to scorch the bones, and then together they broke them open and spread them on the ground.

Frances asked, "What does it mean?" She knew he didn't know. She closed her eyes and picked up each fragment of bone and set it down again, concentrating as hard as she could, and thought, "Where is Jean Garamond?" She was sure the bones were trying to speak. From the street, a woman's raspy voice interrupted the silence, and then the sound of footsteps and banging shutters. Sighing, Frances opened her eyes. "There is too much noise," she said. "I can't make out what they're saying."

In May, her courses came for the first time, all while her mother gave birth and her father paced, and a thousand Iroquois beset the island of Montréal. No one had time for Frances, so she tried to make do with rags and stoically bore the cramps in her young womb. It lasted five days. But she had the satisfaction of showing off before the other girls and, best of all, scaring Marc with the actual blood.

It was a beautiful spring. There were grouse drumming in the woods and songbirds deliriously singing, and these the Iroquois could not stop. Men shot ducks and geese straight out of the air, and so people ate again and were strong. The tiny black flies sucked their fill. Then the leaves of the northern trees unfurled in waves of translucent pastels: the bronze and peach of maples, lime-green birch, popple, and rusty shrubs coming on, all interwoven with spires of dark fir. Between the raids of the enemy, and the hail and rain of spring storms, the *habitants* did their best to sow the fields. And this too, the Iroquois could not stop.

When Frances again had her courses, her joy was quenched by shame, for the sisters of the Congregation informed her that it was a sign of woman's original sin. And her own sweet *maman* concurred, a blow from which it was difficult to recover. Sullenly, she watched the new baby—a lucky boy—and worked on her sewing and waited for the bleeding to stop. But Marc loved her, in his way, and so on the fourth day, he appeared at the window in the company of an

Indian girl, a convert, and one of their friends. She was Huron, and her Christian name was Marie.

"We brought you a present, Frances." He was beaming. He boosted Marie to the sill and she held out a small round pot, made of pretty ochre-colored clay, incised with divots around the rim.

"It is for cooking, *Française*," she said. "It is only for your courses, every month. You must cook separately or you will cause trouble." Marie giggled. "Marc told me how you scared him! You must be more careful! You must take note of the moon so you'll be ready. Don't you know you are too powerful for the others at those times?"

"I am?"

"*Bien sûr, Française.* You should be more careful."

"Oh!" She was thrilled. "I will be very careful! *Merci, mille fois!*"

On June 26, the entire populace of Montréal celebrated with due pomp and solemnity the feast of Sainte Anne, patron saint of travelers. After Mass, the Sisters led a parade through the streets, attended by the faithful, all meticulously turned out in their best clothes. Bernard Cornet cut his usual imposing figure in his greatcoat of fine Spanish wool. Pauline, his wife, wore her deepest blue Holland linen, and bore in her arms her infant son. Frances, alas, was not wearing a dress. She had come late, wrapped in a fur cloak like the *sauvages*, with a mantle of embroidered leather. She bore a crown of small antlers. She was radiantly happy.

"Are you at least wearing a shift, daughter?" Pauline was already sorry she'd let the girl take this liberty, although it pleased her to annoy Bernard. However, it was clear from the darkness in his eyes that she had gone too far this time.

"*Mais oui maman*, I have my shift," Frances lied, for she found the tickle of fur on her bare skin to be the most delicious of pleasures.

For weeks after, she continued to wear her *sauvage* ensemble whenever she could sneak it out of the house, until the *curé* spoke to her parents, and so Bernard put an end to it. They tried to distract her with chores and prayers, at which she had always excelled, but she preferred to think of the Montagnais and their reindeer, or the *coureurs de bois* who roamed the village. She would slip out with Marc as usual and share her secrets with him. It did not bother Marc to speculate about the whereabouts of Jean Garamond, or "my betrothed" as Frances called him. It was a game, and together they devised all manner of plans to track him and bring him to justice. He had sworn an oath to return, had he not?

30 juillet, 1691
Journal du Bernard Cornet

The best and the worst of luck. Yesterday a small party of canoes came down, one of which carried a most precious harvest of furs from our Garamond. Thick winter furs from very far north. They are worth a king's ransom— I can hardly believe he got them for what I'd sent last fall. He himself does not grace us with his presence, though I do not blame him. His comrades had the very devil of a time with the Iroquois. They are nearly all injured in some way— it is a miracle they are here. And now the powers that be have put a ban on trade with the Sioux. What nonsense! It is meant to be a detriment to our relations with the western allies, the Illinois, Ojibwa, *et cetera*. Well perhaps, for now. But how to get word to our diligent trader? Ha! I can see no way. I am somewhat reassured that G. is not trading with the English on the sly. That is what happened to poor Laverdure— he found out at last. He will prosecute his errant *engagé* for desertion— if he can ever get his hands on him. But our *coureurs de bois* are worth all the trouble, to be sure. No one can fight so well except the Indians themselves. Though we have all grown terribly ruthless. Our *curé* fights with the rest of us, while the good Sisters re-load his guns! The enemy burns us to cinders and we reply in kind. I have been lucky so far, losing only two toes on my right foot to my wounds of last year. Though the frostbite did not help at all. But I killed my share and I am satisfied.

The people called it the Little War, a seemingly endless stretch of stealthy forays, guerrilla tactics, and siege. The Sun King did not help them, beset as he was in his own webs of war in Europe. The long year 1692 dawned in the bleak winter and kept New France in its bloody grasp. Yet, at the appointed time, spring returned. Fields were tended; trade, plied. The colonists were amazed at their own tenacity.

The ships from France came but seldom, and when they did they were laden with letters and many a *cri de coeur*. Amongst the business missives from La Rochelle, Bernard Cornet received a letter from Garamond's uncle in La Flèche, which, as the young man's master, he opened and read. It said, in so many words: There is famine in Anjou. Your mother prays for you every day. If you have a sol to spare for your poor family, *et cetera*.

Bernard refolded the letter, an image of dark empty fields in his mind. He glanced at his wife as she worked at the table; noted the expression of resigned suspicion on her face. How afraid he was that she'd leave him! As always, he hid his qualms behind business.

"I will forward this with the fall run, should we be fortunate enough to have one," he said. Then, handing her the letter, "You should read it, my wife, and be grateful you have left France for good."

31.

A Bird Out of Place

1693

3 mars, 1693
Journal du Bernard Cornet

I confess I have never liked wind. So very blustery today, and as cold as can be. I have just shirked a particularly disagreeable task— that is, fetching cream
from Le Brun's, all the way across the village, and the
obligation to endure Monsieur's endless demagoguery.
Astonishing, the extent of political maneuvering in this
tiny wilderness refuge. But the Englishman's daughter is nowhere to be found and it is necessary to have
cream for the *tarte au sucre*, for today is Demoiselle
Hubert's wedding. Yet another of Cadot's nephews, so
we shall go of course. She has a dowry of 900 livres,
plus the usual household things, including, I believe,
several animals. Such luck!

THEY FOUND FRANCES wading a muddy back channel of the river—up
to her waist in reeds—after which she was commanded to stay put.

Not much chastened, she retreated to a corner of the *petit aparte-ment* on the rue Saint-Paul, humming to herself and day-dreaming as she dressed her little brother. She was no longer allowed to wear animal costumes, so she took no care with her appearance at all. They had to insist she wear her better dress for the wedding, a soft gray wool with narrow ruffles and white buttons down the front. Her hair, thin and colorless, flew uncontrollably, having escaped at once from the blue ribbon. She was fifteen, tall and thin, and stubborn as winter in Canada.

"An unlucky combination," Bernard had remarked at least thrice, "stubborn, impractical, and plain."

She finished with the child and turned to study her mother's clothes laid on a bench by the wall. A heap of pretty scarlets, and on top, the crystal earrings Bernard had bought as an engagement present years ago. Frances stopped humming and stared at them closely, as if measuring their dimensions, and then she got up to help with the pie.

Her good friend Marc also attended the wedding that day. He had grown taller, even, than Frances, and for the most part, full of the ways of grown-up men. But he still liked to play with her, and he sometimes still told her stories. By then, he realized she might never be like other girls he knew, so it was hard to take her seriously. After the ceremony, he humored her as she laid out her latest plan.

She said, "A musket is worth an escort west, wouldn't you say, Marc? *Papa* has a quantity in the warehouse, of course. Jean Gara-mond would have need of help by now, wouldn't you think?"

"I bet he would welcome you with open arms. *Bien sûr*, a musket is worth a lot to anyone, especially with powder and lead. But do you think you could carry all that? Eh? You can't do it, you know." He grinned and winked at his brother nearby.

Frances only smiled serenely. She could remember every line of Garamond's face and body, or so she thought, and his wayward eye and the fact that he'd promised to return. "You may not know that he and I are practically orphans—both of our fathers are dead." She glanced darkly at Bernard Cornet, then went on. "Orphans stick together, Marc. Garamond and I are meant to be together."

"Do you want to go somewhere right now? I haven't kissed you for a long time, Frances, *jolie* Frances—" He glanced around for any hovering sharp-eyed elders, but all these were engaged elsewhere. "Now's our chance, eh?"

She ignored him. "I have begun to collect some things to trade on my way," she said loftily. "And, if the *sauvages* can track animals, so can I."

"Oh, *quelle folie*! Just forget about it, will you?" He stood up abruptly and pushed her away, then left to join the crowd at the table.

Frances did not take offense, and in fact may not even have noticed his rudeness, for she seemed always to be thinking of other things. She went home early from the wedding, feigning a stomach ache, and so she had the place all to herself. She went directly to her mattress and felt for the slit that she'd made. Finding it, she reached into the musty, scratchy straw and retrieved a packet of glass beads. She took them to the window along with her needle and thread and her fullest petticoat. She worked for an hour, as long as she could see in the fading light, carefully sewing beads into hidden folds of white linen. Then she put it all away, and returned to the wedding feast. "I feel ever so much better," she told everyone, and happily joined in the *gigue*.

On a day in May, Marc returned to the village with a party of woodcutters, and, seeing Frances on her way to the wharf, split off to join her. He was feeling particularly mischievous, and told her, all innocently, "There are Montagnais north of the mountain, *mon amie*. Montagnais going home to hunt reindeer! What do you think?"

She stopped in her tracks. "Truly, Marc?"

He stopped, too, for a moment, laughing, and then turned back the way he'd come. He answered her over his shoulder, "*Mais oui*, it's true. I saw them with my own eyes not two days ago. If you hurry, you may catch them."

But he did not laugh at all when he heard the next day that the Cornet girl had disappeared. She had gone and taken a musket and her mother's crystal earrings. Soon the whole village knew and a search party was assembled and sent out. Everyone was to be on the lookout for the tall fair girl in a gray dress and deerskin cloak. Only Marc did not go, for he was dying of shame in his heart, and whenever he tried to tell his uncle about the Montagnais, the words fell to pieces. The Montréalers searched for three days, but then they returned, for the fields were filling with weeds and the vegetables had to be set, repairs made, bargains struck. It seemed that the girl had simply vanished into the deep forest, league after league of hemlock and maple, a confusion of dark columns in a mist of new green leaves. There was nothing to be done.

Spring became summer, then mid-summer, and far to the north of the island of Montréal, a party of Huron Indians encamped for the night on the banks of a small river. This river, really no more than a stream, wound through a valley of cedar swamps, and, though it seemed somewhat aimless, provided a shortcut to a portage to another, larger river running south and west. Here, they were at the northern-most point of their detour around the Iroquois blockades. It was a long way from Québec and still longer from their destination, their village at Missilimackinac. The party comprised men of all ages, some twenty in all, and two women: a new bride and her mother. The women had dwelt in Lorette, a Huron village near Québec. Just then these two were beginning to feel the effects of homesickness, which of course they hid from the Missilimackinac men.

That evening, many of the party had already dozed off to sleep. A few still played a quiet game of chance by the fire. There were two scouts at opposite ends of the camp who periodically walked an imaginary line through the forest. At about the time of total darkness, one of these yelled a warning, and a crashing in underbrush ensued. The dogs of the camp proceeded to howl. People stumbled to their feet and then the scout appeared in the firelight dragging a woman. He thrust her into the midst of the amazed Hurons. It was Frances Cornet—long pale hair flying in her face; gray tattered dress. She rose to her feet, smiling pleasantly as if completely at ease, and said, "*Bonsoir mes amis. Je suis perdue, n'est-ce pas?*"

There was a moment of shocked silence before everyone started to shout. They understood her perfectly well, but to think that a *Française* could appear out of nowhere, fifty leagues from her people, and merely to say she was lost, was completely outrageous. Someone pushed her to her knees and things could not have looked worse—"*Miséricorde!*" she cried—but then one very strong and self-assured man intervened.

He loomed over the crouching girl, pointing sternly in her face, and said, "Do not trifle with us, *Française*. Who are you and why have you come upon us like a thief? Or a spy?"

She was panting by then, her eyes darting about as they waited for her to speak. At last she set her face into a mask of calm and, staring directly at the air in front of her, said, "I am only going to my husband in the west, but the Montagnais took me and forced me to go with them instead! I have escaped and now I am lost—"

"Why would the Montagnais take you," he demanded. "There are no French women in the west! Who is your husband?"

"He is Jean Garamond, a great trader! You are Huron? He is your ally! Do you not know of him?"

"I know of that man," someone said from the back. "He was at Missilimackinac when we arrived last year."

Then another said, "I think he was at Bowating—" Speculative murmurs ran through the crowd and Frances took heart. She rose again to her feet but the self-assured man pushed her back down. "Why did the Montagnais take you? Do not lie," he said.

At this, she could not help but look guilty and the people saw this instantly. Suspicion, then anger and loud muttering whirled around her again.

"*Écoutez-moi!* They abused me! They forced me into sin after sin! Do you doubt it? Look at me—" She gestured at her torn dress.

The man, Jiwatena, gazed shrewdly at her for a moment and asked, "What else did you give them?"

"A musket, some powder, some lead. But they ripped out all my beads! They were all colors! That is the truth, Monsieur."

The truth was close to that, but it was she who had searched out and found the Montagnais—it had taken all her strength to catch them—and it was she who begged them to take her. They had done so reluctantly in exchange for the musket and various lies, and for entertainment. But the Montagnais had quickly tired of the *Fran-çaise* and worried she'd be found with them. They'd thought of killing her, but in the end, when they discovered the Huron encampment, they seized the chance to simply discard her instead. By the time Frances was telling her story, the Montagnais were long gone.

If Jiwatena guessed any of this, he did not let on. "I am the master of this trade route," he said, "and I wonder what you have for *us*. Anything? Why should we take you to your husband?"

Frances looked steadily at the ground for a long moment, then she reached into her bodice. Everyone tensed, but then she withdrew her hand and in it was a wad of stained white cloth, no doubt the one used for her courses. Undeterred, Jiwatena took it from her and opened it, and smiled, for inside was a pair of graceful crystal earrings. She'd kept them hidden all that time, for Frances Cornet had grown very quickly adept in the art of deception.

Jiwatena decided to keep her for the night, at least. He set a double watch and bade everyone be ready to depart before dawn, just in case the girl was a decoy or an agent for some mischief. Then he turned her over to the Lorette women so he could think and consult with his comrades. Should they not return her to the settlements and earn some goodwill thereby? But what if she were an outcast, a sinner, as she herself said? Would it not be safer to kill her secretly here, far away where it would never be found out? They did not debate long for it seemed a better idea to take her with them, should she be no trouble, and to put her husband, should he exist, in their debt. Jiwatena's cousin, husband of the Lorette bride, was sure the

Français trader had been most recently at the Nipigon post, so perhaps they could send a party that way. Depending on how things went. Most likely, the traders or the black gowns would take her out of the hands of the Hurons.

"It is doubtful she knows where she is," Jiwatena concluded. "We can always say it was too far to return her. If we get her past Bowating, there is always copper to trade for at Nipigon."

His companions assented. The oldest man cast a pinch of tobacco on the fire to sanctify the decision, and thus the immediate future of Frances Cornet was set.

Blue Wing, the elderly, tattooed mother of the Lorette bride, regarded the *Française* with the utmost distrust. So outlandish—the burnt red skin, white hair, white eyes, that ruined flouncy dress! She reached over to finger the wool, judged it unsalvageable, and grunted in disgust.

"Look at her," she said to her daughter in their own tongue, "she is a spectacle, a foreign bird! I hope we can do away with her before she jinxes us." The girl gave them her most engaging smile, but Blue Wing was not fooled. She thought, This one is full of guile.

The daughter, Dawn, laughed and asked the girl, "*D'où êtes-vous?* Where are you from?"

Frances said, "From God and France."

"What is your name?"

"*Fille d'Anjou.*"

"Anjou?"

"France."

The Lorette women chuckled. Blue Wing said loudly in French, "She is ridiculous. Still, she is alive and that is something."

"She is as tall as me, *anan*, my mother."

"Yes, she bears watching all right." Blue Wing leaned forward suddenly to glare at Frances. "Heh, Anjou, we will watch you very closely!"

To their surprise, the girl narrowed her colorless eyes, smile gone, and growled. Very softly, she growled at them like a beast. Dawn and Blue Wing started back and glanced at each other in dismay.

"*Oki*," Dawn murmured.

Blue Wing leaned forward and cuffed the *Française*, once, twice to be sure, and commanded, "You will behave, Anjou. Do you understand?"

Frances said nothing, but lowered her eyes.

Now Blue Wing was an expert observer. A witness of sorts, as commanded by her own precious dreams. She was old and her body failing, and this journey with her youngest daughter would be her last. Unbeknownst to anyone, she saw everything through a veil of pain, but this pain was the means by which she focused her attention on matters of import: the deeds of spirits, the beauties and wonders of the world. She could ignore what she deemed trivial, at will, effortlessly. Just that day, for example, a meaningless quarrel between her daughter and son-in-law had left her unscathed, all while she witnessed, in the bright light of afternoon, the dark hearts of trees, deep-set in glowing aureoles of green leaves. Blue Wing saw such things all the time, for her dreams commanded her to be a witness, and she obeyed with joy.

The next morning, before anyone had spoken to the *Française*, Blue Wing took her aside and asked boldly, "What did you dream, Anjou?"

"I never remember," Frances lied. In fact, she dreamed every night of flying, or running, or swimming like a fish. But she refused to give anyone any clues, whatsoever, and so Blue Wing could only wonder.

Dawn said, "No doubt, her soul desires to have relations with her husband. And that is why she is so—"

"Huh! You think only of sex and husbands," Blue Wing said as she packed their bundles in the canoe. "Her soul desires relations, but maybe not with her husband. We will see."

The women traveled together with Tiron, Dawn's husband, in a small, narrow canoe. This arrangement was only accomplished after several bundles and a dog were apportioned to other canoes, for they were all thoroughly burdened with goods from Québec. So there was Frances, pale as a fluttering flag in the bow, tattooed Blue Wing, and red-beaded Dawn, and the man—all but Frances bare-breasted in the summer heat. For several days, they paddled without incident, only stopping to fish. Every night, they raised their bark shelters and cooked savory *sagamité* and small cakes of bread. Twice they met other Indians—Algonquin, Ottawa, Nipissing—and then they encamped together to trade and gossip and show off the *Française*. It came out that Jean Garamond had indeed been seen at Nipigon that summer, and so they made their plans more definite on that score. But no one was sanguine they could smuggle the girl past the black gowns who reputedly kept watch over all that passed at the Sault. They needn't have worried, for Frances had plans of her own. In the meantime, she behaved perfectly.

Blue Wing watched the *Française* with deep expectations. She had a feeling she was going to witness something stupendous. And she was a tiny bit grateful, for the girl paddled in her place, and for once, the old woman could sit at her ease in the canoe, and look and think her fill. Soon enough, she saw what she was looking for.

It began early one evening, when they'd pulled in to the shore of a lake. Though the day had been fair, a storm now approached from the south and so they hurried to make fast the camp, trying to ignore the startling white of gulls flying low over dark blue water. Within minutes the storm broke over them in a gale, as if it had been long pent up and suddenly released. Rain hurled itself to earth until the air seemed liquid and the noise of it drowned everything. The people doggedly continued to set up their camp. But then the thunder and lightning commenced, pummeling them with heart-stopping crashes of white and peals of thunder that shook the insides of their bodies. Groping together in the dark, they gathered into a knot of frightened people, cringing under blankets and skins. No one noticed the absence of the *Française* except Blue Wing.

"Heh!" she shouted to her daughter, "where is Anjou?"

"The *Française* is gone!" Dawn shouted to her husband and the news swept outward from him.

Everyone searched the darkness with their eyes, but no one stirred, and the storm continued to whirl itself into madness. There was a monstrous flash of lightning that illuminated the shore and the adjoining woods for a moment. "Look!" someone cried over the din. They had found her—she had climbed up into a ruined tree, like a gray, sodden flower, and perched there invoking, what? Her God? The Thunderbirds?

"*Oki*," people said to themselves, to each other, and shook their heads. Not a soul among them thought of fetching her down. Instead, they watched her, frozen in each bolt of white, and listened to fragments of laughter as she swayed with the storm.

The man, Jiwatena, thought of the crystal earrings he'd taken from the girl. He thought, They are charms! I shall never part with them.

The young woman, Dawn, thought of pity and thanked the spirits for her husband and her own good luck.

But the old woman thought of the ramifications of *ondinnock*, the desires of the soul that demand satisfaction. She thought, This journey will be remembered forever! I must see everything. I must not rest.

32.

The Artists

Winter 1907

"I HAVE FELT a similar ecstasy while painting."

The young pregnant woman speaks hesitantly; she is not used to speaking her heart, Heaven knows. She would never dream of uttering such nonsense at home.

Mrs. Frances Anne Hopkins gives her a piercing look. "Mademoiselle Cornet was surely a most headstrong girl," she says. "Such intemperance is not to be emulated, my dears. Discipline, discipline is what you need to be an artist."

"However, what is one to do about the ecstasy?"

"Contain it, of course. *Train* it to do your bidding."

Mrs. Turner breaks in, as is her way, somewhat clumsy and forceful and shy all at once. "One must not indulge in fancies when travelling the wild country. It is not wise. You must make no mistake—art is a wild country."

They are waiting at the Bull-and-Bower, high on the crest of Hampstead, looking out across the Heath toward London. It is winter and they have met for their twice-yearly luncheon, four women artists, two of whom are students, and two, elders.

They have arrived in full panoply; indeed it is a point of pride to them to dress with the utmost care for the luncheons. Their beauti-fully wrought costumes have an air of ceremony, and rightfully so, for these women must work so hard and so well to be artists in a world that disdains them, that the luncheon at which they break bread together has become a sacrament, and their mutual trust, a mission. They are waiting because there is one chair yet open at the table, reserved for a third student, the maverick of the group, Miss Beatrice Brooks.

"Perhaps we may start with the wine," Mrs. Hopkins tells the waiter. She has chosen a midnight-blue, velvet Empire coat with matching skirt, a snowy white waist; her hat is a crown of purple, blue, black, and white feathers. The Empire coat is trimmed in gray fox. She is a widow now and rarely sees any of her husband's old colleagues from the Hudson's Bay Company. She resides in a small house on Fitzjohns, where she paints and gives lessons in the after-noon. The lost children are not forgotten, but there are also the ones who thrived, and these have left her now for lives of their own. She is still a handsome woman, though grown somewhat small and delicate.

Mrs. Turner paints landscapes and has also lived in Canada. This is a strong bond between the two elders. Mrs. Turner is tightly wrapped in a tailored suit of gray broadcloth, a white tucked waist with red piping. Her one concession to gaiety, a nosegay of red silk flowers on her hat. She has accompanied Mrs. Marjorie Kinney, the young pregnant woman, from London.

Mrs. Kinney's misfortune is to be married to an intolerant man, and everyone else pities her greatly. She works *en pointilliste* in the subtle, somber colors of interiors and winter gardens. This day she wears garments of dark brown and silvered lace—more like shadows than colors—and a smoldering swath of burnt orange. There is a twining of bittersweet berries on the silvered lace of her hat, and a coat trimmed with close-speckled brown fur. Her talent is unique and soon to be temporarily subsumed in motherhood. She frowns now, still thinking of Frances Cornet.

The young woman by her side is Louise, penniless and unmarried. Louise is imbued with quiet joy and more self-assurance than any other person dining at the Bull-and-Bower. She paints portraits "for almost nothing," and takes in sewing, and avoids the snares of her class. Mrs. Hopkins gives her lessons *gratis*. Louise has donned her usual costume, a hand-made affair gleaned from remainders, mended and cunningly disguised with embroidery and Irish crochet. She has fashioned it to give the effect of a camellia, flower and leaves together, for the dress is ivory silk trimmed with ruffles of dusky dark green, and the hat also, a mound of ivory chiffon and dark green set on her braided blond hair. Louise must hide the stains on her gloves by holding her wine glass just so. Her old, black worsted paletot is tucked out of sight under her chair.

Finally, Miss Beatrice enters and approaches the table. She is hatless and offers no apology. Her hair, a dark cloud trailing curls. She flings off an enormous fur coat—black karakul, of course—to reveal a narrow skirt and waist with tight gigot sleeves, all in brilliant yellow *moiré*, as if the noon-day summer sun had come to luncheon. There are audible gasps from other tables in the room. She is not pretty, but possesses a flawless hourglass figure, molded, as all their bodies are to varying degrees, by merciless corsetry. Beatrice longs for an atelier in Paris, bare and cold and close to the raw currents of art to be found in that city. Meanwhile, her wealthy family endeavors to marry her off as soon as possible.

"I am so very anxious to see a Cézanne!" she says now, with real despair in her voice.

With studied grace, the women lean forward to begin their discussion in earnest. They waste no time on trifles, but cover thoroughly every puzzling, weighty concern that has mulled in their minds for six months: rumors from Paris, suffragettes at home, the relative merits of impasto versus gouache, who had gone to the varnishing, membership in good standing with the Society of Women Artists, *et cetera*. This talk is like balm to their souls. Anon, luncheon is served. There are two roasted capons with savory dressing, apple tarts, and more wine. Then tea and sweets and more tea. As always, Miss Beatrice pays for Louise, though no one, not even Louise, acknowledges the act. It becomes somewhat late in the afternoon, and the lamps are turned up. London is a dim crenellation on the southern horizon, toward which they all gaze during a pause.

Louise smiles, then laughs, to break the spell. "It's been done, I imagine."

"Yes," says Mrs. Turner, "But one may paint it in one's own way."

"*If* one knows one's way," Mrs. Kinney adds.

Miss Beatrice throws up her hands, as if to cry, "At last!" for this is what really troubles her. She says, "But there are so many ways, so many choices—I am resolved to try everything! It is impossible, of course! How *do* you choose what to paint, Mrs. H?"

"Oh, well—" Mrs. Hopkins is at a loss for a moment; she feels an unaccustomed flush on her cheeks. "I suppose I choose to paint the subjects for which I care most deeply." Then she thinks to herself with chagrin, How quaint I've become!

She does not say that painting, for her, is like touching the things that she loves, like caressing what is impossible to caress.

At half past three, they gather their things, and rise to exchange hugs and advice for their respective journeys home. Mrs. Kinney dabs at her eyes and says bravely, "I shall see you all this summer with babe in arms!"

"Of course you will, my dear!" they reply in chorus. Then the five of them kiss good-byes and, reluctantly, depart from the Bull-and-Bower.

Mrs. Hopkins has already decided to walk part-way home over the Heath, however worn out she may be from the luncheon. The talk has inspired her, as usual, and the Heath, she knows, with its muted winter colors, will provide a perfect foil for her imagination. It pleases her that high Hampstead is the source of ancient rivers—the Tyburn, the Fleet, the Brent, and the Westbourne—buried or neglected now, but flowing, all the same, downhill to the sea. She strikes out with some energy, her old muscles aching but warming as she goes. She thinks, I must finish the Superior picture by tomorrow, in the morning with the good light.

Up ahead, she sees Miss Beatrice's trap returning to meet her and bear her safely home.

33.

Lake Superior

Winter 2020

Gentle Reader,

Of what, one may wonder, does Kitchi Gami dream? Of the sea far below? The whale that cleaves the water? The wide wings of albatross?

I venture that there exists a kind of maritime kinship among large bodies of water on this earth. Superior, one of a select few, is called an inland sea, the evidence of which is overwhelmingly apparent to, for example, the mariner. How easy to lose sight of all land on Lake Superior! Like the sea, this uppermost of the Great Lakes is massive enough to brew its own weather; when provoked by storm, it bends all to its will. Its currents swirl in vast eddies before coalescence and departure via Saint Marys River. It is large enough to feel a faint pull from the moon.

And at bottom, Lake Superior shares much the same sort of rock that makes the floors of the oceans—dark, dense floods of basalt. In the ocean, this rock finds its way from the interior in molten state and flows outward in suffocating sheets, heavy with minerals sucked from the earth's mantle. It is like a magnificent subterranean simmering that occasionally boils over. Most often this occurs along deep ocean ridges, but sometimes within the fastnesses of continents. There was a period of time, over a billion years past, when such a mid-continent rift appeared beneath the land that now lies beneath Lake Superior. This rift sliced an arc from Kansas north to the lake, and south again through southernmost Michigan. All along the rift, basaltic lava issued forth and hardened into rock— twenty, thirty, forty *thousand* feet thick. And then volcanoes, of the usual type found on continents; from these erupted a lighter, more pugnacious lava, which also hardened into new rock. It went on for a hundred million years. Would the continent part? In geologic terms it was a near thing, but in the end the sundering was thwarted by mountains rising in the east.

The great weight of the new rock caused its own subsidence, pressing the arc of the rift down along its length, including the apex in the north, so that the layers began to buckle into folds and faults. Thus, the syncline of ancient rock that underlies Lake Superior. It is oriented from west to east, and, interbedded with the colorful, comely rocks that came both before and after, it accounts for many of the scenic delights of our time. Isle Royale and the Keweenaw Peninsula, two limbs of a bowed layer of rock. The dark range of heights round Thunder Bay; the protective cap of twelve-hundred-foot Sibley Peninsula. In the east, there is the blue-gray soaring wall of Old Woman Bay, and Gros Cap near the Soo, and far, far from most places, there is Michipicoten Island.

It is well to remember that these billion-year-old rocks cover others still older—greenstones and granites and gneisses of the Canadian Shield, and sandstones left from ancient seas, seas without life, and later, seas that nurtured the first organisms, the first photosynthesizers. All of these, and the great rift-born rocks, too, were subsequently washed again by seas, those of the Cambrian, Silurian, Devonian, *et cetera*, ages beyond comprehension—it is only by their record in stone that we know of, but do not comprehend, their passage. Does it help to think of the land under Lake Superior as dwelling once in the southern hemisphere? Much has changed. But when the seas drained away at last, the lowlands of the old rift syncline gathered the rain and the springs into ancestral rivers. One river flowed west, then south; another east and south; and possibly there was another running north along a faultline to today's Lake Nipigon. One more item of note before we think of Ice, and that is Space, for sometime after the rifting, a meteorite—a meteorite!—hurtled into the Superior basin, the results of which conflagration are the Slate Islands. (So we must always be looking over our shoulders.)

The great cooling began about two million years ago, roughly coincident with the Pleistocene epoch, and deepened until ice accumulated into thick sheets on the order of magnitude of continents. Here, we are concerned with the Laurentide ice sheet. In the environs of today's Hudson Bay, the Laurentide grew so thick it could not endure its own weight and so flowed outward from its center in monstrous, towering lobes. Its advances and retreats were numerous, but inch by inch, the ice bulldozed everything in its path. At first, it followed the lowlands, such as Superior's basin, excavating there a two-thousand-foot trench from east to west before nosing south. Eventually the ice overflowed up onto the highlands and had its way with everything as far as Missouri, save only for a driftless and possibly magical piece of southwest Wisconsin.

The ice ages ruled long and did not begin to give way until just fifteen thousand years ago. It was during the giving way that giant, freshwater lakes formed between the ice and higher land. These lakes, called "proglacial," existed in an ever-shifting configuration of drainage patterns for some seven millennia before condensing into their descendants: Great Bear Lake, Great Slave Lake, Athabasca, Manitoba-Winnepegosis and Winnipeg; and eastward: Superior, Michigan, Huron, Erie, Ontario. They are a satellite-eye semicircle on the northwest, west, and southern edges of the Canadian Shield. Their proglacial counterparts were McConnell, Agassiz (four times larger than Lake Superior), Keweenaw-Duluth, Chicago-Algonquin, Maumee, and Iroquois. Lastly and farther north, there appeared Lake Ojibway, continuous with Agassiz to its west; but Ojibway drained catastrophically and did not leave a true heir. There is a treacherous, mercurial element to the phenomenon of a melting sheet of ice. Years upon years go peacefully by as the lakes grow and the glacier wanes, and then, a rotten spur will collapse, or a dam is breached, and the deluge follows. Uncountable tons of water are simply unleashed, bounding downwards at millions of cubic feet per second, carving canyons, erasing life, and what is left is a mudscape, stretching, perhaps, from one horizon to the other. The devastation is colonized by ragweed (horrors!) and such, and then small trees and grasses until the next flood. The insecurity of such an environment is astounding, surpassing even life on the lip of a sleeping volcano. Either way, one knows that disaster will come.

But the proglacial lakes changed in more tranquil ways too, as when a lower outlet emerged from the ice. The old outlet would be left on high and the new one would fill, gradually lowering the lake until temporary equilibrium was found. It was in this way that fish and other organisms journeyed from one watershed to another, until, for example, the range of the northern pike extended from the Mississippi River to the Mackenzie.

Lake Superior's proglacial ancestor opened from west to east, beginning about twelve thousand years ago. The first was Lake Keweenaw, a western fragment that drained away to the Mississippi River. It should be noted that the ice did not give up easily; several times it reclaimed territory, but eventually a stage was reached that produced Lake Duluth. This lake chose the Bois Brule-St. Croix route to the Mississippi, in the process cutting a beautiful gorge in the St. Croix valley. How proud our Daniel Greysolon would be had he witnessed the work of his namesake! The ice continued to recede until an outlet lower still appeared, the Au Train and White-fish rivers in today's Upper Peninsula of Michigan, and thence to Lake Michigan. Finally, between nine and ten thousand years ago, St. Marys River was freed and thereafter remained the outlet of the lake. This stage is called Lake Minong, larger than our Lake Superior, for when the ice melted far to the east and opened the mouth of the Fleuve Saint-Laurent, the upper lake levels fell. One imagines a long whoosh as they drained to the sea. At this stage, Superior is called Lake Houghton, and together with Huron, flowed directly to the Ottawa River by way of Nipissing, the exact route followed by latter-day voyageurs.

So Quebec rose again, relieved of its burden of ice, and this post-melting rebound leaves evidence all through the glaciated lands in the form of beaches, terraces, and abandoned outlets, stranded high above water. Tributaries on rising land plunge down rapids and falls to the lakes. The Bois Brule, for example, switched its flow to become a tributary to Lake Superior, while St. Croix remains true to the Mississippi. The headwaters of the two rivers are separated by a patch of wet land that was once a much-used portage trail, now obscure. The Superior basin is still rising and also tilting, so that the northern shores of both mainland and islands stand taller than those of the southern. 'Round about seven thousand years ago, the lay of the land drew close to that of our time. Barring irreparable effects from human meddling, the ice may return one day; it lingers now in its arctic strongholds, like Canada's Baffin Island. From the air, it is like a huge flattened dome of white porcelain. In the meantime, we have five Great Lakes, interlinked and glorious and bound for communion with the wide blue Atlantic.

Where were the people in all that time? It is possible that they'd been on this continent for tens of thousands of years, but the evidence falters. We do know they crossed a temporary land-bridge from Asia, a fortuitous consequence of the fact that water frozen in ice sheets cannot quite fill up the seas. By circa twelve thousand years ago, people had found the southern edge of the ice sheet, and over the following millennia, they trickled throughout both North and South America. But some took their stand in the shadow of ice, where they hunted the megafauna of the times, mastodons and others, and caribou feasting on lichen. The people of the Pleistocene followed the animals; the animals followed the plants; all moved in sync with the retreats and returns of the ice. In the land around Superior there were as early as ten thousand years ago the Plano people, so called by us moderns. They were succeeded by the Shield-Archaic people, then the Laurel, and lastly in our time, the Woodland people, of whom the Ojibway count as one nation. The earliest people no doubt witnessed the terrible floods of the melting. Think of the stories! All the same, people love water, and so there remains evidence of long habitation at the mouths of tributary rivers: St. Marys, Pic River, the White and the Willow, and Michipicoten, to name a few.

A mysterious catastrophe occurred at the end of the Pleistocene: the nearly simultaneous extinctions of as many as forty species of large mammals. Some grim coincidence of competition in the growing warmth and the unenlightened hunting techniques of Pleistocene people, as well as, no doubt, other as yet unidentified factors. It took scarcely three thousand years. In the northern forests, the survivors were moose, timber wolves, caribou, elk, black bears, cougars, deer, and just fifty miles southwest of Duluth, dark streaming herds of bison. The swimmers survived as well, cradled in Superior's basin. All these and the native people remained, *co-evolvers* with Kitchi Gami.

And who knows what curiosities of antiquity still find refuge in the lake? There are rumors and legends and half-seen dreams. Any mariner can tell (with dread) of the little ice devils that congeal in a ship's rigging until their weight pulls it down. There are the storm-spawned sister waves, hunting together in threes. There is *La Vieille*, much-feared old woman of the wind. There is a little spirit cedar tree. It is said that Lake Superior is ruled by Mishi-bizheu, the great lynx, counterpart of Thunderbirds; he dwells in chasms and deeps, but he is not the only one. The ice water of Kitchi Gami is also home to the *nebaunaubaewuk*, the sleek and glimmering merfolk, and their motives are hidden from us.

34.

A Revelation

Summer 1693

As Frances Cornet and the Hurons descended to the great northern sweetwater seas, the weather closed in around them with fog and drizzle. Still they pressed on to the west. Near where the way split between Missilimackinac and the Sault Sainte Marie, they met several parties of traders, both Indian and French, all going down to Montréal with some three years' worth of furs. Though they were starting out in casual bunches, they planned to gather at the Lac Nipissing and to burst through the Iroquois blockades in a mass. There would be hundreds of canoes, Jiwatena and his people were informed. With each encounter, the Huron had to explain the presence of the girl. The eyes of the traders, especially those that looked out from homesick souls, lingered long on the blond. It was extraordinary to see her there. Her eyes cast down, she answered the rain of questions and off-color jokes with talk of marriage, or of deals, or even of joining the Jesuit fathers at their post—all utter nonsense. Always, she would say the name of Jean Garamond, Jean Garamond, with every other breath. Because that name was known rather well in the country by then, they let her pass, for the traders were all going one way, and the Hurons and the girl, another. Perhaps it was thought she would never get by the post at the Sault.

But when, after so many weeks of journeying, they approached that place, Frances took her fate in her hands and slipped away in the middle of a starless night. She had determined to take no chances with men of authority of any sort.

The Hurons, on finding the *Française* gone, could not say whether they were saddened or relieved. There were some who raged, thinking themselves duped, and some wiser ones who laughed. After the incident of the storm, almost all of these people had come to feel an obligation to take the girl to her husband if they could. That it was a matter of soul desire, no one doubted. In this, they deferred to the old woman, Blue Wing, who had taken over the care of the *oki*. So it was Blue Wing whom Jiwatena asked first for counsel when the girl disappeared.

"*Anan*, we must decide what to do," he said. "My brothers wish to turn back to Missilimackinac to rejoin the others. Tiron and your daughter would look for the girl. I am thinking we should tell the people at the post, but I would hear your thoughts on this matter."

Blue Wing did not hesitate. "We must go on as if she were with us. Say nothing to the traders. Then we will see."

The people wondered much at this. Some muttered it was amusement gone far enough. Others were fired by the idea of a journey to Nipigon, for some had never been there, and all wanted part of the trade in copper and Cree medicines, and it was the willingness of these that finally decided Jiwatena. And he was curious to see what would come of Blue Wing's advice. So ten of the people in three canoes went on, at a leisurely pace, up the river to the post.

"Do you think we will see the *Française* again?" Dawn asked her mother as they left. "She has run off like an Iroquois slave."

Blue Wing only shrugged. She was not surprised when the girl hailed them from shore, two days later, and far beyond the post.

When the skies cleared at last, they were cruising the north and east shore of the Rivière Sainte Marie, there more than a league across and redolent of big lake. On either shore were gathered towering headlands that guarded the entrance to the Lac Supérieur. They rounded the one on the east—Gros Cap. Here, they tucked neatly into a small cleft of a bay with a beach of pink and gray cobbles, for they knew there were berries to pick on the steeps of the cape. Frances declined to go with them, for her feet were still battered from her flight through the woods.

The little beach was wreathed in cedar, pine, and rock, and so hidden at the foot of Gros Cap that she felt as if, being there, she were part of a lovely secret. This pleased her very much. The lake was still, and a loon, its black and white feathers glistening, hunted for fish therein. There were smooth, flat rocks at the waterline reaching out to the lake, red and pink, just ankle-deep beneath the surface. After a while, thinking to cleanse and numb her feet, Frances walked out onto one of the slabs. The pain of the cold water was immediate and intense. She tried to concentrate instead on the view before her. The far headland lay on the western edge of the horizon, and beyond that, another point receded to just beyond sight. To her right was a low island, far away. To the north, the lake flowed away in a stainless expanse, a clean slate, and there her gaze was fixed. How long did she look? The only sounds were the soft lap of water and the muffled splash of the loon. The air was sunlit, but cool as if edged in frost. It was if all these things conspired to mesmerize Frances Cornet, not in the way of madness, but in the sudden brilliance of clarity, in the realization of what she really did want. At some point, she dropped to her knees, her gray skirt floating in the water, and uttered one small, thrilled cry. In that moment, the man Garamond was forgotten, as well as the entire edifice of her life, her people, and her family. Frances Cornet was aware that she only desired one thing in the world, and that was to stay with the Lac Supérieur.

The others returned to the beach at mid-day, bearing a quantity of ripe berries. The old woman, Blue Wing, came last down the slippery trail exclaiming, "Ah!" for she'd skinned her knuckles again on the rocks. Berry-picking had done her no good at all, and now she parried stabs of pain with every step. She noticed right away there was something different about the *Française*, who was sitting primly on a boulder, waiting for them, all innocence. But there was something—

"Heh, Anjou, what have you been up to?" Blue Wing eased herself down next to the girl. "Let me see your feet," she said.

Obediently, Frances unwrapped her feet, red and sore, but also wrinkled from standing in water. Blue Wing studied the feet and glanced searchingly several times at the girl's fathomless expression.

"We will give you a grease to heal your feet," she said casually, fishing for clues. But the girl's only reply was a radiant smile.

The next week, they camped and paddled their way north along beaches, cliffs, and broad pleasant bays. The days were fair, the breezes mild. Even so, they prudently saved travel for mornings and nights, and whiled away their afternoons on shore, so that the sand was decorated with purple beach peas and grasses, canoes and sleeping brown bodies. Sometimes the wind did come up, and so they stayed for the night. Every morning, Blue Wing observed that immediately on waking, the *Française* went to kneel at the water's edge, and there, it seemed, she paid a kind of homage. There was only one more occurrence of note before they left the mainland for the Île Michipicoton, and that was when they passed an especially haunted chasm, a dark rent in the rock. Everyone saw how a winter wind issued from this infamous chasm and touched the *Française*, alone among them, so that her fluttering hair flew straight up to the sky. There was a dry, clacking noise of insects, and the girl looked around in delight, as if summoned by some familiar. But then they passed the chasm, and no one spoke their thoughts aloud. They fell back to routine: ten paddles dipped in pleasant syncopation; three bark hulls slicing water. The north grew large and the south disappeared.

There was one thing the Hurons desired very much on this journey, and that was to hunt caribou on the floating island, the Île Michipicoton. This island, perhaps four or five leagues off the nearest coast, was both blessed and cursed, for treasure and spirits of all temper were found in abundance there. The island had come to be known as Michipicoton to the Indians and the *coureurs de bois*, but it had other names, many left unsaid, and many faces.

Jiwatena, as they turned to the west for the nearest approach to the island, kept watch on the sky and the mood of the lake. They would only try the crossing if the island stood firm on the horizon and retained its shape every moment. It did so, and the days passed serenely as they had for a fortnight, so Jiwatena rose at dawn, took a last long look, and gave the signal to cross.

"No tricks, now," he muttered to the powers of the world. He even cast a stern glance at the *Française* and the old woman.

It did no good. Just past half way, the island started to shiver and to gently lift itself up. The people would blink their eyes and it solidified, only to resume its play moments later. By the time they touched shore, both they and the island were bathed in smoking mist.

Despite this questionable beginning, the hunting was excellent. In two days, four caribou were killed. Fires were built on the red cobble beaches, hides were cured, meat smoked. They ate all they wanted. Still, the feasting was marred by nerves, and on the fourth day the wind swooped down on the island. After that, not one more animal was seen, and the people unanimously abandoned any idea of more hunting. Should the wind die, they would escape to the mainland as quickly as they could.

Every morning for three more days, Jiwatena took up his vigil and watched the shapes of the hurtling waves on the beach. Sometimes there was a lull, and the people made ready to leave, but he knew better. The wind rose again from another quarter and so they waited. Then, one night, Blue Wing woke with a headache and knew right away that the *Française* was gone. Within an hour, it was raining with a vengeance.

The Hurons, of course, were formidable trackers, but in finding the trail of the girl, they had no success. They looked all that day, through the rain and after, and when the sky cleared and the lake turned mellow and summery, they buried their desire to leave and looked for her still. "Anjou, Anjou!" Blue Wind called ceaselessly, "Where have you gone?" There was never any answer or sign.

Jiwatena looked again to Blue Wing for advice, for he was sure the time to cross had come. Yet, he was loth to leave the *Française*.

"I have taken her under my protection, *anan*. Still, the island will not bear us long," he said.

"I know it." Blue Wing also knew in her heart they would not find the girl. She knew that the girl had gone to seek her soul desire, and that the husband was not her object was perfectly clear.

"We cannot hinder her," she said slowly. She had never felt more exhausted. "We shall be driven away, no matter what you think you should do."

At that, Jiwatena lost no more time in deciding and told the people to prepare to leave at first light for the mainland. He and two others would go on to Nipigon to trade and to search for the man, Garamond. Tiron, the women, and the rest would return to Missilimackinac and inform the black gowns or the soldiers, whomever they should see first, of the fate of the girl.

"We shall leave here some of the meat we have cured and Tiron's corn, and one of the hides. Bundle it," he gestured to Dawn and Blue Wing, "and mark it so she may find it if she returns to this place."

At his words, audible relief ran through the camp. They had all had enough of the Île Michipicoton, and all save the old woman were more than happy to be rid of the *oki Française*. Had she not brought only trouble? Now, perhaps, they would be blamed, despite all their pains on her behalf.

They assembled the precious cache for the lost *Française*, and, in the last red light of day, piled a cairn of stones above it. When no one was looking, Dawn slipped in her new husband's flint and firesteel. Then Blue Wing tied long strips of leather to a pole that she planted in the stones, and thus they marked it.

In the morning, so benign and so clear, the lake spread before them as still as blue ice. The Hurons departed. In one canoe, the young bride looked back at the island, perhaps wistfully, and said, "Do you think she is already dead?"

"No! Do not think so," said Blue Wing, looking straight ahead to the mainland. "The *Française* is alive and she will even find the cache." After a moment, she added, more softly, "I am wondering, if *les chrétiens* forsake their saints to consort with spirits, who can tell what will happen next?" The daughter did not reply, but the spirits did, for a little breeze sprang up to push them north.

35.

What I Know About Michipicoten Island

Summer 1992

DURING HIS ONE year of college, my son Walt had become something of a scholar—unfortunately *outside* of class. And he was far too tuned in to other peoples' needs for his own good. I had only mentioned my desire to get to the island on this trip, and within a week, he had mailed me several photocopied pages on the geology, ecology, history, and current status of eastern Lake Superior, including Michipicoten Island. It makes me worry that Walt is not so happy in Madison, that it's a bit too big, a little too loose, and that he's taken refuge in doing things for Mom. I called him right away to see what was going on, but he said, "No, everything's great," too breezily, and I resolved to pay him a surprise visit in August. He will hate that, but I, of course, cannot be avoided.

Anyway, the information about the island was very interesting. Except for a handful of private inholdings and a couple lighthouses, it is complete wilderness. Ontario has made it a provincial park, and so it is likely to remain wild for the duration, as they say, especially because it is so hard to reach. There is no regular boat service. You must have your own hull and motor, or you must hitch a ride with someone, and precious few people are going that way. My heart sank at that.

The island is a rocky, forbidding thing, like much of the northern shores of Lake Superior. It is made out of lava, 1.1 billion years old—how young I feel—that cooled into red rhyolites and andesites to the south, and somber basalt to the north. There is black obsidian, shiny and rare for having survived uncrushed for so long, and also agates on the beaches. This last I remember hearing from Grandma Beth, so it must be true; something about a Lady Duffey? Dufferin? Another wealthy Victorian tourist in long skirts, this one searching for pretty stones while she waited for her steamer to refuel. I decided I must look for agates if I ever get to Michipicoten Island. It would be like a treasure hunt.

The island is high and hilly, a thousand feet above the lake at its loftiest point, and many of these heights are arranged in east-west ridges. There is an island chain off the southern shore, also trending east-west. The ridges rise abruptly to their north and gently to their south. Around the circumference of the island, forty or so miles, there are occasional beaches and caves stranded above the water because the island has risen, you see, as the glaciers melted and drained away. They call this "isostatic rebound," and apparently it's still happening wherever the big ice had been and gone.

Inhabiting all this rugged terrain is a peculiar assortment of animals: woodland caribou, large and fearless beavers, mice, birds, snowshoe hares, eye of newt, et cetera, but there are no deer, moose, bears, or wolves. The largest, but not the only predator of consequence (for there are weasels) is the red fox. All the vegetation in this place is typical of the mainland, that is, boreal forest, especially down low, and northern hardwoods adorning the ridges. In the coldest pockets, relict plants of the arctic still thrive; small and strange or deceptively pretty, they are tough enough to grow at the glacier's edge, should the glacier ever return. In the meantime, the forest, exceptionally lush and thick, dominates. It has escaped fire, for the most part, and large-scale logging, and in any case, it is bathed year in and year out by the moist, tempering atmosphere of the lake.

The island is about nine miles south of a long curving sweep of the mainland, but that short distance hardly counts as an easy crossing, because if you're thinking of launching from the coast there, it is all ramparts of rock, and no friendly, civilized amenities like docks and fuel pumps. Even today, the nearest road is over forty miles away at Michipicoten Harbor, near Wawa. So people make the boat trip from there, which keeps the riff-raff out, as Dad would say. Of course, the stout-hearted could paddle, following the coast and camping, until coming even with that deceptively short nine-mile crossing. But so much can happen on Lake Superior in the time it takes to paddle that distance. The most seasoned of sea kayakers think long and hard, and likely stay put in the end. This from Irv.

Not that there's ever been much of a rush to Michipicoten Island. The Ojibway did not want to go there, and perhaps they still don't. We read about the Sarah Pucaswa legend, while killing time in Hattie Cove: Sarah and her husband Joe and her sons were an Ojibway family living on the island in days gone by. Sarah and Joe argued one day, and Sarah set off in a canoe to escape her husband's wrath. He caught up with her and murdered her. There is a certain amount of what we used to call "bad karma," in our innocent way. I remember well the dire tone of voice that Grandma Beth always used to speak of it. But, I thought, it's all just hearsay, isn't it?

As for the whites, they came and they went; a few stayed. As early as 1647, the French had drawn the island on their maps, calling it "Missipacouatong," though no one seems to know just what that means. Does it name the mainland cliffs, or the harbor, or the river that leads to James Bay, or the island? The translations have merged into a linguistic stew of "high bluffs" and "sand." Then, for a while, the island was called Île Maurepas, after some French official, a bigwig in a wig, I am sure. The Brits took over in the mid-1700s, and finally the name "Michipicoten" attained semi-permanence.

It was the British, and then the Canadians and Americans who made a serious try for the island's riches, for it was thought to bear rich veins of copper, silver, nickel, and iron like Michigan's Upper Peninsula, Isle Royale, and the Sibley Peninsula. Various schemes were executed at the bidding of bright-eyed adventurers and money. Shafts sank on the western and northern shores; miners toiled with the sort of heedless fortitude of which people are sometimes capable, though not often in these days. The island stubbornly refused to yield.

But there was fishing. In fact, it was the Hudson's Bay Company, Frances Anne Hopkins's benefactor, that set up a fishing camp in the 1800s to help provide food for their voyageurs. Though the fur trade was winding down by then. They gave it up to an American, a Mr. Booth, whose company pulled fish from the lake until the 1930s. Then there was the Purvis family—locals—for several decades more, and finally Ferroclad Fisheries. All this went on at the Quebec Harbor fishing station on the south shore of the island, which is virtually deserted now. You see, that dread foreigner, the sea lamprey, did a number on the fish of all the Great Lakes, and Kitchi Gami did not escape. But a modest recovery has begun and the fishing still goes on. Today, some of the boats on which modern-day tourists can ride to Michipicoten Island are commercial fishing boats, bound for its whitefish-bearing reefs.

And there's shipping: ferries in the old days to and from the island, and today, freighters, plying the lanes between Thunder Bay, Duluth, and Sault Sainte Marie. Storms have often dictated the exact rendering of these routes, and storms have claimed hundreds of vessels on Lake Superior. There are seven (or more) wrecks round the shores of Michipicoten, and in fact, our famous *Edmund Fitzgerald* may have hit a shoal between there and Caribou Island to the south, and that sealed its fate. The weather never seems to improve for any length of time on this lake, what with gales, fog, and freezing rain; thus the lighthouses. There are three on Michipicoten, two of which are very beautiful, and no doubt they've averted countless disasters. But are they effective against mirage? Against bad karma? That is my burning question.

Grandma Beth says this about Michipicoten Island, "My dear, the island floats like a castle; it stretches and hunches like a very big inchworm. It often grows vast broad-brimmed hats."

It's common knowledge that many islands are prone to mirage when seen from afar, but that doesn't satisfy me. There's something else going on here, I mean, would Michipicoten settle down if it were settled? Well, perhaps I'm doing some fishing myself. I can't help it though; the possibility of going to this floating daydream of an island, to see it for myself, has taken on an urgency all out of proportion to everything else that has happened this past year. I can feel how the time I've spent on the Pukaskwa coast has slowed my pace, stilled me inside enough to know certain things. That Irv will leave, that Jerry is still gone forever, that Marinette wants me but maybe there are other places, other people. I am looking for a crystal ball, or failing that, clues, and I think they are waiting for me on the island. Yes, that's crazy talk. What else would you expect when you consider the source—not me, but the one I'm named for, Frances Cornet?

36.

A Tweak of Fate

Summer 1693

GARAMOND OF ANJOU, resplendent in fringes and paint and long strings of beads, sat fuming on a shady hillock above a beach. He was oscillating swiftly between guilt and resentment, back and forth, over and over, until he was driven to ramble uncertainly on moccasined feet. Then he sat down again by the letters strewn on the ground and ran his hands through his black, curly hair, grown long now, almost to the middle of his back. His fingers flashed with rings as they slid through his hair.

His companion, one Saint Pierre, sat farther back in the trees where they'd set up their camp. There was a fire in a pit of stones with a kettle dangling above, a row of bundles and kegs, neatly arrayed, and the canoe, its seams newly sealed and drying slowly out of the sun. On the bow of the canoe was painted a vividly blue and cheerful soaring jay.

Saint Pierre had set himself the task of melting lead into balls for the muskets. He had spread all of his implements in a semicircle before him: slim bars of lead, ladle, hatchet, molds. A clean leather mat on which to catch the shiny new ammunition. He was all ready to start; still he waited, glancing curiously at the *Anjevin*.

What could those letters say to agitate his partner so? Saint Pierre did not know the riddles of the written word, for which, at the moment, he was sorry.

They were encamped on the Point aux Pins, a low, flat peninsula some way above the settlement at the Sault Sainte Marie. The peninsula was cool and calm beneath a waving canopy of pine. The beach alternated agreeably from golden sand to smooth, colored pebbles. It was a good place to hide out and think.

Saint Pierre could no longer contain himself and called out loudly, "Heh! What is the matter?"

Garamond flung him a look over his shoulder. He did not retort, "That is none of your concern!" for it surely would be if he, Garamond, went off on a fool's errand instead of tending to business as he ought. Or ought he? That was the question. But how was he to know where the little girl was? It would be impossible to find her.

That he and Saint Pierre were heading west and not east was according to plan, after all. Having left Nipigon in the spring, they and the others of Grand Père's cohort had assembled at Missilimackinac with the hundreds of traders and all of their furs, poised to pour heedlessly into the glutted beaver markets of the east. By the early days of August, the hordes had gone with an echoing sigh of farewell, so that the whole region of the Straits and the Sault seemed unpeopled. A few remained, and Garamond and Saint Pierre were two of these. They'd filled their canoe to capacity with trade goods skimmed from the supposed re-garrisoning of the posts—there was, of course, a war on, though that was forgotten now and then—and they'd stowed the rest in Mercier's stout little warehouse for later. Now, they would make for the post at Chegouwameeagan where Grand Père himself waited in dignified repose. Unless there were complications.

"I am thinking," Garamond answered at last, "whether I should have taken the sacraments, you know?"

Saint Pierre gave a snort. "All right, keep your secrets."

Garamond stretched out on his back to stare up at the lacy green of the pines. He *was* thinking about penance and the possibility that he was long overdue. He had striven for three years to become an *homme honnête*, as Cornet had instructed, and he had done so and enriched his masters. However, he had not thought seriously of going back east in the meantime. Rather, he followed Grand Père's example: his trade was not limited to furs, and he tended his business from the Northwest, the *pays d'en haut*, comfortably far from the colony. Even though his contract with Cornet was fulfilled the past summer, Garamond did not care to test his freedom in Montréal. Instead, he went back to the village of Issati to harvest rice and to see the old woman Yellow Deer, and also the forbidden fruit—Sitka Toh. Just as he'd done every fall.

There were, by then, many women in the north who thought passionately of the *Anjevin* trader and his charming foreign ways. He had enjoyed himself very much. Still, he never gave up on the Dakota woman; each year he'd contrived to make his proposal, "Come away from here with me." Now, as he chafed in purgatory on the Point aux Pins, he thought only of delay and the thwarting of his will. He thought, I should be halfway to Chegouwameeagan by now, and in his mind's eye, he envisioned all the rivers and streams and lakes between that place and the Issatis.

He picked up one of the letters that lay next to him. It was the only one he wanted to read: the usual business missive from Cornet, Laverdure, and Cadot, dated 20 *mars*, a meticulous record of the goods they were sending, and the fervent hope that he could come down with the brigade. All seemed well. But another letter had been included with that one, one which filled him with frustration and worry. He did not read it again now. It was the letter from his family in famine-ridden Anjou: their money was worth nothing; his brother was taken by Louis' army; the fields were dust. *Merci de Dieu!* All the woe, all the dire chances of life in France came back over Garamond in a queasy flood. He turned over on his stomach and cried, "Bah!" Saint Pierre got up and walked away in disgust.

Then there was the third letter, the desperate appeal of Bernard

Cornet, made doubly alarming by the fact that a steady, respectable merchant was actually pleading without shame for a peasant's help. "She is looking for you!" the man's voice blared in Garamond's head, "She is just a child and knows nothing. I beg you, if you are an honorable man, you must find her and bring her back to her poor mother. If the girl is not returned, *ma femme* swears she will leave New France. Think, Jean Garamond, of all the favors I have done you." There was no hint of acknowledgment that the task was hopeless.

Garamond rolled over and sat up. His face was set in determination. He took up again a quill and a sheet of brown paper; he shook the jar of ink, dipped, and began writing furiously. Within moments, he'd crumpled the precious paper and cast it on the ground, where it lay among the others in the ferns.

Just north of the Point aux Pins, where the escarpment of Gros Cap heaved its mass from the water, the party of Hurons that included Blue Wing, her daughter, and her son-in-law, advanced with all speed to the Sault. That night, they came to rest on the southern shore of the cape. There was the usual evening discussion: Should they divulge the whereabouts of the *Française*? Or would it be wiser to let the whole thing slide?

"It will come out by and by," said the man, Tiron, trying to impress his bride with his *savoir faire*. "We would be seen as remiss if it were discovered against our will."

"Yes, and perhaps not!" retorted another, a younger man who enjoyed a good argument. Their current dilemma gave him endless openings and so, irresponsibly, he relished it. "Perhaps the soldiers will enslave us or plunder our houses! Who knows what they may do if—"

"All this is useless talk," the old woman broke in.

They wrangled for another hour or so. In the morning, the sharp-eyed young bride claimed to see smoke rising from the peninsula to the south, "It is an encampment!" she cried, but others were sure it was mist. So they passed it by.

Two days later, Garamond, still tarrying at the Point aux Pins, spied a canoe with three Indian men paddling up from the Sault. He watched them silently, his heart gradually constricting, and hoped against hope they would pass and Saint Pierre would see nothing. But they pulled directly onto the shore near his camp and called out. He didn't move. Saint Pierre went out to them and soon they were conversing and gesturing, and Garamond heard his name being spoken. Two of the men were Huron, but the third was Ottawa, and with a start, Garamond realized it was Little Owl, his old adversary.

Smiling broadly, the men on the beach turned to look up at the camp—to his hiding place. He knew he was discovered. "*Quel tête de con, petit hibou*, you have me," he muttered. Resigned, he got up and walked out of the trees and into the sun, and said, "That is me; I am Jean Garamond."

37.

Frances in Paradise

Summer 1693

THE GIRL, FRANCES Cornet, had been looking for something else all her life, and the farther west she proceeded, the warmer she got. Canada was the door to the world she suspected and there was no doubt she would leave her mother's house to go through that door. On her journeys with the Montagnais, and then the Huron, she forgot the past and reveled in a sudden, complete unfolding of her senses. What did she love about the wilderness? It engulfed her.

She spent her days on the Île Michipicoton rambling reindeer trails and the streams that trickled throughout. The elements, to her joy, toyed with her continually, first giving fog, then bright sun, heat, drizzle that soaked her thin dress, then cold whipping wind. Her world changed before her eyes at every turn and directed her footsteps accordingly. When it rained, she wandered among green trees under long, silver lines of rain, hopping from mound to mound, splashing through ponds and bogs. In the sun, she kept to the cobble beaches and rocks. She ate insects, raw fish, and crustaceans indiscriminately, casually, and berries when she found them. Like all children, she knew how to snare small animals, such as birds and hares. Once, a rather sluggish beaver fell prey to her arts. She could not get close to the quick-fire foxes, nor could she brave the baleful stares of the reindeer. But she survived. Even, by accident, she found the cache the Huron had left, and feasted ravenously. Then she wandered away, and forgot where it was, and then forgot it existed. She had other things on her mind.

The mosquitoes by then had bitten her so thoroughly that her body ignored them; only occasionally, if one whined too loudly in her ear, she would snatch it like lightning and curiously examine the tiny corpse in her hand. Sometimes she was lonely. So she thought to save the skins and bones of the animals she killed, and with tender care, refashion them into small effigies that she set round her for company. More and more, she came to mimic the creatures, for she thought them charming beyond compare. Once, there was a bird, so graceful as it preened and fanned its feathers, she was smitten and could not look away. It paid her no mind, as if it were an actress on a stage, and soon she was stretching her own limbs like the bird and luxuriously combing her bleached tangled hair with her fingers. But the best companions ever were the *nebaunaubaewuk* in the lake. She discovered them one day as she skipped down the shore, picking pretty agates and throwing them down. The *nebaunaubaewuk* swam in the lake, just out of sight, but coloring the atmosphere with their presence. She flirted with them, and they loved her, for she was innocent and open as the sky, as if she'd just awakened from the womb.

One night she dreamed of the *nebaunaubaewuk*—they were naked, slick, and they came to her and caressed her beyond all bounds. When she woke, she remembered for the first time in a long time her *maman*, the little home on the rue Saint-Paul, and especially clearly, the strictures of the Roman Catholic Church. The *nebaunaubaewuk* then seemed like devils. She remembered the insistent prodding of the *curé*—"Confess, daughter, before it's too late!" The example of the good sisters of the Congregation swam before her eyes. For a while, she chastised her thin body and begged forgiveness of God and Jesus, and especially of the Virgin in Heaven, surrounded by all the angels. Frances relished the pain well at first. It seemed an accomplishment of a sort, one she could show the *curé*. But it *did* hurt, and finally, when her legs and arms burned under a red lace of cuts, she stopped and waded into Kitchi Gami's icy water. She looked up and saw, not angels, but fantastic flying beasts. Soon the kindly *nebaunaubaewuk* came to wash her skin and numb her pain, and then all her thoughts turned to sex. She did not resist long. Wave after wave came to her, tickling her thighs with cool gentle fingers until she stripped off her dress, and shed her shame for good.

That evening, she found herself at the westernmost tip of the island. She had killed a gull with a stone and eaten it, and now she clambered at leisure on the rocks near the water. At her feet, nests of saxifrage and purple harebells glowed in the light of sunset. She sat down to watch all the colors, like long tremulous waves, against the dusky curve of the mainland, far away. The evening was very fine, but warm so that her wounds stung and throbbed. She watched until the colors deepened to black velvet. Then she felt her way to a crevice and tucked herself away for the night. Uncharacteristically, she slept until late in the morning.

When she woke, the first thing that caught her attention was a curious piece of driftwood, possessed of a silvery sheen, and, most remarkably, pierced with two round eyeholes. She took it up in delight and began to play with it, as if she were a lady at a ball or a spy. She loved how the mask made a frame around everything she saw. Everything seemed farther away or cast in shade. There was a cliff that rose straight up from a corner of the beach, and toward this she gradually made her way. Once there, she found a cleft in the rock that led along the base of the cliffs, and still clutching the mask, she advanced perhaps fifty yards and came to a small grotto. Here was an astonishing sight. She lowered the mask and gaped: there was a huge egg-shaped boulder wedged in the rocks. Above, a slab the size of a cottage threw all into dark shade so that only a few ferns grew here and there, like fugitives. Frances gazed longingly at the egg boulder and forgot that it was wedged in its singular position; it seemed rather, to be suspended in air beneath the giant slab. The place was like the center of the world; irresistibly, it drew her in to crouch in the small space below the boulder. A strange excitement changed her mood; her heart began to pound in answer to the power of the mass of rock above. She stayed there, frozen, until she remembered the driftwood mask in her hand and raised it to her eyes. At a distance, she could see the lake, shining in fragments through gaps in the foliage. Of a sudden, she felt a bracing jolt of objectivity, unfamiliar to be sure, and she clearly realized, deep in her wild undisciplined heart, that if she chose between the two worlds she had found, the choice would be irrevocable—that the gods would not forget. From beyond, the lake glinted and winked at Frances. When she gave in to its allure, the choice was made. Her clarity vanished as if it had never been, and there was instead the weight of the center of the world above her; it grew with unbearable pressure and she knew the place would crush her. So, in a burst of determination, she threw down the mask, scooted out, and ran away down the cleft to the beach. Too late.

38.

The Approach

Summer 1992

THURSDAY, OUR LAST day on Otter Island. Before lunch, I had hiked up to the lighthouse for one last stupendous view: north, the Pukaskwa coast, like the foothills of the Rockies dropped on the edge of Lake Superior; south, the faint smudge of Michipicoten Island; west, an endless sheet of blue. The ferry picked us up in the afternoon; the trip was scenic and uneventful. I've never been any good at anti-climax, so I was anxious to get back to Hattie Cove and put Pukaskwa behind me. I wanted to know what would happen next.

It turned out that Nicolette's advisor and his wife had come in that morning. They were expected, I guess, but I found their presence irritating. They had picked out a campsite and everything was all set up; poor Nicolette was having to account for herself from the moment she got off the ferry. We transferred all the gear, put up our tents, and then Irv and I stole away to indulge in the joy of showers.

"Hey," he said when we were done and sweet-smelling, "did you see all the wine they brought?"

"It's the least they can do, don't you think? Let's keep our distance 'til tonight, though." I grinned, combing my wet hair with my fingers. "Then we'll help 'em out with all that booze."

We wandered down to the gift shop/HQ and browsed through the souvenirs and books, and it was then that I got up my nerve to inquire about how one would get to the island. It was, after all, another Canadian park.

"Well, sometimes you can get a ride out there." This from the ranger. "You can ask around at the marina on the river, down from the highway at Wawa. Or, you can try Bergquist's. That's a fishing boat, but he'll take people out there," she smiled, "for a price. Or if he's going out anyway, he might give you a deal."

"What about a big tandem sea kayak?" I asked.

"Sure, they can put it right inside. In fact, the outfitters use Bergquist—you should try them first. Let me see if I can find some phone numbers for you." She started to rumple through desk drawers.

"Isn't that great?" I said to Irv. "Even if we could just go out for a day. We could still get back by Monday morning if we drive straight through." My head was starting to buzz with happy little plans. "I can stop for cash in Wawa—"

But he hesitated, and I eyed him with sudden attention. "Yeah." He studied the map behind the desk. "That'd be amazing. Maybe we could work it in, yeah."

I thought, No way is he going to the island; this was one clue I could read very well.

"Really, we should leave tonight, then," I said, pushing it.

"No, we have to get things squared away with Nicolette."

Reluctantly, I agreed this was necessary.

"I can't seem to find anything," the ranger looked up apologetically. "But if you just stop first thing in Wawa and make some calls, eh? The marina and Bergquist's are both in the book."

We returned to the campsite, accompanied all the way by the sound of angry red squirrels, like tiny jack hammers. I resolved to get drunk on wine if possible, and to not sleep with Irv.

The upshot of all this is that Irv backed out and I got ready to drive to Wawa myself early in the morning. Irv would stay to help Nicolette and perhaps hook back up with me on Sunday. We left it hanging because chances were that I wouldn't be able to get to the island, in which case I might come back to Hattie, or I might just head home. We were being very casual and pseudo-adult about it, but even Nicolette could detect the tension, this through her own chagrin that her advisor had essentially taken over our project in the space of two hours. We were all three putting on a brave face. The wine actually did mellow things out, for that night at least. Irv said I could use his boat, and though this did not make up for his defection—we were going to explore the soul of wilderness together and search for signs of a legend, were we not?—it gave me something to grab on to. The boat meant I would be able to paddle along the shore of Michipicoten Island. The romance of it all was almost too much; I stopped drinking at eleven so I wouldn't have too bad a hangover.

Not surprisingly, things were worse in the sober morning. Aside from the bleariness, there was Irv urging me to stay for all the wrong reasons. "What do you want to go out there for?" he was demanding before I'd even unzipped my bag. "It's not really healthy, you know, all this fixation on that girl in the story. You should stay here and finish up with us—"

"Unhealthy? Fixation?" This really pissed me off and I wonder now if he did it on purpose. I know he thought he was being the voice of reason. Well maybe he was, and usually I'm one to listen to that voice. Just not that day. I lay there and thought again of taking shortcuts through alleys, dusty ditches, old fields. Hadn't there always been something in me that did things like that? Wasn't I free now to do those things?

"You can't even afford it."

"It's just something I want to do, Irv. Who knows if I'll ever get back here? Just leave it!"

We got up. We didn't talk much after that. It was Nicolette who helped me load the boats—the other vehicles didn't have roof-racks—and my camping gear and miscellaneous junk, which seemed to fill the car to capacity.

"See, there's no room for Irv, anyway." I said.

She gave me an unsettlingly shrewd look. "So you're staying in Marinette, huh?"

"Probably."

"Good, you can be my contact at the UW. You're taking another class, right?"

I sighed. "Damn, I don't know. Maybe I should, and forget about men completely. I'm sure it wouldn't have been long before the *other woman* got to Irv, anyways."

"No, he seems like a pretty good guy."

"I give him a week, two weeks, in Madison before she finds him."

"She?"

"Yeah, he definitely isn't gay."

Nicolette said coolly, as if just making conversation, "I was the other woman once. And I have no regrets."

I could have screamed—I should have screamed—but at the time, I was just too surprised.

I was behind the wheel by 7:45, just steaming mad and roaring down Highway 17 rather faster than one hundred kilometers per hour. Wawa or bust, I guess. I was too mad to appreciate the scenery— what happened to "I might never get here again?"—and instead I cranked up the radio and chewed on my thoughts. Of course, I was furious with everyone, though I soon forgave Nicolette. Her admission didn't seem to count somehow, when stacked up against all her good points. It was perplexing, did not compute, so I pushed it to the background. You know, really, the issue was men. Man. What the hell? I thought, They are sure free to indulge their own fantasies, but let a woman— I abruptly changed the station, some goofy talk show. Idiots! It took half an hour of smooth, fast driving before I calmed down. I pulled over to take a long drink of water, and thought, What do I want from men? Instantly, my own parents appeared in my mind's eye. It was that simple.

"Look at them," I said to the trees, the road, the rocks. "They've stuck together without fail all these years and I have no doubt what-soever they'll be together when they die. That's the kind of marriage I wanted."

I smacked the dashboard hard and let out an "Argh!" It felt good. After that, I put on my tapes and drove without thinking.

Made Wawa—the big goose!—by 9:30 A.M., got gas, and found a phone. Riffled through the phone book for the outfitters, but they had no trips going just then, so they suggested the marina on the Michipicoten River.

"Oh, a sea kayak, huh? Okay." I found the man's voice gratingly innocent. "Well, we have some clients out fishing now. S'posed to come back pretty soon. I could radio them, but I'm not sure it'd work out. Did you try Bergquist's?"

"Not yet."

"Well, if he's going out, you could get a ride with him, no prob-lem. Then, depending, you might come back with my guys. Whyn't you call him and get back to me? I gotta be honest; it'll cost a bit."

I called Edward Bergquist Fisheries, but there was no answer. I thought, How bad do I want this? I asked the service station guy for directions, jumped back in the car, and drove right on down there. I guess that answered my question. Oh, and like a fool, I stopped at a cash machine.

The road to Bergquist's was pretty rough on the Escort so I was relieved when I caught a glimpse of the establishment, so to speak, on a small cove of its own. Half a dozen utilitarian buildings; every-thing spic and span. As soon as I came to a stop, Bergquist presented himself out of nowhere and said, "What're you doing down here, miss? Missed a turn, eh?"

I laughed nervously and spilled my guts without even getting out of the car. He listened and nodded; meanwhile a couple other guys showed up and drifted toward us.

"Yah, well, *sport fishermen*," Mr. B. said dryly, "If you can get 'em to pick you up, you can ride out with us tomorrow. We can swing by there, I guess. Cost ya though." He winked.

So I called the marina from there and set it up. I could leave in the morning, do an overnight on the island, and come back on Sunday with the marina bunch, "the *other* tourists," I heard someone say. Oh yes, by then my job at St. Joseph's seemed far away indeed, and besides, I thought, I could still make it home if I drove straight through. I went for it, all right. But I was still feeling a little sensitive about the whole issue of *men*, and so I could barely hide my resentment for being at their mercy. I thought suddenly of Jerry and gritted my teeth. The marina guy named his price.

"*How* much?"

"Well, 'cause of all the running around."

"Shit," I said under my breath. Then, "Can I charge it?" Bergquist and his guys watched me curiously. Affirmation on the credit card. I thought, This is the most reckless thing I have ever done. Then I gave more money to Bergquist.

"*Captain* Bergquist," he said, and winked again. "Hey Warren, help her with the kayak, eh? We'll load it now and save time. D'ya have a map of the island?"

"Oh yes." I thought of the horrid mess in the car.

"Right, be here at 6:30 or we leave without you. D'ya get seasick?"

"I don't think so."

The man named Warren approached. He was an Indian, and in spite of my general discomfiture, I felt a little thrill because, you know, I'd never once spoken to an Indian. A Native American. Warren was middle-aged, handsome, a bit stout. He was wearing a cap dramatically emblazoned with "*Montréal Canadiens.*"

"Hey," he said.

We untied the kayak and carried it down to the dock. There, floating serenely was the entirety of the Bergquist enterprise, the *Palmina*. Forty or fifty feet long, painted crimson and white, and shaped like a plug. The sliding metal doors on her side were open now, and so Warren and I crossed over a wooden plank and stepped straight inside. I took a quick look around; *Palmina* was scrupulously clean and festooned with coils, nozzles, and various outsized implements, all bearing marks of hard use. I could not smell any fish. We laid the kayak against the wall, just inside of the sliding door.

"Have any gear to put in?" Warren asked.

"No, not yet. I'll need my stuff tonight."

"Been out there before?"

"No, I just always wanted to," my voice trailed off. I was acutely aware that I, the phenologist observer/recorder was the one being observed at that moment. I glanced at Warren, but his demeanor was only polite, non-committal. Still. I rallied and told him about the lichen project; in reply he told me about an Ojibway tradition of bathing newborns in some sort of lichen tea. He was nice, but I had the feeling that he was only making conversation in order to keep me under the microscope, so to speak, and I became more and more self-conscious until I blurted out some fiction about "doing a little lichen survey out on the island," as if I were the only one who had time, or whatever. He looked at me doubtfully. I thought, How stupid am I, and sulked for a brief moment. But then, you know, I was tired of being belligerent, so I decided to let it go.

"Do you think I could camp somewhere around here? Frankly, Warren, I am now too broke to motel it."

He laughed and gave me directions to a "nice little beach, a bit stony."

Back to Wawa to buy a roll of film, tea, peanut butter, fruit, hard rolls, and candy. A sixteen-ounce can of beef stew. I splurged on a restaurant meal, but ordered the cheapest thing on the menu— grilled cheese sandwich and potatoes. There was one waitress for the whole place, poor thing, and seeing her was like seeing myself in a different incarnation. I was feeling more tired by the minute, but I made myself go out and dig through the car for Walt's map while there was still light. Found it—how inadequate it looked—and went back in for my sandwich.

"Could I buy a bottle of beer to take with me?" I asked.

"Yeah, of course." I thought she sounded a little sympathetic, which made me feel almost weepy, for God's sake.

I found the beach easily enough and by 7 P.M., I was drinking the beer and setting up camp. All was calm and beautiful and deserted. How satisfying it was to set up my little camp: just a low tarp and bug net for shelter, my sleeping bag and pad, my duffel full of miscellany and makeshift drybags. My small but crotchety stove, ready for tea. Really, it was amazing how the routine of camping had become body-familiar; my movements were deliberate and comfortable by then, without the fumbling awkwardness of the first couple days in Pukaskwa. I sat down to watch the lake and to listen to the clicking of thousands of small stones as each wave ebbed, a sound like static electricity, which, only if I concentrated, resolved into stones and water. Clicking and hissing. I imagined I could see Michipicoten Island, way, way off, and then the clicking and hissing became downright annoying. I could not help but wrestle with my motives for a while. Hopeless. It was my very first night alone—let alone camping alone—in, how long? I could not remember; it must have been at the house in Fort. I thought, Good grief, what would they think of me now?

I am sure that Grandma Beth would be deeply worried, and probably my sons, too. But Mother and Dad? No way; I am sure that they'd be, each in his or her own way, waiting expectantly to see what I'd do next. That, at least, was a comfort, and I realized how lucky I'd been to grow up under the care of open-minded people. I remembered also that Frances Anne Hopkins would have surely passed my beach on her way to the Sault, and that, too, was a comfort. I thought vaguely of taking photos and souvenirs for everyone at home. It wasn't long before, overcome with the events of the day, I tucked into my bag to sleep.

I found no reprieve there. I don't know how many times I woke that night, and with a start every time, nor how many dreams I had—disturbing, vivid, persistent dreams that left my heart pounding and eyes wide open. The worst was the one with the crazy man and his wild eyes and red voyageur's cap. He waylaid me somehow, even after I'd gotten such careful directions from the locals, and held me captive. He knew I was an imposter, which seemed to madden him even more, and then I overheard him whispering to the lake, getting instructions, *et cetera*. Fortunately, I had my data sheets along and a painting conspicuously signed "FAH." I woke up and was saved. It was four o'clock and the moon was heading for the western horizon. I had to pee, but I didn't want to leave the cover of my tarp. I lay there debating, gave up, emerged. Walked gingerly over the cold cobbles of the beach, found a place, squatted. And then I looked up. There, the northern lights, faint white spears on this night, streaked downward, spear after spear, as if trying to plunge to earth. I finished and wandered back to the tarp, but did not go under. Instead I stood there, shivering and watching; I didn't even try to go back to sleep. As soon as it was just light enough to see, sometime after 4:30, I packed and hit the road for Bergquist's.

39.

Elusion

Summer 1693

FRANCES CORNET SAT demurely, attentively, on the lip of a round shallow cave high above the water of the Lac Supérieur, the transparency of which was tinted, that day, in aquamarine, while the depths sank away into jade. She was waiting for the fogs and mist, for she knew the *nebaunaubaewuk* would then venture near, and she could look again on their beautiful faces and bodies. This was her favorite spot so far. To get to the cave, one of many giving out from the northern coast of the Île Michipicoton, she had crept down a fissure from steep cliffs above, taking great care to move her limbs precise distances and only in a certain sequence, lest she tumble headlong into the lake. She waited now in full confidence, for the air began to gauze over prettily. But, in a while, it was not the voices of the *nebaunaubaewuk* she heard, but the unmistakable dip and swirl of canoe paddles, and the rustle of water against bark. Her head shot up; her blue eyes narrowed as she listened. In the stillness, she could hear the patter of droplets falling from paddle blades, and she could picture the graceful arc that they made.

Before the fog set in, Garamond and Saint Pierre were both sure they'd seen the smudge of a campfire ascending from the island's north shore directly in the path of their crossing. They made straight toward it, keeping the sun, now just a silver ghost, off their right shoulders and listening with all their might for the sounds of waves on rock. Perhaps two hours after departing the mainland, they found the island and glided up to the base of the cliffs. They did not like the looks of the dark gaping caves that perforated the rock faces, nor the streaming mist that climbed the heights above so eerily. There was no sign of any person whatsoever. Garamond gave a shout, but the answering quiet was so thick, it seemed to forbid his voice, and so they paddled along gently, searching in silence.

"Do you smell the fire?" Saint Pierre asked.

"Maybe. No, I'm not sure."

They noticed then that the canoe was being lifted and let down rather more than it had been, and that little waves had begun to slosh worryingly among the rocks.

Garamond said, "Let us find a place to land."

"Yes, and quickly. They say there are beaches east of here, but it could be far. We shall have to hike back here." Saint Pierre sighed in resignation. The *Anjevin* would have his way, and so here they were, on this dreaded isle, looking, no doubt for a corpse. "We go around once only, eh? Then back. That is what we agreed."

"*Oui, oui,*" Garamond steered the canoe around and they set out toward the east. The going was too easy, so they knew that a wind had risen and was pushing them from behind with silky fingers. There was more and more noise of surf and the fog lifted suddenly to reveal a china blue sky. As they rounded a great headland, the rising wind was cut off somewhat, and so, once they found a cobble beach, it was not too much trouble to land. Then they pulled everything up and walked back along the shore the way they'd come. As soon as they'd begun, Saint Pierre, eyeing the steepness of the terrain, turned around and went back for rope.

While he waited, Garamond gazed across the lake to where the mainland should have been. Instead, there was a suspended roll of gray cloud over which faint pink clouds hovered. Before his eyes, the gray became overlaid with mist. Far out on the lake, he could see the suggestion of whitecaps. Not for the first time, he regretted his ridiculous notions of honor and tried to invent some plausible escape. But Saint Pierre soon returned, face flushed with the climb and laden with life-saving tools, and so Garamond's evil thoughts disappeared.

"Saint Pierre, you are a mule, eh? I'll let you do all the work from now on."

"You and your accursed ideas, *Anjevin*."

They divided up the gear and set off again, this time, feeling like heroes. It was a tough scramble but, truth be known, they both relished the challenge, and the strength and skill with which their bodies responded. The higher they climbed, the more they caught the breeze, which cooled them and blew away the bugs. The sun blazed pleasantly and the air was crisp. Sometime after mid-day, Garamond noticed that the lake had turned dark blue, fringed with white. There was a line of towering clouds in the distance, and the roll of gray fog had resolved itself into dark, broody highlands. At the same time, they caught a definite whiff of wood smoke.

"There! Do you smell it? Up there!"

Garamond pulled up short behind Saint Pierre. They scrutinized the densely wooded ridges, but they could not see the origin of the smoke.

"Do you think we are past those caves?"

"No," Saint Pierre squinted, calculating. "We're just even with them. We should spread out a little, what do you think? It's too windy to shout, and maybe the girl would hide from us, or run away."

Garamond thought of Frances with a flash of pity. Who could tell what she'd do? "You're right," he said. "I shall work down to the cliffs and you could go up there, around the base of that hill, *d'accord?*"

Saint Pierre nodded. "Take care near those cliffs, my friend. Call out if you find anything, and I will, too."

"Rejoin in an hour? Here, let us set up a signal."

They parted and quickly lost sight of each other in the thick green growth. The wind by then was rumpling the boughs of the trees every which way, so that it was difficult to see a way through, and together with the treacherous, tilted ground beneath, Garamond had all he could do to keep his footing. Sooner than he expected, he came to the brink of the cliffs. A few more yards and he saw her—she was crouching on the edge of a cliff with her back to him, looking down. He was struck with relief, like a wave of forgiveness. He didn't know whether to call her or steal up quietly and grab her before anything else could happen, so he dithered, the wind blowing hard and muffling all other sounds. He decided to get just a little closer. He advanced perhaps halfway, and then she started to rise to her feet.

"Demoiselle Cornet," he called to her softly, carefully, "It is me, Jean Garamond. Remember me? I've come to get you, to take you home—"

Frances turned to face him and his heart nearly stopped, for she was thin as a wraith. Her dress, a whitish, indeterminate color, hung in rags about her, and on her face was an expression he'd never seen. He could not tell what it was, but he felt a distinct chill. *Oki*, he remembered the Huron man had called her.

"Frances? Is it you?"

Then, for a moment, she smiled and was the piquant young girl he remembered, only grown as tall as her mother. But she spoke like a woman; she said, "Welcome, Jean Garamond of Anjou," as if she really were a *comtesse*, the grand *maîtresse* of the island, "Have you come to live here with me?"

He laughed uncertainly and her eyes turned hard.

"Well, of course, sometimes, we may come back here, you know? On our travels. Together! We will travel together, but first, don't you think, we must pay a visit to your *maman*." He moved toward her, he hoped, unobtrusively, all the while trying whatever dissimulation entered his head. She listened to all of it, her eyes fixed upon him with the uncompromising gaze of an animal. He had the stray thought that the bright sun of afternoon was too strong a light for her, that she should be tenderly and mysteriously wrapped in mist. With just a hint of panic, he thought, "What shall I do?"

At that moment, she smirked. Mortally confused, he stopped both talking and moving, and then in disbelief, watched as she turned to the cliff.

"No, no! Frances!"

He leaped forward, thrashing and half falling through the bushes toward her. "You must come with me, back to your *maman*, your *papa*. Wait! It is a sin—"

"I will not go," she called back over her shoulder.

He stumbled and got up. The wind was making it difficult to think, but then he had a sudden inspiration. "Frances! Remember, we have a pact, we have a pact, you and me—"

But it appeared that she was going to break the pact without a second thought. As she turned away, she receded toward the cliff, dress and hair floating and whipping around her until he was no longer sure where she was. He continued to run toward her but his legs had begun to wobble, for he knew what was coming. He would be just a few steps too late. It was possible then, that she slipped. As she fell, her body twirled slowly around until she gazed up at him, her lips apart. She held up her arms as if to invite him to follow, as if asking him to save her. Her dress and hair billowed around her face like petals of a pale flower. This last sight of her went on for hours until he himself diminished to a point and vanished. The glittering silver water concealed her instantly. Garamond did not hear his own cry, nor the cry of the greedy *nebaunaubaewuk* as the waves washed Frances away. He ran back and forth searching for anything, but there was nothing at all to see.

40.

Passing, Not Stopping

Summer 1869

"AFTER FRANCES CORNET fell into the arms of the *nebaunaubaewuk*," Xavier, unseen by his listeners, crossed himself piously, "Jean Garamond of Anjou was never the same. He tried to find the Sioux woman, his lover, but with no success. He never returned to the east, and no matter how he tried, he could not dull his pain. And now I will tell you the sad end of Garamond: he was faced with *une portage terrible*, one so steep and so rough that, even in those days, it already had claimed the lives or the limbs of countless traders. He was so weary that day of his grief, of the journey, and of so much he could not explain. He had with him an enormous load of furs, worth a fortune, more than anyone had ever got, but he needed to carry the furs up that portage. He stood at the foot of the trail and he could not decide what to do. *Voilà*, he hoisted the whole load to his shoulders—it weighed thirty stone. He staggered up the trail. He was close to the top when he collapsed; he fell, and died. *Merci de Dieu.*"

A chorus of protest broke out from Xavier's audience. The two canoes paddled side by side, so that everyone could hear the tale, and now it appeared that the ending was not acceptable.

The White Shell was the first to make himself heard. "That is not correct, *Métis*," he said. "Everyone knows the *Anjevin* went mad and leaped in after the girl!"

"That is not how I heard it, at the knees of my own *grandmaman*," the elder Canadian brother called out from the other canoe. "He should never have broken the pact! And so he was punished by God in Heaven—"

"Rubbish!" cried Mr. Baker. "It is almost certainly the same tale I heard at Swan River—"

"He had lost too much! His heart was broken!" The young bow-man, Denis, had stopped paddling abruptly, overcome with drama.

"I said, I heard it at Swan River, a decade ago or more! The hero went off with the Indian princess, and the girl turned into a *mermaid*." Baker and Mr. Marsh burst into laughter at this.

"I tell you, he was derelict of his senses for the rest of his life."

"He was Garamond of Anjou! He shook it off and went on! But the girl tricked him one day, she called him from the water—"

Here, Xavier interrupted smoothly, saying, "There is no doubt that the death of the girl affected him deeply, and perhaps he was not sure anymore which world he was in." In fact, Xavier knew there were as many endings to the story as story-tellers. He himself had told it several ways over the years. At present, there was his experimental healing of Mrs. Hopkins's grief to consider—like cures like, *n'est-ce pas*? Besides, he had always found the demise of foreigners to be a more satisfying end to a tale. He was still thinking of the two Yankees who wanted Ojibway trees.

They were paddling in fog just then, dove-gray and strangely under-lit from the sun, far above. It seemed in the brief silence that their voices could still be heard, echoing around them. Someone, one hitherto light-hearted Iroquois youth from Québec, intoned, "Thou shalt not meddle with spirits."

"Ha!" Mr. Baker said, but did not elaborate.

The White Shell spoke up again, "The girl was bewitched by Misshepezhieu; she felt his breath issuing from the chasm—we all know that place."

Surprisingly, everyone agreed, and they began to speculate on the precise nature of the girl's relations with the *nebaunaubaewuk*. That she had been utterly lost from the beginning, there was no doubt, but the motivations of the beings that did her in were always open to question. Was it anger? Jealousy? Love? How, exactly, could one appease them and *remain in the world*?

It was here that Edward lost all patience. He was incensed by Xavier's tale; he could not bear it.

"What a waste!" he roared, silencing everyone. "It is preposterous! Inconceivable!" He turned around in his seat to berate Xavier. Xavier looked back at him placidly.

"How typical of a half-breed to concoct such degenerate fiction!"

A wave of subdued menace swept through the ranks, but Xavier did not miss a stroke. He said, "Frances and Garamond were strangers here, Monsieur; they did not know how to live."

Frances placed her hand on her husband's arm, soothing him with a glance. Inside, she was startled, even flustered by the *métis'* words, but she knew her first duty was to maintain decorum, for how else could they remain in the world? Edward lifted his chin with scorn, carefully hiding a flood of gratitude toward his wife. He only muttered to save face, "Impudent wretch." But Xavier was a most valuable *gouvernail*.

The fog was so thick by then, like a film that could not be brushed from their eyes, that they slowed their pace and steered closer to shore, which soon reappeared as a dark mass on the left. They were hoping to make the bay of the Floating Heart River before the weather turned, as The White Shell was sure it would. Nine miles to their south, Michipicoten Island drifted unseen.

Mrs. Hopkins had not slept well the night before, but no one had. They'd camped at a deceptively pretty place with a small brook jumping down a hill in the woods and running out onto the beach. But there'd also been wide stony shallows on which Lake Superior's waves broke in diagonal curls, the booming of which reverberated disturbingly beneath their beds all night long. In the morning, everyone seemed restless, perhaps thinking of the day's journey at the mercy of southwest winds. Or perhaps it was the island, all mysterious on the horizon, for, when it came to telling stories, Xavier was a man consummately skilled in timing. The island disappeared and reappeared, playing slow tricks on their eyes. At mid-day, they had passed the mouth of Pipe River, with its sandy cove and islets, and it was there, before the fog set in, that the island had solidified into a huge, sprawling mass. At its closest approach, it took more than half of the view to the south. But the fog did come, shrouding completely the site of the *dénouement* of Xavier's tale. He was more than satisfied at this, thinking that it was the greatest good fortune of all. Relaxed, content, he leaned back on the high curve of his place in the stern, poised lightly between many worlds, and said, "*Mes amis*, none of these things should surprise us. That island has always caused trouble."

The disputants fell quiet then, and the fog became a light rain. The water was still, rent only slightly by their passage. The *bourgeois* donned their oilskins, but Frances, not wishing to crush her coiffure until necessary, opened her black parasol edged in lace. She gazed steadily south to the island, or where she deemed it must be, and pondered the fate of the girl. All around her, millions of raindrops fell to the lake until its surface was covered with minute silver crosses and floating, frosted globes.

41.

Mercy

Fall 1693

GARAMOND OF ANJOU, great trader and *voyageur* of the north, stood swaying at the foot of a long, winding portage. He looked up, but did not see the trail. Instead, the dream of the night had returned in full strength and assailed his staring eyes: the Île Michipicoton, having grown for itself long, dark wings, was flying across the sky. He dropped his bundle in frustration and fear.

"*Sacre le diable!*" he cried, "Go away!"

The trail reappeared. Saint Pierre, coming up behind, shook his head in pity, and said, "Eh Garamond, the sacraments didn't take?"

"What did I tell you? That priest at the Sault was a fraud, I am sure of it. *Merde!*" He could still hear the wing beats, deep-voiced and hypnotically slow. With a sigh, he sank down, holding his pounding head. "I am sorry, old friend, but I don't want to go to Issati."

Saint Pierre let out a long breath. "Are you sure? We have a lot of goods, eh? We have come pretty far." He sat down next to his partner and gave him a critical look. "We can camp here a little while and think about it, what do you say?"

"There is no use. I am going back to Chegouwameeagan to be with Grand Père. At least he knows what he talks of, when he talks about living with devils. I am sorry, Saint Pierre, but you know, I'm doing stupid things now, forgetting things. Last night, I forgot to tie the canoe. This morning, I scalded my hand. I don't want to travel anymore."

So they turned back the next day and paddled to the mouth of the Rivière aux Aunages, boiling with Kitchi Gami's incoming waves. Garamond missed a stroke and they almost capsized. Saint Pierre was finding it more and more difficult to hold his tongue. When he thought of the girl, Frances Cornet, he grimaced with contempt.

But there were no more incidents, and two days later they arrived at La Pointe, the new post at Chegouwameeagan, on the island of Saint Esprit. Grand Père was awaiting them on the shore of the lagoon. By then, Garamond was not surprised by anything and without a word, started handing bundles up to the old man.

They settled in for the winter—chopping firewood, raising buildings, fishing, and hunting in the woods—for the fall season was already well on its way. Saint Pierre, more than happy to leave Garamond, went to live with his old comrades in a cabin as far away from Grand Père's as possible. Most of the traders and all of the Indians gave the haunted *Anjevin* a wide berth, and many a campfire revived the story that, after all, he was a wendigo, and that perhaps they should all take care that winter.

Grand Père was torn between his desire to help Garamond and his yearning to hear of the dreams. This last, he mastered after a brief but strenuous struggle, and so the old man and the young shared their small household, but kept their thoughts to themselves. Garamond was forbidden to go off by himself at any time, lest the devils gather. Yet the dreams and visions continued anyway—the soaring island, the spectral face of the girl he could not save. He bore them stoically and bided his time. Seemingly. One day, when the leaves fell in profusion, as if fleeing the trees, he found his voice.

He said, "Monsieur, I cannot help but wonder about all those things that I lost. First, my own father, and so I had nothing; I left

France. Then poor Miron; he hit his head. The canoe and Mercier's jerky! Remember—it was gone in the morning!" He paused a moment. "Eh *bien*, you were not there, I guess. Well, and the woman Sitka Toh. Of course, I survived Monsieur, I survived everything. But now, Cornet's little girl. What next, eh? My senses? My life? Perhaps I didn't deserve all that luck, you know?" He looked earnestly into the pot he was stirring, then added, "It doesn't pay to be greedy, Monsieur. *Non, pas du tout.*"

Grand Père had never felt so old as he did then, not even in the years when he himself had been lost. In despair, he watched as all he had worked for threatened to vanish, now that Garamond was failing before his eyes. Grand Père had taught him everything: the best routes, the names and characters of every key personage, the values of goods to different peoples, and the proper times to trade. Only a part of these matters had anything to do with furs. His staples were still corn and medicines, maple sugar and rice, but there were also treasures and curiosities from all the far reaches of America, for Grand Père had labored long to link himself into the Indians' ancient web of trade. In all his days in the north, there had not been a pupil so apt as Jean Garamond. The young man's strength and luck, and his canny ways with both Indians and fellow traders had set Grand Père's mind at ease—he could face God at last, assured that he had done his best to make a bridge between peoples. Now, sadly, he looked into Garamond's vacant eyes and thought, "The devils have won."

Soon came the storm-wrung month of November, and the Lac Supérieur undertook its yearly catharsis. Then the snow started and fell every day until all the *pays d'en haut* was covered deep. At Chegouwameeagan, the new year was welcomed with an eruption of liquor and carnal excess, and then, ever so slowly, the days began to grow longer again. Garamond was not cured, but at least he grew no worse, and so Grand Père dared to have hope.

In February, there was a fracas between some of the traders and the soldiers who'd come up with Pierre Le Sueur in the summer. Le Sueur himself had gone back with the brigade, so with no one to control them the soldiers had run amok in earnest. The fight began near the little fort, late on a snowy evening, and escalated swiftly until everyone came out to either participate or watch. It was the kind of situation in which Garamond ordinarily took part as a peacemaker—he was known for this throughout the country. He burrowed in as usual, dodging drunken fists and head butts, and made for the hot center of the dispute: the trader, Decaux, and two soldiers, the brothers Songis.

"Heh, heh!" he bellowed and dragged the assailants apart. Decaux aimed a savage kick at him, but missed.

"*Cochons!*" Garamond grabbed the smaller Songis and tucked him under his arm, glaring around at the circle of raging men. "Enough! We have weeks of winter yet, *mes amis*. It's a pretty small place, eh? Too small for fighting."

There was a lull as all eyes turned on the *Anjevin*. Someone called out, "Heh, wendigo, what are you trying to make up for, eh? You can do all the good deeds you want—"

Decaux walked bristling up to Garamond and shoved his face up close. "Who are you to tell us what to do? What really happened on that island, *Anjevin*? What happened to the *petite jeune fille*, eh?"

"*Fous le camp.*" Garamond pushed him away and then cried out in surprise, for the smaller Songis had just bit his hand. He dropped the little soldier and held the injured hand to the firelight. "*Merde!* Look what you've done!"

"What have *you* done, wendigo?"

All at once, everyone was clamoring for explanations, letting all their pent-up curiosity and dark suspicions out in a rush. Saint Pierre was conspicuously absent, and Grand Père's old voice was lost in the din. Random, ridiculous notions came hurtling toward the would-be peacemaker, until finally someone—perhaps one of the Ojibwa hunters—began to laugh. Seeing his chance, Garamond started to edge away into the snowy dark, just like, he thought, a lurking monster wendigo. But one of the soldiers stood abruptly in his path.

"*Anjevin*, don't go too far," said the man, who was not as drunk as the others. "We may take you down in the spring, eh? Perhaps it is a matter for judgment. *Oui, oui*, perhaps you should stand trial at Montréal. I shall personally accompany you, I think, for sport," he smiled, "I mean, to see justice done."

Garamond didn't answer. He kept on edging away until he broke free of the little mob and out into the night. Behind him, the brawl reignited in all its former ferocity.

"*Imbéciles!*" he grumbled, "I hope they kill themselves."

He held up his bitten hand to see the wound, but it was too dark. It throbbed with pain, so he went in search of the little spring that lay nearby. He found it, bubbling heedlessly within its square wooden crib before foaming away in a brook toward the lagoon. With a sigh, he plunged his hand into the icy water. He felt very calm, for he had come to a decision.

Before long, footsteps came crunching toward him. It was Grand Père with a precious roll of clean bandages. He said, "It would behoove you, my little son, to remain obscure for a time."

Garamond chuckled and let the old man bind his hand. "You know, Monsieur, they are right about one thing. I haven't told everything yet."

Grand Père feigned shock. "Go on, by all means."

"Before I left Montréal, I made a little oath to that girl, as a joke, or maybe to shut her up. She was very pesky." He cleared his throat, uncomfortable to divulge such a silly sin. "She was just a child, I thought she would forget. In the end, she did forget, or she stopped caring about such things. But somehow I think that oath started all the trouble." He glanced at the shadowy form of the old man and frowned. "I should never have made it."

"What will you do?"

"I think I must go back to Montréal, and face Cornet and the mother." He paused, for he knew that uttering the words would fix the new course. "I will go back for a while, and whatever happens, happens."

"You have become an *homme honnête* after all, my young friend," Grand Père said softly. "And, perhaps it is for the best that you give an account of yourself, perhaps it will cure you of the visions." He clapped Garamond on his shoulder. "Rest assured, *Anjevin*, I will help you in any way I can."

True to his word, Grand Père made quiet arrangements over the next fortnight. He conferred with the Ojibwas encamped at Chegouwameeagan for the winter, thinking it best to pass over the good *coureurs de bois*. At length, he secured a promise of aid from the elders, who held the old *Français* in high esteem. They would send a young nephew to paddle with Garamond to the Sault Sainte Marie. After that, he would have to find another partner and perhaps a company he could join for the journey east, for the Iroquois still harried travelers on the lower reaches of the Rivière Outaouais.

The ice did not break until mid-April in that spring of 1694. At last Garamond was ready to leave for the east and whatever his fate would be. The Ojibwa youth, called Maeengan, insisted on paddling in the stern of the canoe to keep an eye on his charge, for such were Grand Père's instructions.

"And take care that he is never alone," the old man had lectured, "He is weak, no matter how strong he seems."

Maeengan nodded gravely, "I will try my best, Grandfather."

Grand Père turned to Garamond and said, "I may not be here when you return, for there are too many soldiers here now. I will go to the Cree and stay there, I think, forever. *Adieu*."

They left him standing guard on the shore and paddled away, loaded with Ojibwa furs, provisions, and rice to sell at the Sault. A painted blue jay gamboled on the bow of the bark canoe. It was a calm evening, and they disappeared from view within minutes.

Garamond still suffered from nightmares and visions, but he'd learned somewhat to live with these. He would sit quietly and listen for the sounds of the real world to leak through. To these he would cling and wait for the dream to dissolve. Maeengan became adept at sensing these episodes and would set up a determined chatter in his best French to bring his trader back. It became a routine in no time. Thus the days flew swiftly by as the shore unwound to the east and rolled away in the west. There were no storms, as if the lake were making amends. They passed several parties of traders and travelers coming up-lake, and there was much talk when they came near, but Garamond did not call attention to himself or his name. No one troubled him.

However, he did not know that his progress was tracked with affection and great interest by the creatures *within* the lake—the *nebaunaubaewuk*. They followed the little canoe from the islands of Chegouwameeagan, on past long sandy shores and the mouths of rivers swollen with spring water and choked with red clay. They followed past looming hills and lonely coastlines, always studying their wondrous object, the man Garamond. They lost him at the portage across the Kionon, but they found him again some days later, and rejoiced, and laid their plans.

They were coming then to the painted cliffs, whose heights Garamond had never climbed. He thought, I may not have the chance again. So he called to Maeengan that they should look for a place to land. Maeengan was eager to get out and stretch his legs, and perhaps even to hunt in the forest. They found a tiny cove, unloaded, and carried up the canoe. Then they hiked off together, working their way upward to come out by the cliffs. It was a glorious spring day with sunlight enmeshed in the branches above, and the forest resounding with chirps and trills and the drumming of hidden grouse. With every step, they crushed the spring flowers that drifted the forest floor. Soon they were sweating and puffing.

"Look, *Français!*" Maeengan whispered and pointed to a deer. The deer stared back at them for a heartbeat, then bounded away. Maeengan sprang after, drawing his bow and arrow, and Garamond ran after the youth. It did not take long for them to lose each other.

"Maeengan! Where did you go?" Garamond slowed to a stop and swore. "Now what can I do?"

There was no answering shout and he had no wish to search for the boy. He had come there to see the view from the painted cliffs. He held his breath for a moment and listened. Faintly he could hear what sounded like small waves on a shore, and so he headed in that direction, thinking he would meet the boy at the canoe. He kept listening for the surf until he realized that the sound had become the familiar slow wing beats of the island. His heart began to pound.

"Maeengan!" he cried. "Come and find me!"

But he kept on toward the lake. He topped a little rise and there was Kitchi Gami spread below him to the far horizon, glowing blue as stones from the desert, going deeper and darker with distance, until Garamond was minded of the ocean he had crossed, just five years before. He crept to the cliff and looked down. The sound of wing beats faded into surf, but mingled now with watery cries and laughter from another realm. Then he saw them—he was not surprised—the *nebaunaubaewuk* playing in the waves below. And there was the girl, Frances Cornet, among them.

"*Merci de Dieu!*" He crossed himself and backed away. But he couldn't help himself—how he yearned for another look! Madly, he thought, What if she needs my help? What if I could save her even now?

Again, he stepped up to the cliff and then out on the rock. Perhaps there was a way down. There *was*, but it entailed, not a scramble, but a slipping on the wet, transparent film of slime that covered the rock. Out went his moccasined feet from under him, and down he went on the slick tilted rock, toward the waves, four fathoms below.

From somewhere inside him came a yell. Absurdly, he had time to think, I must not hit my head! As he slid, his body took over for him, spread-eagled, and somehow slowed of itself, and suddenly he saw at the very edge of vision a small, stunted bush clinging to rock, as if the earth had extended a hand. Summoning all his strength, he reached out to grasp it and pulled himself up from the cliff.

42.

Michipicoten Island

Summer 1992

WEIRD HOW THE morning sun did nothing to illuminate the way to Michipicoten Island. We'd set off aboard *Palmina* at 6:30 sharp, as promised, under clear, eggshell-blue skies, and before we'd even lost sight of the dock, the mist closed in and hid the entire world. There seemed to be no wind, but there were long smooth rollers that materialized before us, lifting, passing, then disappearing astern as if they'd never been. Bergquist huddled over his console of buttons and speakers and dials, and ignored me. The others had curled up in various corners, trying to sleep before the fishing frenzy, I guess. So I tried to read my paperback, unopened all this time, but soon lost interest, and instead I found myself staring out at the white and listening to the bone-rattling, metal-reverberating noise of the engine. With no one to talk to and nothing to see, as *Palmina* braved the fog and the rollers westward, inevitably, I thought about Jerry.

Quite easily it came to me that our marriage had been doomed, not necessarily because of unfaithfulness, but because of a deep divide between him and me, which had never been spoken of or bridged. At some point, my Jerry had become a cynic, until by the time we split up, I am sure that nothing satisfied him anymore and that he felt he couldn't trust anyone, not even me. Everything had become a joke to him, usually a bad joke, or a lie. Integrity, tradition, beauty, certainly any idea of the value of wilderness—how he'd sneer if he could see me now. Was it the war? I wondered. All those returnees in caskets set against his own escape via marriage and asthma? Which I knew he still thought of as weakness. The problem with cynicism, let alone the undermining of simple happiness, was that he no longer saw things as they were; he had fooled himself. This had been a thing that I sensed, but could not tell him—to my grief. I understood at that moment that I could walk away from my bitterness without feeling I was leaving a part of myself, because nothing could make me a cynic; in my heart of hearts, I remained as enraptured as the day I was born. As for Jerry, for the first time in seven years, I wished him well.

Palmina throbbed on, unaffected by epiphanies. I started again to read my book, advanced perhaps a dozen pages, but then I surrendered to the general droning somnolence of the trip and fell asleep.

I woke up when the engine got louder, but really it wasn't that. It was just that the rollers had gone flat and the air more still, even, than before, for we'd made the lee of the island. Still, there was nothing to see, but I gathered from the increasing activity on-deck and the glances to starboard, you know, to our *right*, that we were cruising west along the southeast shore. Presently, the engine cut to an idle and Bergquist appeared.

"That's Cozen's Cove," he pointed at the gray outside. "Where's your map?"

I produced it swiftly, and he jabbed at various points on the now-incomprehensible mass of squiggles.

"If you go that way, there's East Sand Bay, nice place to camp. Then over here farther is Quebec Harbor. Can't miss it; Davieaux's on your left, just follow the shore. You'll get to where they can pick y'up. Now it's noon tomorrow, right?"

I nodded, suddenly feeling my throat tighten up. He gave me a hard look.

"Just stay in there, right? They can come in a lot closer than I can, so they'll see you." He continued with his instructions, warning me against trespassing on private docks, and/or being plain stupid, *et cetera*.

"Are there any caves around this part of the shore?" I asked, for I dearly wanted to see one of the infamous look-outs of Frances Cornet's, though of course, I said nothing about *her*.

"No, they're on the north side. Can't take ya there; too exposed to weather."

"Jeez, it's pretty calm, isn't it?"

Bergquist flatly refused. While this conversation was going on, one of the crew had dragged the kayak to the open door. "Where's your stuff?" he called out. I realized I'd wasted my chance to neatly and carefully pack, and that now, all would have to be smashed pell-mell inside the boat. They were going to release me straight off the deck like a fingerling fish. I rushed to my gear. A flurry of ten minutes, and the kayak was let out with a soft splash while I teetered on the walkway above. Bergquist grabbed my wrist, not very courteously, and I slithered down into the cockpit of the Hydra. I thought, Bastard!—but I laughed. And then I was looking up at them from the familiar proximity of the water surface. My self-confidence returned; I smiled, waved, and backed off. Bergquist disappeared and soon the engine rose again to its deafening pitch, and off went *Palmina* in a haze of gasoline. Before me, I could see the shore, a vague darkness—Cozen's Cove.

"Better get over there before it disappears," I said out loud. So I did, but then, obtusely, I turned right along the shore, to go east and north, warnings be damned; I wanted to see the north shore. The act of paddling was an instant balm; I was peaceful, alert, curious, happy. The kayak cut through gentle swells as if they were soft butter. What I could see of the shore was dark and red, that rhyolite rock most likely. I paddled over red and white striped slabs, peppered with potholes. I made one quick pit-stop, devoured a roll and peanut butter, and continued on until Point Maurepas at the eastern tip of the island. Here, a handsome white lighthouse stood watch. It was an open, flowery spot, so I pulled in to stretch my legs. Not a soul to be seen, but I knew all the lighthouses were automated now, so that was no surprise. Still, it was odd to walk on such a remote piece of pavement. For a while, I watched the clouds of dragonflies, feasting on something or other, and then I departed again. It was two o'clock.

All this time, the mist was either retreating from or veiling the inland terrain. As I left the lighthouse, the shore began to turn a little west of north, and not too much farther on, I rounded a headland and encountered a brisk faceful of wind. The fog gave way and I could see for the first time, the shore bending away out of sight. I had second thoughts. I sniffed that wind like a dog; it was nice, fresh, but for some reason ominous—probably that was Bergquist scolding in the back of my mind. I checked my watch and tried to study the map as I bobbed, until a little gust plucked my cap from my head and carried it off. I had a hell of time retrieving that thing. I estimated four miles to East Sand Bay from that point, and I realized that was enough to fill up the day and then some, especially if I wanted to poke around on shore, too. I thought, Maybe I'm not cut out for the caves.

"Yeah, middle-aged and too damned careful." I jammed on my cap, smiling ruefully, and turned around.

But I took my time. The fog came and went, lending a pretty kind of rhythm to the landscape, and everything was pure and wondrous. I stopped once at a narrow red beach where, lo and behold, I found caribou tracks. I explored there a while, thinking maybe I'd see one, but that of course would be too lucky. The going was terribly thick away from the beach, but in an opening I found a luxuriant growth of *Cladina rangiferina*, like an old, comforting friend.

East Sand Bay was a wide crescent of a beach with a small stream flowing down to the lake. I was by then so ravenous that I fixed supper before shelter, a no-no, according to Irv, but oh how good that beef stew tasted, chased down with peppermint tea; a handful of caramels for dessert. It was good to sit right down by the boat and hang out. There was just enough sun to stay warm and just enough mist to stay cool—perfect. Curtains of white mist climbed the forested slopes behind the beach. I spied the shiny brown head of a beaver in the water; overhead, a hunting hawk. I busied myself for a while, cleaning up, unpacking, rearranging. I set up my tarp and pulled out the bug dope. I watched a trio of loons arrive and settle in for some fishing. Meanwhile, the light had turned fantastic, a combination of white mist and blue sky. The mist flowed by like microscopic, dry confetti, which permeated the air up in the conifer forest, gilding it like something out of *Fantasia*.

So there I was. It was still a novelty to be alone, though I could see when it wouldn't be. Since I'd already thought about everyone else, there was nothing left to do but to think about Frances Cornet. Of course, the way they put it to me when I was little was that she'd become a mermaid and lived happily ever after in Lake Superior. It wasn't until I was, oh, junior high school age that I got the real story. So tragic, and so *personal*, what with our names being the same, notwithstanding the intervention of Frances Anne Hopkins's life. Tragic and eerie, but you hear about such things, don't you? Lunatics, saints, prophets. What is it they see? What is it that seems always embedded in the wildest places on earth?

I'm not superstitious. I know perfectly well there is nothing special about Michipicoten Island; it is the same as any place that has been left alone in a natural state. It was only the personal tie to the island that made it different to me, and that's what I hoped to mine for insight into my life. Perhaps I had already found it, coming over on *Palmina*—that thing about Jerry. Perhaps that was enough, I thought, as I sat watching the mist. And there was some of the act of paying homage, I guess, in my being there. And a tiny bit of curiosity to feel what Frances Cornet had felt, that is, if she really existed at all. Oh, I'm not above that: how amazing to, what, merge with the universe? I looked around expectantly. But I firmly put away the notion that she and I had much in common except our names. Right then, I consciously put that away. I knew that had been what was bothering Irv.

I decided to make a campfire, and went off to forage for wood while it was still light. The moon, near full now, brightened as the daylight waned, and placed a glowing impression of itself on the water, this, inspiring the three loons to sing. The three of them in full voice beneath a huge white moon in an indigo sky. Really, I should have been tired, what with the bad dreams and wakefulness of the night before, and just the strangeness of the day. But I felt as if I'd drunk a gallon of strong coffee. I got the fire going. Its crackling sounded like rain spilling from a roof. I kept building it bigger and hotter, for company? until I was quite overheated.

Dutifully, I tried to read my future: all the things that were fuzzy, all the options, the clues. I tried to be systematic. I could make nothing of it. I kept watch by my fire for a long time, as long as it took for the moon to shrink to its normal size and the loons to depart. Nothing else happened and nothing came to mind, and in fact, I was pretty sure the only revelation I'd ever get would be by the grace of some sort of altered state via drugs or fasting or self-hypnosis. But I'm too old for that sort of thing. Still I had to do something, so I set out my warmest clothes by the fire, then stripped and waded out in the shallows, splashing and screeching like a banshee. It was a sort of baptism, a commemoration of the trip, suitably earned by braving Kitchi Gami's cold fire. I don't know what time that was, but afterward I was calm, as if I'd done the right thing. A while later I crawled under the tarp and into my bag, and slept soundly for hours on end.

In the morning, the air went bone dry under a bright, hot sun. I ate breakfast, washed up, and was doing some serious tanning, stretched out in bliss on the rocks, when the sound of an outboard ruined everything.

"Shit!" I yelled to the gods.

I shaded my eyes in the direction of the offending noise, and soon a small motorboat turned into my bay. It came to rest at the far end—they must have seen my tarp—and a family, clearly a mom and dad and their child, waded up to the beach. Probably visitors to the people in Quebec Harbor? Cozen's Cove? Though I'd seen no one there. They were lugging coolers and all the accoutrements of a weekend outing. I sighed, or was it a growl? When the kid pulled out one of those crazy plastic dolphins—it was bigger than he was—I was sure that my little quest was coming to a banal and inglorious end.

Still, there was a mellow surf on the bay, muffling extraneous sounds. I settled back and closed my eyes, regretting that nude sunbathing was out of the question. "Goddamnit," I grumbled. I tried to imagine how it would feel, all my pores open to the sky, the kiss of air and heat. It was rather easier to imagine than I thought it would be, so I kept at it. Some minutes passed and I thought to check on my unwanted companions. Perhaps I'd heard something. Mom and Dad were industriously setting up what seemed like a patio full of lawn chairs, blankets, sun shades. Their offspring, a little boy, maybe six or seven, had wandered to my end of the beach, no doubt drawn to the strange sight of a sea kayak turned upside-down and a woman camping by herself. He was dragging the plastic dolphin by a string; actually a very cute kid, and the mother in me wanted to indulge him with a smile, but I frowned instead. I was feeling that ornery.

I closed my eyes again, resolutely thinking of nudity and melting into the rock beneath me. It was too easy. I could feel the sun streaming down on my body, like a rain of hot energy, and for fun, I imagined these streams arcing back and forth between me and the rock and the lake and the kid and his dolphin until we were all connected. The insides of my eyelids were red as flames by then, which should have tipped me off. I heard the bounce of plastic on cobbles and looked up. The boy was dancing at the edge of the surf, his toy dolphin discarded. I could see how open and innocent he was, and felt a wave of sympathy, but he'd forgotten all about me. He was playing, apparently, with the quicksilver dolphins, the real ones, in the water. There transpired then long moments of alarm during which I witnessed this dance. I could not understand what I was seeing, and you know, there was really nothing there, yet the hairs stood up on the back of my neck. I have never felt such relief as when I heard the mother call:

"Jess, what're you doing? Come back by us."

"Okay!" But the kid had turned around and was staring at me. I realized that, at some point, I'd gotten to my feet and was now stumbling slowly toward him, like some kind of zombie. I stopped, embarrassed, and then Dad approached, dolphin in tow, and took Jess's hand.

"How's it going?" he asked politely. I recognized the look on his face—the look of the parent whose sixth sense has been tweaked. Jess's eyes never left my face. There was something and we both knew it. He was trying so hard to reach me, in that wordless way children have, and my heart went out to him—but I refused.

"Oh great," I answered, then lied, "I camped overnight on a dare, and now I'm about to pack up. I'm going to collect fifty bucks and get a ride from Quebec Harbor."

"Ah," he said and laughed, not believing me. We made brief small talk. Yes, they were visiting relatives for a week on vacation. Beautiful weather, *et cetera*. Father and son departed for their corner of the beach. I thought, Jesus, I am a complete idiot. Feverishly, I started to tear down my camp. Let's go, let's go, let's go.

I used the work and the packing to calm myself down. All those little bits and pieces had to fit in my boat, like a ragtag, 3-D jigsaw puzzle. It was an art and I was proud of my work when I finished. I brushed my teeth thoroughly. Then I launched the Hydra into the surf. I passed the family in their little pavilion; they waved—the boy with joyful abandon—and I waved back. When I didn't stop paddling, I could almost feel his smile fade. I glanced back; he just stood there looking after me, sad and baffled.

"He's a kid," I said softly, meaning he'd be on to the next thing in five minutes. But would I?

I found the broad entrance to Quebec Harbor in an hour or so, that would be 10:30-ish. First there'd been Hope Island on my left, then the lighthouse on Davieaux, a pinpoint flashing in the sun. I stayed on the near shore and looked for a spot to wait for my ride. Thank God there was no fog; my guys would see me and the orange kayak, no problem, and by then, I admitted, I could hardly wait—it was definitely time to go home. I could not have cared less about agates.

But did it have to be such a fretful wait? The stroke of noon crawled nearer, hovered, passed. Then one o'clock. A couple powerboats buzzed past. I had to retreat to the shade of the bushes, but then I was terrified I'd miss it—what? the *Golden Doll*? *Golden Troll*? I couldn't remember the damned name. I was starting to curse whatever imaginary names I could come up with, when, not the sport-fishers, but the scarlet hull of *Palmina* turned into the harbor near two in the afternoon. "Hey!" I yelled, jumping up and running shamelessly toward them. An arm waved from the deck. And so, you see, I was saved again.

I'd been unfair to the crew of the *Doll*, it turned out. They'd first called Bergquist about me, then had gone off to help someone stranded at Pukaskwa River. Fouled plugs or something. So, unbeknownst to me, it had all been arranged and flawlessly executed by *men*; I'd been gallantly rescued, taken tender care of by men—how I loved them! The ride back was quite fun, jolly even, with the chatting and flirting and hobnobbing, at least on my part, and I only looked back once. We were perhaps a mile or two from the island, impossible to tell, and already the thing had risen into the air. I did not look again. When the guys got tired of talking to me, I buried myself in my book and read all the way to the Edward Bergquist Fisheries dock.

There, I disembarked, Mr. B. himself helping me carry the kayak. I was absolutely heart-warmed to see Warren again and Nicolette, of all people, leaning together on a railing and sharing a soda. They both ducked their heads when they saw me, as if they'd been indulging some guilty pleasure—I knew they'd been talking about lichen.

"Hey," I said, beaming.

"How was the island?" This from Nicolette. She was looking beautiful, I thought, in her northern-Italy way, dark wavy hair set loose. "Thought I'd drop by," she continued. "You forgot to take these." She held up a sheaf of papers. They were the forms I'd need to fill out to get course credit for our project. Yet another voice of reason.

"Thanks," I said. I took the forms.

Irv had apparently already left with Nicolette's advisor—I could imagine them talking science—the wide-eyed grad student and the wise P.I. It was a good move for Irv, I allowed, and I suppose I wasn't ready to see him, anyway. Nicolette was going to turn right around and head back to Hattie Cove where she'd spend at least a couple more days with the lichens of Pukaskwa. So she'd made a special trip down here for me. Once again, it was she who helped me load the boat and shove my stuff in the car. This time, we gave each other a quick hug and promised to phone. Mutual respect, I guess. I had no doubt we'd stay in touch.

I pulled out around 6 p.m. for the big drive. I felt good at first, even a little euphoric. Right away, the views were fantastic: the spooky cliffs at Old Woman Bay; the forest like a giant, sprawling emerald lamp; and farther on, the wide blue sheen of Agawa. But rustling around in the background were the boy and his quicksilver dolphins. It was just a daydream or a fantasy or heatstroke, I'm sure, but in the end I couldn't *not* think about it, and by the time I approached Batchawana my cheeriness had gone, and instead I felt twitchy, uneasy, late. I kept driving. Soon I knew, the light would be gone and with it all distractions. In the last bright hour of sunset, I could see white blooms of froth and waves on the shore, and I marveled, from the safety of my car and the silent highway, how the sight gave no hint of the force of water falling on rock. I tried again to find a station out of Sault Sainte Marie; failed.

43.

The Seed Exchange

Summer 1869

It was hard gaining entrance to the mouth of the Michipicoten River as it collided in turmoil with the lake and the stiff westerlies they'd been bucking all morning. The two *canots de maître* of the Hopkins's party lined up a good way out, and then, with voyageurs digging for all they were worth, shot through like juggernauts of bark, past the tossing, tethered York boats, and never slowed until they were safely in between the steep sand banks of the river. They did not stop at the Ojibway encampment there, but proceeded on upstream, the wind rumpling the water backwards until they slipped round a bend in the river. There was the rattle of a kingfisher, and then silence except for the shush of leaves, far above.

Frances rearranged her gown and looked ahead expectantly. A few more bends would bring them to the Company post where Peter Bell, an old friend, ruled as chief factor. Best of all, to Frances, who was by then craving the company of women, they would also find Mrs. Bell, living there with her husband for a year. Presently, they heard the dogs barking, and soon an exuberant pair of spaniels came crashing along the shore. The post, a scattering of brave, homespun buildings, appeared next, and the hails of Company *engagés* followed after.

"We're here!" Frances laughed and turned coquettishly to her husband. "Am I quite presentable?" He chuckled but did not answer; he was already thinking of the bed they'd share that night.

The canoes each came to rest at the wharf. There the four *bourgeois* alighted and, leaving the work of unloading behind, hiked briskly up the trail, surrounded by beach peas, shrub willow, flowering asters and goldenrod, all growing from fine white sand. Mr. and Mrs. Bell emerged smiling from the main house.

Tea and refreshments were served in a small parlor, brimming with the graces of civilization. There were flowers in vases, chinaware, a velvet-upholstered settee. That there were clean linens on the beds and a well-laid table to look forward to, no one had any doubt. Here was, not luxury, but comfort in a humble Company post.

"You must tell everything from the beginning," said Mrs. Bell as she stooped to pour Edward's tea. "Ever since I knew you were coming, I've been so excited, it's been impossible to be patient! Mr. Bell has had a time of it, I can tell you."

"Quite so," said he, "Precious few gentlefolk out here, as you know. How kind of you to stop on your tour."

Edward and Mr. Baker launched into a report of the canoe trip so far, telling of the weather, the silver island, and news from Fort William. Mr. Bell informed them that word had come down from James Bay that caribou had been sighted again after many years of absence. "Here, here!" everyone cheered. And that Mr. Horetzky would come down with both wife and daughter, and that he—Mr. Bell—hoped that Baker and Marsh would enjoy their sojourn in Horetzky's place. The two clerks smiled wanly, "Oh yes sir," said Mr. Baker, "Looking forward to it, indeed." Then the existence of the Dominion of Canada was discussed at length, as well as rumors of bloody insurrection at Red River. They shook their heads in disapproval, drank their tea, and wondered aloud how bad things would get. The Bell's parlor seemed a refuge then, one both temporary and frail, that could too easily be swept away by events.

After tea, Mr. Bell, Mr. Baker, Mr. Marsh, and Edward left for a tour of the post. Mrs. Bell took Frances upstairs to a spare room, painstakingly set up for guests, where a young girl had already laid out the Hopkins's things.

Mrs. Bell said, "Would you like us to freshen your dress? Is there anything I can lend you? Canoe travel—" Her voice faded as she touched the black sleeve. "How dreadful for you, my dear Frances. I am so sorry!"

Frances hesitated for a moment, unprepared for such heartfelt sympathy. She stared blankly down at the bed, and Mrs. Bell gave her a quick embrace.

"I'm on the mend, I'm on the mend."

"My dear, is there anything I can do?"

"Just be your own delightful self, as you cannot help to do. It is quite wonderful to see you."

Tactfully, Mrs. Bell busied herself with the window curtains, which had fallen slightly askew. She looked out on the river below for a moment, then said, "You were telling me earlier of your tale-telling *gouvernail*."

"Oh yes. Very compelling, in a way. I daresay he's a bit of an up-start. It was the legend of Frances and Garamond, a tragedy in the wilderness. Have you ever heard it?"

"No, I don't believe so. However, our local Indians have some in-genious stories, I am sure. We have our social visits, very important, and every so often I am told a tale. How curious that the heroine has your Christian name—"

"Oh I am sure that was part of the plan. It seems there was a plan. Edward was rather wroth about it all. The story ended on your Michipicoten Island with the heroine's demise." Frances smiled faintly. "She fell into the arms of the *nebaunaubaewuk*."

"How romantic."

"Very. Still, it was amusing for me, and so very little has seemed amusing. I do feel better about the rest of our little journey. I've been hoping all along we could stop at the island; I've always wanted to search for agates there."

"But only last week, there was a steamer going out. What a pity you missed it! I shall give you an agate as a memento. I have several lovely ones from the island. What colors do you like?"

They set about sorting the Hopkins's parcels and personal things, laying some in drawers, and leaving out others for overnight laundering. Mrs. Bell helped Frances out of her dress and sent for the girl to fetch it. More tea, piping hot and fragrant, arrived. Frances, lounging in a borrowed pale yellow wrapper, felt completely at ease.

"Do you know," she ventured, "how terribly difficult it's been to paint? It's only now I can do anything at all."

"Poor thing!"

"Look, here is all I have to show for myself." She drew out a bare sketch of Paquanah, on which she'd roughed in suggestions of color: white mist, turquoise sky. "I've had this packed away with the watercolors, fortunately. My sketchbook fell into the drink!"

They laughed. Mrs. Bell was a practical, stoical woman, despite her considerable skill as a hostess, and she did not understand why any woman would paint other than as an accomplishment. She smoothed her auburn hair and regarded Frances with steady, appraising, British blue eyes. She was unaware that her friend had already considered these features as a pleasingly balanced composition. But that is what Frances *did*.

"And I have even had an unexpected pupil, a poor boy, a *milieu* in our canoe. Can you imagine? He wants to be an artist and I believe he has designs on my brushes." With truly guileless arrogance, she added, "I shall make a present to him of my spoilt sketchbook. Surely there is some sort of sheet paper I could buy at the Sault. I shall just have to make do with that."

They were just two days late for Edward's forty-ninth birthday, and so, before dinner, they trooped out to the high sand banks of the river for a toast. The river ran clear and swift below them, and unruffled so that the sun laid bands of bronze and gold on its face. Occasional trickles of sand fell down the banks to the water. Just downstream, a child played with the spaniels, shouting and leaping with abandon, and across the river, the post's small cemetery perched high on the banks.

Mr. Bell cleared his throat ceremoniously and said, "To your health, Hopkins, and good fortune to you, sir!"

They raised their glasses and drained them, even the women, who stood arm in arm. As expected, Mr. Bell had provided an excellent wine, and Edward discreetly refrained from inquiring of its cost. Perhaps, he thought, our worthy host has got it with his own money, however, most likely not. He smiled broadly and asked for more.

When the sun sank and the wine disappeared, the hungry *bourgeois* turned back to the post. Edward followed behind Frances, noting with satisfaction and anticipation the narrow curve of her waist. How lightly she stepped up the path, he thought, with all her skirts and jewels weighing her down, hindering her, perhaps. He wondered for a moment how she did it, how did any woman do it? He did not think of her as strong, but rather, enchanting, graceful, comely. Yet she *was* strong, he was dimly aware, and as determined, in her way, as any man. He came up close behind her in order to take her arm when the path became wide, and so, together they advanced to evening dinner at the Bells.'

Sometime in the night, a cold wash of arctic air swept over Lake Superior, including the environs of the H. B. Co. post at Michipicoten River. The temperature dropped under calm, star-struck skies, and by dawn, every surface was drenched in dew. The Hopkinses emerged for breakfast promptly at half past six, but they were too early, for the fire in the kitchen would *not* take hold in the damp, and so all was delayed.

"My dear," Mrs. Bell said to Frances, "Won't you come and see my hyperborean garden? It is not at all far, and I'm sure," she cast an admonishing glance at the flustered young girl, flying into the kitchen, "I am sure that all will be ready upon our return."

"Of course, how lovely. It is like my morning constitutionals at home. Edward, would you mind?"

He graciously did not. The two women stepped outside, breathing deep of pure, cool morning. They each took a basket from the porch, and holding their skirts out of the wet, crossed the yard, passed the dairy and the chickens, and set out smartly down a trail through the woods. The trail was lined with ripe raspberries.

"We shall pick them on our way back," said Mrs. Bell. "Do you know, my husband has been so terribly immersed in his plans for the house here, and that is admirable, but I confess to you, my dear, that I'd far rather spend time pottering about with my plants."

A clearing up ahead signaled the garden, which to Frances's amusement, was one vast patch of potatoes, broad leaves glistening with dew, and ranged all around with the fir and spruce and pine of the forest, still steeped in gloom.

"Surprise," Mrs. Bell chuckled. With unmistakable pleasure, she surveyed her domain, hands on hips. "We can grow nothing else because of the soil, or the sand, rather. I do the best I can with manure—" She smiled in embarrassment, but Frances laughed and squeezed her hand. They wandered down the rows, Mrs. Bell calling out each variety they passed: Seneca Horns, Purple Peruvians, Ozettes, and Early Blues, all in varying states of ripeness and vigor. And a few as-yet unnamed varieties of which Mrs. Bell seemed especially proud.

"Where have you procured them all, Eileen? For a potato patch, it is rather impressive."

"Oh! That is a wonderful story. We here at Michipicoten have become a sort of locus, an exchange point for seeds and plants. I have everything coming through here—I even keep records. I'll show you, with your indulgence of course, but I find it all very fascinating indeed."

"I should love to see."

"Most all of it gets sent on to our more agriculturally favored posts, but I have my choice of potatoes! Don't you think I'm due that? These mystery plants here," she bent to inspect the rough, reddish leaves, "these were native seeds that came all the way from Fort Garry. Our Indians 'round here are as avid as I am for seeds. We have some spirited discussions, I can tell you!"

From the east, at last, a stream of bright rays filtered through the trees, lighting the garden and sparking the dew. There was a suggestion of warmth, to Mrs. Bell's satisfaction, for the northern summer was short and needed all the sun it could get. She knelt again in another row, making a rose-colored pool of her dress, and forgetting her guest for a moment, sent her testing fingers deep into the soil. "Not ready, yet," she said softly, and wiped her hands clean on her skirt.

44.

How Matters Stand

Fall 1693

GRAND PÈRE SITS on the bank of a swift river far to the north in the Cree lands. He begins to speak: "When I was lost, I dreamed that God came to me as a lustful woman. She said that I and my people were on the wrong path, and that the wrong paths shall be ruthlessly winnowed out. Then she kissed me full on my lips—*Deo gratias*! That dream has haunted me ever since. It is now over forty years I have lived in this country, and I lived in France forty years before that. I have learned, at great risk, hardship, and joy how to tread a line between these worlds. I have made my peace with God, with the *nebaunaubaewuk*, the animals, the Jesuits, the Cree, the Ojibwa and the Sioux, and with the Five Nations of the Iroquois. How I have loved to walk these trails and follow these stone-hearted streams in a bark canoe! I have learned to protect myself with the company of others—my colleagues, my friends, and the peerless women I have known. I have learned how to laugh at the jokes God plays on me, and to guiltlessly use this land and its creatures to sustain my body. I had only to open my eyes to see the beauty of surviving here, for it is a crowning achievement, and not a degradation as I first thought. But dying is easy, and I fear my peace is short-lived. The girl, Fran-

ces Cornet, had no armor against the *largesse* of the world. Garamond, whom I loved, has left. Peace be unto thee, my friend! I am
too old to journey again with a young man like that. Now, to whom
shall I tell all I know?"

45.

A Drive in the Dark

Summer 1992

I CALLED CHRIS from the Canadian side of the Sault. "Where are you?" she demanded. I told her; she scolded.

"I know, I know, but I'm driving straight through. I should be back by midnight or so, okay?"

"Yeah, well, a lot has happened," she paused dramatically. She was right. The first thing was that the regular gal had returned to her post at St. Joseph's, "to help out," and, in the event, my temp job was now kaput. I had a crashing sense of panic as I envisioned my up-coming credit card bill, not to mention the house payment, *et cetera*.

"What else?"

"Well, it's possible that your son Mike is engaged."

"*What?*"

"And your other son has decided to quit school. According to your mother, he has taken up with the Commies in Madison," she laughed, "and you know what *that* means."

"No, I really don't," I lied, thinking with alarm about the rami-fications of an interrupted college education. I thought, Oh no you don't, Walter; you will quit over my dead body.

Chris said, "Oh, and this is kind of sad, Franny. I think they're making arrangements for Grandma Beth at that nursing home, you know the one by the clinic?"

"Damn, how could so much happen in two weeks? Anything else, for God's sake?"

"Well, let's see. It's been friggin' cold here. I'm losing the tomatoes for sure."

I hung up the phone and went in search of some fast food, the faster the better. My head was spinning. Then, in the restroom, I discovered my period had started with a vengeance, right on schedule, all right. It's just that I had forgotten the schedule. Frantic digging through the car for tampons and another pair of jeans. I'd even left a small spot on the seat of the Escort. I ate, fueled up, and hit the road, or rather the strip of chains and car lots into town.

God, there was construction all over the place, a confusing, blinking, honking mess in the dark, headlights coming from every direction. It all seemed so haphazard, worthless, offensive. I felt a stab of missing Irv—another of many to come, I was sure—and his deliberate way of living. I crossed the bridge, high over the imprisoned Saint Marys River, and landed back in the U.S.A. where the usual welter of tourism and asphalt reigned. I escaped without incident and headed west into the U.P. night. The relief of leaving the town was overwhelming. It was nine o'clock on a Sunday night, so I had the road—I chose a narrow state highway, still a pretty straight shot—to myself. Maybe, I thought, what everything comes down to is space, space to think, to spread out, to be yourself. I settled down to follow my slender, headlight-illuminated route, and to sort out my problems.

First, no matter how late I got back, I had to show up for work in the morning, scrubbed and presentable. Let them tell me to my face, I thought, and besides, perhaps there were options. Or at least, references. Something would come up, I was sure, but I knew I'd be working twelve-hour days again, temping somewhere and most likely waitressing; so much for UW classes, at least this semester. And Walt would have to be rounded up, and Mike cautioned in the strongest of terms. A trip to Fort would be expected, but phone calls would have to do. As I drove, I could feel the natural beauties of the past weeks slipping away through my fingers like strings of jewels, and a part of me—the girl with the *edge*—came sulking and insisting, What about me? I swore and rubbed my eyes.

Really, there were too many options. Where *was* my natural home? Marinette? Kitchi Gami? I thought affectionately of the fields and woodlots and deep-thinking streams of southern Wisconsin—but what did I want? To live in a wilderness paradise with Irv? I thought of running after him, moving to Madison, stealing his heart, kidnapping him. Getting younger. Right.

But I wouldn't give up everything; I wanted more camping, not less. I wanted a sea kayak of my own. I knew I'd be hanging out at Du Nord's with the other paddlers; I was one of them now, and with them, I'd find ways to get out. To get *out*. That had become a necessity; my expectations had been irreversibly enlarged. I needed to get out to be complete—just not too far. I thought again of the boy on Michipicoten Island. That had been, what, ten or twelve hours ago? The whole scene leaped back in my mind. *What had happened?* There was something there all right, but nothing, I realized, I could use for my own ends, nothing to make choices *for* me. There was something there; it would always be there. I thought of Frances Cornet, and then I gave it up, because, you know, to see what she saw, I'd have to throw everything out and start over. And that would never fly. So I thought a little about Frances Anne Hopkins and decided, yes, she was still worth learning from. Yet Irv had a say in things, too, he and Nicolette, my mother, my father, and Chris with her gardens. They were all living at least a part of their lives in a state of grace. If I could take what I needed from each one of them, I'd be there, finally, that is, *home*. About this time I realized I'd passed the turn-off for Highway 77.

"Oh shit." I turned around. Retraced my way six miles, found the intersection, turned south. I knew I was getting too tired to drive, but there was always warm soda and tunes. I popped a can and skipped around on the radio. Not much doing. There was a bridge coming up and a pretty wide place to pull over, so I did and proceeded to search through my tapes. I glanced out the passenger window; there, the full moon had laid a path of pearls on the surface of a river, straight to me.

"Hey there, Moon River."

I shut off the engine and got out. The odor of a river at night is unmistakable: earth-rich, secret, awake. I breathed it in deep; I listened to the water running over shallows, shaking the reeds and alders. I knew the little river was whispering clues, perilous clues, ones no doubt prone to dire misinterpretation by mortals like me. No, I didn't understand, but I was thrilled nonetheless by the sound of the voice. I was feeling revived, actually, when two headlights abruptly appeared on the road ahead, then two more, then the rushing sound of fast-moving metal. I retreated to the car and locked my doors, waiting for the vehicles to slow down, check me out, and move on, which they did. Time flies, Frances, said the red taillights—time to go.

So I drove on and crossed more rivers, flowing beneath my wheels, faithfully down to the sea. All my troubles crowded back, and I wondered, Is it all just one huge continuum? From the pettiness of everyday all the way through the bad times, the good times, the times of ecstasy in the wilderness, and beyond? I knew I was in way over my head.

"Back up the truck, people," I muttered. "Highway 2, lookin' for Highway 2."

There it was, the sign for Manistique. I turned west and then south again. Passed over another creek; I sensed its cool exhalation, the hints and the hunches, streaming in through my open windows. I asked, "Am I doing right?"

Silly, I know. But I couldn't help asking, and couldn't help but to listen, no matter how unintelligible the response, because it was clear to me then, if not now or ever again or even later that same night, that much as I know I can't trust them, clues are all I have.

46.

Hampstead

Winter 1907

THE MORNING SUN, gently blurred by the translucence of the English atmosphere, has finally risen high enough to illuminate Mrs. Hopkins's studio. She has been waiting for the light, sitting calmly before a large, unfinished painting, an empty tea cup pushed away to one corner of the table. She wears her usual spattered, brown smock. Her implements and paints lay ready—burnt umber, ultramarine, carmine, sienna—her own palette of perhaps a dozen colors.

The painting describes a droll but lovely scene. To one side, Lake Superior batters a shoreline with heavy blue surf. A party of Hudson's Bay Company voyageurs has drawn two canoes up the beach. They have spread their possessions on every bush and rock to dry, like so much pretty detritus. Bolts of fabric flutter in the wind. One man kneels to light a fire in the shelter of rocks. Mrs. Hopkins remembers the man's face very well. The rocks, all stoic and twisted by time, mark the edge of the scene, and beyond is the forest, climbing distant heights.

She still enjoys the glow of yesterday's luncheon with her colleagues, and is confident of finishing the picture in time for framing with the others. She glances around the walls of her studio, hung from ceiling to floor with unsold pictures, as is the whole house. But she does not worry about that. Outside, the cries of the rooks, descending from bare trees and rooftops, ricochet down the streets of Hampstead. The day is cold, she knows, having stepped out early, and the studio, while gradually warming from the fire in the grate, is still cold enough to stiffen her fingers. She closes her eyes for a moment, and blows warm breath on her hands. She dips her brush in the umber, mixes it with white, and waits for her heart to remember. It is but a moment, and then, with loving care, she touches her brush to the rocks, the sweet and resolute northern trees, the sky, and the cleansing water.

The End

Epilogue:
Chasing Synthesis

Winter 2020

SYNTHESIS, I own, is a labor, a pilgrimage that never shall end. Must never end lest life drain away too soon. But I stop here, dear reader, to commend you on your steadfastness, for you are a pilgrim the same as me—or the pieces of me who people these pages—and we love you for that. To journey in any wilderness, or rather to dance and to weave within it, one must be nimble, clear-eyed, kindly, and brave—a tall order in a daunting world!

Consider that wilderness is beautiful, nourishing, and pitiless. Questions arise: Does one love it, need it, or endure it? Those of us who think in terms of words on a page are at some disadvantage here. Still one must try. I offer you a beautiful day in spring, the requirements of our genes, and the fact that our life spans are finite as tentative answers; so yes, yes, and yes. But that is just the beginning. More questions and replies float like an unstrung tapestry; each thread glows on its own account and reflects the light of its fellows. There is the thread of the merchant and the thread of the mystic. Those of explorers, artists, and scientists. Mother, greenhorn, failing ancient. Native-born and prodigal child. All these may twine themselves together, one dares to hope, given some moments of stillness. That mere moments are all we have to admire our work is a fate to be borne as best we may; the tapestry frays in a sudden wind, it is lost, or laid aside and forgotten. We must start over, sometimes with a brand new design, one that may or may not harmonize with others' or with what we've made before. A humbling prospect, to be sure, but I've learned my lesson well: not even an old encyclopedist may rest when the loom calls for weave.

Sources for Quotations

PAGE 2

"The Governor's was the most beautiful thing of the kind I ever saw; beautiful in its 'lines' of faultless fineness, and in its form and every feature; the bow, a magnificent curve of bark, gaudily but tastefully painted, that would have made a Roman rostrum of old hide its diminished head. The paddles painted red with vermilion, were made to match, and the whole thing in its kind, was of faultless grace and beauty—beauty in the sense of graceful and perfect fitness to its end."

McDonald, Archibald and Malcolm McLeod. *Peace River: A Canoe Voyage from Hudson's Bay to (the) Pacific by the Late Sir George Simpson, Governor, Hon. Hudson's Bay Company in 1828, Journal of the Late Chief Factor, Archibald McDonald, Hon. Hudson's Bay Company, Who Accompanied Him.* Malcolm McLeod, editor. Ottawa: J. Durie and Son, 1872. 41.

PAGE 10

"this adventurous Traffick"

Innis, Harold A. *The Fur Trade in Canada: An Introduction to Canadian Economic History.* Toronto: University of Toronto Press, 1999. 248.

PAGE 22

"Ami, veux-tu voyager sur l'onde de tous les vents? Les flots et la tempête grondent cruellement. Les vagues changent tous les jours. . ."

La Rue, F.-A.-H. *Le Foyer Canadien: Recueil Littéraire et Historiques.* Quebec: Bureaux du Foyer Canadien, v. 1, 1863. 372.

PAGE 52

" . . . Nature is nothing else than God himself acting by certain laws which he has established of his own free will. So that the works of Nature are not less the effect of the power of God than miracles, and suppose as great a power as miracles, it being altogether as difficult to form a man by natural laws of generation as to raise him from the dead."

Robinson, Howard. *Bayle the Sceptic.* New York: Columbia University Press, 1931. 25.

PAGE 53

"So when something in Nature appears to us as ridiculous, absurd, or evil, this is due to the fact that our knowledge is only partial, that we are largely ignorant of the order and coherence of the whole of Nature and want all things to be arranged to suit our reason. Yet that which our reason declares to be evil is not evil in respect of the order and laws of universal Nature, but only in respect of the laws of our own nature."

Spinoza, Baruch. *Tractatus Theologico-Politicus.* Samuel Shirley, translator. Leiden: E.J. Brill, 1989. 238-239.

PAGE 54

"This is what I see and what troubles me. I look around in every direction and all I see is darkness. Nature has nothing to offer me that does not give rise to doubt and anxiety. If I saw no sign there of a Divinity I should decide on a negative solution: if I saw signs of a Creator everywhere I should peacefully settle down in the faith.

But, seeing too much to deny and not enough to affirm, I am in a pitiful state, where I have wished a hundred times over that, if there is a God supporting nature, she should unequivocally proclaim him, and that, if the signs in nature are deceptive, they should be completely erased; that nature should say all or nothing so that I could see what course I ought to follow."

Pascal, Blaise. *Pensées*. A. J. Krailsheimer, translator. London: Penguin Books, 1966. 162-163.

PAGE 57

"I am as free as Nature first made man . . ."

Dryden, John. *Dryden: The Dramatic Works*. Montague Summers, editor. London: The Nonesuch Press, 1932. 34.

PAGE 105

"All the rivers run into the sea; yet the sea is not full; unto the place from whence the rivers come, thither they return again." — Ecclesiastes 1:7

The Holy Bible. Cambridge: University Press. 589-590.

PAGE 142

"The Fish and the Cormorant"

La Fontaine, Jean de. *The Complete Fables of Jean de la Fontaine* (Book Ten). Edited and translated by Norman B. Spector. Evanston, Illinois: Northwestern University Press, 1988. 169-170.

PAGE 188

"The heavier soils were typically covered by mixed conifer-hardwoods, with white pine, hemlock, balsam fir, and white spruce as the conifers, and sugar maple, basswood, yellow birch, beech, American elm, red oak, and ironwood as the deciduous species."

PAGE 188

"The dry lands were dominated by pine, with jack and red pine on the lighter sands and white pine on the sandy loams."

PAGE 189

"The wet lands contained either conifer swamps, dominated by tamarack, black spruce, and white cedar, or hardwood swamps with black ash and yellow birch."

Curtis, John T. *The Vegetation of Wisconsin*. Madison, Wisconsin: The University of Wisconsin Press, 1971. 177.

Further Reading

Abbey, Edward. *Desert Solitaire: A Season in the Wilderness*. New York: Ballantine Books, 1968.

Bosher, J.F. *Business and Religion in the Age of New France, 1600-1760: 22 Studies*. Toronto: Canadian Scholars Press, 1994.

Bowles, Paul. *The Sheltering Sky*. New York: Ecco Press, 1949.

Brown, Jennifer S.H. *Strangers in Blood: Fur Trade Company Families in Indian Country*. Vancouver: University of British Columbia Press, 1980.

Cash, Joseph H. and Gerald W. Wolff. *The Ottawa People*. Henry F. Dobyns, editor. Phoenix: Indian Tribal Series, 1976.

Chisholm, Barbara and Andrea Gutsche. *Lake Superior: Under the Shadow of the Gods*. Toronto: Lynx Images, Inc., 1999.

Clark, Janet E. and Robert Stacey. *Frances Anne Hopkins, 1838-1919: Canadian scenery*. Thunder Bay, Ontario: Thunder Bay Art Gallery, 1990.

Diamond, Jared M. *Guns, Germs, and Steel: The Fates of Human Societies*. New York: W.W. Norton & Co., 1999.

Durant, Will and Ariel. *The Age of Louis XIV* in *The Story of Civilization*. New York: MJF Books, 1963.

Eccles, W.J. *The French in North America 1500-1783*. East Lansing, Michigan: Michigan University Press, 1998.

Fischer, David Hackett. *Champlain's Dream*. New York: Simon & Schuster Inc., 2008.

Forster, E.M. *A Passage to India*. New York: Harcourt, Brace and Co., 1924.

Gilman, Carolyn. *Where Two Worlds Meet: The Great Lakes Fur Trade*. St. Paul: Minnesota Historical Society Press, 1982.

Gilman, Carolyn with research by Alan R. Woolworth. *The Grand Portage Story*. St. Paul: Minnesota Historical Society Press, 1992.

Handbook of North American Indians. William C. Sturtevant, editor. Washington D.C.: Smithsonain Institution, 1978—.

Huppert, George. *After the Black Death*. Bloomington/Indianapolis: Indiana University Press, 1986.

Innis, Harold A. *The Fur Trade in Canada: An Introduction to Canadian Economic History*. New Haven: Yale University Press, 1962.

Johnston, Basil. *The Manitous*. New York: HarperCollins Publishers, 1995.

Kent, Timothy J. *Birchbark Canoes of the Fur Trade*. Ossineke, Michigan: Silver Fox Enterprises, 1997.

Krech, Shepard, III. *The Ecological Indian: Myth and History*. New York/London: W.W. Norton & Co, 1999.

Leopold, Aldo. *A Sand County Almanac*. New York: Oxford University Press, 1949; New York: Ballantine Books, 1970.

McPhee, John. *The Survival of the Bark Canoe*. New York: The Noonday Press/Farrar, Straus and Geroux, 1975.

McGuffin, Gary and Joanie. *Superior: Journeys on an Inland Sea*. Minocqua, Wisconsin: NorthWord Press, 1995.

Morse, Eric W. *Fur Trade Canoe Routes of Canada: Then and Now*. Toronto: University of Toronto Press, 1979.

Nute, Grace Lee. *The Voyageur*. New York/London: D. Appleton and Co., 1931.

Olson, Sigurd F. *Runes of the North*. New York: Alfred A. Knopf, Inc., 1963; Minneapolis: University of Minnesota Press, 1997.

Pielou, E.C. *After the Ice Age: The Return of Life to Glaciated North America*. Chicago: University of Chicago Press, 1991.

Pond, Samuel W. *The Dakota or Sioux in Minnesota as They Were in 1834*. St. Paul: Minnesota Historical Society Press, 1986.

Schutze, Thomas. *Frances Anne Hopkins: Images from Canada*. Manotick, Ontario: Penumbra Press, 2008.

Seed, John, Joanna Macy, Pat Fleming and Arne Naess. *Thinking Like a Mountain: Towards a Council of All Beings.* Philadelphia: New Society Publishers, 1988.

Shepard, Paul. *The Tender Carnivore and the Sacred Game.* New York: Scribner, 1973.

Shepard, Paul. *Coming Home to the Pleistocene.* Washington D.C.: Island Press, 1998.

Skinner, Claiborne A. *The Upper Country: French Enterprise in the Colonial Great Lakes.* Baltimore: Johns Hopkins University Press, 2008.

Trigger, Bruce G. *The Huron: Farmers of the North.* Fort Worth: Holt, Rinehart and Winston, 1990.

Warren, William W. *History of the Ojibway Nation.* Minneapolis: Ross and Haines, 1885; St. Paul: Minnesota Historical Society Press, 1974.

Whyte, David C. *An Introduction to Michipicoten Island: Lake Superior's Wild Heart.* Jackson's Point, Ontario: David C. Whyte, 2001.

For more information, free maps, or to order copies of *Journey to Michipicoten*, visit the Web site: www.journeytomichi.com.

Maps:

- Northern Fur Trade Routes
- France in the Seventeenth Century
- Lake Superior

Patricia Kay Lucas writes fiction and non-fiction from an unmanicured, marshy corner of Madison, Wisconsin. Much of *Journey to Michipicoten* is based on the author's first-hand wilderness experiences and her travels to historical sites in the United States, Canada, and England.

www.ingramcontent.com/pod-product-compliance
Lightning Source LLC
Chambersburg PA
CBHW031415240626
47154CB00001B/54